To all the women in my life who have funneled so much love into me. And to the men who taught me how to be one.

<u>Those We Leave Behind</u>

Chapter 1

The earth was warm and dark and soft under the shovel, and it gave easily to his step, but it was far too wet for proper digging, so it clung to the blade, and he had to beat it off on a stone or a stick, or rake it off with his boot. The snowfall had given way to a light misting rain and the clean white cover was slowly becoming mush. It was getting dark quickly now.

Harley stopped digging and pulled his hat low over his eyes. The sun hadn't shone all day because of the low, gray clouds, and finally its feeble February light was giving out altogether. The hole was not half finished, but he would stay until it was done. He went back to work, stabbing, bending, lifting, clearing; the rhythm of his movements playing cadence in the cold evening quiet.

Soon the bottom was too deep to reach from above, so he stepped down into the hole, working from one end to the other, keeping the floor level.

He was on the knoll behind the house, and he could see the lights shining through the windows down there. He could still make out smoke from the chimney rising through the gloom. Ellie would probably have preferred the willow copse down near the creek, but the ground stayed too wet there. Wood doesn't last very long in wet ground. This was a pretty spot though; you can see the whole farm from here, and you can see this knoll from anywhere on the farm.

By the time full dark covered Harley and his land, he stood waist deep in the hole. He heard someone coming up the hill behind him, but he kept his pace, not turning to see who it was.

"Doc says come on and eat, Pa." It was Cy. "Let me do some while you go."

"Tell Doc I'll be down directly," Harley said, without looking up. "Go on back and tend to your brothers."

"Please, Pa, I want to do some."

Harley stopped digging and turned to look at his boy. Cy was tall for his age, and lean. He was a big help on the farm, a far bigger help than any twelve-year-old should be. Even in the dark Harley could see his son's eyes wet and shining. He wanted to say something, but he was afraid to let Cy hear his voice now.

"Can I help just a little?" Cy pleaded.

Harley turned and went back to his work without answering. He heard the boy walk away.

"I'm sorry, son," he said, after the boy was long gone.

*

By ten o'clock Harley could no longer see over the top of the hole, and he reckoned he was about done. Wearily, he cleaned the loose dirt from the bottom and prepared to climb out. It had been a long day, and a long last night, and a long day before that. He had not slept in more than forty hours, since before five o'clock yesterday morning. He leaned the shovel against the side, using it to boost himself up. He scrambled to the top and pulled the shovel out behind him, paused, and looked down into the hole, then put the shovel over his shoulder and started down the hill toward the house.

The rain had finally stopped and the snow was nearly gone, leaving only pale white traces in the folds and creases of the land. He walked in the company of nothing but the cold, his breath clouding before him, and the quiet of winter night. The boys were all in bed by now, he knew, but he saw Doc Hall's automobile parked in front of the house. The lights were still on, and he knew that the Doctor and his wife Olivia would be waiting for him. Duke did not run up to meet him when he reached the porch as he usually did, rather he sidled slowly up, barely wagging his tail.

"Atta boy, Duke," Harley said, scratching the dog's ears, "you're a good dog, aren't you?" He stood looking across the fields, the dog quiet at his side. In the distance they heard some hounds running a trail, listening as the short barks turned long and mournful. Harley guessed they were up on Short Ridge, and that it was Doodie Howard's dogs. He imagined Doodie at the fire, and probably Tom Post and Paulie too, and Doodie saying, 'Got 'em treed, boys, let's walk...' He pictured the coon as well, quivering in the high branches,

4

snarling down at the dogs, waiting for the men. Harley opened the door and went inside.

Ben Hall sat slouched wearily in the rocker by the fireplace, a book in his hand, leaning toward the lamp beside him. When he heard the door open he shut the book and stood up.

"Livie's got supper warming, Harl, c'mon," he said, taking Harley's arm and leading him to the kitchen. Harley followed, mainly because it was easier to do than protest that he only wanted to go to bed now. "She's with the baby. She ought to be done soon," said the doctor.

Harley hadn't realized how hungry he was until he started eating. Ham and beans, cornbread, sliced onion, and buttermilk. He ate hard and fast, while Ben sat silently at the table reading his book. As Harley sopped the last of the cornbread around, cleaning his plate, Ben looked up and spoke.

"I'll be going to town in the morning. I've got to see some folks, but Liv'll be here till afterwards."

"Sure, Doc, I know. I appreciate everything..." he trailed off, watching the steam rising from the bean pot on the stove.

"She's taught Cy and Seth all she could," said the doctor, "but she'll need a couple of hours with you tomorrow. Better early, before everyone gets here."

"Yeah, early," said Harley flatly. "But I'm taking the boys for a walk first thing. Soon as we get back. I'll see her then."

"She'll likely be back Friday. Anna Mae'll be here in the meantime."

"Yeah, we'll manage fine." He looked up at Ben. "You and Liv have been great."

In the back of the house the baby began to squall. They heard a door squeak slowly to, followed by Olivia's footsteps coming down the bare wood floor toward them.

"Hello, Harley," she said coming into the kitchen, going straight to the stove. "You get enough to eat?" Behind her the baby carried on something awful. "She's just mad," said Livie, stirring beans. "A real spit-fire, that one is..."

"Yessum. Plenty. Just what I needed, Liv, thanks."

"I'll give her a few minutes."

"She'll be all right."

The fire popped and a red ember flew out onto the hearth. Harley watched its smoke curl back into the fire as the coal grew black and cold. For long moments there was no sound but the hiss of fire.

"Well, I'll be going to bed now," Liv said, going to her husband and kissing his forehead. "Night, honey," she whispered. "Goodnight, Harley," she said. The two men watched her disappear through the front room, and then heard the baby begin to quiet.

"Harley," Doc Hall began, "I'm sorry..." he let his words drift off, sighing heavily.

"Me too, Ben," said Harley. "It ain't your doing, or mine, and we're both sorry." He sighed as well, looking at his hands, hard and muddy on the table before him. He pushed his chair back and stood. "Me too."

Excusing himself, he went outside and washed up, looking into the crisp winter stars the whole while. When he finally went back in the house, all was dark. He lay down on the sofa under his grandmother's quilt for a very long time and tried to make himself sleep. Finally he gave up and went and spent the night sitting with Ellie.

*

Before sunrise, before the eastern sky had even begun to lighten, Harley went to the boy's room and began gently shaking Cy.

"Wake up, son, help me with your brothers."

Cy rubbed his eyes, climbed out of bed without saying a word, and began pulling on his trousers. Harley went to Bert's bed and began waking him, while Cy went to Seth. When the three older boys were dressed, Harley picked little Amos from the makeshift pallet on the floor and wrapped a blanket around him, then led his children outside.

Though the sun was still not yet above the horizon there was enough hint of coming light to see the fields lying fallow around the house, and the silhouettes of the barn and the corncrib and the smokehouse, and the low, heavy clouds in the sky above them. Without a word he led them across the front yard, through the front gate, and out over the crunching, frosted grass. They walked in a rough line: Harley in front carrying Amos, Seth and Bert next, Cy in the rear.

By the time they reached the first fence row, the cocks were stirring in the barn. The sun, though they couldn't see it through the clouds, was up, and crows were beginning to chatter down by the creek.

"I gotta pee, Pa," said Bert, and everyone waited while he and Seth emptied themselves. Harley watched the steam rising in front of the boys, while Cy just looked back at the house. Bert finished, and then Seth said, "Okay," as he refastened his britches, and they started back up the hill.

As they neared the crest Amos began to fuss, then to cry. He was used to being fed when he woke, and to being warm. Harley raised him close to his face and ssshhh'ed. The child quieted, eyes working this way and that at the odd morning.

"Ouch!" cried Seth. At his father's look, Bert backed away from his brother. Even at five, he knew that look.

When they reached the grave, Harley handed Amos to Seth and put his arms around him and Bert, pulling them to the edge. Cy stood at the foot of the hole, staring down into it. They stood there for perhaps two or three minutes in the quiet dawn, hearing only their own breathing and the wind moaning through the big chestnut tree behind them. Finally Harley spoke.

"Boys, this is where we'll lay your Ma."

Bert fidgeted a little, pushing dirt clods around with his foot. Seth sniffed.

"Here to the left's where I'll lay one day," Harley said, looking pointedly at Cy.

"Momma?" said little Amos, and Seth sniffed again. Down at the house Harley saw Doc Hall in the back yard, picking up an armload of firewood. He watched Ben disappear through the back door, kicking it shut behind him. He strained to hear the sound of the slam, but it was too far away. He looked over to Cy again, standing alone, still staring into the hole. Away in the distance, toward the river, a single shot rang out, and a few seconds later, another. Harley knew a deer was down over there, and he thought about that for a minute.

"Momma," said baby Amos. "Di-puh."

Harley took his arms from around Bert and Seth and stooped over the lip of the hole. Hopping down into it, he turned and reached up to Bert. The child hesitated a moment, then took his father's hand and joined him in the grave. Harley held his arms up to Seth, and Seth gave Amos to him, and then jumped down. Cy stood above, looking down at his family. He turned and looked back the way they had come. The wind whipped his pants legs around his ankles, blowing his dark, too long hair (Ellie's hair), across his eyes.

"Come on, son," Harley said softly, and Cy obeyed.

It was warmer down in the hole. The dirt walls gave off little wisps of steam. Harley knelt, bowing his head, and his sons followed suit. The wind blew hard across the top of the grave above them, sounding like a sigh that wouldn't end.

It was cramped down in the hole, so they once again formed a rough line, Seth and Cy on either end, Bert next to his father who held Amos in his arms. Amos squirmed to get down, so Harley leaned over and set him on his feet, taking one of his little hands and giving the other to Seth. Seth took Bert's hand and Bert reached out to Cy. Harley reached for Cy's other hand.

"Lord," Harley began, "accept our thanks for your bounty." Seth sniffed, and so did Cy. "Bless this soul which has joined you. Make her welcome."

"Berr," called Amos to a wren that lit on a branch above them.

"Give us the strength to accept your way, and the courage to persevere."

Seth began sobbing openly, which scared Bert, who began to cry also. Harley paused for a long while, wondering what else he should say.

They heard the whir of the wren's wings above them.

"Berr gone," said Amos.

"Amen." Said Harley.

"Amen." Said Cy and Seth. Bert continued crying, though he wasn't sure exactly what for.

"Berr?" said Amos looking up. "Berr?"

Harley straightened, handed Amos to Cy, and climbed from the hole. Reaching down he pulled Seth up, then helped Bert, who was still crying, out. Cy handed Amos up, then took his father's hand and was pulled out.

It began misting a fine rain as they all stood there for a moment in the cold. Seth pulled his sleeve across his eyes, and Harley did too. Bertie cried loudly across the hilltop.

"Hush, Berty," said Cy. "Ma's with the angels now."

"Foo," said Amos. "Foo. Ead."

A carriage sat down at the house, with a pair of roans still hitched to it. Harley heard an automobile chugging up the hollow. 'That'd be the Anderson's,' he thought.

"Seth, take Amos and Bert on down and get 'em fed. Cy, put Mr. Mosely's team away and get started on your feeding. I'm gonna move the cattle over to the bottom. I'll be along directly to help you milk."

Harley saw smoke coming strong from the chimney now, and turned the collar of his coat up over his neck.

"Foo, Momma," said Amos. "Ead now, Momma."

*

It was nearly noon before Harley and Cy finished their chores, and Seth's and Bert's too. Although they worked at times side by side, they worked silently and neither spoke until they were washing up at the pump house. Harley worked the pump while Cy washed, then Cy did the same for his father. The water was thick from the cold.

"Fifteen of 'em, Pa," counted Cy, "seven wagons and eight autos."

Harley looked up at his crowded yard, then back to his scrubbing. "When you get inside be polite to everyone, then go see that your brothers are all dressed." He pulled his coat from the nail and shrugged it over his shoulders. "I'll be at the shop."

"Yes, sir," said Cy. Then a second or two later, "Pa?"

"What, son?" Harley stood still, giving the boy his full attention; waiting, tense.

Cy looked his father full in the eye for perhaps ten seconds before looking away and bending to pick up his coat.

"Pa, I ..."

"Harl?" came a voice from the direction of the house. It sounded like Burley White. "Harley, you in there?"

"Just a minute, Burley," Harley answered. Then lowering his voice, "What is it, son?"

The boy watched his own feet shuffle in the dirt floor of the spring house for a minute, then looked up into his father's eyes again. They stood there, two feet apart, and this time Harley looked away first.

"I ... I don't know, Pa. I don't know..." Still the boy looked squarely at his father.

Harley made himself look back up, and he felt the reins breaking. He took a step and pulled his son to his chest.

"I don't know either, Cy. I don't either..." and it all broke loose, for both of them, and they hugged each other, and wept.

*

Somewhere through the everyday sounds of the barnyard, through the clucking of the hens and the grunting of the hogs, music began to play, low and mournful. Someone had brought the church organ, and the notes of Addie Harper's version of 'On a Hill Faraway' drifted into them. The dirge had begun. Harley found himself on his knees, Cy was stooping over him, his face buried in his father's collar. A tentative rap at the door made them both jump.

"Harley, you okay?" asked Burley softly.

Father and son squeezed tighter for a second. Then Cy said, "Just a minute, Mr. White."

Harley wiped his eyes while Cy put on his coat, stepped through the doorway, and blinked as he emerged into the light of day.

"The Reverend sent me, Harl. They're about ready."

"Okay, Burley, thanks." Harley put his arm around his son and they followed their neighbor into the house.

They went up the back porch and in through the kitchen so they could change clothes before they met everyone. Livie and Maggie Akin were tending the cook stove. Cy strode through without a word and disappeared into the boys' room, but Olivia stopped Harley by grabbing his hand. She gave it a gentle squeeze, but didn't say anything. Harley let go and went on into the bedroom.

The parlor was packed when he came back out five minutes later, as well as the dining room and the hallway. At least forty people were jammed into the front half of a house that measured no more than thirty feet by thirty feet, square. Harley looked past the friends that greeted him morosely, and saw Bert and Seth sitting on the organ bench watching Addie play. Little Amos sat on Anna Mae Hodgkin's lap in the corner, playing with a gaudy costume bracelet which he grinningly held up to show his daddy across the room.

The casket rested on the dining room table, which had been pushed up near the far wall. Thankfully, it was closed. They had never discussed that, he and Ellie, but he was glad it was closed. Addie was playing 'Nearer My God To Thee' now, and slowly, immutably, the tide of people revolved around the point where Harley stood at the hall door. The men mostly took his hand and clasped his shoulder and said things like: "Let us help you, Harley, I'll be by," or "Hell of a thing, just a hell of a thing." The women mostly just hugged him and sniffed into their hankies. Harley didn't see Cy anywhere.

After a few minutes Reverend Adams stood up before the coffin and cleared his throat, and the low murmur that permeated the house died immediately. Sam Adams cleared his throat once more and somebody in the dining room coughed.

"Friends and neighbors," the gray old preacher began. "Christians. We're gathered here today to give the soul of Elenor Hayes Felts to our Lord and Savior, Jesus Christ Almighty. And to give her body back to the earth from which it came." A couple of low 'Amens' echoed in the room.

"She was called from this family; from Harley there, and from young Cyrus and from Seth and from Bertram, and from baby Amos, to a higher place, a higher life." The room was silent now, except for the chatter of Amos in the corner.

"Gree," he said, still holding the bracelet. "Boo," he said, pointing at one of the beads. An image of Ellie sitting with Amos, teaching him colors just a few days before struck at Harley, drawing a choke from deep down his throat

"She was a fine mother," said the preacher. "She was a fine wife," he said, "and she was a fine neighbor. We're all going to miss her; we're all going to mourn her passing. But we're all going to get on with our worldly things like she'd want us to. We all know that we'll see her again, that she's making a place for us." Again a few low, scattered 'Amens' wavered in the thick air.

"Harley," he said looking across the room, "Bless you. And Bless young Cyrus," but Cy was nowhere to be seen, "and Seth and Bert and Amos. Take peace in the Lord, may your hearts be eased."

Addie started playing 'When You Walk With Him', as low and as slow as she could play it.

"Boys," said the preacher, nodding to the men that sat in front of him. Six of Harley's friends stood up and quietly walked to the dining room table, three to a side.

"Let us pray," said Reverend Adams.

"Momma?" Said Amos in the quiet. "Momma?" His little head craned as he searched the crowded room.

"Oh, Lord, teach our hearts to know that life is eternal, and that your love is immortal. That death is only another horizon, and that a horizon is nothing save a limit of our sight. Lift us up that we may see further. Cleanse our eyes that we may see more clearly. Through Jesus Christ Our Lord, we pray. Amen."

Amens went up around the room, and Harley found his hands shaking. He clasped them together in front of him, but still they shook.

"Errrmmmm," said Amos, rolling the beaded bracelet across his thigh.

Slowly, quietly, everyone filed out of the house and began filling the wagons that would carry them to the knoll. Mr. Mosely's wagon stood at the head of the line, empty save a granite slab pushed under the seat, bundled with straw and wrapped in burlap. At last only Harley and the six pallbearers and Reverend Adams remained inside. The men took hold of the casket and prepared to lift it.

"Wait," Harley said softly. "Wait outside a minute, please."

The Reverend nodded, and he and the men went out. Harley pulled up a chair beside the coffin and sat down.

*

When he stepped out the door, the first thing he noticed was how bright the day had become. The clouds were breaking up and the sun shone through in patches, mottling the rich farmland around him. The quiet assaulted him. Forty people sat silently in the wagons, not making a sound, except for a few low sobs from some of the women.

12

Harley wanted to say "Okay," but he was afraid to break the quiet. So he simply nodded at Burley, and the six went inside.

After a couple of minutes they came shuffling back out, carrying the box. They took it to Mr. Mosely's wagon and slid it gingerly into the back. Harley took his seat up front, between Bert and Seth, wondering vaguely where Cy was. Mr. Mosely stood up and turned around, like a trail boss surveying his herd before a long drive. When he was satisfied that all was ready, he sat down and snapped the reins, and the procession started up the hill.

The day had turned mild indeed, much milder than anyone had a right to expect in mid-February. The horses snorted out huge puffs of steam as they pulled against the rise, and when Harley turned to look behind him he saw dozens of little puffs rising above the heads of his friends and family. But sunlight shone full upon them now and it didn't seem cold at all, at least not to Harley. Bert shivered on the seat next to him, so Harley put his arm around the boy. A hawk screeched far above, and though Harley himself didn't look up, he knew, could feel, most of the eyes behind him rising. He looked at Seth.

"Have you seen your brother?" he asked.

"No, Pa. Not since he came in with you," said Seth. Harley nodded and watched the warm little cloud of his son's words float away, dissipating into the high blue above, where the hawk screeched again.

They were nearing the top of the hill when Seth said suddenly, "There he is, Pa, up there." He pointed to the great old chestnut tree that dominated the hill, just right of the graveyard. Harley shook his head as he realized that he was already thinking of it in those terms. The graveyard. Two days ago it had simply been the knoll, the highest point on the farm, and nothing more. Suddenly, it was the graveyard. He looked past Seth's out-stretched arm and saw Cy, still in his work clothes, sitting on the bottom limb of the chestnut, swinging his legs under him. Even from this distance, he plainly saw that Cy was starIng down into the hole. He never once looked up as the procession approached.

Finally, they reached the top and Mr. Mosely pulled his team between the tree and the grave, so Cy had to lift his legs up to let them pass. When they stopped, the boy was directly above the box in the back of the wagon. Harley stood up, and the limb on which Cy perched was at eye-level. He held his hand out to the boy. Cy looked at it, then at the hole.

"You should've let me help," he said. "I needed to help."

Harley lifted the two younger boys from the wagon and went to get Amos from Anna Mae. Everyone unloaded and formed a rough circle around the grave. The six brought out three lengths of rope and laid them across the grave, then went and gently slid the box from the back of the wagon. Slowly, ever so slowly, they carried it to the center of the circle of mourners and lowered it onto the ropes, each being careful to stand on his own end. Ellie hung there suspended over the gaping dark below. One of the horses snorted and pawed at the ground, and Reverend Adams began.

"We come from the ground, and there shall we all return," he said. Cy was humming softly up in the tree, but Harley couldn't quite catch the tune.

"Ashes to ashes and dust to dust," said the Reverend. He bent to pick up a handful of soil, but it was crusted over and frozen hard, so it took him a few seconds to break some loose. Finally he straightened and threw the cold dirt onto the lid of the coffin. "Let us pray," he said, as Cy hummed on.

"Lord, make our fleeting life rich in usefulness, eager yet unhurried, on high tasks intent, dauntless in loyalty, vision led and love anointed, till the dark enwraps and Death hangs his sickle at our gate."

Seth began to sob, and as Harley pulled him tight to his side, he recognized the tune Cy hummed. How did the words go?

"When the day is done, sometime, somewhere, at Thy behest, give us to see what here is dim."

He should know it; Ellie sang it to all the kids...

"And by Thy grace, render a higher service in a clearer light."

"Thi," said Amos, looking up from Harley's arms. "Thi?" he called to his big brother perched in the tree above them

"Amen," said the Reverend.

"Amen," said the gathered.

As the six bent to grab the rope ends on which they stood, there came a loud thump from the back of Mr. Mosely's wagon. Cy jumped from the bed of the wagon and ran to the grave, tugging at the back pocket of his too-small, too-worn overalls. He pulled something

14

out and Harley saw a flash of red as Cy threw something into the hole beneath the casket, then step back, bowing his head.

"Thi," said Amos. "Mere, Thi."

Harley wanted to look up to see if the hawk was still circling overhead, but he couldn't look up; he just couldn't.

"The Lord is my shepherd; I shall not want. He maketh me lie down in green pastures...."

At the sign from Reverend Adams, the six began to play the rope out, hand over hand, and they lowered Ellie into the earth.

*

Late that night, after all the hands had been shook and all the hugs hugged, Harley went to his room — it was his room now; how quickly things change — and began to get undressed. Carefully, he folded his tie and suspenders and put them in the top drawer of the bureau, where they belonged, then hung his suit coat and good shirt in the chifforobe, next to Ellie's good dresses, just where he had found them. But as he began to unbutton his pants, he stopped and picked up the kerosene lamp from the nightstand and went into the hall. He paused outside the boy's room, listening to the even rhythm of the breathing in there. Yes, they were all asleep now, even Amos, who was spending only his second night sleeping with his brothers. Harley longed to go in and stroke each brow, gaze into each face. But instead he crossed the hall and stepped through the door there, opposite. He paused and listened, but he couldn't hear it. Quietly, he walked over to the cradle and saw why. The baby, Cassie, lay there, not making a sound, her eyes wide open. She blinked at the flame of the lamp. Harley watched her great brown eyes flick back and forth from his face to the light of the lamp. Deep, deep in there he saw himself reflected behind the light, and, just for a second, he thought he saw Ellie too.

He set the lamp on the table and reached in and picked up his new baby girl. He realized that this was the first time he had held her, and was amazed at the way she molded into his breast. He sat down in the rocking chair, and very softly began talking to his fresh, new, daughter.

After a time, he became aware that the baby was asleep, and that he had probably been dozing too. Moving as slowly as able, he stood, placed her back in the cradle, and covered her. He watched her for a minute, listening to her breathe in tiny hmmms, then picked up the lamp and tiptoed from the room. He went back to his room and pulled off his pants and climbed into bed, but as he reached to shut out the lamp, he stopped and stood back up. He went through the hall into the dining room, to the sideboard where Ellie kept the good dishes. He set the lamp on it and pulled open the top drawer, and before he even looked, he knew that the paper valentine that he and the boys had made for Ellie would be gone.

Chapter 2

Harley woke to the faintly reassuring smell of lilac, and she was there with him, on his pillow, in the bedclothes. It was the familiar flowery scent that roused him, not the strong mid-morning sun that streamed through the window, even though he could not remember ever having slept through a dawn before. He reached across the bed and realized even before his arm fell empty on the cold sheet where he was, and he winced. There came the sounds of frying from the kitchen, and a quiet feminine voice, and it was all too real for him, and he nearly cried.

Liv was talking to someone above the skillet, but whoever it was wasn't answering. Bacon smell came and drowned out the lilac, and Harley pulled himself up and got dressed. He could tell by the light that it was at least nine o'clock and he felt guilty, and he was grateful to feel even that.

When he stepped into the kitchen, Liv looked up from the baby. "Morning, Harley," she said.

"Morning, Liv," he answered. The baby coughed on the bottle. "I sent the boys to school," said Livia Hall. "I didn't think Cy would go, but finally he did. Bert's playing with Amos in their room."

Harley nodded, went to the coffeepot, and poured himself a cup. The bacon was curling and beginning to blacken on the edges. He turned it as he sipped. The day outside the window shone bright and clear, a rare winter hint of the coming spring. He walked to the table where Liv was feeding Cassie, and sat down.

"She's such a lovely child," said Liv.

Harley looked at the little girl for the first time in full light. She was still wrinkled and ruddy, and sparse wisps of black hair clung wet and matted on her tiny head. She sucked at the bottle that Liv held, eyes closed, tiny fists clenched on her chest.

"Yeah," said Harley looking away. "Yeah, I reckon she is."

Across the hall he heard Amos squeal, and then Bert say, "Hush, Amie, Daddy's sleeping."

"You want to finish her?" Liv asked, holding the bottle across the table. The child began to fuss and squirm, her little mouth searching.

"No, Liv, you go ahead," he said, rising and going to the stove. He fished the bacon out piece by piece, laying it across one of Ellie's blue and white Currier plates. There was a winter scene there, depicting a family pulling up to a cabin in a one-horse sleigh. When Harley pulled the last piece out and covered the clouds at the top of the picture, he walked out of the kitchen and across the hall.

Bert and Amos were lying on the floor, face to face on their bellies, playing with their old wooden blocks. Bert jumped up, running to his daddy, hugging his waist.

"Da!" said Amos.

"How're my men this morning?" Harley asked, tousling Bert's dark hair.

"Good, Pa," said Bert. "Amie's building a boat," he said pointing, "he did it all himself."

"Bo," said Amos, pointing. "Bo."

Harley bent to his youngest son. "That's a fine boat, Amie, mighty fine." Amos grinned and sat another block on the pile.

"Mrs. Hall says we have to keep inside, Pa," said Bert. "Can I go out now?"

"Sure, Berty, you go on out and play. But feed your chickens first, okay?"

"Okay, Pa," said Bert, grabbing his coat and running out the door.

Harley hefted Amos up and went back to the kitchen. Liv put Cassie into the cradle by the stove and began breaking eggs into a pan that sizzled with butter. Cassie lay sleeping with a fist pushed into her mouth.

"See your sissie, Amos? Ain't she pretty?" said Harley, leaning over the baby. Amos reached out and grabbed at Cassie's face.

"No, don't touch, just look," Harley told him.

"Bay-bee," said Amos. Cassie frowned in her sleep and tried to roll away, shutting her eyes tightly.

"How many eggs do you want, Harley?" asked Liv.

"I'm not really hungry this morning, Liv," he said, "I'll just have a little bacon."

"Well, I've got two in here. Let me know if you want more."

"Thanks, Liv." He sat Amos down and turned to face her. "Thanks for everything."

Amos waddled immediately to his new sister.

"Just look now, Amos, don't touch," said Harley. The boy put his hands behind his back and leaned deep into the cradle.

"You like 'em over light, don't you, Harley?" Liv asked.

"Sure, that's fine."

She brought a plate to him and gently pushed him into a chair.

"Bay-bee," said Amos.

As Harley began to eat, Liv sat down opposite him. The whites of the eggs were a little runny, but he made himself eat them anyway. Bert's voice drifted from outside.

"Chick, chick, chick," he called. Liv watched Harley eat in silence. Finishing, he spoke.

"I really want to thank you for all you've done. You and Ben."

"Don't even give it a thought," she said.

"You need to be getting back to yours."

"Ben'll be here to get me in the morning. I just couldn't leave."

"There's no need, I'll carry you home this evening."

"Now, I've got all my things with me, and Ben can manage the kids just fine."

"I know, Liv, and you've been a blessing, but the sooner we get on our own the better," Harley said, rising, picking up his empty plate. "I'll take you as soon as the boys get home."

"Whatever you think, Harley, but I'd like to stay."

"I know Liv, and I appreciate it, but...."

"Okay, Harley," she walked to the sink and patted his arm. "Whatever you think."

He gripped the basin hard and stared out the window at Bert, sitting on the top rail of the hog pen, framed by the hills beyond. Behind him, Harley heard Amos shitting audibly in his diaper. Liv went and lifted Amos and carried him from the room.

"Poo," said Amos as they left. "Di-puh."

*

As strong as the sun was, it was still cold out, and Harley was grateful for the sting in his lungs and for the work that still needed to be done. Bert followed him for a while as he fed the hogs and pumped water for the house, but he made the boy stay when he went to see to the cattle. Alone in the fields, his eyes kept straying to the knoll that rose above him wherever he was, and as soon as the chores were done he walked inevitably to it. Before he reached the top, he stopped and looked back across his farm: at the little house nestled by the creek, at the stock scattered away to the west, at the fields waiting to be sown. The wind blew strong up here, and he shivered against the chill. High wispy clouds were moving in and the sky hung low and dark to the northwest, promising a return to the grayness of winter. Everything looked as it always had, as it should, but it all felt so different. He pulled the collar of his coat up as he turned to make the last twenty yards to the crest of the hill.

The heavy limbs of the old chestnut creaked in the wind ahead, and the sunshine vacillated before the oncoming front. Because of the rise, he couldn't see the tombstone until he was within twenty feet of it. The cold, sudden nearness of it stopped him in his tracks. No matter how ready he'd thought he was, the hardness of its reality took him. He stood a dozen paces short of it and sighed. The wind gushed loud around him, seeming to push him on. But he stayed his ground and read the inscription from a distance.

"Eleanor Hayes Felts" It shouted above the wind.

"B. 6/3/1903"

"D. 2/13/1933," it said.

"Wife, Mother, Friend"

"Rest In Peace," it cried.

Harley looked at the raw dirt pile and tried to remember where he had been when they had covered her up, and who it was that had covered her. He took a few steps nearer and sat down, and he prayed, and he fought to keep the anger from his prayers.

Somewhere, through his lowered darkness, he became aware of movement, of another presence. Slowly, fearfully, he looked up. Everything was as he remembered it: stark and still and cold. Then he saw a flash of cloth at the side of the stone, and he knew. He stood up and turned away from the grave.

Spreading away below the valley was silent and still, save the smoke that tore from the chimney of his home. He swallowed hard and took a deep breath.

"It's awful pretty up here," he said aloud. Nothing but the wind answered.

20

"She wants us to go on," he said, and this time he heard the sob, barely.

He turned back to Ellie's place and walked toward the stone. Cy sat huddled on the back side; knees drawn up to the face that he cradled in his hands. Harley squatted next to his son. As badly as he wanted to, he didn't touch the boy, or even speak to him. He just sat there on his haunches, waiting. He heard a sob again, faint and deep, and waited more. Just when he thought he couldn't bear it any longer, the boy spoke.

"She didn't want anymore." Cy's voice sounded small and distant, more thought than speech. "She was happy with us. I heard her say so," he choked on his own voice. "Why'd you make her? Why didn't you leave her alone?"

Harley drew a deep breath and looked at the bowed head of his son. The chestnut groaned in the wind over them.

"You've got a little sister down there, son," Harley said. "Your momma named her last fall. Cassie. Your momma loves her as much as she does you," he went on, "or your brothers. Or me."

Cy didn't speak. Harley sat wishing he would.

"She wants us to go on," he said finally to his son.

Cy raised his head and looked at his father, and the sight of the pain in his son's eyes felt as if it would tear Harley's heart from his chest. They stared deeply at one another for a full minute, then two, then three. Cy put his head back down.

"We were enough. We should have been enough."

Harley reached out and put his arm around the boy's shoulders.

"You were enough, Cy. Seth was enough. Bert and Amos were enough," he whispered. "And now Cassie is enough."

The squall line hovered above them, and the sun went in for what Harley knew would be the last time.

Slowly, inexorably, Cy leaned into his father's hug, until the two of them sat clutching each other, leaning against the tombstone that broke the wind that blew up the hill at them. Harley put his lips against the sad young head under his arm and smelled the freshness.

"Damn," said the son.

"Damn," said the father.

*

There are springs, and there are springs, but the seasons of youth dawn with a clarity and suddenness that flee mature comprehension. Only in innocence can time be divided into sharp, clear lines, and seemingly endless anticipations be finally rewarded, before the blurring guilt of age steals away the awe.

It was drawing on to noon when the single drop of sweat fell upon the blade of the hoe, and Cy's long winter ended. The bluebirds and the gnats had been back for weeks, but they, like the boy, had been simply biding their time, waiting for the change. Cy stopped his work and stood tall, arching his back, hands thrown wide behind him, and he knew that it had finally come. He looked down the endless furrows of dark clumped soil, dotted with pale green sprouts, and he felt the warmth of the breeze on his bare shoulders.

He could see Seth across the field, small and dark, bending to his work. Cy looked up into the incredible blue above, clear as blown azure glass, and thought about the stars that hung invisibly there. The boy in him came to the fore and he suddenly whooped as he flung his hoe high into the air. He broke into a dash for the shade of the hardwoods that stood hewn back from the field.

"C'mon, Seth," he yelled into the quiet air through which he rushed. "We're going to the creek!" He saw Seth pause and straighten up, and even from three hundred yards he could see the question on his brother's face.

"C'mon!" cried Cy, turning and running backwards across the tiny ridges and valleys of freshly plowed ground. "Rotten egg!"

Seth stood for a moment watching his older brother, apparently gone mad, then something in his expression changed. He dropped his hoe and sprinted toward the woods, angling to cut off Cy's path. As Cy turned to run forward, he tripped on the uneven ground and fell tumbling into the clean, rich soil, laughing. He sprang up and ran across the furrows in the smooth, leaping bound of the young, the wild, the free.

When he crossed into the tree line, the coolness hit him like a kiss, and he flew in zigging glee, hitting the gaps between the trees and bushes with uncanny precision. He heard Seth crashing along behind him, to his left. Cy shouted straight ahead, not daring to take his eyes off the maze before him.

"Whooooo-weee!"

"Yeeeee-haaa!" Seth came back, and Cy knew he was outpacing the younger boy. Grinning, he leapt over a fungus covered rotting log, and he began to smell water.

When at last he reached the slow winding curve in Willow Branch that was the swimming hole, he threw himself down onto a bed of cool moss and listened to the sound of his own labored breathing. The water gurgled quietly below him as he pressed himself low and tried to slow his racing heart. Grasshoppers and cicadas buzzed around him and a shaft of golden sunlight penetrated the canopy above and fell on his hand, lighting it in golden aura. He heard the footfalls of Seth nearing and he stifled a giggle as he eased behind the trunk of a huge white oak whose roots lay bare in the bank of earth that the water had cut into the land. Suddenly Seth stopped and all was quiet again, save the buzzing of cicadas and the babble of water.

"Cy?" Came the tentative call. "You there, Cy?"

Cy heard the slow, sneaking steps grow nearer. In his mind's eye he saw the approach of his brother – low, and crouching, and wary.

"Come on, Cy, I know you're here."

Cy's panting was gone now. He drew imperceptibly into himself, coiling. He heard the soft steps pass his tree and he saw Seth gently easing up the creek bank, hunting. Cy counted silently: "One. Two. Three!" and he sprang with the immortal ferocity of the ageless predator. Seth never had a chance. He was knocked down from behind and pinned without ever hearing the pounce. Cy grabbed a handful of moss and held it to his brother's mouth.

"Say it or eat it," he grinned.

Seth twisted his head violently, but Cy grabbed his hair and pushed the moss to Seth's lips. "Say it."

Disgust showed plainly in Seth's eyes, but he knew he was caught, and when he opened his mouth to comply, he tasted the verdant fungal bite of what was held there.

"My, my, good old Cy," he spat.

Cy climbed off, laughing, leaving the moss resting on Seth's mouth. As soon as his back was turned, Seth took the clump and hurled it at Cy, hitting him squarely in the back of the head. Cy whirled, grinning, and the two circled one another cautiously before falling into a squealing, giggling, fight to the death.

After they swam and splashed and dunked for over an hour, they lay drying on the bank in a patch of light that slanted low under the trees. Cy looked at the sun through his closed eyes, watching the color of his lids change from yellow to red to violet as he clinched them tighter and tighter.

"What're we having for supper tonight?" he asked.

"I dunno," answered Seth. "Chicken, I guess."

"Chicken again! Don't you know how to fix anything else?"

"You try it bigshot! You try cooking for a while."

"Yeah, and you're going to tote bales all evening, right?" said Cy. "Chicken. Ugh! Sometimes I think I'm going to grow feathers."

"Yeah, well you just try doing it, Mr. Big-shot. You just try it sometime." Seth, seeing the look in his brother's eyes jumped up, grabbed his clothes and began running toward home. "Mr. Big-shot!" he called over his shoulder. "Mr. Big-shit!"

Cy raised his face and squeezed his eyes tight, loving the heat as the light turned indigo inside him.

When finally he dressed and headed to the house, the evening was nearly upon him. The sounds of afternoon were quieting and the sun lay dying red in the pink and blue sky before him.

Seth had actually become a decent cook in the time since Ma. At first the meals had been horrendous. Once, all of them — even Pa — had lain sick for a full day, waiting to die of food poisoning. But they'd survived, and now the food was beginning to taste again, rather than gag.

Bert and Amos were playing on the front porch as he approached the house. When they saw him, they came running.

"Thy! Thy!" called Amos, slamming into the gate. "Thpin me, Thy!"

Cy grabbed the little boy by the arms and whirled him around and around until he got too dizzy to keep it up. He slowed, easing the two-year-old into the bright Easter-colored grass.

"Me next," demanded Bert, and after Cy gave him a turn, the younger boys followed their big brother onto the porch, where the smell of frying chicken sifted through the screen door. It reminded Cy of the smells of so long ago. He loved that smell. They went inside and Bert immediately began setting the table.

Seth grumped over the stove, "Toting bales, huh? You're just lazy, Cy Felts."

Cy cuffed his brother lightly on the ear and said, "Where's Pa? Ain't he back yet?"

"No," said Seth, "But he'll hear plenty when he gets here, believe me."

Cy cuffed him again, much to Amos' delight. Seth just scowled.

"I'll spit on your piece."

"Do it and die," said Cy, scooping Amos up and carrying him out to the pump to wash up. Bert followed along.

"Ya'll been swimming, ain't ya?" asked Bert.

"Mind your own business," said Cy, "And wash them hands good."

By the time they got back into the house, Seth was clearing the stove and supper was ready.

"Looks like Pa's going to be late," he said. "Let's go on and eat while it's hot." Cy sat Amos in the highchair, and Bert and Seth went to their places. The children all looked to Cy, and he bowed his head.

"Lord," he began, "Thank you for this food."

"Amen," said Amos.

"Not yet, Amie," said Cy. Seconds of quiet passed before he spoke again. "Thank you for the roof over our heads. Thank you for the sunshine and for the songbirds, and for us." Outside, the hogs snorted in a quarrel. "And bless Ma too, God, tell her we all miss her." The silence again. "Amen."

"Amen," repeated Seth and Bert.

"Uh-huh," said Amos.

And they ate.

It was full dark, and the boys were all in bed before Harley came in with Cassie. Cy heard the door slam, and the familiar heavy footsteps in the hall as his father carried the baby to her room. He heard the steps go into the kitchen, and Cy knew his Pa was at the sink, gnawing on a piece of chicken. He could easily picture his daddy's big frame bent before the window, eyes scrolling across the dim farmyard as he slowly chewed. Whenever Pa looked out at the land like that, his huge dark eyes took on an absence, and Cy could never decide whether they looked vacant, or intense. It was almost as if Pa was out there, being a part of that, rather than here, peering through his pupils. It didn't really scare Cy, but he was never entirely comfortable around his Pa when he was like that; he always felt like some kind of intruder, or spy.

He heard a chicken bone splash into the stockpot, then heard footsteps starting from the kitchen. Cy watched the wavering light of the lamp coming down the hall. He could see Amie, already asleep on his pallet by the window. The door creaked open, and Bert was immediately across the floor and into his Daddy's arms.

"Hi, Pa! What took you so long tonight?"

Seth propped himself up on one elbow. "Hey, Pa."

"Evenin', boys," said Harley, rubbing Bert's back. He leaned over and kissed a shock of the boy's hair, then went to Seth and kissed his forehead. Cy laid with his arms crossed behind his head and Harley patted his chest as he walked by to bend over Amos.

"Where you been, Pa?" Bert asked again.

"I just had a little meeting tonight, Bertie, and I reckon us men have got to have us a talk about it," said Harley.

"What about, Pa?" asked Seth, sitting up. Cy rolled onto his side and raised his head off the pillow.

"Well, after I picked your little sister up, we went over to the Gambil's house for a visit..."

"Across the river!" cried Bert. "Why didn't you take us across the river with you, Pa!"

"Now, Bertie, you know the Halls live halfway to the river from here. By the time I got done in the tobacco, if I'd come all the way back here to get you little boogers, we wouldn't be at the Gambil's place yet. Besides, the ferry quits running at sundown. We'd have had to spend the night."

"But, Pa, across the river!" said Bert, nearly breathless.

"Next time, Bertie, next time."

"What kind of business?" Cy asked quietly from the corner.

Harley straightened up and went to the lamp on the bureau where he had set it, and lowered the wick. When he turned back to face the boys, the dim flame was behind him, plunging his face into shadow.

"You all know Mr. and Mrs. Gambil from church," he began, taking a breath. "Well, I was talking to them, and we came to a little ... uh, arrangement."

Amos let out a small sigh in his sleep, and Seth and Cy glanced over at one another.

"Ya'll know how hard it's been around here the last few weeks." He stopped and looked at his feet for a moment. "And I've got to say you boys have all done real good around the place here. I'm mighty proud of all of you." Harley looked over to Cy, who was staring down at Amos on the floor. Bert yawned. The flame behind Harley flickered, and Cy looked up, watching the immense shadow of his Pa, cast jumping and wavering across the ceiling.

"Mrs. Gambil's niece, Sara is coming down from Maryland on the train the day after tomorrow. She was going to go live with her aunt and uncle for a few months, but like everyone else around here they're in kind of a squeeze right now." Harley paused, and Bert yawned again, rolling over.

"Sara's going to be coming to stay with us for a while. She's..."

"Pa!" cried Cy sitting up suddenly. "We don't need no girl around here. We're getting along fine." He looked square at Harley for a moment before laying back down, crossing his arms over his chest. "We're getting along fine," he said again.

"Sure we are, son. We're doing just fine, every one of us. But Cassie's not here during the day and we can't expect Mrs. Hall to raise her forever, can we?" Harley's shadow rose a bit higher on the ceiling. "And you know that you and Seth aren't supposed to go off together and leave your little brothers here alone." He said, looking knowingly at Cy, then at Seth. "But how're we going to get the crops in if one of you has to stay near the house all day?" Seth sneaked a look over to Cy, who was having none of it. Harley turned sideways, and a thin crescent of his profile showed in the dim yellow light.

"She's on her way, tomorrow. There aren't any jobs for a young girl around here, and we all agreed that it'd work out best for everyone if she came over here and watched after Cassie a while. Bert and Amos too. For her keep."

The wick in the lamp began to dry and the light began to die.

"She'll be coming home with us after church on Sunday. She's to be welcomed into our home and treated as one of our own," he said, looking at the two older boys. Bert had joined Amos, sleeping. The lamp began to sputter and its feeble light gave out nearly all together. But before it did Harley went to Seth and rubbed his chest, and then to Cy, who had turned to face the wall. He kissed the back of his son's head.

"Good night, boys," he said, pausing at the doorway. A ray of early moonlight fell through the window, lighting Amos's face in pale angelic innocence.

"Night, Pa," said Seth.

The light went out with a soft spit, plunging the room into darkness.

Chapter 3

There is a place on the western foot of the highland rim where the low, even country of the great Mississippi Valley first encounters the rippling hill country that spreads out from under the majestic Appalachians. The slow, broad waters of the Tennessee River mark the boundaries with almost clerical precision, and only occasionally do the thin-soiled limestone ridges of the east cross; and for every acre they claim, the rich flat bottoms of the west retaliate, broaching into the highlands. But on the whole, the two realms keep each to its side, respecting the jurisdiction of the river, perhaps because it is the spawn of their conflict, in a rare, mystical place where a major American river flows from south to north. Or perhaps simply because sharply defined ending and beginning points, though harder to swallow, are much more reliable than gray blendings.

Just at one of those gray areas, where the water takes a sudden and unfair turn to the west, there lies a bay of land, thirty miles wide and fifteen deep, bounded north and south and west by the river. Here, neither side lays claim, nor relinquishes; hollows and ridges flow into the fertile lowland, and smooth cotton bottoms stand shoulder to shoulder with rugged corn patch and cattle country. Through the middle of this bay runs Indian Creek, mostly shin deep, and wide and quick and cold running, but sometimes curving back on itself into lazy, deep green pools where fat catfish lay. It spills into the Tennessee about twenty miles below the great battlefields at Shiloh and Pittsburg Landing, where twenty thousand souls poured their juice into the land for Union or for State, and its clear water can be seen downstream along the eastern bank of the great river for more than a mile. Traveling upstream along the Indian, in seven or eight miles there joins from the north a nondescript little stream called Willow Branch, and four miles along it, at its very head, a small stone and cedar spring house spews forth water from hundreds of feet below; water as pure and cold and clean as the day God made it; water that will feed the Gulf of Mexico a fortnight later; water that will briefly flow from the south to the north, to serve as fleeting guardian between the high and the low, the one and the other.

The spring house lies tucked in perpetual shade at the crotch of a hollow, and so, is largely covered with moss; rock and shake alike. The small oak door, less than four feet high, faces downstream and shows the wear of eternal damp, though it is the fourth of its kind to guard this portal in the past hundred years — since the continent was still fresh and clean. Twelve generations of bluebird have nested and raised young between the rear wall cap and the left gable rafter, and there is a worn hole in the dirt and stone floor that actually connects to a fox den, though this is a place haunted by man.

The earthwater roils up into a dim, chiseled stone basin before spilling under the door and disappearing into a wide, flat, wintergreen marsh. About twenty yards away, it collects itself and rolls into a deep, narrow channel, and Willow Branch begins.

Eighty yards farther on the tall hardwoods fall away and the water passes along the edge of a small glade, and in the glade is a short-walled cemetery of about a dozen graves, a lodge pole picnic shelter, and a wood-frame hall with a very steep roof, topped by a steeple.

Bess plodded up the lane that wound along the banks of the creek, her hooves raising little clouds of dust with each step. It was still too early in the year for the trees to be leafed over, so the morning sun shone strong, glistening in the patches of foam on the horse's flank. The morning air hung thick and redolent with the smell of new green and blossom.

Harley sat high on the creaking wagon seat holding the reins loosely in his rough hands. He gave ole Bess her head; she didn't need to be driven on such a familiar path. He listened to the birds singing the new spring on, and to the groaning complaint of the wagon through the ruts, and he thought about another ride he had made down this road, on just this kind of day, a lifetime ago. It was near this very spot, though heading in the opposite direction, that he had proposed to Ellie. Sweet, tender, Ellie. So very long ago, so very far away...

Seth sat on the seat beside him holding Cassie, cooing and grinning down at her.

"Look, Pa, she smiled back," he said. "She's getting to be kind of fun, you know. Like she's really a person, not just a crying machine."

"Yeah, I know," said Harley, looking at his little girl. "You're right, son."

Bert sat in the wagon bed behind the seat, teaching Amos to tie his shoes.

"No, Amie! This one goes under."

"I know," said Amos, still pulling the string over the top.

Cy sat swinging his legs off the back of the wagon, looking at the road behind them.

As Bess swung into the last bend before the church, they began to hear the faint organ music and the strains of the congregation's singing. The hymn was "On a Hill Faraway".

"We're late again, Pa," said Cy. Harley heard the edge in his son's voice. "We shouldn't even of come."

Harley pulled the reins in. The creaking of the wagon and the clop of Bess's hooves ceased, and the only sounds were of the birds above and the water below. Harley turned in the seat.

"Now listen, son, I'm going to say this one more time and that's the end of it," he said, very quietly. Bert and Amos stilled, looking up at their father. "The decision has been made, and you can't change it. We're not going to argue about it anymore. I've listened to everything you and your brothers have had to say about this," he looked at Seth, "and you've heard what I've said. If I knew another way I'd take it, but I don't." Harley looked back at Cy. Cassie gurgled on Seth's lap. "Get your brother's shoes tied, Berty." He snapped the reins and they lurched into motion.

It was Homecoming Sunday and the pews were nearly full when they walked into the stuffy little chapel. The singing was over, and a small sea of paper fans waved in the room as the choir walked quietly to sit with their families. Harley took a seat in the back row with Bert on one side, Amos on the other and Cassie on his lap. Cy and Seth stood against the back wall with some of the other boys.

"Hello, Harley," said the Reverend Adams from the pulpit. "Glad you could make it." Harley heard Cy cough behind him. "Standing room only!" Said Reverend Adams, beaming at the boys lined across the back. "Isn't it wonderful we could all make it here this fine and glorious morning!"

The sermon was homecoming oriented, about fellowship and the value of keeping in touch with old friends and the duty of Christians to one another. It ran on longer than usual, proportionate to the increased audience. When finally the benediction and invitation had been given, and the Lord's Supper and the collection taken, the reverend led in the closing hymn, 'Nearer My God To Thee'. Harley heard a giggle behind him and turned to see if it was one of his boys, but it was one of the Anderson kids.

As the last line of the song died away the only sounds were of the closing of hymnbooks and the elders filing slowly out. When they reached the door and pulled it open, sunlight flowed back down the aisle and struck the foot of the pulpit.

People began to stand and the room broke into a score of loud conversations while the children headed for the door. By the time Harley talked himself out of the chapel and past the elders, the kids were already scattered about the lawn and along the creek and the women were carrying food to the picnic shelter. Harley walked toward the creek, knowing that was where his boys would be. He spotted Seth, floating sticks downstream with four or five other boys. As he headed for them across the grass, which was recently mown and spiked with the long stems of fast-growing wild onion, he felt more at ease than he had in a long time. All around him were people he'd known all his life, and the sounds of happy voices and children playing in the sun. Everywhere the land spoke of fresh growth, of rebirth.

The boys stopped their play and looked up at Harley as he reached the bank above them.

"Hello, boys," he said, nodding around. "Seth, how about going and getting those beans you cooked?" A couple of the boys snickered.

"Aww, Pa, can't Cy fetch 'em?" said Seth shyly. Harley saw the small face begin to flush. "I had to cook 'em." There were more giggles.

Seth squinted at his father, standing on the bank with the sun at his shoulder. Harley could feel its heat on his ears.

"That's okay, son," said Harley, "I just thought you might pull the wagon in a little closer while you were up there, is all."

Even into the sun, the child's eyes threw wide.

"Really, Pa?" He said, almost in a whisper. "You mean it? Drive the Wagon?"

"Sure," said Harley, winking at Seth, "take it down there by the willows. Get Bess some shade."

32

"Okay, Pa," said Seth as he looked around at the other boys, "I'll get them beans for you." He stood squinting up at his Pa. Harley could see his own reflection in the irises of his son, brown as topsoil in the bottoms. Seth sprang up the bank like a doe startled in the brush, and the other boys scrambled after him.

As Harley made his way to the picnic shelter, his eyes searched the crowd that was gathering there, beginning the line down the long rough-sawn oak table, bowed heavy with food. He saw the Gambils standing near the cemetery talking with Sam Adams, and he headed that way.

The reverend had his back to Harley, and as usual was doing most of the talking. Rig Gambil and his wife Clorise were facing each other on the other side of Sam. The girl stood opposite the preacher, leaning back on her hands atop the cemetery wall.

She wore a fine white linen dress that stood out from the calico and gingham of most of the ladies. Her hair was long and straight and blonde almost beyond hint of yellow. Harley saw her look up past the gesturing of Sam and the nodding of her aunt and uncle, and he stuttered a half step when he saw her eyes. He had never seen eyes so pale. They were nearly as white as they were blue, like evening sky behind cirrus clouds.

She watched Harley's approach until Sam noticed her focus. He stopped talking in mid-sentence and looked around.

"Well, hello there, Harley!" He said, turning. "We were just talking about you." He clapped an arm around Harley's shoulder and drew him in. The girl looked back across the tombstones behind her.

"Hello, Sam," said Harley. "Rig." He shook Rig's hand. "Hello, Clorise."

"Hello, Harley," said Clorise. "My, those boys are growing up fast!"

"They sure are," answered Harley. "They sure are," he said again, without knowing why.

"Harley, this here's Sara," said Rig. The girl turned back around. "Sara, say hello to Mr. Felts."

"Hello," she said. Her voice was as pale as her eyes, as faint as her hair.

"Hello, Sara," said Harley. At the serving line a loud burst of laughter rang out.

Reverend Adams still had his arm around Harley's shoulder. "Beautiful day for Homecoming, ain't it?" he said happily, and they all agreed. A brief, miserable second went by when no one spoke, broken when Seth came running up, carrying a cast iron pot wrapped in a towel.

"I got the beans, Pa," he said, beaming at Harley. He held the pot up to his father. "Thanks for letting me get 'em."

Harley took the pot from Seth. "Son, you remember Mr. and Mrs. Gambil don't you?"

"Yes sir. Hello, Mr. Gambil. Mrs. Gambil."

"And this is Sara."

Seth looked at Sara for the first time, and she at him. There was another moment of silence.

"Hello, Seth," she said quietly.

"Gosh..." said the boy. "Umm, I mean, hello."

The preacher leaned down to Seth. "Sara's all the way from Maryland," he said, rubbing Seth's hair, "Imagine that."

"Yeah," said Seth. Harley saw the girl smile shyly back at his son.

"We'd better get these over to the table," he said, lifting the bean pot. He looked at Sam. "You're going to have that horseshoe arm ready aren't you, partner?"

"You bet," said Sam. Harley thought it was the shortest sentence he'd ever heard the man speak. He looked at Rig. "Why don't ya'll eat with us over at the table by the spring?"

"Sure, Harley," Rig answered.

"Clorise," Harley nodded, taking his leave. "Sara," he nodded again, "pleased to meet you."

The girl looked him in the eye for the first time since his approach.

"The pleasure is mine," she said. Her voice sounded to Harley like it was very far away.

"Come on, Pa," said Seth, grabbing Harley's arm. "Let's go." He looked at the other grown-ups. "Reverend. Mr. Gambil, Mrs. Gambil," he said, leaning slightly forward in a half bowing motion. As he started to pull Harley away, he called back, "See you, Sara,".

"See you, Seth," said Sara.

By the time Harley gathered his boys together, most everyone else had been through the food line, except the children, who were always last. As he shepherded his brood through the line he joked and teased with the other kids around him, alternately towering over them and bending to them. When they finally had all their plates filled, Harley handed his to Cy.

"How about carrying this over to the spring," he said nodding toward the table under the huge old cedar where the Gambils sat. "I'm going to get your sister from the ladies."

"Can't I go eat with Jody and Billy, Pa?" Asked Cy. "I promised them I would."

"No, son, we're all going to eat together today," said Harley, "as a family." Cy turned and walked away.

Harley went and took Cassie from the clump of women who had been fussing over her. Marlene Howard, Doodie's spinster sister handed her to Harley, grinning her crooked-toothed grin at him. "She's such a hoot, Harley! I'd love to see her more often." Her eyes were blinking so rapidly that Harley thought a gnat had flown into one of them before he realized.

"Sure, Marlene. We'll be here next Sunday. She can sit with you if you like."

Then Charlsie Polk said, "Put your tongue back in your mouth, Marlene," and all the ladies laughed, except Marlene, who just kept grinning at Harley. She didn't even blush. But he did.

"Thank you girls for watching after Cass," he said, leaving.

The tables were all full with the adults, and the kids sat scattered about the lawn, balancing their plates on their knees. The loud jovial talk had faded into the quiet catching up of mealtime. Cassie grabbed at Harley's face as he carried her across the lawn.

The Gambils were almost through eating when he got there. He spread Cassie's blanket in the shade of the cedar and laid her on it. She immediately rolled onto her side and shoved her thumb into her mouth. Bert and Seth sat next to Amos at the table while Bert talked excitedly to Sara about his two box turtles, Jason and Hercules. Harley's plate sat balancing on the end of the table. He looked at Cy, who sat on the ground with his back to the gnarled trunk of the cedar. His plate sat on the ground at his side, untouched. Harley sat down opposite Rig.

"I see everyone's been introduced," he said.

"Not really," said Rig, nodding toward Cy. The boy sat watching the creek flow by.

"Sara's nice, Pa," said Bert. "She rode the train here."

Harley smiled at Bert. "You need to do a little less talking and a little more eating."

"Yes, sir," replied Bert.

Harley and Rig talked about the weather and the prospects for the year's crops as they ate. Sara picked at her food, smiling politely at Bert and Amos' contest for her attention. When they had all finished eating Clorise stood up and gathered the plates.

"I'll go rinse these off," she said. "Would you like some more tea, Harley? Rig?"

"No thanks, dear," said her husband. Harley shook his head. "Thanks, Clorise."

"I'll come help you, Aunt Clo," offered Sara, rising.

"No, honey, I can manage," she said, laying a hand on the girl's shoulder, easing her back down. "You just sit here and visit a bit."

Harley watched Clorise take Cy's full plate from his side. He looked at Rig and sighed.

"Cy, come here a minute," he called.

Cy looked at his father for a second, then rose and took two steps toward the table.

"Sara, this is Cy," said Harley, "Cy, Sara." The flies that had gathered for the food buzzed in the air.

"Hello, Cy," said the girl quietly.

"Hello." Cy never looked up from his feet.

"How's that calf of yours doing, Cy?" asked Rig.

"Fine," said Cy. "She's up to eighty-two pounds. Pa says she'll be bigger than her momma." He looked up at Harley. "Can I go to the creek now?"

"Sure, son, go ahead."

"Me too?" asked Bert.

"Me too!" echoed Amos.

"Go on," Harley smiled. "Bert, keep your little brother out of the water."

"Okay, Pa," said Bert, already bounding away.

"Wait, Berty," cried little Amos, running after.

"They're good kids, Harley," said Rig. "All of 'em."

"Yeah, I know they are, Rig. Thanks."

Cassie was sleeping soundly, and Harley bent to shoo a fly from her face. A crow landed in a treetop across the creek and cawed loudly. An answer came from behind the church.

Seth stood up from the table. "Want to go see the spring house, Sara?"

The girl looked at Rig, and he nodded.

"Surely," she said, rising. "Excuse me, Uncle Rig." She looked directly at Harley for the first time since he had sat down. "Mr. Felts," she said. She followed Seth down the hill, walking slowly with her hands clasped behind her back.

The two men watched until they reached the little building, then Rig turned to Harley.

"I wonder how much water's flowed out of there since you and me and Bobby tried to race sticks down it all the way to the river."

Harley turned and followed the creek downstream with his eyes. It sounded the same. It looked the same, though maybe a little wider, a little slower. Cy was down there, throwing rocks at a floating can.

"Oceans." He said.

Rig looked at the little cemetery. "Did you ever dream about it? I still dream about it sometimes."

Cy hit the can square, knocking it under and a second later Harley heard the clank.

"Yeah, I have, Rig. I'm afraid I have."

A boy waded in to fish the can out while the others loaded up on stones.

Rig turned back to Harley. "I appreciate you doing this, Harley," he said.

"Well, it's fine of you to thank me for it, but you know it's not just you I'm doing it for," said Harley. Cassie was waking and she cried a little, then hushed.

"She really seems like a nice girl," said Rig, "and a decent enough cook, for a nineteen-year-old. There just wasn't any way we could take her on now, so when Clorise mentioned you a week after she got the letter from Sally, I figured it might just work out the best for everybody."

"Yeah, it will, one way or the other," said Harley, watching the boys at the creek. "Cassie'll be walking by next spring, and Bert'll be nearly six, old enough to watch the little ones. It'll work out."

"The timing's almost like it was just meant to be, isn't it?" said Rig. Cassie began to cry again. Without answering, Harley got up and went to her.

Around three o'clock a stiff breeze began to push the treetops toward the southeast, and a bank of dark, dense clouds showed itself in the western sky. People began to load up their cars and their wagons, and hug and smile at friends they would not see until another season. Harley sat on the cemetery wall giving Cassie her bottle. He was at the exact same spot he and Ellie had sat so long ago, and he talked softly to the feeding child, telling her. He watched the assembly breaking apart and the glade growing sparse. Across the way, walking slowly to the parking lot between her aunt and uncle, he saw the golden shine of the girl's hair swinging evenly between her shoulder blades. When they reached Rig's old Ford, Rig put his arm around his wife and they stood there facing the girl, talking. Then they each hugged her, and Rig reached into the back seat and pulled out a large black bag.

Harley stood up and bent his head low to Cassie. He hummed one of Ellie's rhymes as he walked slowly to the wagon.

*

They were less than a mile from the church when the sun went in and the wind began blowing fiercely, kicking dust into their faces. Thunder rolled off in the distance, low and long, building as it went, like the sound at the end of a battery of cannon. The trees along the road swayed violently, and the girl's long hair whipped at Harley's face.

"Better unroll the tarp," he called to Cy in the back. Bess snorted into the wind, stepping quick.

Cy pulled the tarp from under the seat and spread it across the bed. It smelled of corn.

"Seth, get Bert and Amos under the seat." Harley had to shout above the roar of the rising wind. "Cy, I want you up here helping me hold the tarp when it hits."

"Okay, Pa," yelled Cy.

A flash of lightning blazed the sky, and thunder boomed a second behind it. Very close. Harley felt Sara flinch nearly off the seat. He smiled.

"Lightning's good," he told her, "It puts nitrogen in the soil. And thunder puts the fear of God in you."

She pulled a rope of hair from her mouth. "How far is it?" She asked above the wind.

"About half an hour," he shouted back, "or forty-five minutes."

"Oh," said Sara.

A bolt from the sky flashed down on a tree behind them and a limb as thick as a man's waist crashed onto the road, leaving a coppery taste lingering in the air. Cy climbed into the seat, pulling the canvas with him as rain began to pat in huge, random splotches. Harley took one corner of the tarp, and Cy held up the other.

"Oh," mouthed Sara.

"Git on, Bessie," cried Harley snapping the reins. The horse eagerly obeyed.

It was the epitome of spring storm in the mid-south; of the kind that come only once every few years. Combining all the ferocity of late summer squalls with the staying power of winter weather, it lashed across the land like God gone mad, blurring the creek and bending the life. The rain beat on the tarp like stones on tin and blew under it no matter how Harley and Cy tried to hold it. They had to shout across Sara in full voice to be heard. She tried to help them hold the tarp against the wind, but she didn't have a corner to grip and it kept ripping from her hand. Harley could hear Amos crying loudly under him, and Cassie too. He worried if they would get to the ford in time.

The southeast corner of the farm was marked by the junction of Willow Branch and Indian Creek. The property lines followed the water north and west, and steep ridges lay to the south and east, boxing in a little over four hundred acres all tolled, effectively limiting access to one place: a gravel bar on Indian Creek just below Willow Branch. From there it was less than a half mile to the house. Bess reached the crossing and pulled up before Harley even realized they were there. The thunder and lightning had moved away to the south and the rain was slacking a bit, but still it drove down in stinging sheets. When Harley saw the ford, it was worse than he'd hoped, but not as bad as he'd imagined. He gave his side of the tarp to Sara and the reins to Cy.

"Hold tight on Bess," he yelled, "I'm going to go have a look." He climbed off the wagon and into the storm. He went first and rubbed Bess's neck and spoke calmly into her ear. She stepped her front hooves high, clomping them down into the gravel, but she didn't pull. He went to the edge of the torrent that spilled across his drive and looked at how high it ran against the roots of the big sycamore on the opposite bank. He looked across the fields toward the house, then walked back to the wagon on Cy's side.

"It's under four feet," he called. "I'm going to try and lead her through." Cy nodded at his father. "Tell Seth to hold Amos, and give Cassie to Sara. Get Bert up there on the seat between you two." While the children rearranged, Harley picked up the largest rocks he could find and piled them on the back of the wagon. When he was satisfied, he went back to Cy.

"Don't pull her back any, just keep her turned upstream," he said.

"Okay, Pa," shouted Cy. The rain was weakening by the minute, but the water rose by the second. Harley went to Bess and scratched behind her ears and rubbed her neck.

"C'mon now, girl," he told her, "We're going home."

He took a good hold on the halter and led her to the water. She pulled back at first, then followed Harley into the seething yellow-brown and white rage. The water was cold and fast, tugging at Harley's legs, trying to sweep his feet from under him. He stepped slow and cautious, finding good purchase with each step before releasing his last.

By the time they reached mid-way, the water was splashing off the under-carriage of Bess's ribs. Harley pulled her head hard upstream and talked her on. He saw the back of the wagon try to float, and for one horrifying instant, he thought it was gone, but it settled back to the bottom. His foot hit a slick spot and his legs swept to his side, nearly horizontal. He held his grip on Bess's harness, his hands yanking on one side of her neck while his boots bobbed to the surface on her far side. He pulled himself tight to her face, trying to fight his legs back beneath him, and when he saw the wild-eyed look of her pupils just inches from his, it scared him far more than when the wagon bed had raised in the water. If she panicked it was all over. He looked deep at her, caught her foreleg with his ankle, and she stood firm. He wrapped his other leg around her shin, and was able to stand. Only then did he take his eye from hers. Only then did she take her eye from his. And just as she started to pull for the far bank, there came a dull thud from the creek above them. Harley turned and saw a tree trunk twice the size of a railroad tie twisting around the bend toward them.

"Git up now!" He shouted into Bess's ear. The horse leaned hard against the current, and the wagon eased forward, then caught and sunk.

"Git!" He fairly screamed, trying to keep fear from his voice. "Git, Bess!"

She lowered her head so that her snout was brushing the wake before her, and the wagon lurched, then her ribs cleared the water, and suddenly they were on dry land, just as the log slammed its way past, just missing the wagon behind them. Harley heard it go by, and he heard Cy let out a loud whoop and heard Bess blow out water. And he heard Sara laughing, high and clear.

By the time they reached the house they were all soaked through and through. Harley stood and helped them all down.

"Seth, take Sara and show her to her room. Cy, you fetch her bag. I'm going to put Bess away."

He stood and watched them disappear through the front door before walking Bess to the barn. As he rubbed the mare down and praised her in the dim quiet, he remembered the sun of the morning, and how it shone.

He heard footsteps running through the mud, and Cy appeared in the doorway, silhouetted in gray.

"Sara wants to know," said the boy, "What do you want for supper?"

Chapter 4

It rained all night, but the viciousness was gone, rumbling and flashing away into the southern sky. The water fell in the slow, even manner that fills the earth and lies so dear to the heart of the farmer. Harley stood at the door of the barn watching darkness overtake the land, blotting out detail. The washed air smelled cool and clean before him, blending with the sharpness of the stalls behind.

He'd fed all the stock and checked the hog, old Weena, who was overdue to drop a litter. The sow lay snorting quietly in the muck of her stall as he poked and prodded, trying to tell if she was in distress. He prowled the loft, searching out leaks in the roof and marking them so he could patch when they got dry. He even straightened the tack room, something he'd been putting off for months. Then he just stood and listened to the drumming of the rain, watching the storm move off into the distance, and the lights in the house wink out one by one. All the while Duke sat by his master's side, peering into the night.

When only the kitchen window still glowed, he blew out the lantern in the barn and walked slowly to the house.

He stopped on the porch and hung his jacket and cap on the hook by the door. As he took off his boots, the sky lit for an instant with distant lightening and he saw the chestnut tree on the knoll, silhouetted through the rain. Harley scratched Duke's ears and went into the house.

It was still and dim and quiet inside, so the ticking of the mantle clock seemed loud and distinct, counting out the night. The smell of stew filled the air and Harley realized he was hungry. He went through the dining room toward the light of the kitchen.

He was startled to see the girl sitting at the table, her head resting on her hands on the tabletop. He stopped, and heard the faint weeping.

"Sara?" he said tentatively.

Her head jerked up and he heard her gasp softly.

"I didn't mean to scare you," he said.

"That's okay, Mr. Felts," she said, standing. "I was just a little startled, that's all." She went to the stove. "I kept some soup warm," she said. Harley watched her dab at her eyes as she stirred the pot.

"Harley," he said. "Call me Harley."

He went to the cupboard and took out a bowl and a spoon.

"Smells good," he said. He saw the back of her head nod and she sniffed loudly, drawing her sleeve across her face. Low thunder rolled off in the distance.

Harley went to the stove and held his bowl while she ladled soup into it. He marveled at how small and pale her hand was against the big wooden spoon. Sara studied her task, careful not to spill. When the bowl was full, Harley went to the table and sat and began to eat. The clink of his spoon against the bowl and the sound of the hot soup in his mouth — even his swallows — seemed incredibly loud to him.

"This is good," he said.

Sara sniffed again, softer this time, and turned to face him.

"Thank you," she said. One of the boys coughed in his sleep across the hall.

"They been to bed long?" Harley asked, nodding toward the door.

"About a half an hour," said Sara.

"Oh," said Harley. He took a spoonful of soup.

"They're nice boys," Sara said, taking the pot from the stove. "Amos is a doll."

"Yeah," said Harley, "he is. A doll."

"Will you be wanting any more?" Sara asked.

"Maybe a little," said Harley. "Just leave it. I'll give what's left to Duke. He hasn't been fed yet."

"Oh," said Sara, wiping her hands on her apron. On Ellie's apron.

"You can go on to bed," said Harley, "I'll see to Cassie when she wakes." It suddenly seemed warm in the room and Harley felt flushed. Heat flashed through him redly, and a wave of dizziness.

The girl hesitated a moment then reached behind her back, untying the apron. She pulled it over her head, shaking out her long yellow hair, and hung it on the pantry door. Where it belonged. She paused again, watching Harley eat, then walked to the hall doorway. She stopped and turned.

"Good night, Mr. Felts," she said.

"Harley," he answered over the soup, "Call me Harley."

Cassie woke twice during the night, and both times she took her bottle and went easily back to sleep. She really was a good baby, Harley thought as he tucked the quilt around her the second time. She fussed far less than any of the boys had, and whenever Harley was feeding her she watched his eyes with a brown unwavering stare that spoke to him of pure love and trust and contentment. He had come to treasure her calls in the night — the sound of her sucking and the warmth of her tiny body.

As he crawled back into bed he heard the clock chime one, two, three, four times. He had over an hour to sleep till dawn. Even under the heavy covers, he felt chilled and couldn't get comfortable. The rain still fell on the roof, but it was soft now, hardly a patter. Tomorrow would be a slow day, too wet to work in any of the fields. He decided he'd grease the wagon. Maybe he'd turn Bess into the bottom for a couple of days. They wouldn't be going anywhere for a while; she didn't have to pull to the Hall's and back every day now. Good ole Bess.

Bert's shriek split the air like an ax through green poplar. The nightmare again. Poor Berty, how long would he suffer through the terror that haunted his dreams? Would it ever leave him alone? Harley was up and to the door before he remembered. He stopped and went back to get his trousers. As he fumbled in the dark, searching, he heard Bert scream again.

When he finally reached the boy's room, Bert was moaning softly. Sara sat on the edge of his son's bed, rocking Bert gently in her arms.

"Ssssshhh," cooed Sara, "It's alright. It's alright now."

"Take it off. Make them take it off," cried Bert softly.

"Ssssshhh," said the girl. "It's off now. Sara'll make them take it off. It's off now."

Harley stood in the doorway, watching as she stroked his son's brow, as she lay down with him.

"Sara's here, Bert," she whispered. "It's okay. Everything is okay."

Quietly, Harley turned and went back down the hall. He passed the door of his room and went out the front, onto the porch. Duke raised his head drowsily, his thick tail thumping slowly on the planks of the porch floor. Harley sat down and began lacing his boots.

*

    Dawn came late through the clouds in the east, lighting slowly, greyly. A stiff breeze blew behind yesterday's front, chilling Harley in his wet clothes. Gradually his farm spread out of the darkness below him: wide and neat and familiar. He knew every field, every tree, every fence row, like he knew his own hands; they were always before his eyes, they always had been.

    Duke lay thirty yards away, low and quiet, watching carefully. Harley had ordered him home twice, but the dog was unwilling to leave his master, choosing rarely instead to disobey, while keeping a respectful distance. His yellow fur clung wetly to his side and small shivers ran across him periodically, but his head never turned from Harley.

    To the north, where the wind came from, Indian Creek ran swollen and yellow, slicing Harley's farm from the country about. Whitecaps blinked and wavered in the muddy, rushing water, never still, never flowing away. Harley leaned back, feeling the cold stone on his spine and the water running down his face. No birds welcomed the new day; no warmth came with the light. All about him was only quiet and cold and anguish.

    God! How I miss you.

    God, how could you.

    God. How?

    Only the wind answered, and the rain. Only God knew, and God wasn't talking.

*

    Far, far, away a voice was calling. At first hollow and weak, then stronger and solid: summoning, reaching.

    "Yes?" said Harley.

    Duke's head was raised, ears pricked. Buds sat on the tips of the limbs of the chestnut, straining to open.

    "Yes?" said Harley again. But he couldn't hear.

    "Yes."

The wind cried through the tree above him, the rain almost done. Away to the west, a hint of blue peeked at the horizon. The voice was gone now, Harley knew, but he still sat, listening to its echo playing in his ears.

He sat until the sun was high above him and the storm was just a fading memory. He sat there long after Duke had come and licked his hand and trotted away down the hill. He sat there when Cy found him.

"Pa?" said the son.

"Damn," thought the father.

*

Harley lay sick in bed with the fever for three days, and all he remembered of that time was the chill, and the heat, and Sara. The boys were there, of course, but timidly, sporadically, fearfully. Sara was a constant, dim and faithful. Wiping his brow with the cool cloth; holding his head up to pour down water or cider; feeding him tiny sips of chicken broth; she was what he saw when he opened his eyes, and when he closed them. She is how he remembers those days. Blonde and soft and delirious.

He had never imagined a man could be so sick, and survive. He had never before felt like he wanted to die. He lived, for a time, in the lap of angels, at the mercy of the demons in his heat. He swirled within himself, lost in an existence where neither time nor space had any power, nor meaning. Reality lay totally within his tortured skull, misery and ecstasy, now and then, here and now. No world. No sense. No reason. Nothing but the battle.

Traveling back along the finely woven web of human memory, there comes a point where the main radiating spokes no longer serve, and one must leave the straight lines of clear awareness and follow the inwardly spiraling overlay. Somewhere short of the hub, this ever-diminishing circle finally and inevitably entangles the mind, and recollections can go no further. It is here that the pitiable moths of cognizance struggle vainly, awaiting the oblivion carried by the bite of the spider; finally and ultimately recognizing that the light is unattainable.

46

Somewhat nearer the axis than most lies the en-shrouded moth of Kellis Harland Felts, and his cocoon contains this:

It is fine and bright and warm, and the bare grass tickles and itches at once as the close hum of bugs fills the ear. All is verdant green below and endless blue above, and between lays the scent of wildflowers: lavender and crimson and yellow. The firm, lifting grip spins the world as the earth falls away and baby Harley flies high above the shining, upturned smile of Daddy, feeling the wash of breeze across his face and the thrill of consuming motion. The wrapping hands rise farther and farther into the air as the giggles spill downward, and the count begins. "One," starts the game. "Two," tenses the muscles. "Three!" signals the free fall, a split second of total un-connectedness, where dwells neither earth nor sky nor man; only thrill. Then there is return to life, with the smooth nestling into the strong, sure arms. Close by, clear and high, mother's laughter mingles with father's and son's, and even the new spring chant of robin and thrush seems pale next to the song of the young family. All the world is good, and fair, and safe.

Next:

Harley the boy lay in bed with his eyes closed, thinking he was awake. The heavy summer sun streamed through the open window, beading sweat on his forehead, where a quiet breeze immediately dried it. He could hear the wrens and sparrows tittering in the trees outside, and the low whine of the chickens below, but mostly, he heard the buzzing of the fly; louder now, then fading to quiet, then loud again as it made its rounds, searching.

Finally, in abrupt cessation, it settled onto his cheek, and no sound was from within the room, save his torpid breathing. He felt a faint tickle as the thing walked to the crust at the corner of his eye, but he made no move to shoo it. The wind stirred the curtains and the fly buzzed again, fading across the room.

Far away, there came a dim rapping at the front door, then footsteps in the hall below. He heard the quiet murmur of voices drawing nearer through the creaking of the stairs, but he fell asleep before they reached his door.

His eyes were pulled open, and he could see himself reflected in the dark pupils that hung over him. A strange voice said, "Can you stick out your tongue?" and in answer, he did. A cold stick pressed into his mouth and he gagged.

"Hmmmm," said the voice, and the eyes went away.

Then his mother was above him, stroking his forehead with her cool, soft hand.

"Ssshhh," she whispered. "Go back to sleep now." He was reassured by her smell. As she pulled away he turned his head to follow her. She went to the bed opposite his and stood beside the back of the strange man. He wanted to call her back, but his throat burned so badly that he dared not try.

They leaned over the bed there, and he strained to focus his eyes. His mother's hands were balled on the back of her tired dress, fingers kneading, as the man worked on a dark form on the other bed.

"Kellis?" Said the man. "Can you hear me, Kellis?"

The light in the window dimmed for a moment as the shadow of a cloud scudded under the sun, and the fly buzzed again, passing. He watched as the man walked around the foot of the bed to the other side. His mother said something softly that he couldn't understand. He turned his head a little farther, and he saw a face staring closed-eyed up from the pillow there, as still and red as sunset, and he realized that it was his father's face.

The fly swooped down and landed on his daddy's eyelid, flicking at the salty wet there. He saw his mother fan it away once, then twice, then a third time, as it refused to be deterred by her feeble protections. Then the man on the other side of the bed said something to Momma and came around and took her arm. As he led her from the room, she pulled away and came and kissed Harley on the forehead, then went and tucked the blankets tight around his daddy's neck and kissed him lightly. She went to the window and shut it. Then she and the stranger left the room. He could hear them talking quietly in the hall as he drifted into sleep, and sleeping, he dreamed of snow.

When next he woke, it was to the cool strokes of the damp wash rag that his mother wiped across his brow. It seemed to him to be early morning, so he knew he had slept a long time. The heat that had plagued his body for the past few days was gone, and his vision had cleared somewhat, so the blurry dimness had left as well. He swallowed experimentally and found that the fire in his throat had subsided.

"Harley," whispered his mother leaning close. "How do you feel, Baby?"

He looked up into her pool green eyes and smiled weakly. He swallowed again, enjoying the freedom to do it without the wrenching pain.

"Water," he croaked, surprising himself with the raspiness of his own voice.

"Of course, Darling!" She sprang up and hurried to the basin and pitcher on the stand by the door, filling a glass with shaking hands. She came back to him and helped him ease into a sitting position, holding the glass to his lips as he gulped hungrily. The sweet relief he felt in his bones was caught and magnified by her beaming smile.

She sat with him all that day, as he drifted in and out of sleep. Toward evening, she brought him some soup and fed it to him with eager patience, and when he asked for more she leaned and hugged him, laughing. He thought it odd that she laughed while tears streamed down her cheeks.

When he finished eating, she washed his face with the cold, wet rag, and drew close to his ear.

"Can you make it to the outhouse?" She asked.

"Yessum, I think so," he said.

She pulled back the covers and helped him from the bed. His legs were so weak that she had to support him for a minute while they remembered how to stand. As she helped him on with his robe he looked at the other bed, smooth and well made, and that seemed important to him, somehow. She led him to the door, and he heard quiet voices floating up from downstairs.

"Have we got company, Momma?" He asked.

"Yes, dear," she said, "Now watch these steps."

In the front room, Aunt Mary and Uncle Ted sat talking with Mr. and Mrs. Justice, and the Reverend. Their conversation stopped when they saw his mother leading him down the stairs.

"Hello, Harley," said Aunt Mary gently. "How are you today?"

"I'm okay," he said. No one else spoke as he and Momma passed on into the kitchen. The cook stove was boiling away in full steam, and Mrs. Pargh sat at the table cutting dough.

"Why, Harley! Welcome back to the world!" she said in her squeaky voice. "How was the soup?"

Harley smiled and nodded, and his mother took him outside.

A half-dozen kids were running and shrieking through the back yard, playing tag. Harley's eyes brightened at the sight of his cousins and the Justice boys. When the children saw him they stopped their game immediately, standing as they were. Harley looked at his mother questioningly.

"Hey, Chuck! Hey, Molly! When'd you guys get here?"

His cousin Molly murmured a shy "Hello, Harley," looking at her feet. He noticed that none of the others were looking at him.

"Come on, Harley, we're almost there," said his mother. The kids ran around the house to the front yard.

"Momma, what's wrong?"

They reached the door of the outhouse and his mother made as if to go in with him.

"No, Momma, I can," he said. But instead of going on in, he turned and looked back at the house, growing dim in the gathering dusk. Someone was standing at the bright window of the parlor, and they pulled away when they saw his face.

"Momma, where's Daddy?"

His mother drew herself up very tall for a moment; then she stooped beside him and wrapped him in her arms. He stood awkwardly, feeling the strength of her grip, and her hair about his face, and the fading heat of the day. He listened to the tree frogs and the crickets and the whippoorwill away off in the distance; and he waited. After a time, she took his cheeks in her hands and lifted his head.

'See how pretty the sunset is?" she asked. "Can you see all the colors?"

*

Harley came to himself slowly, dimly. Awareness leaked back into him in tiny drops, filling his mind with minute details of the world around him. The blankets on him felt damp and heavy. It was evening. The sun had already fallen below the horizon but its glow still filled his window, silvery-yellow at the bottom and slate gray at the top. Close by, a whippoorwill pulsed its staccato call, and pausing, was answered from afar. Out in the yard there was shouting and laughter — the boys. It sounded like they were playing hide and seek. Harley heard a high squeal, and tried to guess who had just been caught.

The easy breeze that sifted through the window screen felt hot and dry. It held no hint of the scent of wet ground, and Harley wondered about that. He felt very thirsty. When he turned his head to look past his feet toward the water basin, he saw the small shape kneeling over the edge of the bed, head bent as if in prayer. He raised his hand and cupped it around the shining hair.

Cy looked up into his father's weakly smiling face.

"Pa? Is it you?" asked the boy.

"Of course it's me. Who'd you think it was?" Harley croaked thinly.

"I mean, are you okay? Are you awake?" asked Cy.

"Don't I look awake? What's got into you, son?" Harley's throat scratched when he talked. "How about getting me some water?"

While Cy went to the pitcher and poured a glass Harley thought about the boy's odd questions.

"Is this Tuesday?" he asked.

"No, Pa," said Cy, returning with the water. "This is Thursday." He held out the glass.

"Help me sit up," said Harley.

Cy sat the glass on the floor and grabbed his Pa under the arms. Together they got Harley into a half-sitting position. Cy arranged the pillows and stepped back. Suddenly he lunged at his father, throwing his arms around Harley's neck and burying his head in Harley's chest.

"Oh, Pa!" cried the boy, "I didn't think you'd come back. I really didn't."

Harley stroked the young back. "Back from where?" You know I'd never leave you boys. I just had a little touch of a cold, that's all. Had to sleep it off."

"I was scared, Pa. Awful scared."

"Don't fret anymore, son. We're fine." Harley kissed the top of his son's head. "Now, how about that water?"

Laughter ran in the front door, slamming the screen behind it, and Harley heard the breathless chatter of his children.

"You didn't either tag me, Berty. You missed by a mile," came Seth's voice.

"Did not, Seth Felts," protested Bert, "I got you, and you know it!"

Cy handed Harley his glass.

"Hey, everyone!" He shouted. "Pa's awake!"

"Pa!" Bert squealed, and a stampede of footsteps started down the hall.

"Come on, Amie, let's go see your daddy!"

When Harley heard the eager feminine voice, his heart stopped. Could it all have been just ...

Then he remembered. Her. Sara. That's who he'd heard. His whole life burst into the room and leapt onto his bed, shrieking and covering him with kisses and hugs. All four boys talked at once, and their voices were medicine. Harley looked up and saw Sara standing in the doorway, watching. She caught his glance for a moment and then looked quickly down at her feet.

"Come see Daddy, Thera!" called Amos. Harley grabbed Amie on the ribs and sent the child into a giggling fit. He looked back up to the door as the child squirmed helplessly in his grip.

"You're probably famished," said Sara, turning away. "I'll go see to supper."

"I'll help!" cried Bert, jumping down from his father's lap.

"Me too!" said Amos, and they both ran through the door, following the light footsteps down the hall.

"Where'd you learn to be such a good 'it', Sara? I didn't think girls were any good at tag," Harley heard Bert say. Sara laughed.

"Well, don't believe everything you hear, Bert. Isn't that right, Amie?" she said, fading into the kitchen.

"She never left you, Pa, except to cook, and to feed Cassie," said Seth. "And she walked all the way to the Hall's to fetch the Doc. Can you believe she walked all the way there and had him back in three hours? I thought she'd be gone half the night."

"I could have made it a lot quicker, if she'd let me take Bess," said Cy. "I could have done it a lot quicker."

"Well, you couldn't have walked it any faster," said Seth.

"Could too," said Cy, "I bet I could."

"No way," retorted Seth.

Harley laid back and listened to the sounds of his family. He felt a wave of gratitude sweep over him, and he felt oddly strong. He had been through his ordeal and he had weathered it, with their help.

"How about bringing Cassie in here," he said to Seth. "I need to see her."

Chapter 5

The dream was never the same, but the feeling never varied, and the sweat was always there — cold and sticky — when he woke in the night, wide-eyed and thudding. Mostly it was Ellie who pulled him out of it, kissing his brow and stroking his chest as she rocked him in her arms. But now he was all alone with his gasping and his memory. On these nights he rarely went back to sleep, he just laid, remembering.

He remembered how the pitiless sun bore down on the world so that you could almost hear the moisture sucking away into the sky. He remembered how his back had burned that night. He remembered how the day had drawn on, careless and free and steaming.

There was a commonality to the dreams, threads that ran through all of them. Bobby — the youngest of the three — running, always running, sandy-haired and freckled. He was always there at the start. His eager laugh tolled in Harley's sleeping head, and his grinning face shone through Harley's tight eyelids. That's how it always began. With the sight and sound and motion of Bobby Mangrum. And it always ended there too, with Bobby.

But the middle got muddled up a lot; it changed from one time to the next, so Harley was always surprised when it came back to the all too familiar end.

They were at the spring house, Bobby and Harley and Rig, wasting a summer Saturday in the languid way of boys with nothing to do. The fields were slow; the planting was done and the harvest was still far away, waiting for the crops to soak in their ration of sunshine. It was rare for the children of farms to have a full day to themselves, so they were novices at spending it. It was Harley who came up with the idea of following the water from the door of the spring all the way to the river. And it was Rig who thought of using floating sticks to track it. And it was Bobby who named it a race.

They spent a quarter-hour searching for sticks; all opting for short smooth ones, less likely to snag. And it was decided that no one could touch his stick with his hands, but that long pushing sticks would be allowed, to free the floaters from the roots and eddies along the way.

The sun was mid-way up the eastern sky as they stood at the spring house door. Harley gave the count. "One...two...three!" The sticks hit the water and the boys began pushing their own through the wintergreen, toward the narrow channel twenty feet downstream. The race was on.

Though Rig's craft took an early lead, and generally maintained it, the three were never separated by more than a dozen paces. Shouting and laughter followed them down the water course, with cries of "Hey, you hit my stick!" and "What 'cha doing way back there, slowpoke?" and "You guys ain't got a chance." Fish darted ahead and crows watched from behind as the competition made its way down the length of Willow Branch, into Indian Creek.

By the time the boys reached the railroad trestle next to the highway, their tan young backs glistened with sweat as the sticks flowed into the slow, wide pool under the bridges in a dead heat.

"I'm hungry, guys," puffed Bobby. "Let's stop and eat."

"The water'll get away," said Rig, whipping behind his floater with the long, slender sapling he used as a pusher.

"Darn the water," said Bobby with just a hint of a whine. "It's lunch time." A truck whizzed by on the highway bridge ahead.

"Aw, you're just a baby," called Rig to the younger boy. Harley looked at the steep banks that rose up on either side of the bridges.

"He's right, Rig," he said, "I'm bushed. Let's eat on the trestle. The water ain't going anywhere."

"Oh, I reckon so," said Rig. "But we gotta put back in at the exact spot we take out." They pulled their sticks out and climbed up onto the tracks to eat.

The three boys sat in a silent row on the steel rail, eating the sandwiches they'd brought. Between the cross-ties at their feet they could see the deep, green water flowing silently past. The sun bore brilliantly down upon them, strobing off the creek twenty feet below, and when they looked down the railroad bed stretching away into infinity, heat waves shimmered through the distance.

Harley took out the pocketknife his Uncle Teddy had given him for his tenth birthday and began whittling the end of his push stick into a sharp point.

"Ya'll ever been down the creek across the highway?" he asked.

"No, I ain't," said Rig. "You?"

Bobby spoke up. "Me and my daddy fished a bluff around the next bend one time."

Harley spit into the water, watching the small drop of him fall away and flow under the bridge, picking up speed as it went.

"I came to it from the back of the Trotter place one time," he said, spitting again. "It's pretty steep down there. It goes through a limestone cut where it squeezes in and starts runnin' like the dickens. We'll have to hump to keep up."

"So what?" said Rig, "I can keep up, can't you?"

"Sure I can!" Harley shot back. "Sure I can. I was just sayin'... That's all."

"I can keep up!" said Bobby.

"That nub of yours'll never make it to the river," said Rig nodding at Bobby's floater on the rail beside him.

"Will too!" cried Bobby indignantly. "And it'll get there long before that lump you've got."

"We'll see, half-pint. We'll see," said Rig.

Harley watched the over-sized ears of the younger boy go red through the thick shocks of hair that locked around them. He stood up.

"We'd better go if we're gonna get back home before dark."

As Harley said it, a train whistle moaned long and low in the distance. All three boys laid their ears on the steel rail — shiny on top and rusty red on the sides — and listened to the hum in the steel, rumbling with the distant power of coal-fired thunder.

When they could hear the rattle of the cars through the heat-soaked air, they scrambled down the dirt banks to the spot where they had taken out their sticks to watch the train roar by.

"Count 'em!" yelled Rig, as the smoking black locomotive passed. Harley stood in the creek with the water up to his ankles, watching the line of boxcars and scuttle-cars careen above him, feeling the hot wind draft on his face.

"Here comes the caboose," shouted Bobby's small voice, nearly lost in the roar.

The red tail of the train rocketed past and the noise died with the suddenness of a rifle shot rolling away between the ridges. Harley saw two trainmen leaning on the back rail of the caboose as it grew smaller and smaller with distance.

"Ninety-two!" shouted Rig, unadjusted to the renewing quiet of the water.

"Eighty-nine!" said Bobby, only a little softer.

"Wasn't either," said Rig, "you just can't count fast enough. Tell'em, Harley, ninety-two."

"It was ninety-four of 'em," Harley said, above the murmur of the creek. "Count off the drop, Bobby, let's get going."

"One...two...three!" counted Bobby, and they were off.

Rig's maple root took an immediate lead.

"Hey, you threw it downstream," cried Bobby, "that's cheatin'."

"Didn't either," called Rig over his shoulder. "See you chumps at the river!" He slapped at his floater with his push stick and disappeared under the highway bridge.

A car whizzed by above and glints of chrome bumper flashed in Harley's eyes. There was a loud splash ahead and the sounds of thrashing and spitting.

"Shit!" Hollered Rig. Bobby grinned at Harley.

"He fell in," said Bobby, "I'm going over."

He scrambled up the bank toward the road. Harley could hear the faint whistle of the train as it approached the grade crossing near the ferry. He went under the bridge to help Rig out of the water. The mud banks were soft and damp under the bridge, covered with slick, scummy moss. Harley almost fell in himself as he reached Rig who stood sputtering and fuming in the creek.

"Where'd my floater go?" asked Rig.

"Don't worry," laughed Harley, "you can keep up with it."

He leaned over and grabbed Rig's hand to pull him up. The screech of tires and the blast of a car horn tore the air.

"What're you trying to do, you crazy kid," came a man's voice from above. Bobby scrambled down the bank in front of them.

"You're snagged, Rig, you're snagged," he taunted gleefully. "See you at the river!"

"I'll catch up with you, shrimp!" called Rig. Harley ran after his own floater.

After an hour of chasing along the creek-side Rig was still behind — though barely — Harley figured they'd be at the river in another thirty minutes or so. He saw the cut at Joe Trotter's place ahead, and heard the rush of Indian Creek as it pushed over the limestone boulders that poked through the water. He nudged his floater to the middle of the creek and sprang ahead of Bobby, running up the foot of the bluff.

There was a ledge of dirt between the creek and the rock wall, about three feet wide and six or eight feet above the water. Harley's stick spun in the backwash of a boulder in the middle of the stream, and he watched helplessly as Bobby's craft shot past.

"Let me by! Let me by!" shouted Bobby.

Harley leaned out over the water as far as he dared. His floater was just out of the reach of the long willow limb that was his push stick.

"Balance me," he said, holding his hand out to Bobby. The younger boy braced his foot against a rock and took Harley's hand. Again, Harley leaned out over the bank. He strained against Bobby's hand, leaning farther and farther, feeding his push stick through his hand until he gripped it at the very end. His floater bobbed in little circles, bouncing off the rock that blocked its way. Harley timed its revolutions, and when it reached the point nearest the bank, he swung his stick down, slapping the water. The tip hit his floater, nudging it around the rock, and it headed downstream.

"Get it out of my way!" shouted Rig, racing up behind them. He tried to step between Bobby and the bluff, and Harley felt Bobby's grip slip. Slowly, as if in dream, Harley felt himself fall. It seemed to take minutes to reach the rocks, only seven feet below. He saw where he would land, he saw how he would land, and he tried to put his hands out to catch himself.

His right hand hit first, wedging between two rocks with an agonizing sound. He still held his push stick, his fingers bent crazily back on it. His breath was knocked out of him and he sucked water as he gasped to refill his lungs. Then dead weight thudded into his back, pounding him into blackness on the rocks.

He was out for only a few seconds, and when he came to, it was to the sound of Rig's voice, screaming down at him. Something was pushing his head into the water and he had to struggle to lift his mouth out enough to breathe. Water gurgled in his ear as he strained to push the weight off his back, and then the gurgling was all around him, and the hoarse sound of Rig, shouting.

Harley knew his hand was broken. It was wedged under him with the push stick pointed up between his arm and his waist. With a sudden jerk, he pulled his hand free.

"Aaaaaaaauuuuuurrgggh!"

His cry silenced Rig, and then he could hear nothing but the gurgling, and the birds.

Slowly, dimly, Harley eased his way from beneath Bobby and rolled onto his back, wincing into the sun.

"Harley?" Barely above a church whisper.

"Harley?" Rig was leaning over him. "Are you okay?"

The rock under Harley was warm, and he listened to the calls around him: cardinal, thrush, sparrow, crow (from far away), and mockingbird. The sun burned his face, reminding him of bonfires in the winter, and standing too close. Someone coughed in his ear.

"Jeez, Harley," said Rig, "Jeez..."

Harley turned his face away from the sun. Bobby was there, on top of him, wide-eyed and freckled. Bobby coughed and Harley felt it hit his face, warm and wet. His eyes stared wild into Harley's, pulling with his pupils just as hard as he had pulled on his hand seconds before. Bobby hiccupped, and red foam ran from his mouth. Suddenly Harley felt the stickiness under his belly. Bobby didn't say a word. He just stared vacantly at the red tip of Harley's push stick, impaled through him into the sky above.

*

Cy was bored. Suckering tobacco had always been one of his least favorite chores. It was always hot when they suckered — hot and dry and endless. And he had to stoop all day long, working up one interminable row and down the other, plucking the pale sprouts from the bottom of the stalks. Cy spat and watched the little puff of dust that rose above his little saliva pool. A cow ant hurried across the furrow at his feet, and he spat again, hitting the bug.

Suckering seemed pointless to Cy. He knew it had to be done for the plants to yield properly, but by the time he and Seth covered the acres of tobacco patch, the insidious little shoots were already reappearing on the plants they had started with. In a couple of weeks they'd be doing it all over again, and it'd be just as hot as it was now. Maybe hotter. Cy didn't mind the other work in tobacco so much.

Gassing the beds was kind of neat, and when they set the plants he could stand back at the end of the day and look across a field that had been barren the day before and now was dotted rich green. Cutting and spiking was okay even though it was by far the hardest work, leaving him sore and weak in the dog days of August. But the satisfaction was there when you cut, returning the field to barrenness, banking the crop. And he actually looked forward to the hanging. For the past two years he had gotten to work the top of the barn, climbing through the dim tiers of horizontal cedar poles that stretched from side to side, taking his position above the three sets of hands that relayed stakes up from the scaffold twenty feet below. Cy had never felt more important than when he sat high up there in the stifling heat, watching the chain of men passing the year's harvest to him. He took the heavy sticks — five plants on each— and filed them carefully between the joist poles, keeping just the right spacing so the stakes wouldn't fall and the smoke could circulate between the rows. He worked his way down the tiers until he reached the bottom, then he'd hand the crop off the wagon to the men that filled the last row from the ground. He liked firing the tobacco, liked the smell of smoldering sawdust, and the coolness that crept into the air when it was firing time. But most of all he liked the stripping.

It was always cold when they stripped, and damp. The tobacco wouldn't come into order until the rains filled the air with the moisture that kept the leaves from crumbling when they were pulled from the stalk. And everybody helped strip; man, woman, and child. Whole families gathered around wood stoves in one stripping room after another, until everyone's crop was baled and ready for market.

Cy loved stripping season. He knew no place on earth as warm and friendly and safe as a stripping room; with the grown-ups sitting by the fire, telling tales on each other, and of people long passed: of grandparents, and of grandparents of grandparents; of unknown uncles and cousins with vivid names like 'Cletus' and 'Enora'; of times of war and times of plenty. The children sat and listened to their histories amid the quiet background of the crackling fire and the rustle and snap of leaves being pulled. One soft, slow voice at a time punctuated the quiet, receiving full attention. Cy always saw the wistfulness in the eyes and always heard the fondness in the voices of the grown-ups when they spoke of the past.

He would never forget the time Ma told everyone how Pa had proposed to her, and the way she smiled at Pa while she talked, teasing him. Pa got real red in the face and on his ears; and when she'd got through making fun of him, he stood up and went and kissed her right in front of everybody, and everyone clapped and hooted at them, at Ma and Pa, standing there hugging and grinning and staring into one another's eyes. Cy would never forget that.

But suckering sucked. Cy hated it. The thinning and pruning, the solitude, the repetition; he hated it all. The men never suckered, they left it up to the kids. Cy stood and stretched his back. He was just tall enough to see over the tops of the plants, dark and green and broad leafed, stretching row after row before him. Seth bent two rows over and ten feet back.

"Hottest day of the year so far," said Cy, stretching and arching toward the high puffy clouds that dotted the blue inferno above.

"Yeah, why don't you remind me again, in case I forget," Seth grumbled without looking up.

Cy looked across the field. The tobacco would be in full bloom in a week or two, and hints of pink blossom were already scattered about. Bumblebees buzzed through the air, seeking the early flowers.

"I bet it's ninety degrees at least, and not even ten o'clock yet," said Cy.

Seth plucked his way down his row in practiced rhythm without answering.

"Might be a hundred 'fore we're done,' said Cy, as he bent back to his work. "We ain't seen nothing yet."

Dinnertime came and went, and no one showed up with the sandwiches. Usually, when he and Seth were in the fields, Pa would come around about noon, carrying an oilpaper bundle of ham and hard bread, and they'd all eat together before Pa checked the morning's work. But Cy reckoned it was after one o'clock already, and still no sign of lunch. Seth had caught his row up, and Cy could see his brother through the plants, two rows over. Seth's stomach growled loudly across the summer hum of bugs.

"Maybe we ought to go on to the house," said the younger boy.

"Not yet," said his brother, "We'll work a bit more first."

"Fine. You work ahead. I'm going to go get me something to eat," said Seth.

Cy felt his own stomach rumble hungrily.

"Fine," he said, "I reckon I'll just go with you." The boys grinned at one another, and started down the rows toward the house.

Just before they reached the edge of the field, they heard the rustling coming toward them.

"Seth?" Came the cry. "Cy? Where are you?"

Cy looked at Seth and rolled his eyes. "We're right here, Sara," he said, putting great emphasis on the last word.

"Where, here?" she called back. Cy looked at Seth and began to squat slowly, putting a finger to his lips. They could hear her thrashing about the plants on their left somewhere.

"Where?" She called again, clueless.

Cy put his hand over his mouth to stifle the snicker that welled up there. He could see his brother crouching in the green-dappled shade nearby.

"Seth?" Sara called plaintively. Cy grinned at Seth. Seth looked back seriously, and Cy's smile fell from his face like honey off a comb as he watched his brother straighten up and call out.

"Over here, Sara."

"Shitbird," spat Cy. "Baby little shitbird."

She'd brought the babies with her, and when Seth walked out of the patch, Cy heard Amos' squeal.

" 'Mawn, Theth, ead at the creek!"

Then Bert chimed in. "We brought a picnic!"

With a hard breath, Cy stood and walked toward the shade.

Willow Branch ran tree-lined and dark alongside the tobacco field, cool even in the mid-day sun. Cy was the first one to get there, and he waited while the rest of the Felts children, and Sara, made their way to him. Bert came first, lugging the picnic basket, followed by Amos, who was clutching a tea jug to his chest, then came Sara carrying Cassie, led by Seth.

"Here you are, Cy," she said. "I hope you're hungry."

"Who wouldn't be, this late in the day," he said, scowling toward Seth.

"I suppose you're right," said Sara lightly. "It's not easy getting these three all moving in the same direction at once. But better late than never, right, Amie?"

"Uh-huh," said Amos.

"Let's eat!" said Bert, which they did.

There was fried chicken and spring squash, sausage left over from breakfast, fresh biscuits with molasses, and pecans for desert — already shelled. In spite of himself, Cy thought it was the best meal he'd ever had outside of the house. But Seth kept raving about how good everything tasted, and how pretty it was here by the creek, and how nice everything was, until Cy couldn't listen to anymore. He got up and walked out into the middle of the creek and stood there, feeling the water flow around his ankles, gently pulling the sand from beneath his feet. He stood staring upturned and closed-eyed at the sky beyond his lids.

"Never had anything like it," he heard Seth say.

"Can we come back tomorrow?" Bert asked.

"I wanna go thwim, Thera. Will you go thwim with me?" said Amos.

Cassie cooed in Sara's lap, and Seth started in again about how great everything was.

Cy spun suddenly on his heals, splashing the water loudly.

"Why don't you all just get it over with and go ahead and crown her!" he spat. "Just go on a do it!" He strode out the opposite side of the creek and disappeared into the woods.

The worst heat of the day was done and things were beginning to cool a bit when he re-crossed the creek and climbed the bank. Bert and Amos sat on a quilt at the edge of the tree line while Cassie slept at their side.

"What're ya'll doing still here, Bertie?" asked Cy.

Bert looked up from the daisy chain he was trying to tie. "Sara says wait here," he said. Cy looked at Cassie, who was fidgeting on the blanket. Amos just stared at Cy, listening.

"You look after your brother and sister, Bertie," said Cy. "Where's Sara?"

"Over there," said Bert, pointing across the tobacco. "She said stay here."

"Well, you stay here. And keep them out of trouble." Cy looked once more at the kids and started out across the field.

He found Seth and Sara working side by side near the middle of the field, both drenched in sweat. Sara bowed into the work with a vengeance, her thin, fine hair matted to her forehead, grunting with every tug. For a novice — and a girl to boot — she moved surprisingly fast through the plants, leaving the suckers piled in the furrow behind her. Cy could see drops of blood on her fingertips. As he reached her row and stopped, she glanced up through her wet face and hunched stance, then kept right on working. Cy stood there for a minute, mustering to say what was on his mind. Sara and Seth moved on down the row, oblivious to his presence. He let out a long sigh, then stepped between the plants to his right, stooped, and began silently pulling suckers.

It was well onto evening and the sun was almost down when Cy heard the call, angry and indignant, from the direction of the creek.

"Sara!" It was Pa.

"Cy! Get over here! Seth!"

Sara stopped in her row next to Seth and looked toward the voice. Cy called back.

"Over here, Pa!" As he started across the field he heard Seth and Sara following.

Pa held Cassie in one arm, with his other around Amos, who stood leaning against his leg. Bert slept soundly on the blanket at his feet.

"What's the meaning of this, Sara?" said Pa. "How dare you leave my children alone here by the creek!"

Sara looked helplessly at Harley, then turned and looked back across the field behind her, as if for help.

"Do you have any idea what could happen to these babies all alone here in the woods? Any idea? How long have they been here?" Cy watched his father's fist clinching and un-clinching at his side.

"For a while," said Sara meekly. "I just thought I'd help..."

She looked back across the field again.

"Help! You thought you'd help? Thought, hell!" roared Harley. Cy had never heard his father curse at anyone before. Cassie began to cry in Harley's arm.

"You never thought! You're supposed to help with the babies. If I needed a field hand I'd hire one days, not move it into my house!" Amos ran to Sara and hugged her leg.

"Daddy, thop!" he cried.

Harley checked himself and turned away. He breathed slowly and heavily. Without turning back, he spoke, very quietly and evenly.

"You have no idea. You just don't know what could happen here by the creek." He turned to face her. She held her breath as he gathered himself up to continue.

"Pa, I told her I'd watch the kids," said Cy.

Harley turned to his oldest.

"You were supposed to be working. She's supposed to be baby-sitting."

"I know, Pa, but she wanted to help. I was getting dizzy from the heat and all, and she offered. It's all my fault, Pa. I shouldn't have. I'm sorry, Pa."

Harley looked hard at his son, then at the girl. Sara stepped forward. "Mr. Felts... I..."

"I don't want to hear about it," he cut her off. "You just don't know what could happen. You can't even imagine what could happen here by the creek."

No one spoke for a long time. They all stood there listening to the quiet hum of the dying day.

"Come on, Seth," said Harley finally. Let's you and me get these young'uns home."

Chapter 6

It was unusually quiet around the dinner table that evening. Harley worked late in the barn and when he finally washed up and came into the kitchen, Sara was already serving the boys — veal that looked overdone, as usual, stewed tomatoes and canned string beans. Beans that Ellie had put up last fall; beans that Harley had helped her shell on a dull and satisfying evening. He remembered her sitting with the straw basket held in the hammock of her dress between her spread knees, pushed out of its usual spot by the belly that was just beginning to swell over her lap. They sat quietly and easily, experimenting with names for the new baby.

"What about James if it's a boy, or Nathaniel. I always liked the name Nathaniel," said Harley. "Nate. Nat."

"It won't be a boy, I told you. We'll need girl's names. Soft names. Warm names."

"Maybe you're right, El, but we should be prepared either way. You said the same thing about Amos, remember? Nate. It's got a good solid sound to it, and Nathaniel sounds very dignified."

"You're wasting your time, Harley. This time I'm sure. It was just a hunch with Amos, but this time I know. Faith. How about Faith? No, not that, Jilly Burton had a cousin named Faith, and an absolute brat she was too."

"Alright then, you pick for girls and I'll pick for boys. I reckon that's the way it ought to be anyhow. But do you like Nate? What do you think about Nate, or Nat?"

"I think it's a horrid name for a dainty little girl to have to carry. Far too cold and uncomforting. A girl should have a comforting name."

"Okay, okay, whatever you say, momma."

Seth came out, carrying his lesson book to ask Harley about a problem in arithmetic. After a suitable period passed, Ellie gave him the answer. The boys always came to Harley with their study problems, though it was usually Ellie who gave them help.

She shivered in the fall evening chill.

"Seth, be a darling and go fetch Momma's cassinette, would you? It's hanging in my chifforobe."

"Sure, Momma."

They both smiled after him as he left.

"He's a fine one," Harley said, leaning over and patting his wife's knee. "They're all fine, all mighty fine. You've done a swell job, Mrs. Felts. Turned out a fine brood," he winked and grinned, "but then I always had an eye for good breeding stock." They laughed together as she slapped his hand away in feigned indignation.

"Seth is the sensitive one," Ellie replied. "He should have been the girl; his feelings go deeper than the others do. But I'll have my little girl yet. I'll keep on till I get one, even if it means giving you a full baseball team of boys along the way."

Harley rolled his eyes. "Then I expect we'll have to move into the barn; keep the stock in this little cracker box of a house."

"Well, don't start toting the furniture just yet. This'll be the one, mark my word. She'll be just lovely, then we'll quit."

"Alright, have it your way. What about Maggie? That's a nice feminine name, but strong too, somehow. Sturdy."

Now it was Ellie's turn to roll her eyes.

"I'll not be picking my baby's name for sturdiness. She'll want a gentle name."

"A sissy name you mean," said Seth, the screen door slamming behind him. He held up a short wool jacket. "Is this what you wanted? Is this a cas... , a cassin..."

"Cassinette, dear. Yes, that's it. Thank you."

The boy draped the wrap over his mother's shoulders, taking great care and exaggeration in tucking it around her neck. He patted her back and kissed the top of her head.

"Well, here's her widdle cassie to keep her warm and comfy," he said in his best baby talk.

"Okay, son, you've had your laugh. Now go tell your brothers to get ready for bed. We'll be in directly to tuck ya'll in," smiled Harley.

After he was gone Harley and Ellie shelled their beans in silence for a few minutes, then Harley said:

"It is getting a might crisp out here. Do you want to go in?"

"No," said Ellie, gazing out across the farm. "No, let's finish this batch. It's really quite nice out here, as long as I've got my widdle cassie to keep me warm."

So long ago. So far away. Harley took a bite of the beans. They'd been stewed way too long, to the point they were almost mush, flat and tasteless. Not like Ellie cooked them, for sure. Not even close. They ate pretty much in silence, and when Harley finished, he excused himself and went to sit in the old rocker on the porch. His great granddaddy had made the chair when he'd first settled this land. It was a fixture on the front porch, had always stood in the exact spot it was now, by the front door, where the rough-sawn oak flooring was worn smooth and dark by generations of tired feet resting after long days. The night was stiflingly hot and humid; not even a whisper of a breeze stirred among the loud, lazy drone of crickets and cicadas, and the little chirpers down by the stock pond. A big bullfrog groaned down there too, and Harley thought maybe they'd be having frog legs for dinner soon.

The clink and rattle of dish washing faded from the kitchen, and the boys came slamming out the door across the porch.

"Wanna play hide and seek with us, Pa?" as they blurred past.

"Not tonight, guys. Ya'll go ahead. I'm just going to sit and rest a spell."

It was awfully satisfying to sit and rock, comforted by the familiar creek and craw of the old rocker; by the squeals and laughter of the boys, invisible in the yard. Almost too satisfying by Harley's mind. Back in the house he heard Cassie begin to cry, then hush as the faint notes of a lullaby wafted through the screen. Harley had a lot to be thankful for, he knew. He closed his eyes and talked to God, thanking him for what blessings he did have. And eventually, without realizing it, he dozed.

He woke with a start at the sound of the spring of the screen door stretching out. Sara gently eased the door back to.

"I didn't mean to startle you," she said, going to sit on the wooden steps leading up to the porch.

"That's okay. I was just resting a spell," answered Harley, watching her back as she settled in against the cedar post that supported the porch roof. She wore a white dress, and her long blonde hair cascaded down to the small of her back; a pale ghost figure framed by the dark beyond.

"Come on and play, Sara," came Seth's voice out of the night.

"I don't think so, Seth. But thanks." She turned a little sideways on the step so she was half facing Harley.

"The garden is looking real good. It's been a good season for growing." She looked down at her hands knitted on her lap. "I'll get the rest of those weeds out tomorrow."

Harley watched her hands, fluttering like a pair of chrysanthemum moths dancing at a candle. He caught himself glancing at her tiny waist, looking for a sign of a bulge, but he looked away quickly, before he could tell.

"About this afternoon..." she started, looking up at him.

"No need to go into that. It's done," said Harley, staring out into the night.

"I'm sorry, that's all. It won't happen again."

"I appreciate that." He paused. "And maybe I was a little harsh. Maybe I overreacted a bit." He looked her full in the face, into her shining, luminescent eyes. "It's just that... They're all I've got, the boys. And the baby. They're my whole world. All I have." She stared directly back, her eyes locked and focused on his. Then she looked away, turning back to the yard.

"I know. I'm sorry."

"I see you, Cy! Come on down, you're caught," called Bert, who was apparently 'it'. "No fair going in the tree. I can't reach."

"That's just too bad for you, shorty," came the answer.

Just then Sara shrieked, jumping up onto the porch. She tripped on the top step and fell into Harley and the rocker. There was a loud snap as the arm of the chair broke under her momentum. Seth came laughing out from under the porch.

"Gotcha good, didn't I, Sara?" Then he saw Sara draped across his daddy's lap, and the splintered arm dangling beside them. "Oh, Pa," he began, eyes widening, "Gee, Pa, I..." He stopped at his father's look.

Harley helped Sara to her feet, stood up himself, looked at the chair and then at Sara.

"Seth's done it now!" cried Cy from his perch in the blackness.

Harley looked back at Seth, and his teeth began to show as he burst into a quick laugh.

God, how long had it been since he'd laughed? It felt good, and he kept on laughing until Sara and the boys joined him.

"Heck, the old thing needed re-caning anyway," he said. "It can be fixed.

"And now you'd all better find a good hiding place, 'cause I'm 'it' now. Me and Amie. With a vengeance."

Footsteps scattered gleefully about the yard, mingled with cries of "Daddy's 'it'!"

Harley looked at the girl beside him.

"You too, Sara. You'd better hide good, cause we're hunters from way back, ain't that right, Amos?" Amie bobbed his head in eager agreement.

Sara looked hard at Harley for a second, before turning and disappearing into the giggling night.

*

After Harley and his youngest son had tracked them all down, after they had been caught by Bert and Seth, and after they had eluded Cy and Sara in their turns, he sat down on the porch, beaded with sweat and puffing hard.

"Okay, boys, we'd better call it a night."

"Aw, Pa, can't we play one more round, please."

"No, it's late. We'll play again another time. Now go get yourselves ready for bed."

"Okay, Pa, but can we tomorrow night?"

"We'll see. We'll see when tomorrow gets here."

The boys filed past into the house. Sara came last. After the screen door slammed for the last time, she stopped and looked at Harley, her baby-fine hair matted humidly around her face. She stood for a moment, not speaking, and then said:

"Goodnight, Mr. Fel..."

Her hands dropped to her side. "Goodnight, Harley."

*

The Fourth of July is the biggest thing that happens to the small town of Cuthcutt. On Independence Day, the little river stop transforms into a gaily bannered, red, white, and blue festooned excuse for a town, like a country whore dressed for Saturday night in the big city. The Main Street merchants (all seven of them) go all out to celebrate the birthday of the U.S.A., pinning gaudy crepe paper to the shop windows, hoisting tattered and worn American flags onto rusty steel poles, and tolerating the non-stop strings of firecrackers at their doorsteps. Totally a river town, Cuthcutt is laid out along the banks of the Tennessee, with Main Street teeing off perpendicular. Cuthcutt was founded half-heartedly, and has been dying ever since. From the river it seems almost impressive, suddenly showing up one bend away from the endless hardwood forests that line the banks for miles and miles, upstream and down. Impressive sheerly by dint of size; by the scope of the tobacco warehouses that line the waterfront for nearly a quarter mile. Impressive at first glance, until a closer look from the landing shows the true color of rust, rot, and despair. Impressive from the river side; depressive from the town side. Huge, imposing warehouses perch on the river bank above the rows and rows of wharves built for uploading the season's crop. Then there is Main Street, branching straight off from the ferry landing, a dusty (or muddy, depending on the season) track lined by the bank, the hardware, the grocery, the dry goods, the millinery, the 'hotel', and of course, the saloon. Stick-framed, clapboard, peeling-paint buildings all, one not much different from the others, all terraced up by a wooden sidewalk, huddled before the trees that stand quietly waiting to retake their rightful domain. Traffic is light, usually, almost non-existent in the strictest sense, except on the Fourth of July; a magical day in the humdrum, sleepy-eyed life of Cuthcutt when the folks of the countryside turn out, gather up, and parade through their sorry little town, made gay for a day.

From the ferry ramp across the river, it was about all that little Bert, the traveler at heart, could stand. It was the magic kingdom, the way of the world, and the star of Tennessee, to his five-year-old eyes.

"Look-ee, Pa, at all them buildings!" he bubbled, as Harley ushered his brood onto the ferry. "Gosh!"

"Half of 'em's empty, Berty," said Cy. "They ain't all that much, really. Just a bunch of wood boxes, termite food."

But Sara saw the bigger boy lick his lips as he spoke, saw the gleam in his eyes, the grin under his scowl.

"Now, Cy, don't spoil it for you little brother. Let him have his dreams."

"He can dream. I hope he does. But let him dream about Paris, or New York. Why waste dreams on a hole-in-the-wall like this?"

"Is Paris as big as this?" asked Bert, "or Baltimore? Tell me about Baltimore again, Sara. Tell me about the halls again, and the muse-see'ems."

Sara scooped Bert up into her arms, facing him toward the bow of the flat-rafted ferry. She wore an A-line dress that hid her figure quite well usually, but there on the deck of the ferry, plowing cross the river into the wind, it billowed out behind, along with her baby-fine hair, making her into a blonde maidenhead, showing the ever-growing bulge above her waist.

"Later, Bertie, another time. Just enjoy this, while you can."

The day was bright, clear, and hot — a model summer day, southern-style. It had been dry and sticky on the long ride to the river, but here on the water there was a breath of breeze; there was always wind over the water. Harley was back in the stern with Jeremiah, the steersman, talking fish and baits and such, watching his family lined before him, leaning eagerly against the wooden rails, urging the raft on to the far shore. Amos sat amidships, playing with the puzzle that Sara had brought to keep him occupied for the ride and the crossing. Seth was at Sara's side, as he always seemed to be lately, and Cy stood with his feet on the lower front rail, hips locked against the top rail, leaning a bit too far out, showing off, pushing the limits.

"Stand down, Cy," said Harley, interrupting Jeremiah's account of almost landing a twenty, or maybe even thirty, pound channel catfish, just last week.

Cy didn't look back, didn't acknowledge he'd even heard, except to step down from the rail and spit into the modest wake ahead of them.

Harley started to speak again to the boy, then thought better and just let it go. He turned back to Jeremiah instead.

"When'll you be making your last run tonight?"

"No tellin'. I'll be staying on till after the dance at least," he replied, spitting his plug of tobacco into the wake behind them, as he reached immediately for a fresh chaw from the foil wrapper in his back pocket. "Whenever everybody's back acrost, I reckon. Whenever that is."

"We won't be too late ourselves," Harley told him. "We'll likely leave first run back, soon as you get your dancing out of your system. We won't be staying much after the fireworks, if I can drag you away from your darlin's, that is."

"I wish," said the little boatman, biting off a fresh chew from his plug. Harley watched the brown juice run down Jeremiah's stained chin, right where the last had left off.

"Maybe this year," said Jeremiah.

"Maybe," said Harley. "You never know. Maybe so."

"Nope. Never can tell, can ya?" He looked ahead, toward the front of the ferry, grinning a big brown-toothed grin, and tried at a wink, though it came out more of a squint. "Grab that rope, will ya? You dog, you. We're fixin' to land. Tie us off, will ya, dog?" he said, looking beyond Harley.

Harley followed Jeremiah's gaze, then stepped to the front and picked up the docking rope that lay next to Sara and his boys. He kept his mouth shut about it, in case he was wrong.

"Okay. Sure thing."

"Dog her good now, you dog you."

The ferry slid into the junction of Main and the Tennessee with a soft cush and Jeremiah made his way forward to crank down the loading ramp.

"You children have yourselves a big time now," he said, working at the wench. He winked and nodded toward Sara. "That includes you too, missy."

It was a good thing Harley liked Jeremiah. He tied off the ferry and didn't say anything more.

They were plenty early, climbing the rise onto Main at something before one o'clock. The games wouldn't start for better than an hour yet, and the parade wasn't scheduled until 3:30, but the town was filling with people already. When they got to the corner of Main and Commerce at the top of the hill, Harley gathered his brood around, and Sara too.

"I promised Burley I'd meet him soon as I got here. Cy, you've got the order for the feed store, right?"

"Yes, sir," answered Cy.

"Good, go give it to Mr. Vance. Sara, why don't you take the others and find us a spot on the grounds, and get the boys signed up for their games, okay?"

"Yes, I'll do that," she said.

"Good. It's settled then. See ya'll in an hour or so..."

He turned and walked away.

"See ya," said Cy over his shoulder as he left too.

Sara hitched Cassie higher on her hip and looked at Seth, then Bert, then Amos.

"Come on, guys. Let's go find us a spot."

The Hog's Head was every bit as dim and stale smelling as it ever was, though a bit more crowded and a bit louder than usual. Harley hesitated in the doorway, allowing his eyes adjust to the lack of light, giving his nose time to adjust to the scent of spilt liquor tanged with a whiff of old urine. All the regulars were there — the Mangrum brothers, Hubert Tazwell, Hair Bear, and the rest, reminding Harley why he didn't come here much. He sucked in his breath and started toward the bar.

"Harl! Over here."

Harley turned and saw Burley grinning from a corner table, sitting with Paulie Whitson and Rig. He grinned back and went to join them.

"Howdy, boys. Good to see you."

"Have a seat. We've been saving one for you," said Burley, holding out his hand. Harley took it and shook it.

"Thanks, Burl, I could use one about now." He shook with Paulie and Rig too, then pulled up a chair.

"I've got what you need right here," said Rig, uncorking the bottle of Jim Beam that sat on the table. He poured a shot glass full and slid it toward Harley, then topped off his and Burley's and Paulie's.

"To the good life," he said, raising his glass.

"May we live forever," chimed Paulie. And they drank.

Rig refilled all around.

"Great to see you, feller," he said. "I been meaning to get over your way, to see how things were going. But what with the season settin' in and all... You know, hard to make time."

"Yeah, I know that, for sure."

"So, how's it working out? She doing okay?"

"Yeah. Sure. Things are fine. Sara's doing fine."

"I'll bet she is. I told you, I knew she'd fit in."

Harley swirled his glass and took another sip.

"The boys love her. She's good with the little 'uns," he sipped again. "She's a good girl."

"You bet. I figured that right off." Rig sat with his back to a window, so it was hard to see his face with the glare behind. Harley thought he saw a wink, but couldn't be sure. "She sure struck me that a way. Right off. A good 'un, that girl is, and every bit as purdy as her mother."

Dust mites floated in the light shafts that streamed through the grimy window behind Rig. Harley swigged again and set his empty glass on the table just loud enough to say 'another'. This time it was Burley who picked up the bottle and poured.

"How's your crop coming, Harley? Good enough weather so far, eh?"

"Yep, couldn't ask for better. Looking strong so far, looking good. Yours?"

"Great. Could be record poundage this year, way things are going. Earliest blooms I can remember, and tallest plants too, for July."

"Mine too," said Paulie, "I've never seen fatter leaves, nor fuller, than this crop."

"Yup."

"Amen."

"Got that right." The table agreed. The glasses were filled again and Paulie gave a toast to a fine harvest, and the glasses were drained. Rig did the honors again, pouring out another round. But the bottle went dry before the last shot glass was quite full. He waited till the final ready drop fell into Paulie's glass, then held it up high, neck down, and whistled loud across the room.

"Charley," he called to the bartender, "Give us another."

"No more for me, guys. I gotta be going," said Harley, reaching into his pocket, "but let me chip in on the last."

"No need, Harley," said Burley. "Finish your drink. This'ns on me."

"Now, Burl..."

"Now, Harl. Your turn next. I'll hold you to it."

"Deal," said Harley. "I owe you."

"Deal," said Burley. "But forget the owing. It ain't about keeping score, now is it? It's the future that's ours; the past is always over and done."

"I reckon not. I reckon that's the least of it, for sure." Harley ran his fingers around the rim of his glass as the table fell uncomfortably silent for a moment.

It was Rig who spoke next:

"Whatever," he said, slamming down his drink. "But a little word to the wise... I hear tell from my Uncle Jack, down Jackson way, that they've had a touch of the blue mold showing up the last couple of weeks. Best keep an eye out, we had. Things going this good, that's just when the blight shows up and slaps you down. Best be on guard. Things is going too damn good. Kinda scares me, it does."

"I heard that," said Paulie, "I know what you mean. Just when a man gets comfortable, that's when the slappin' back down comes. Can't be this good without bad lurking around."

Charley brought a fresh bottle, uncapped it, and set it on the table.

"Hey there, Harley. Good to see you again, been a long time," he said, wringing his barman's apron in his pudgy hands, as he was prone to do, waiting.

"This one's mine," said Burley, tossing a silver two-bit piece on the table. "My tab, Charley."

"You got it, Burley," Charley scooped the tip from the table and turned to go, only to run smack into Frank Mangrum, who had followed the liquor from the bar.

"Excuse me," he tried to sidestep, only to run into Lloyd, who inevitably followed behind his brother, and liquor.

"Excuse's ass, you fat fuck!" snarled Frank.

"Yeah," chorused Lloyd, always the slower, dimmer, shadow version of his brother. "Yeah, Fatty."

Charley knew them both, knew them day in and day out. The little guy with the big mouth and the big guy that backed him up.

"Sorry," he nodded, and went on his way.

"Afternoon, gentlemen," said Frank. "Mind if me and my brother join you? I told him you wouldn't, seein' as it's a holiday and all..." He pulled up a chair, not waiting for a response, leaving Lloyd standing at his back.

"Bring us a couple more glasses, Charley. We needs to toast to Uncle Sam's birthday," he called over his shoulder, grabbing the bottle by the neck.

Harley stood up. "I was just leaving. I've got things to tend to."

Mangrum leered openly. "Yeah, so I've heered. I reckon you do, Felts. Have tending to do, that is... Can't say as I blame you, from what I've heered." He winked at Lloyd as he said it. He threw down a slug of whisky and tilted his head forward, leering through his unruly brows. "Best take better care of her than you did my cousin Bobby, else she's liable to find herself a real man to cozy too. The she'll be gone as sure as he is."

Harley took a half a step toward Mangrum, and Lloyd took a half a step toward Harley. Burley pushed his chair back and stood also.

"We were all just about to go," he said quietly.

Rig and Paulie finished their glasses and stood, and Burley poured two of the empties up. He motioned Lloyd to his vacant seat.

"On us, boys. Enjoy."

"Shame ya'll gotta run off. But the day's young yet. We'll be seeing ya." Mangrum looked at his brother and clicked his tongue. "Won't we, Lloyd?"

Lloyd grinned stupidly back, trying to nod and drink his shot at the same time, so that he wound up pouring most of it down the front of his shirt.

Harley found Sara and the boys sitting on a blanket spread out along the first base line of the ball field on the southeast corner of the square. It was a good spot, he thought, close to all the game fields, and a good place to watch the parade as well. They were setting out the picnic, Seth and Bert and Amos, all stumbling over one another trying to be the most helpful. Harley stood back and watched a moment before he strode over to them.

"Perfect place," he said rubbing Bert's hair, picking Amos up. "Ya'll found a great spot,"

"Seth, you got us signed up for the three-legged race, didn't you?"

"Yessir! We're number 4," he replied, holding up two squares of linen marked with large black fours. He handed one to his dad.

"Just remember — right, left, right, left, along my count. Okay?"

"I will, Pa. Just give me the mark."

"It'll be a piece of cake. They'll never know what hit 'em"

"Now, don't you guys go collecting your ribbons so soon," said Sara. "Save that till after the race," she grinned.

"Aw, that's just a formality, ain't that right, Pa?"

"Yeah, we'll let the rest keep hope, and then we'll show 'em."
He looked down at the spread on the ground before him. "Dinner
looks great, Sara, really great."

She smiled and looked down at her lap, deflecting the
compliment.

"I'll go find Cy and we'll be back before the horse-shoe
pitching starts. I hope the Reverend's on his game today," Harley
said.

"Go get 'em, Pa," said Bertie, squinting up at his Dad.

Harley winked backed.

"You bet Bert. We'll get 'em, or at least go down trying." He
turned and walked away, easily and erectly.

Before he reached the street he saw Cy ambling toward him.
Harley draped an arm around his son's shoulder and led him back to
their circle of loved ones.

And so the afternoon wore on, an air of leisure anticipation
permeating the grounds, the people, the town. Reverend Adams and
Harley won first place in horseshoes; he and Seth earned a green
ribbon for third place in the three legged race, but had by far the most
vocal gallery during the race and during the awards. Cy won a red
ribbon in the sprints, which Sara proudly pinned to his shirt as the
whole family clapped and bravo-ed. They sat and watched the parade,
which consisted of the school band marching past, a hay wagon
decorated to depict the Battle of Bunker Hill, pulled by Tom Houk's
spanking new Massey Ferguson tractor, and of Mayor Richey riding
in a black Ford convertible beside Eula Wallace, this year's 'Miss
Liberty'. And the veterans marched. Of course the veterans.

Cy stood close by his Pa watching the columns file past; some
old and withered, some hardly older than Harley. The elders hobbled
along on canes and bent spines, many with empty sleeves or pant legs;
the youngers much the same, except a bit more upright, a bit livelier
in their step. Harley laid a hand on Cy's shoulder and let it rest there
until the last of the soldiers were past, and then some, hoping the boy
didn't feel the tremble in his touch.

"How old were you during the Great War, Pa?" Cy finally
asked.

"Oh," said Harley, letting go, "not a whole lot older than you,
Cy."

The crowd was filing away now, eager to partake of the county-wide potluck supper that awaited them. But Harley and Cy stood there looking at the empty street almost expectantly, as if they saw more to the parade than what they had just witnessed with their eyes.

The air between them vibrated with the question, so Harley said, carefully, "Henry was Sara's age when he went. And David was gone as soon as he turned 18."

Cy knew, had always known, why he had no uncles. But he had never until that moment considered the fact that his daddy had no brothers.

Finally, without a word, they turned and began following the crowd. No sooner had they than they heard a cry, faint and far before them.

"Paaaaaaa?" It drew on long, like lowing.

"Thyyyyy?" it called, "Where are youuuuu?"

It drew onto dim as they ate, and dark by the time they were done.

Sara was clearing everyone's dishes when the brass band began warming up at the gazebo, where the dance would be held.

"Mighty fine," said Harley, standing. "That was a mighty fine meal, wasn't it, boys?"

Everyone heartily agreed.

"Come on y'all," Harley motioned. "Let's find your Aunt Clo and Uncle Rig, Sara, and go listen to some music."

"You all go ahead, Harley. I'm going to finish loading the basket and carry it down to the ferry. I'll meet you guys at the bandstand once the music starts."

"Okay, we'll see you there." Harley picked Cassie up and motioned to the boys again, and they all started away. Sara gathered up the blanket and folded it over the wicker picnic basket and watched as the Felts family was swallowed by the crowd. Then she turned with her load and headed toward the river, just as the band launched into 'Bicycle Built For Two'. It was a beautiful night out.

The ferry had long since made its last run into town, and sat empty, tied to the wharf while Jeremiah enjoyed the festivities. Sara climbed aboard and went to the back and shoved the basket under a bench. But instead of turning and going immediately back up the hill, she sat down and leaned over, perching her chin on the top railing. The water was black and silent, an empty abyss between her and the silhouette of the hills on the opposite shore. Even though she couldn't see it, she had a strong feeling of its flow past her; was aware of constant motion around her, making her feel as if she were the one moving, sliding upstream on a glass snake. She put both hands on her stomach to ease the queasiness that welled up there. Olivia Hall had said the baby should begin kicking soon. Maybe then it'd become real for Sara. She looked up into the stars, bright and clear and high, and when she looked back down, she noticed them reflected in the river, her eyes adjusting to the darkness. She sat there for several minutes, thinking, praying, and just resting. Aside from the bone deep weariness that came with staying up to late in the night cooking and back at it before dawn, aside from the gnawing at her mind of the growing in her belly, it really was a lovely night.

"Evenin' there, missy."

At the sudden unexpected voice Sara started so violently it made her hiccup. She hadn't heard anyone step onto the boat. She turned around and saw a stranger standing no more than four feet from her; a small, unshaven man with greasy black hair and close-set, leering eyes set beneath bushy brows.

"Didn't mean to startle you, ma'am. I saw you come down and thought I'd come on down and join you for a spell."

Sara could smell him. He obviously hadn't bathed in some time.

"Name's Mangrum," said the man, stepping closer, holding out his hand. "Frank Mangrum. I'm a friend of Harley's. He said he was going to introduce us. This way saves him some trouble."

Sara shook the man's hand. "Pleased to meet you, I'm sure."

He didn't let go. He just stood there with her hand in his awful, grubby, paw, grinning at her.

"I really should be getting back," said Sara trying to withdraw her hand from his. But he held firm.

"No need to rush off, missy. You and me oughta get acquainted, doncha ya think?" Mangrum said, winking at Sara. "Bein' sorta neighbors and all, I mean, ya know."

"Please let me go," said Sara. "They're expecting me back."

Mangrum just grinned, gap toothed, and took a step closer.

As the dance got into full swing, Addie Harper came over to where Harley stood holding Cassie. The kids were all in the ball field behind the bandstand, playing red rover.

"Let me have that little angel, Harley. My, how she's growing!" Harley handed Cassie to her. "I'm going to take her with me for a bit, show her around to the ladies. Why don't you go dance and have a good time."

"Oh, you know I ain't much on dancing, Addie."

"Funny, Ellie always seemed to be able to get you out there," she paused, looked away briefly. "And you cut a pretty mean rug, best I remember."

Harley looked past her at all the couples swinging about the lawn. They were playing 'Matilda's Waltz' now, one of Ellie's favorites.

"At least mingle around anyway. I'll bring Cass back directly."

"Okay, Addie. Sure. Thanks."

"Come on, little girl, let's me and you go to your first social." She waved over her shoulder. "You have fun, Harley."

"You too, Addie. See you in a bit." He wandered into the crowd that ringed the dance area.

"Hey, Pa," Harley turned. It was Cy.

"I thought you were playing with the kids."

"I was, but I'm getting too old for that stuff. I thought I'd come watch the dance."

He stared out at the sway and crunch of the dancers. "Is it hard, Pa?"

"What's that, son?"

"Dancing. Is it as hard as it looks?"

"Naw, it ain't hard. Just move your feet in a box, corner to corner to corner. Let the music get in you and it comes natural."

"I expect I'd like to try it sometime." Harley noticed there in the dark that his boy was getting within a few inches as tall as he. Cy scanned the crowd.

"You seen Sara, Pa?" he said, turning. "Wonder where she is. She's been really looking forward to music. Funny she ain't around."

"She was going down to the dock to put the basket away. But she has been gone for a good bit, maybe we ought to go help her."

Harley put an arm around Cy's shoulder and led him toward Main Street.

They had just reached the corner of Commerce Street when Cy said, "Look yonder, Pa. What's going on, you reckon?"

Harley looked down past the pier. There were two dim shapes on the ferry. They seemed to be struggling. Then came the scream, Sara's voice. Cy got the step and bolted down the hill, with Harley close behind. Cy had legs like a deer, and ran well. Harley couldn't keep up so it was Cy who gained the boat first. He grabbed Mangrum by the arms and Harley saw the man swing around and catch the boy square in the head with a hammering fist. Cy crumpled and went down in a heap. With a roar Harley charged onto the boat, tackling Mangrum. Sara stepped back to the stern, her dress torn from her shoulder. Harley had Mangrum by the throat.

"I'll kill you, you little..." he began. But he was hit from behind before he could finish, and kicked off of Mangrum. Lloyd was on him in a heartbeat, wrestling Harley up, pinning his arms behind him.

"You ain't killing nobody, Felts," sneered Frank, and he buried his fist in Harley's stomach. The blow took Harley's breath. He struggled to free himself, but Lloyd was a monster, out-weighing him by thirty pounds, at least.

"You Felts's always thought you was better'n us Mangrums, didn't ya?" Frank took another shot, to the face this time. Harley heard his nose crunch as blood began to flow down his face. Mangrum swung again, then again. He reached into his pocket and pulled out a four-inch jack knife, flipping the blade open with one hand.

"I've been waiting for years to take care of you," Mangrum hissed. "Just like you took care of my cousin Bobby."

Harley felt himself leaking into the night, blacking out, when he heard a loud crack, and Lloyd turned loose of his arms. He spun and swung at the man, but Lloyd was already sinking to his knees, so all Harley caught was the top of his hat. Sara stood behind him, gripping the splintered handle of an oar in her shaking hands. She reared it back like a ball bat and swung it again with all her might, catching the back of Lloyd's skull with a sickening thud. The big man fell face forward onto the deck. Harley turned to face Frank, but the little weasel was already running up the gangway. Before Harley could collect himself, Frank jumped to shore and took off up the hill, leaving a hushed "whoo-hoo" echoing behind him. As Harley started after him he heard another thud behind him, and then another. Sara was leaning over Lloyd, flailing away with the oar handle. Harley stepped over the crumpled heap of man and grabbed Sara's arms.

"Enough. That's enough. He can't do you no harm now."

Sara looked at the prone body under her, dropped the oar, and staggered back against the rail, staring vacantly across the river.

Harley immediately went and bent over Cy.

"Son!" he said shaking the boy. "Cy! You all right, son?"

Cy opened one eye. His left was already swollen nearly shut.

"Oowww," he moaned.

"Are you okay, son? Can you sit up?"

"I think so," said Cy. "Oohh," he moaned again. "What a wallop."

Harley helped him stand. Sara was still cringing against the back of the boat, staring down at Lloyd with terrified eyes.

"Think you can make it up the hill, boy?"

"Yeah, Pa, I'm okay."

"Good. Go fetch the sheriff. Find Mrs. Hall and help her gather up your brothers. We'll be up directly."

"Okay, Pa." Cy started wobbly across the ferry, but by the time he hit the ground, he broke into a slow trot up the hill. A gasp came from Sara, then another, as she slowly sank onto the deck into a heaving puddle of gasping and sobs. Harley went and sat down beside her, cradling her as she leaned into his chest, crying hysterically. Harley stroked her hair, leaned over and put his lips on her forehead, the way Ellis always did whenever anyone got a boo-boo.

"There, there, Sara. It's over. Everything's all right now. It's over." She continued crying but she looked up at him, then back down at Lloyd.

"I killed him. I think I killed him."

"No, Sara, he ain't dead." He took her chin and pulled her up to face him and smiled at her. "But he'll have one hell of a headache for a while, that's for sure." Sara caught her breath and smiled weakly back. "You're a regular hell-cat aren't you, girl? Remind me to never piss you off, okay?" She smiled bigger, and Harley chuckled.

"Ouch," he said.

"You're a mess, Harley. You've got blood all over you. Are you okay?"

"Yeah. I'm fine. It only hurts when I laugh. And when I don't."

"Here, let me clean you up some." She took the hem of her dress and began daubing at his face. She had hiccups left over from crying.

"No, don't worry about me. You just sit here and slow your heart down before it explodes." He could feel it pounding against his chest. She settled into his hug and he began stroking her long, soft hair. They sat like that until the sheriff and the others arrived.

*

By the time they got back to the dance, 'the incident' was the buzz of the night. The men surrounded Harley right off.

"Heard you cold-cocked the big one. I've always wanted to do that," said Burley, taking Harley by the arm. "You're a sight, sure enough. Let's go get you cleaned up, pard."

"It was Sara that cold-cocked him. All I did was get beat on."

"Damn shame Frank got away. Reckon we should go hunt him?"

"No, Burl. Time to let well enough alone. The sheriff even let Lloyd go. Sara insisted, no charges."

"Well, Frank's got his coming, all I can say. He'd best be scarce for a while."

"Leave it be, Burley. Come on to the pump and tell me when I've got all the blood off."

"Sure, killer, whatever you say. Just don't hit me like you did Lloyd."

"Ha-ha, Burl. I told you, it was Sara done the hittin', not me."

While Harley leaned over the pump washing his face, two men he didn't know walked past.

"What'd she think, going down to the river with Mangrum anyway. Ask me, she got what she asked for," one of them said, "sneaking off with such."

"Yeah. At least she would have if they hadn't got caught," said the other. Their guffaws faded into the noise of the crowd as they moved on. Harley stood up and watched them go as he dried his face on his shirt tail.

When he and Burley came back to the bandstand, the boys all swarmed around.

"You poked him good, didn't you, Pa?" cried Bert.

Seth chimed in, "Too bad they ain't giving out boxing ribbons. We could add to our collection."

"You boys get back to your fun. I'm just going to sit here a spell before we head home."

"Not before the fireworks, Pa. Gee, we can stay till then can't we?"

"We're going back Jeremiah's first trip. The river is the best place to watch the display anyway. Now ya'll get along."

"Okay, Pa," said Seth, swinging his fist in front of him, "Way to go!"

"Get now!" Harley couldn't help but grin after them.

Sara walked up then, accompanied by Olivia Hall. "Don't pay no never mind to those old biddies," Liv was saying. Sara's dress was fastened at the shoulder with a large mother-of-pearl safety pin. Her hair was brushed smooth and shiny, but her eyes were still puffy and red-ringed. "Nobody listens to their gossip anyway." She spotted Harley.

"Why hey there, Harley. Bit of excitement, eh? How are you doing?"

"I'm fine, Liv, and you?"

"Oh, we're okay," she looked over Harley's shoulder and waved.

"Ben!" she called, "Over here!"

Ben Hall joined the group, shaking Harley's hand. Turning to Sara, he asked, "Are you all right, Sara? Did he hurt you?"

"No, he didn't hurt me. Just scared me a little. A lot. I'm just glad Harley and Cy came along when they did."

"Good. It's a good thing from what I hear. How about you, Harley? Let's have a look at that nose." He took Harley's swollen nose gingerly between his thumb and forefinger.

"Ow!" said Harley.

"I'd say you've broken it right proper. Nothing to do but let it heal though. Want me to give you something for pain?"

"No, Ben, I'll be fine. Thanks though."

"How about you, Cy? Come over here and let me see your eye."

Cy stepped over and the doctor took the boy's head in his hands, turning it this way and that to examine the eye in the light cast by the dim overhead strings of bulbs.

"Going to have a whale of a shiner, that's for sure. Looks like he might have busted a blood vessel too. Now your eyeball matches that ribbon you're wearing," he grinned, rubbing Cy's hair. Turning to Harley he added, "Just keep an eye on him tonight. If he gets nauseous or drowsy, bring him to me, okay?"

"Sure, Ben. Thanks again."

"No problem, Harl. Any party can always use some livening up." He turned to his wife, "And now, Mrs. Hall," he said, "Would you do me the honor of a dance?"

"Certainly, Mr. Hall," she said, taking his arm, "I'd be delighted." They made their way into the crowd, Livia waving over her shoulder. "See ya'll later."

As they left, Cy cleared his throat.

"Sara," he began, looking down at the toe of his shoe, pushing the grass around, "I might not be so good at it, but do you think you could teach me how to dance?"

"I'd love to, Cyrus!" she said, offering her elbow. The boy took it and led her in the direction the Halls had gone. Sara turned and winked at Harley as they made their way to the center of the dance. When they got to the middle of the crowd, Cy just stood there. Sara took his left hand and put it on her waist, then took his right in hers, and off they went. Harley smiled at Cy's first halting, clumsy steps, but soon the boy began to catch the rhythm, and the intervals between his stepping on Sara's feet widened. He could see Sara talking to Cy the whole while, occasionally throwing her head back and laughing. Harley could hear her laughter ringing clear and high as a bell, even above the music and chatter of the crowd. They danced two full dances, then on the third Sara reversed their positions and took the lead, and they swirled smoothly through the crowd. She was obviously in her element, comfortable and graceful.

"Look at Cy, Pa!" Seth laughed, "Talk about clumsy! Two left feet ain't the word for it."

"You'd best hush. Your time'll be coming soon enough."

At the end of the third song they made their way back to where Harley stood, Cy puffing and Sara's hair stuck tight in a ring about her glistening face.

"That's too much like work," Cy breathed.

"You did just fine, Cy. You make a fine dance partner," Sara smiled.

"It seems that Anderson girl thinks so," winked Harley. "She didn't take her eyes off you the whole time."

"Oh, Pa. She's just a kid!"

Sara turned to Seth. "How about helping me get us all some lemonade, Seth?" She held her arm out to him, to be escorted.

"Me too!" chimed Bert. "I can help."

"Me too," said Amos.

She picked Amos up and nestled him onto her hip, then offered her other arm to Bert.

"Come on then, guys. I feel like the most popular girl at the dance, surrounded by all you handsome men."

As they left, Cy looked at his pa. The band started another song. A circle of people a few feet to their right burst into loud, raucous laughter.

"I think Momma would like Sara, Pa." He hesitated before adding, "I think they'd get along just fine."

"I think so too, son... I think so too." Then they stood and watched the song, neither saying more.

The coronet band began packing up their instruments, making way for the fiddles and banjos of the hoe-down. Ben and Liv returned.

"Mighty warm out there tonight," said Ben. "Going to be even hotter, once the square-dancing starts."

"Yeah, I expect it would be," said Harley, watching Sara and the boys making their way back, all of them carrying paper cups, Bert hugging two to his chest and Amos carefully balancing one held before him at arm's length.

"We got there just in time," Sara said, handing a cup to Harley, "We got the last of the ice."

"Once again, your timing is perfect," he said, holding her eye. "I've got to thank you. You really saved my skin with that oar, you know?"

"Oh, it was you guys who saved me. I don't know what would have happened if ya'll hadn't come along."

Harley took a sip.

"This is good stuff," he said. "Not too sweet and not too sour. Just the way I like it." He held his cup up and raised his voice. "How about a toast?" The boys all raised theirs.

"Yeah, let's have us a toast!"

"Toast?" said Amos, looking around quizzically. "Toast?"

"Get in here, Sara." Harley paused...

"To the best durn family in Decatur County!"

"To us!" echoed Seth. They touched cups all around and drank.

Behind them the screeching and plunking of the band tuning up began to fade as Buck Thorton, the caller, took the stage.

"Can I go to the playground, Pa?" asked Seth.

"Sure. But take your little brothers with you."

"Aww gee, Pa. I don't want to lug after them all night."

"Here," said Harley, fishing in his pocket. "Here's some money to buy you all some sparklers. They want to play too."

"Okay," said Seth, taking the coins. "Come on, Bertie. Grab Amos."

"You keep an eye on 'em now, Seth, you hear. Don't let Amie burn himself."

"I will, Pa."

"And meet us back here as soon as they start setting up the fireworks."

"Yes, sir."

"And ya'll behave!"

"Have fun, guys!" Sara called after them. "See you later!"

The tuning noises stopped and Buck said something to the band before turning to face the crowd.

"Evenin' Folks!" he called out in his rich, deep drawl, "Mighty hot out here, ain't it?" The crowd responded with a lively mixed chorus of agreement.

"Well, we're fixin' to really heat it up." He turned to the band, "Ready Boys?"

When they all nodded at him he turned once more to the crowd. "Gents, grab your darlin's, cause we're fixin' to HOOOOO-DOOOOOWN!" A cheer went up from the throng and the band launched into 'Little Joe and the Wrangler'.

Olivia nudged Harley's side.

"Why don't you go get in the stag line, Harley? I know for a fact you won't be there long. There's been two or three ladies I know of asking about you."

"I don't think so, Liv. I'm not ready to go there just yet."

"It's up to you Harley. Just thought I'd let you know, there's a lot of interest out there."

Harley grinned. "When I need a match-maker I'll be sure and let you know, Liv."

"You'd better," she turned to Ben, "Shall we then, Mr. Hall?"

"I'm getting too old for this," Ben mock protested, as he let her drag him onto the lawn. "Get yourself out here, Harl. If I've got to, you can too." Then they were gone, swallowed into the swirling, stomping mass.

"You've got a lot of good friends, Harley," Sara said beside him. "You're a lucky man."

"Yessum. A lot of good folks out there. I reckon I am at that. I've a lot to be thankful for."

They stood quietly for a bit, watching the reel before them. Harley found his toe tapping the ground under him. He shifted his weight to the other leg. Sara was intent on the dance. She began to bounce lightly in time to the music.

"Swing her left! Swing her right! Swing her 'round and 'round tonight!" Buck called, directing the flow. Sara was clapping along now, bobbing, her hair swaying across her back in rhythm.

"It looks so much fun!" She had to lean close to be heard, so close that a strand of her hair caught in his mouth; so close he scented a hint of peach lotion and July musk.

"Are you any good? Do you know how to do it?" She was beaming; happier looking than he'd ever seen her. Suddenly she was a bright-toothed, wide-eyed, clapping-stomping blonde-halo-ed little girl, having fun.

"I've done it a time or two. Not that I'm much good at it. But yeah, I know how."

"Would you teach me?"

She slipped her hand into his and tugged lightly. It felt so small, so pale, so warm.

"Please?" her tug insisted.

Harley looked at the people around him, the ones that ringed the dance. Old folks mostly, leaning forward in their lawn chairs, wishing they were out there one more time. The fat, the homely, the lonely — standing, watching. Pretending not to be jealous of the life that spun and twirled before them. Eager faces, sad hearts. The first song ended and Harley dropped Sara's hand.

"Line 'em up! Belles east, beaus west," cried Buck.

Harley spotted Cy lining up opposite the little Anderson girl, what was her name, Lila? Lily?

"Bow to your partner, gents!"

He watched Cy put one hand to his belt and the other behind his back, palms open, bowing low with the other men.

"Curtsey, ladies, to your man!"

Dresses fanned wide and ankles crossed demurely.

"Hit it, boys!"

The fiddle led off, sawing hard. As the first strains of 'Mary Phagan' filled the night, Harley took Sara's hand back up.

"Sure. Why not..." He stopped, looked at her, and bowed forward. "I mean, I'd be honored, Ma'am."

And they joined the dance.

Sara was a natural. She took to it like she'd been doing it all her life. Harley had precious little teaching to do, and was glad of it.

She was laughing every time he passed her off, and laughing every time she came back. Halfway through 'The Old Hen Cackled And The Rooster's Going To Crow', her glee was rubbing off on him, and by the time 'Vibrating Strings' was over, she seemed the old hand and he the novice. Her delight was as pure as it was contagious, not only to Harley, but to the rest as well. Gradually, the sly winks and tight-lipped smiles that Harley'd felt early on turned to broad, genuine grins. Sara spun her way into the crowd; her joy danced about her like a fever.

Harley couldn't remember the last time he'd had such fun. And it felt good. Finally, no matter what, it felt good again.

As the last notes of 'Belle Of The Ball' died away, Buck pulled at the fob that dangled from the front pocket of his overalls. He made a great show of opening his watch and clicking it shut.

"Well, folks, bad as I hate it, and I know you do too, we're late again this year. It's drawing on to nine o'clock, and our good mayor over there," he nodded toward the dark on his left where a hand raised and waved to the hoots and cat-calls of the crowd, "our good Mayor Richey tells me we've got to shut it down for another year. So last call for dancing. Get your honey close, before we call it a night and get ready for the fireworks!"

There was some laughter and much jostling as perhaps a third of the crowd began dispersing from the center lawn. Sara pulled at the front collar of her dress, fanning it in and out.

"I guess we'd better go find the boys," she said, turning to leave.

"I guess so," said Harley, starting after her. But then the band began playing a muted, sorrowful version of 'No place Like Home', he stopped and took her arm.

"One last dance, Miss Sara? To cool off?"

"I'd be delighted, Mr. Felts."

He bowed and she curtsied, and they took up the slow waltz.

She felt so slight, so fragile in his arms. But her bulge pressed hard on his stomach. He felt so very hard, so rough against her, but he held her gently, tenderly. They both felt the music; both swayed to it, silently. For a time.

It was Harley who leaned back first, who looked dead at her, and spoke first.

"I've never been much with words, Sara... I reckon you know that by now, as well as anyone... But when I have something to say I've got to say it."

She stared right back at him without speaking. She didn't say a damn thing. So he went ahead.

"Thank you.

"Thank you for all you've done." He was full into it now, there was no going back, so he went on.

"Thank you for stepping in and loving the boys like you've done. And making them love you. Thank you for mothering Cassie, for giving her what I never could have. Thank you for putting up with no thanks for so long..."

Still, she stared straight at him. He paused and sucked in a breath.

"Sssshhh," she whispered, before he had a chance to go farther. She tightened her grip on him, hand and waist.

"Thank you. It's me that's thanking you."

And then the dance was over. It was time to go.

*

Seth was there, with Bert and Amos in tow, waiting for them, grinning at them as they walked out from under the lights.

"Ya'll have fun?"

"We did. How about ya'll?"

"Seth made me hold Amie's hand the whole time, Daddy," whined Bert. "He wouldn't even let me play."

Amos yawned large. It was way past his bedtime.

"Parklers!" he tried, and yawned again. Harley bent and picked him up.

"There'll be big 'parklers' over the river, soon as we find your sissy and your big brother. Hang on Amie, we're headed home now. Got to get you to bed, baby boy."

Amos yawned again.

"Seen your brother, Seth?" Harley asked.

"There he comes," Seth pointed, "Right behind Miss Hodgkins."

Anna Mae walked up and handed a blanket-bundle full of baby to Sara.

"Here you go, she's all yours again."

Sara took Cassie in her arms, leaning low over her, cooing, "There's my girlfriend. Did you have a big night, little girl? You're worn out aren't you, sweetness?"

"She's so precious," Anna smiled briefly at Sara, "Take care now, and let me know whenever I can help out, you hear?"

"Thanks, Anna Mae. I surely will."

"Come on, gang, let's head across the river," Harley said. "Thank you, Anna, for watching the baby."

"My pleasure, Harley. I loved doing it. She's such a doll."

"Goodnight," Harley said, and he gathered his brood and headed for the river.

They were among the first to board the ferry. Jeremiah was there, preparing for the crossing.

"Glad to see you all didn't break nothin' on my boat, 'cept what needed breaking," he winked first at Cy, then at Sara. "Way to go. Only wish I'd been here to see it, 'stead of wasting my time up on the hill again." As everyone settled aboard, he cocked his ear to the left, to the downstream side, and a steady drumming noise rose from there.

" 'Fraid it'll be a few before we start across. Coal barges coming."

The ferry grew more crowded as the chugging grew louder, so that Harley and his family were slowly pushed to the bench on the stern, next to Jeremiah's helm. Harley sat down, holding Amos, Sara next to him, cradling Cassie, while Cy and Seth fussed over railing space and Bert settled next to the basket under the bench. There was a tug boat pushing a string of a half dozen barges up from the mining country down Chattanooga way when the first flash hit the sky, lighting the faces around them bright and amber, followed by a soft, distant 'pop' as the sky-sparklers fell and dimmed. Two more flashes back-lit the town as the diesel chu-chunked-chu-chunked-chu-chunked upstream behind them. Then 'pop-pop' as the black water turned gold, then green, then black again, while the ferry swayed against the bank in the wake of the barges. Harley tried to turn Amie toward the lights, but it was too late; all he got was a yawn and a sigh as his youngest son turned and nestled into his chest. Cy and Seth stood at the railing waiting for the next explosion, and Bert sat up, wide-eyed once more as the sky went red, redder, gold.

"Wow," breathed Bertie, renewed.

"Pop! Pop-pop!" said the town.

"Chu-chunk-chu-chunk-chu-chunk," said the river, rocking them back and forth. Cassie was hard asleep, eyes clinched and fists tight at her chest, while Sara's eyes shone orange, white, bright. Harley turned Amos in his arms and leaned back.

"Pop-pop-pop."

Fade to black for an instant, then the sky, the water, the eyes around him lit again, reflecting coral shells and waterfalls and shower bursts. Warm and fluid and shining. He felt the warm weight of the child he held. He felt the awe and wonder of the children he beheld.

And he felt the lurch of the ferry as the swell subsided and they started toward the eastern bank. They were going home. Despite it all, it truly was a nice night out.

Chapter 7

It was better than an hour's pull from the ferry landing to the farm. Seth gave out as soon as Bess was hitched, and the family was loaded into the wagon. Cy stayed awake a bit longer, almost to the crossroads that led to Homestead Baptist. Then it was just Harley, Sara, and the night. They rode without speaking for a long while, needing nothing more to be said than the steady clop of Bess's hooves on the hard-pan trail before them, the even breath of sleeping children behind them, and the sounds of summer night. They rode comfortably in silence together for the first time. Finally they had got beyond words. Understanding was coming, finally.

The moon was nearly full out, settling quickly west, but it still hung high enough to mottle the road through the gaps in the high canopy of trees that shrouded them. It was Sara who spoke first.

"She must have been amazing." More whisper than words.

Harley looked up at the sound of her voice, but she wasn't looking back. She watched her hands smoothing her dress across her lap. When she did look up, it was straight at him, hard and fast.

"I wish I could have met her. I almost feel like I have, like I know her, better than my mother, better than my sister. Better than me almost. From the boys, and from you. I feel like I know her. I... I... Feel her. In so many ways."

Sara poured her eyes so deep and damp into Harley that he needed to look away, but he couldn't. His eyes burned hot, misted over, and blurred her from his sight, but he didn't turn away. All he could do was to wait for her go on.

"Maybe I'm out of place here... Maybe I have no right... But, would you tell me something of her? I feel like she's become a part of me. Or I a part of her. And it occurs to me that I don't even know what she looked like. I don't have a picture in my mind, except for the love I see. Except for the loss I feel, for her. And I don't even know who she was, except in my guessing. And in you all."

Harley heard the words from far away, as if they had not come for him, as if they were not aimed at him. Sara's eyes stood pale before him, brimming and fixed and shadowed beyond the dimness of the night, beyond the back lighting of the moon that hung low through the branches over her shoulder. She never flinched, never shifted her gaze; she stayed and waited until he finally looked away. Until he laid the reins loose on Bess's back and whispered to the horse "Get on home, Girl". Until he sighed deep and looked up to the sky, and sighed again. Then she waited more.

"It was on this road," he started, turning his head down to the hands now free on his lap, "right back where we passed about ten minutes ago, that I asked her to marry me." He stopped and cleared his throat. Then he looked back down and watched his hands clasp together, and went on.

"And I reckon it was pretty close along here before she told me "Yes". She knew it was yes before I even asked her. Hell, truth be known, she probably knew I was going to ask her way before I ever did. But she played me out, she made me wait. She had a way of doing that, playing me out. I'd have to say she knew me better than I did myself. She made it all fun. I never had fun really, before Ellie. I never really had time or reason to learn fun, but she taught me. She knew how to have fun. She showed me how. She could make a game out of anything. Before the boys, when we were clearing the pasture along the branch, she'd stay out there all day long with me, working as hard as any man, sweatin' and singing and teasing me right along... Talking about all the heifers that'd be calved right where we were. Calling me Mr. Bull-man, and such. Then she'd moo at me and swish her eyes and make like she was running away, only real slow, so as to make sure I'd catch her..." He stopped, catching himself, feeling his ears go red and hot. He looked up, meaning to apologize.

"I'm sorr..." he began, but before he could finish she cut him off.

"No need to apologize," Sara sat with her hands clasped across her stomach. She leaned back against the wagon seat, shut her eyes and wiggled her fingers in a patting motion against her belly, "Go on. How did you two meet?"

Bert moaned softly and rolled over in his sleep. Harley leaned back and rubbed the boy's shoulder, shifting sideways in the seat so he could reach. He surveyed the dark huddled shapes of the others and went on without turning back around.

"In church. The Hayes' moved here when I was about fifteen or so. I spotted Ellie right off. She was almost two years younger than I was, but she looked and acted like she was way older than that. She had long black hair that hung down her back like a raven's tail, and dark eyes, and high strong cheeks, almost like an Indian, but her skin was as light and smooth as ivory. She wasn't shy, exactly, or standoffish, exactly, but she always held herself high and straight. Proud, sort of. And she had this look about her that at first might make you think she was sad, but when you really looked, her mouth was kind of crooked, like she was smiling with one side and frowning with the other. You never could really tell until you got to know her, or until you saw her really smile, and then she could light up the world like a lightning flash over water. I took a fancy to her right from the start.

"I was out of school by then so I only got to see her on Sundays. When the singing was going on I'd sneak looks at her, and sometimes I'd catch her looking back. And when that happened, the Lord would get so far from my mind I knew I would roast in Hell forever, but I didn't care, if only Ellie Hayes would stand and shed pity on my blighted soul. We went that way for nearly two years, until I got nerve enough to ask her pa if I could call on her. It was just after church and he was standing around with the deacons and other grown-ups, but I had made my mind up, so I just walked up to him and asked. It was about the hardest thing I've ever done, my whole life, to walk up there and interrupt the grown-ups and ask to call on a girl. I'd never called on a girl before so I'm not sure to this day if I was more scared of him saying no, or of him saying okay, because then what would I do? I didn't rightly know the proper way to court. But I had my mind made up, so there I went...

"Mr. Hayes — Mr. Buford I came to call him — he's dead now, came down with consumption just before Cy was born and died before Seth. He was a little man, but he had a long, fierce set of whiskers, halfway down to his belt. Ellie never had no ma that she could remember; she was always told that her ma died on the river in a fishing accident. Mr. Buford was a commercial fisherman and muscle diver by trade, but he always took a funny look whenever Ellie's ma was brought up, and I always wondered if there wasn't more to the story than he let on.

"Anyway, that Sunday when I went up to him and asked to call on Ellie, he took a step back and pulled his hand slowly down that long beard of his, squinting at me through those river-slitted eyes of his, sizing me up like a beached channel cat.

'You're a Felts, ain't you?' he told me more than asked.

"I told him, yes sir I am. Told him my name was Harley, Harley Felts and I held my hand out to shake. I could see Ellie on the steps of the church behind him, pretending to talk to the other girls while she watched me standing there with my sweaty palm stuck out at her father. He didn't take my hand but instead ran his fingers down through his beard again, combing it between them. I dropped my hand to my side and wiped it on my pant leg, feeling like a carp that had fouled his net.

"What are your intentions toward my daughter, Felts?" he asked me.

"To court her, sir," I told him. "To see if she'll have me." He was having a big time, baiting me up, dragging the ordeal out, making a show in front of the whole congregation, it felt like to me, though now I doubt anyone was really taking much notice. I watched and waited as he wound the tip of his beard around his finger, and I began to lose focus of the whole thing. I just wanted to turn and leave and be done with it. I just wanted to get away and forget the whole thing, then a hand slipped into mine, and there was Ellie beside me, smiling with both sides of her mouth, pulling me away."

He paused, turning back forward in the seat, picking up the reins again, snapping them and clicking over Bess.

"The next spring I proposed to her, and the next fall we were married."

His tone said 'the end'. And that brought Sara up from her closed-eyed reverie. She sat up and turned to Harley.

"No fair! You're just getting to the good part."

She waited a decent spell, letting him stare intently into the darkness of the road before them for a full minute or more before she spoke again.

"What did you love about her? The most I mean. What made you pick her to marry?"

Another half minute or so passed before he turned his head in her direction and answered.

"Enough about me. My turn to ask now. Fair is fair."

"Just as soon as you tell me. Then your turn, I promise. But you have to finish first. Isn't that fair?"

Her tone said 'please', so he sighed and turned his head back to the road and sighed again before he went on.

"Fair enough." He glanced, barely, toward her, chewed on his lip a bit, then started again.

"What was it about Ellie? Hard to say, that. Hard to pin-point exactly..." he trailed off. She saw a hint of a smile creep into the corners of his mouth, saw his eyes go far away, and she settled back once more, waiting.

"Her eyes," he said finally. "It was her eyes, more than anything else, that took me first, I reckon." He waited for the tree frogs and late crickets to fill the void, but they only emphasized it, so he went on.

"Ellie always had this 'way' about her. Like she never looked at you, so much as into you... Do you know what I mean? Did you ever know anyone like that?"

But Sara was settled back again, eyes shut yet definitely not asleep; definitely listening. Stubborn as she was, he couldn't help but go on.

"You never felt like she was judging you, never felt like she was doing anything but understanding. Or trying her best. To hear you. To let you show yourself."

Bess pulled up just then, waiting to be told to go or to hold. They were at the ford already. Harley tugged her right rein and she turned and started into the creek.

"She was good people. As good as it gets. Everybody that ever met her knew it right off. She was as good as people get..."

Indian Creek was low with summer, so Bess' clops went wet for only a few seconds before resuming their dry rhythm. Sara saw the brim of Harley's hat turn in her direction, then turn back away. Though his face was hidden by the dark of the night, she had no doubt of the smile in his voice.

"We'd best start waking the boys. We're home now." His hat turned to face the house ahead. "Just don't think you're out of it, missy. You still owe me your turn."

"Okay. A deal's a deal," answered Sara, turning to the back of the wagon without even glancing his way. She reached down to Seth and shook his shoulder gently. "Home now. Stop your dreaming. Help us get your brothers up and to bed." Seth stirred, yawned, and sat up.

"Already? We here already?" he asked, looking around, thick with sleep.

"Yes, already," said Sara. "Home again."

It didn't take long to get the kids to bed; they had been to bed for a while yet, in a way. They rose and walked to the house like zombies, dull-eyed and staring, mumbling "G'nights," and generally grumbling the bile of woken childs. Sara cradled Cassie to the house while Harley took Bess to the barn to unhitch and feed her. By the time he was done the lights in the house had come on and gone out again. He took his time. He wasn't ready to go in yet. The sinking moon still dimly lighted the yard. He looked across his farm and thought how pale and fragile it all was, as if it were no more than gauze floating in ether. Duke followed him to the porch and sat beside him while he unlaced his boots. A screech owl called a series of eerie cries from the distance, once, then twice, and was answered from startlingly close by, from just beyond the barn. The winged hunters were coming home from their hunting, full of field mice and baby rabbit.

"What kind of birds are those?" Harley was startled. He hadn't had a clue Sara was on the porch behind him, sitting in the rocker, in the dark.

"Screech owls," he said turning, trying not to act taken by surprise. She was shrouded in the dark. "Just a couple of night owls coming in. They nest right close by." Again came the faraway call, followed by the close one, responding quicker this time. "They're calling it a night, sounds like."

"Wise old owls," she said. He heard the creak of the rocker begin. "I've always heard that owls are wise birds. Is that true?"

"Can't rightly speak to that, I don't think. They do what they've gotta do, I reckon. Like anybody else," said Harley, setting his boots on the top step beside him. "Like all of us..."

They waited there for a minute, for another round. When it didn't come, he spoke up again, to break the quiet that droned in the night.

"Now crows... Different story, crows. I can speak to that. You want a smart bird, look to the crow." The rocker went on creaking, and he went on staring across the lawn, into the fields beyond the little picket-fenced yard.

"Crows watch men. They know our habits. They covet, just like we do. Crows like shiny things. They like decorations. They like to collect things, just for the sake of shiny, just for the sake of pretty." He turned and peered into the dark of the porch in her direction.

"I learned that early on, when I was just a boy, not even as old as Seth... I was working the fields, hauling hay over at Mr. Totty's place down between the church and the river. Nickel a bale, split between three hands, and we were glad to have it too. Mr. Totty always had the prettiest stands of hay you ever saw. Good land, he had, bottom land, rich and dark as a nigger's butt it was. Good land. Anyway, we were working first cut, spring cut, about the first of May or so, and this bunch of crows would sit up there in the shade trees watching us sweat our asses off for the better part of a week, me and Tommy Post, and your uncle Rig. Anyway, every day at noon, sharp, Miss Ida — Mrs. Totty that is — she'd bring dinner to us in the fields. Us boys and Mr. Totty would all go over to the tree line where it was shady and about two degrees cooler than in the hay-stand, and we'd sit and eat and listen to Mr. Totty spin tales about his Grand-daddy fighting the Yankees in the War Between the States, the War of Northern Aggression as he called it. It was right about the time the Great War was raging across Europe, so us boys were all caught up with war fever and all. And you ain't never heard a tale till you've heard Mr. Totty tell one... He could make you hear the balls whistle past your ears and make you taste the bite of gunpowder smoke, just talking about it. Heck, I'd about nearly have worked for free just for those lunch breaks, to hear him spin his yarns. And you gotta understand, we were all caught up in that kinda stuff then. We listened to the radio every night, us young bucks, wantin' nothing more than to grow up so we could go hang the Kaiser by his damned neck. We couldn't wait for America to join the fray."

The owl called again and Harley paused. The answer came, closer now. He shifted sideways a bit. The rocker creaked behind him, steadily, quietly.

"They're coming home; they've about met up now. They're done for the night." He leaned back and went on.

"Anyway, about the crows. Tommy had this pocket watch. A fine watch, his Granddaddy's watch. He'd gotten it the winter before when his Granddaddy died, from tetanus, I believe it was. Tommy never liked to work much, me and your uncle Rig used to rag him that we should split four and a half cents and Tommy should get the rest. Trying to get him to keep up, you know. But all day long he'd be pulling out that watch, checking the time, looking for noon, looking for dinner and a break. 'Fifteen more minutes', he'd say. Then two minutes later, 'Ten more minutes, boys'. Still to this day I'm not sure he ever knew how to read the damn thing. He was a crow his self, I reckon. Liked the shine of it more than anything. But when we ate, he always set it beside the lunch pails, open-faced so we could see the dial, making out to Mr. Totty like he didn't want to stay one minute over the thirty we took for lunch. But I always reckoned he was more like the crows than anything; he was just caught up in the shine of it more than anything. He just liked showing it off, if you ask me.

"Well, this one day, we were eating and old Mr. Totty was giving us a particularly stirring rendition of how his granddaddy had nearly single-handedly turned the tide at the Battle of Chickamauga. The news from the radio that morning had been that the Great War was all but won, and when lunch time was up and we headed back out to throw bales again, Tommy forgot his watch. He hadn't got more than ten steps from it when one of the crows that had been sittin' and watching and cawing over us every day while we ate, swooped down, scooped Tommy's watch up, and was gone through the trees, chuckling over his shoulder at Tommy. It felt like he was to me anyway." Harley stopped, looked into the dark where the chair was, where he knew Sara was, and laughed, quietly but richly.

"You should have seen it. That crow flying off with his prize and Tommy chasing after, like he could catch up with a flying crow, shouting 'Bring it back! Bring it back!'. And that old crow, lighting in the top of a cedar, holding that silver watch in his beak, laughing down at Tommy. Then all the other crows took it up and they all started cawing and carrying on like they were laughing too. And when Mr. Totty busted out laughing, Tommy left. Stalked off the field. Left me and your uncle Rig to finish the crop ourselves. But we had fun doing it. We laughed like crows at Tommy, right through the last bale of the day."

The creaking stopped just long enough for Harley to hear Sara's giggle over his own chuckling.

"You want a smart bird," he said, "Look to the crow. Can't hardly shoot a crow. They stay out of range.

"They know," he said. "I've heard tell that they live to be up to a hundred years old. They know."

His eyes were used to the dark enough that he could see her smile across the porch. Or at least he thought he could; he could feel it. Either way.

The house lay quiet and dark behind them, until one of the boys coughed in his sleep.

"Seth?" Sara guessed.

"Bert," Harley said with assurance. "He's got sinus."

There was a pause, no owls, no coughs, just dark, until the creaking again.

"Now your turn," he said. "Fair is fair, right?"

The creaking stopped a second or two, then started back. He waited.

It was such a familiar sound; that chair. So comforting, so easy. He waited more.

He couldn't see her smile anymore. Barely heard her sigh. And still he waited.

The crickets were slow. It wasn't as hot as it had been earlier. One of the cows - #43 he guessed, because she was due to calve soon - lowed away off from the south pasture.

When the chair stilled, he knew she was about to begin.

He waited more, in the dark.

The chair rocked once, then twice, then stopped again. Then she spoke.

"He was a jerk."

Harley settled back against the porch post.

"I thought I loved him."

The chair rocked once.

"I thought he loved me." The chair rocked once more, then it began a rhythm again, and she went on.

"Chad. He's a McCormack, of the railroad McCormacks. Chadwick Trevor McCormack. The third. He is every bit as pretty as he is sure of himself, every bit as pretty as he is rich." The chair creaked easily, steadily. Sara peered distantly into the dark fields around.

"It was a fix-up. For my coming out party, when I turned sixteen. He was my date. The only boy I ever dated, it turns out..." She paused.

"Daddy always kept us well off. As well off as a newspaper editor can. But running a paper just isn't the same as owning a

103

railroad. But we were just well off enough for daddy to belong to the same men's club as Chadwick Jr. did. Well off enough to know people such as the McCormacks.

"Lord, mother was so excited that night. She spent all afternoon dressing me up in the new ball gown that she'd spent nearly a month of daddy's salary to buy. She had such fun making me up like a baby doll, chattering away all the time. Telling me how lucky I was. Telling me how to be coquettish. Telling me what fun I was to have, as she painted, squeezed, buffed and brushed me. I never saw her as full of life as she was that afternoon. She'd been raised on the poor side of town; she'd never had a coming out party, or fancy gowns or such, until daddy made it. She was a girl again that day, a giggling, tingling, excited little girl, like I should have been. But I was too busy being prompted and prissed and bustled to be very happy about the whole thing. There was too much pressure for me to be anything but nervous.

"So... Chad showed up in his white tuxedo, in his big white smile, in Chadwick Jr.'s brand new Reo, and he took me to the ball.

"I could tell he liked me right off, or liked what he saw, anyway. He wore me on his arm like a bracelet from that night on. He made me feel like a diamond chain, made me glitter whenever I was with him. We went to all the functions together, from then on. Me at his side.

"Oh, he paid court properly enough, calling on me at home, having luncheons with mother and daddy and I, then later on, having me over to his parent's house — their estate, I should say — to ride horses from their stable, to teach me tennis, to swim in their private pool."

She was settled back in the chair now, hands resting easily on the arms, words flowing freer than Harley had ever heard from her.

"He took me as chattel right from the start, and mother just giggled and cooed and kept making me up, kept telling me what a lucky girl I was to be courted by a McCormack. She kept me on his arm as much as she could. He paid court, the perfect gentleman, for almost two years. And he was bright, and he was witty, and he was awfully pretty, like I said, so by the time he asked me to marry him, I believed it all; believed he loved me and that I loved him; believed in my Mother's dreams. So I said yes. And suddenly, everything changed.

"Once we were engaged, once it was announced, we were allowed new freedoms. We began to have un-chaperoned time together. He began stopping his Reo in lonely spots before he took me home. He became forward in the most insistent way. I tried talking to mother about it many times. I even tried telling daddy once, but all she could see was her daughter becoming a McCormack, and all he could do was blush and stutter. All they could see were the diamonds on Chad's arm. So one night I just gave up. One night I gave in. To him, to them, to all of it."

The chair stopped it's rocking, and Harley felt her gaze fall across the porch at him, strong and steady. He knew her peering, even in the dark. Especially in the dark. But not so much so that he didn't see her hands move to her belly, and rest there.

"And here I am." He heard her say. He couldn't tell, wasn't sure, but it sounded like a smile.

"You know what, Sara?" he started. "He sounds like a crow to me. Not a very smart one though. Might blow my whole theory right there." He grinned in her direction. He looked away, out into the yard where Duke was loudly licking himself, looked away lest she see his look at her, looked away because the dog's loud lapping embarrassed him.

"Duke!" he called, and Duke quit, looking puzzled up at his master for being called down for something so normal.

The chair began again briefly, and then stopped. When she spoke again, it was a whisper, as dim and quiet as the night about.

"What's funny about it all..."

He heard the chair un-creak and he knew she'd risen from it, knew without looking that she was standing, stretching. Made himself not look back at her.

"Funny thing is... I'm not sure if I'd change any of it if I could."

Duke came out of the dark, wagging slowly up the steps, right past Harley, panting loudly to the door where Sara stood.

"I'm here," He heard her say, and Duke shut his panting, as he always did when his ears were getting scratched.

Harley didn't have to turn and look to know that the dog's ears were being scratched. He didn't turn. He didn't stand. He didn't go give the girl a hug.

"It's late," Sara said. "Cassie'll be up before long."

He heard the closer spring on the screen door stretch open, and heard Duke resume his panting.

"Good night." He heard her say.

The door shut softly and Duke came to his side and got his ears scratched once more.

"Good night." Harley said quietly.

Chapter 8

It is most fitting that harvest time for tobacco, the cruelest of crops, comes during the dog days of August, the cruelest time of year. They are called dog days for good reason; Sirius, the dog star, rises and sets with the sun; and it's the time of year that dogs men down, beating them fiercely with sun scorch and sweltering humidity, sucking moisture from the world — man, beast, and earth alike. There is no relief from the oppression of the tobacco fields; no shade, no solace, no mercy. Only daylight to sundown toil, trying to bank the crop while there is time, before even the hardy, near weed plant itself withers away in the sere.

Cy bent to his work with a vengeance. This was the first year they didn't have extra hands helping; it was all up to he and Seth and Pa. Even Bert, though still too small to help with the cutting, was out there with them, laying out the sticks in the rows ahead of them, bringing the water jug by every half hour or so to try and keep dehydration fended off. Sweat rolled down every inch of them all, slicking their backs, pouring stinging into their eyes, causing even hard callused hands to slip and to blister on the handles of the cutting knives. And on top of it all, the thick oozing tar that coated the leaves, and hence the cutters, clogged their pores, adding sick feeling stickiness to the misery.

But one redeeming thing kept them going no matter how faint or beaten they became; this was payday for the year; this was where the money that would clothe and feed and house them for the next twelve months came from. Get it in the barn, get it fired, get it sold, and they would survive another year.

Cy chopped at the bottoms of the inch and a half-thick stalks with practiced rhythm, dropping five plants before putting the metal cone on a hickory stake, picking the batch up plant by plant, and spiking them over the sticks, splitting the stalks at their ankles. He left them in fives like that in the row behind him as he went, where Harley followed to carry the heavy, filed plants to the scaffolds that Bess would pull to the barn. This year was the worst Cy had ever seen for heat. When they'd left the house this morning just after 5:00, the thermometer on the front porch read 82 degrees. Then the sun had risen. Twice already he'd heard Seth puking over on the next row, but Cy had to give the boy credit; he'd not asked to stop and had even protested when Pa made him go sit in the shade for a spell. He was hanging right in there. He was growing up, too.

By three o'clock, huge cumulus clouds dotted the sky in every direction, all around them. Somebody was getting shade. Heck, it seemed like shade had to be everywhere in the county except on this little piece of it. Cy paused his cutting for a minute and arched his back, sore and stiff from eight hours of bending over to slice close to the ground, and caught himself saying a prayer for a thunderstorm. If he could sit for just a little while, feel a breeze, get some cool wet on him that wasn't coming hot from within, he'd be okay. Man, would that feel good!

Harley came up from behind him and picked up two sticks full of crop, laying one over each shoulder like a soldier carrying rifles, the plants clinging heavy to his back.

"You all right, son?" he asked.

"Sure, Pa. I'm doing okay. Dadgummed hot though, ain't it?"

"That it is, for sure." He couldn't stand and hold the load for long. You have to keep moving in the cutting fields, stopping only makes it worse. "Finish this row and we'll take a break, k?"

Before Cy could answer, Pa was gone, puffing his way back down the row. Cy didn't see how Pa could do it; it was all Cy could do to carry one loaded stick at a time.

Just then a cloud scudded over the sun, giving blessed relief from the direct rays. The boy looked up, hoping.

"Think we might be gettin' a shower, Seth," he called over to the next row.

"Uh," was all the answer his brother could muster, and as soon as he grunted it out, the cloud slid away, bringing back the fire.

Cy sighed and spiked another stick full. He had a trick to keep him going at times like this. He let his mind wander. To other places, other times. And sometimes, by the time he came back, a half a row or so would lay behind him. He went there now, remembering...

He was still little, not much more than Bertie's age, and he was mad. Momma was dressing him, early on a crisp fall morning. A cool morning. She was fussing over him, slicking his hair down with a wet comb. It was cold on his head. He didn't want to leave but she was making him.

"Why do I gotta go, Momma? I don't wanna!"

"Sssshhh, baby. You'll like it there, I promise," she cooed at him, stroking his brow with her oh so soft hand, the way she did when he was sick, or sleepy.

"But I don't wanna, I don't wanna, I don't wanna," he whined, then seeing that that wasn't working, he stomped his foot hard on the plank floor of his bedroom, hard enough to jar the lamp on his dresser. "Seth don't have to go! You're keeping baby Seth here with you! How come I have to go and he gets to stay here with you?"

She took his hand and tried to lead him with her to sit on the edge of his bed, but he snatched it away.

"You love Seth better!"

The coaxing smile she'd been wearing fell from her face. She took his hand hard in hers and pulled him up to her lap. He thought she was going to fuss at him; he'd never tried talking back to her before. But what she did caught him by surprise. She leaned over and took both his cheeks in her hands and kissed him, right on the mouth. When she pulled back she stared him right in the eye, her own eyes wet and shiny.

"Cy. Dearest, darling, Cy-boy! Listen to me. Please, baby?"

He felt his snitted muscles un-tense a bit. He'd made Momma cry? How could that be? Still she held his face in her hands; still she stared right into him. Still she held him.

"Honey, Momma doesn't want you to leave her, ever. But Momma's trying to be brave here. Can you help me be brave?"

Cy swallowed and blinked. She pulled him close into her breast and hugged him so hard it almost hurt. This was something big, he knew now.

"Your getting to be a big boy now, Cyrus."

Uh-oh, she called him Cyrus. He was in trouble. She went on.

"Part of me wants to stop that, to keep you my baby forever..."

He could tell by the way she held him though, by the gentle sweetness of her hug, that he wasn't in trouble after all.

"...But there's more to things than what I want. More than what you want, darling." He waited to hear more. "There's another part of me that wants to see you grow up, big and strong, to be a big boy. To be a good man, like your daddy. But now I have to ask you a favor. Will you do Mommy a favor?"

Cy swallowed again. What was going on here? This was all new. "Yes, Ma'am," he said.

"Good. Okay, here's the deal," she paused. The mantle clock ticked in the background. Pa was long into the fields by now and Seth was still asleep. They were all alone. "I need you... Mommy needs your help, Cy. I know that you think your little brother gets more attention than you do. I know you think we love him more. But that's not it at all, honey. That's so far from it you can't even imagine."

Tick. Tock.

"Today is a big day for you. A far greater day than you realize. I'm not sending you away; I'm letting you go. For a little while. There's a huge, big world out there, and you have to learn all about it. If Mommy didn't let you go, you'd stay a baby all your life. You'd never grow up smart and strong like your daddy. You'd never be able to help your little brother when he gets in a jam.

"You do want to be like your daddy one day, don't you?"

"Yes, Ma'am." He did.

"You want to be able help little Seth when he needs help, don't you?"

"Yes, Ma'am." He guessed so.

"You want to make Mommy proud of her little man, don't you?"

This time he just nodded, hard and fast.

"Well, good then. That's what today is all about. This is how you're going to do all those things." She leaned and took his face back into her hands, looking into him again. "This is school, Cy. This is going to be a marvelous thing! They are going to teach you things you never dreamed of. They're going to take you places you can't even imagine; going to show you how to be like Daddy; show you how to make Mommy proud of you. Show you how to look after your little brother — who, by the way, worships the ground you walk on, in case you haven't noticed — and who wants to be like his big brother Cy.

"You understand what I'm trying to tell you, don't you, baby love?"

"I... think so..." He didn't have a clue really. She giggled, she could tell. She could always tell.

"Okay, that's sort of my point. You're going off today to find out what it is I'm talking about. Mommy's going to miss you terribly! But Mommy knows that this is what's best for her baby boy. Mommy knows how much she'll cry after you march out that door, into the big wide world. But Mommy also knows that she has to let you do it. For you.

"Will you be big and strong like your daddy and help Mommy through this? Will you do that for me?"

"Yes, Momma." He would.

"Oh, I love you so much," she said, laughing and kissing him. "Thank you, son. Thank you."

She eased her grip and he knew it was time, so he slid off her lap and stood up.

"Mommy....?" he said.

"Yes, darling?"

"I know you don't really love Seth more than me. I just said that to make you mad."

Again she laughed, and he with her, relieved.

"Cy, Cy, Cy...." She took him back to her lap, kissing his face all over. "If you only knew. One day you will..." Then she did the strangest thing of all. She sat him on the bed and got down on her knees in front of him. She took his hands in hers and looked up at him. Cy had never looked down at Mommy before. It felt weird.

"Cy, dear Cyrus," she stopped as her eyes got wet again. "Mommy loves you more than you'll ever know! If only you could imagine how much I love you!" It got so bad she even stopped to wipe the tears away before she went on. "Okay, I know I shouldn't do this, told myself I'd never say this to you, put this burden on you..."

Tick. Tock.

"But here goes anyway."

Tick.

Tock.

"Here's a secret I'm going to tell you, and I'll never tell it to another soul. Can you keep a secret?"

"Yes, Ma'am." He thought he could.

"Okay," she breathed hard, and he breathed hard too, waiting.

"Cy, you are my first born. You'll always be first in my heart. There'll never be another Cyrus Felts. You're the only one in the whole wide world. You'll always be number one."

He knew what she meant. He didn't say anything back because he knew he didn't have to. He knew.

She stood up and took his hand, starting toward the door. But before she got there she stopped, looked at him, and said, "And if you ever tell anyone I said that..."

"Yes, Ma'am?"

She leaned down and put her hands on his ribs.

"I'll tickle you to death!" And she proceeded to try and do just that.

So long ago, so far away... Cy thought he was laughing, felt the laughter, until it clogged his throat, and then he realized he was choking, coughing, waking up. Pa was there, leaning over him, and Seth and Bertie too. Somewhere, someone was calling his name...

"Ma?" he said weakly. "That you, Ma?" He coughed again, hard, and spit up.

Pa rolled him over onto his stomach and even the dirt against his face felt hot and angry. And he remembered where he really was...

It took them nearly an hour to get Cy back to the house. Harley insisted that he drink and hold down water before they even thought about moving him. His first few sips resulted only in more retching, but after a few tries he was able to hold down minute amounts. Harley sent Bert to the house to tell Sara to fill the wash tub and to bring some ice up from the cave across Indian Creek that served as their icehouse, and then sent Seth to unhitch Bess from the scaffolds and lead her into the field. Cy was burning with fever and Harley feared the boy would go into convulsions if they didn't get his temperature down soon enough. He tried not to remember about that Pinkerton brother who'd died of sunstroke a few years back. It was said the poor man bit his tongue off before he slipped into a coma from which he never woke. Harley broke some of the tobacco stalks over to form a makeshift tent above Cy, to shield him from the sun while he waited for Seth to show up with Bess. And he prayed. He prayed hard, leaning over Cy, clutching him to his chest, talking to the boy.

"Hang in there, Cy. You hold on now, you hear?" Cy's eyes lolled around in his head, only occasionally seeming to look in Harley's direction before fading back into oblivion. The boy's heart was racing a mile a minute, but not nearly as fast as the father's was. "Look at me, Cy! Concentrate!" He was tempted to slap Cy, was ready to do anything to hold on to him; then Cy focused for a minute and got a puzzled look on his face. He mouthed some words, making no sound at all. Harley thought he saw 'Mommy' form on his son's pale lips.

"Oh, dear God. Please..."

"Pa?" It was Seth, trying to bring Bess in. The horse was confused, pulling back on the boy, crushing plants right and left.

"Here, Seth! Talk her over, calm her down." He dared not leave Cy to go help.

Finally, finally, Seth and Bess came crashing into Cy's row, almost right on top of them. Seth stumbled over his brother's feet and Harley jumped up to stop Bess from stepping on Cy. He grabbed her halter and immediately began stroking her neck, whispering softly, soothing her.

"Get up on Bess, Seth. I'll hand Cy up to you." Seth was on the horse almost before Harley finished the words. Harley bent and picked Cy's limp body up and set him carefully in front of Seth.

"Hold him good now. Don't let his head roll. I'll lead her home."

"Is he gonna be all right, Pa?" But Pa was already at the end of the lead, trotting through the crop.

When they got to the house, Bert was at the pump, filling buckets.

"It's almost full, Pa. Sara's gone to the cave again."

Harley led the horse straight to the water trough behind the house. It was over half full and there were large chunks of hastily chopped ice floating in it. He grabbed Cy down before Bess even stopped and laid the boy in the water without taking time to undress him.

"Seth, come hold his head up." He went to take the buckets from Bert, who was struggling toward them. He could hear Cassie crying inside the house. "Go tend to your sister, Bertie," he said. "And Amos too."

He poured the water against the sides of the tub, being careful not to dump it directly on Cy.

"Go help Sara, Seth," he said, putting the palm of his hand on Cy's forehead. The boy was still burning up. And then he waited, and prayed. It was all he could do.

Cy lay with his eyes closed, looking as if sleeping peacefully when Sara and Seth got back, each carrying watermelon-sized chunks of ice in their arms. Harley was leaning close over his son, talking softly into his ear. Sara put her piece of ice into the trough then took the piece Seth held and laid it in as well. Harley never looked up. She put her hand on his shoulder.

"How is he?" she asked. It sounded lame even to her. She could see. Harley still didn't look up, he just kept whispering in Cy's ear.

She turned to Seth, "How about going to see to the kids."

"Yes, Ma'am," and he was gone, relieved to have something he could do.

Sara went around to the other side of the trough, knelt over Cy, and began gently stroking his brow. Cy moaned and half-rolled in her direction. Harley stopped speaking and pulled back, noticing Sara now. She couldn't bear the fear, the pain, the pleading she saw in Harley's eyes. She saw it all in an instant, and it tore her heart. She had to look away, had to have something else to do, because she had no answer for that look. So she spoke to Cy. Took up Harley's liturgy where he'd left off.

"Cy," she breathed. "Cy? Look at me..."

He rolled some more so she took his face in her hands to keep it above water.

"Cy. Wake up, Cy. Please look at me." She leaned over and kissed his cheek.

Cy's eyes fluttered for a moment, then opened. He struggled for focus before closing them again, as a hint of smile crossed over him.

"Ma?" It was slurred, but unmistakable. He picked his head up a bit and squinted at Sara, then turned and looked at Harley. "What happened?" He asked, struggling to push himself up out of the water. Sara put her hand on his chest and eased him back down. He didn't resist; allowed it. He blinked into the late sun slanting down in his face. "How'd I get here?"

"Ssshhhh..." said Sara. "Just hush and lay there now. Ssshhhh..."

Cy laid back, looking up at the sky.

"Durn, I'm dizzy," he said, smiling weakly. But he didn't shut his eyes again. "Durn..."

Once they were sure the heat in him was broken, they helped him out of the tub, and together Harley and Sara walked him to bed. He began protesting as he came back to himself.

"I'm okay, I'm okay," he insisted as they led him along. "Just caught a little faint spell is all." But he let them lead him.

Once they got inside Harley took hold of his son, wrapping his arm around Cy's ribs.

"I'll get him down, Sara. Would you go see to the others?"

"Sure, Harley. Sure." She looked at Cy. "Do as your Pa says now, you hear? You've scared us enough for one day."

Cy tried at a chuckle but it came out as more of a wince.

"Okay, Sara. Okay." He said, "But it weren't too bad. It really weren't," and he smiled, for true. He let Harley pick him up and carry him to his room.

Harley stayed with his son long after Cy fell asleep, long after Sara had put out supper and fed the other children, despite all her askings of him to come and eat something. Cy had a few bites off one of the plates she took them, but Harley hardly touched any. He steadfastly refused to leave Cy's side until long after the boy was deep into sleep, long after his skin had cooled back to normal.

It was drawing onto nine o'clock and all the rest were well in bed before Harley came into the kitchen. Sara was done with the cleaning up and sat at the table hovering over a cup of coffee. She didn't even like coffee, but tonight she was having some. Harley poured himself a cup and sat down. Sara waited for him to speak before she did, and his cup was half gone before he did.

He began with a sigh, long and slow and deep. Then he said it. "I shouldn't have."

He let that lay there a minute, and so did she. He sipped his coffee, and so did she. She waited. Then he went on.

"Dammit. Ain't no crop on earth worth this." She saw his hands clinch before him. "It'll not happen again," he said. "It'll not."

She didn't say a word. She just put her hand on his and squeezed it gently.

They sat that way for some time, until Harley took his hand back.

"I reckon I'll go look in on Cy," he said.

Sara let go and watched him leave the room.

"Goodnight," she said.

She finished her coffee, rinsed the cups, and shut out the kitchen lamp. She resisted the temptation to go see Cy and went to her room. The house was dark and quiet, so she let it be. It was not her place to interrupt. She gently pulled the door shut behind her, hearing how loudly it squeaked in the night, thinking it funny that she'd never noticed how loud it was before. It seemed very loud tonight.

As she pulled her dress over her head she paused and ran her hands over her ever-swelling belly. It felt so very strange to her, the bulge did. Felt like it wasn't even a part of her; still wasn't real. But yet here it was, undeniably. She was tempted for a moment to light the lamp and look at herself, to make it real. But she didn't. She felt it and that was enough, so she slipped her nightgown over her shoulders and lay down. Just as she began her prayers, she felt the light strike from the porch outside her window. At first she resisted, but ultimately she got up and went and peeked.

Harley was there, sitting on the top step where she'd seen him sit so many nights before. But tonight he wasn't relaxing, sloughing off the day as he usually did. Tonight was different. He was lacing up his boots. Not relaxing. Preparing. And when he picked up the lamp and walked away from the house, she followed, slipping on her housecoat as she stepped outside. He was headed toward the field. It came to her what he was doing then, so she stopped and went back into the house, to check on the children and get dressed before she followed any farther. She had plenty of time, she knew. She knew where he was going.

The moon shone over half-full, lighting the way just enough that she didn't need a lamp to get there. She'd taken the trail often enough during daylight to know it by now.

As she neared the tobacco field she spotted a glimmer of the lantern, sitting low among the plants, unmoving. And as she drew nearer she was able to make out Harley's shape, bent over, working swiftly and easily with the cutting knife. She stopped in the dark and watched a moment. He moved down the row with surprising speed, obviously very much at home with this work. She could see the chopped plants laying in the row behind him all the way beyond the hissing light of the lantern.

She walked slowly toward him, careful not to stumble on the uneven ground — she had borrowed a pair of Seth's work boots, even though they were a bit too big for her feet — so she moved quietly and was almost to him before he noticed. He moved down the row in a series of little grunts he made with each stab of his knife.

"I can cut if you'll spike," she said. Harley was so startled he almost fell backwards on his heels.

When he gathered himself and looked up, he saw Sara standing there in a pair of Cy's overalls and a striped felt shirt of his that was very much too large for her, except at the waist. She was wearing an old straw hat and a pair of cotton gardening gloves, all of which hung from her small frame like discarded clothes on a scarecrow. Harley smiled and refrained from saying so.

"What're you doing out here this time of night, missy?"

"Like I said. I came to help. I'll cut and you spike."

Now Harley did laugh. "Girl, you're in no shape to work tobacco." He chuckled more and shook his head. "But I do appreciate the offer." He went back to his cutting.

"Have it your way then," said Sara, picking up a stake and the spiking cone. "You cut and I'll spike. Either way. And that's not an offer, it's a fact." She grabbed the nearest stalk and began struggling to split it over the steel cone she'd placed over the end of the upright stake.

Harley stopped cutting and watched her for a minute, and it took her every bit of a minute to get one plant spiked. He turned his head and spat at the ground, then stood up as she bent to pick up another plant.

"Here you go, mule head." he said, holding out the knife, "I reckon you can cut some, at least till I get these plants spiked and loaded."

She took the knife and grinned at him, bouncing on her toes excitedly, like a little girl just given a treat.

"Durn hard-headed females," he spat again, taking the stake and spike from her. But his smile said 'thanks' before he turned to his work.

They worked for a long time, in the dark of the lantern, and Harley never did quite catch up the spiking, carrying, and loading of the scaffold, to the cutting. He would have stopped her, but each time he came back to fill another stake, Sara was sitting on the ground, humming, slicing, and sliding on her butt down the row. Had he found her bent over, straining just once, he would have stopped her. But she took it easily. She kept ahead of him without straining. So they worked through the night, wordlessly, tirelessly, until the lantern grew faint. When it finally sputtered and flickered and went out, there was still light enough to see; the stars were gone and the sky was rosying on the eastward side, and all around, especially from the creek side, birds were wakening, chattering the morning on. Although he didn't feel the least bit tired, Harley finally called halt to it by sitting down at Sara's side, then laying himself back in the dirt.

"Whew! Girl, you've worn me out." He said, throwing his forearms across his brow.

"Can't keep up, Mr. Man?" she teased back.

"No, Ma'am. Not sure I want to try either."

She giggled a bit, blending her song with the morning birds. She dropped the knife and lay back beside him, feeling the freshly dewed soil on her back.

"Thank you. I was beginning to wonder if you'd ever quit."

"Well, somebody had to, and I got the feeling it wasn't going to be you."

"I quit," she said, with a hint of giggle in her voice.

They lay listening to dawn rise for moments, both enervated by hard work and lack of sleep. Nothing more could be said than the sound of cocks crowing away toward the house, than the creek flowing by toward the shade, than the hum of cicadas waking up, limbering their buzz.

As usual, it was Harley who broke the spell.

"Well, Sara, don't think you'll make a habit of this."

"Well, Harley, don't think you will either. I won't if you don't. Deal?"

He rolled his head to face her, and she rolled hers to him. They found themselves eye to eye, inches apart. And it was he who flinched first, rolling back up to the ever-paling sky.

"The kids'll be waking soon, if they ain't already."

"Yeah," she rolled up as well, "I guess I should be going to see to them. They'll be hungry for breakfast."

"Yessum. I expect they will." He stood and held his hand out to help her up. "What say we go feed 'em?"

Sara smiled, took his hand and let him help her up.

As they walked back to the house the day came full on, lighting the shadows, chasing the stars away. They were halfway home before Harley realized they were still holding hands. He dropped hers, and, needing something to do with his hands, raised his hat with one and wiped his forehead with the other.

"Gonna be another scorcher, looks like," he said.

"Yes. I expect it will be."

Daylight rose full upon them as they walked for a spell, savoring it.

"Harley," Sara began, "Think I could take Bess into town today? I need to run some errands."

"Sure, Sara. Sure you can. Cy won't be working today but he can watch after the young'uns."

"I'll get them squared away before I leave. He won't have to do much. I expect they'll be the ones watching after him, more likely."

"Yeah, I reckon so. I'll let Seth help me till ten or so, then he'll be back to the house. Maybe I'll let him come back out late afternoon..."

Sara stopped. "You're not going back out there this morning?"

"Gotta be done," said Harley, walking on. "Gotta be done."

"Harley..." The plaintiveness in her voice was all the more reason for him to walk on without waiting for her. She knew better than to argue, so she just caught up. They didn't say more across the pasture.

When they reached the gate at the yard Harley opened it and let her through first, then followed and latched it behind him. She was halfway to the back porch before she realized he wasn't following. She stopped and turned and saw him standing alert, surveying.

"What is it?" she asked.

He didn't answer her, except to keep scanning the yard around the house.

"What, Harley?" She sensed, through him, something wrong.

He didn't seem to hear her; he just kept looking around. She felt his tenseness, charging the air between them.

"Duke!" He called. "Here, boy!" Then he whistled.

Sara took a couple of steps back toward Harley.

"He's probably out hunting or something," she tried. But she heard no answering bark. Even she knew Duke would be within range, and would answer back.

"Duke!" he called louder. Still no answer. Harley began striding toward the front porch where Duke usually slept. "Duke!" He called louder, more urgently.

Sara knew the dog should be here. There was no such thing as the yard without Duke in it, unless he was following Harley or the boys somewhere around the farm. Something was not right.

Harley broke into a trot and Sara followed around to the front yard. By the time she got there Harley was already kneeling over the dog, picking up his limp form from the front walk by the gate. Even before she reached them it was obvious to her that Duke was dead. Harley turned to her, Duke in his arms, looking down at the dog, then up to her for an instant, then back to Duke, as he sank to his knees, laying the dog down in the grass.

"Harley... What...?" She stopped, as he placed the dog ever so gently into a normal sleeping position. "Harley...?"

He didn't hear a word she said. He rose from Duke's body and went to the front gate where he stopped and stooped and picked up a slab of raw meat that lay just inside it. He held it to his nose a moment and dropped it, staring across the front pasture. She went to him and put a hand on his shoulder.

"Harley? I don't understand..."

"Arsenic," he said, his eyes scanning the tree line toward Indian Creek.

He opened the gate and went through, squinting, intent on the countryside ahead.

"Go see to the kids." And he was gone.

Chapter 9

When Harley got back, Bert and Amos were up and in the kitchen. Cassie lay cooing by Sara's aide as she cooked breakfast. He rubbed the boys' heads and said good morning to them, kissed Cassie on her chubby little cheek, then went and spoke quietly to Sara.

"There was two of 'em. Riding one horse. They left it tied between here and the ford and walked up."

"Did you see them?" she whispered so the boys wouldn't overhear.

"No, they were gone. But I didn't miss 'em by much. Duke was still warm when we found him."

"Oh, Harley, I'm so sorry. I know how much you loved that dog. Who could've done ..." She trailed off, guessing who might have. "You think it was those awful men from the picnic?"

"Yeah, I expect it was. Don't know anybody else low enough to do such a thing. Should be easy enough to find out. If they had a horse they must've taken the ferry over. I'll ask Jeremiah if they crossed last night."

"I can do it when I go to town," said Sara.

"I'm not so sure that's a good idea now. They might still be on this side, camping by the road somewhere."

"Posh. I'll be fine. Whoever did it is long gone by now."

"You're probably right, but I'm still not so sure that your going off alone is a good idea."

"Don't worry, Harley, it's broad daylight. And if it makes you feel better, I'll carry a boat paddle with me," she said, trying to lighten him up a bit. He did smile, a little.

"Where are Cy and Seth?"

"Cy's sleeping. He's still a trifle feverish, but barely. He was sleeping so peacefully I thought I'd let him, for as long as he would. I told Seth about Duke. He's taken him to the barn to find a box for him. I didn't tell the little ones. I thought it best to leave that to you."

"Thanks, Sara. I'll tell them after they eat so it won't spoil their breakfast."

Seth came in the back door then. It was obvious the boy had been crying. "Pa," he started, "what happened to him? He wasn't all that old."

Harley held a finger to his lips and tilted his head toward Bert and Amos. Sara began filling their plates with eggs and sausage and biscuits, setting the table. Seth and the grown-ups sat down. Harley said grace, and they all began eating. No one said much except for the little ones, who chattered incessantly about the nothing little things that fascinate children so much.

When they were almost done Harley pushed his plate away. "Kids," he began. They stopped to listen to their Pa.

"I've got some bad news this morning..."

Bert jumped up, knocking his chair over backward with a crash. "Where's Cy? Cy!" He shouted. "Where's Cy?!"

"Calm down, son, calm down. Cy's fine, he's just sleeping in this morning. Pick your chair up and sit back down." Bert obeyed, but his eyes were still wide with fear. Harley patted his hand. "Your brother is fine, believe me, he just over-heated his self a bit yesterday. Nothing a little rest won't cure." He glanced at Sara.

"Come here, Amie, come sit on my lap." Amie did.

"It's about old Duke. Duke's dead."

"What, Pa?" asked Bert standing up again. "Where is he? What happened?"

Amos squirmed around in his father's lap and looked up at him.

"I know, Daddy. Did Duke have a baby?"

"No," Harley said, leaning down and kissing his son's forehead, "No, he just laid down and died last night. It was just his time. Maybe your Ma needed a good dog up there in heaven."

"You mean Mommy called him up? He always loved Mommy best."

"Yeah, he did," said Harley. "He surely did."

Just then Cy came into the kitchen, rubbing the sleep from his eyes. "What time is it? What's all the commotion in here?"

"Mommy took Duke with her, Thi," volunteered Amos. "He went to keep her company."

"What?" said Cy, fully awake now. "Pa? What's he talking about?"

"Duke's dead, son. Last night."

"What happened, Pa? That ole black bear come prowling back again?"

"No. No, we just found him in the yard this morning. He died peaceful."

"Of what, Pa? Duke was only six or seven. Dogs don't just lay down and die that young. Where is he?"

"We'll talk about it later, Cy. Seth has already seen to him." He stopped, not knowing what else to say.

"He's with Mommy, Thi."

Cy's eyes searched his father, wanting more.

"We'll talk later. Right now I've got to get to work. It's late already."

"Okay, Pa," said Cy, "I'll be dressed in a jiffy."

"Not today, son..."

"But, Pa, I'm fine. Just give me a minute..."

"Not today, son." His tone left no room for argument. "You're going to rest up today. Besides, Sara needs to run errands. You've got to watch the little'uns."

"But ..." Cy started, then shut up.

"I could work you know. I ought to be out there."

"Maybe tomorrow. We'll see. Seth'll come with me, but he'll be back by ten or so. He'll watch the kids then, while you rest some more."

Now it was Seth's turn. "Pa, I didn't pass out. I can work all day."

"What's that supposed to mean, Seth Felts. I ought to come over there and..."

"Boys! Hush! That's the way it'll be. No more talk of it."

"I want to see Duke," said Cy. And this time his tone left no room for argument.

"Go help Seth hitch Bess to the wagon for Sara. Show your brother where you put him, Seth. Then meet me in the field for a little while."

"Okay, Pa." He said, as the two older brothers left.

"Sara," Harley said, standing. "Since you're going to town, would you mind picking up a load of sawdust for me at the mill? I figure we need one more to get all the firing done. It's going to be a good crop this year."

"Sure, Harley. You mean the sawmill just before the river crossing?"

"Yeah, that's it. Just ask for Eustice. Tell him I sent you and he'll take care of it," he paused. "You'll be back before dark, right?"

"Yes, long before. It shouldn't take me long."

"Good. I'll see you then." Harley picked up his hat, hugged Bert and Amos, and went out the door.

*

It was every bit as hot, every bit as oppressive as it had been for days before. Harley was barely through a half a row when Seth showed up. Neither spoke, it was easier just to work, just to fall into the pace. And so the morning passed...

When the sun reached a quarter to overhead Harley stopped Seth from his cutting.

"Help me get the rest of these plants spiked and loaded, son." Harley saw a flash of protest in Seth's eyes, but the boy never uttered a word of it, he just stopped and did as he was told.

So Seth, Harley thought. Never one to argue or cause a stir. So eager to please, to keep the peace. He and Cy were like daylight and dark — two totally different parts of the same day. Cy lived casting his feelings brightly, heatedly, without relent, while Seth kept his mind shaded, quiet and deep and cool. The two were as true products of Ellie and Harley as could be.

Seth could spike near as fast as his father could, so Harley didn't have to slow his pace much to let Seth keep up. They worked side by side, silently filling a stake each and carrying them together down the rows with Harley leading, holding the front end of a stake on either shoulder, with Seth trailing behind with the bottom ends on his. The morning birds had long since shut and gone to shade, leaving only the insistent day-long call of a mockingbird singing "pretty, pretty, pretty" over and over and over, and the rustle of the plants swinging between them, and the buzzing of day bugs. Despite his weariness, or perhaps because of it, Harley was in his own kind of heaven. Working hard and quiet, with someone he loved. He hated to end it, but he knew he couldn't let it go on.

When the last of the cut plants were spiked and loaded, he sent Seth back to the house.

"Go help your brother a while now, Seth. I'll come fetch you around three o'clock or so."

"Okay, Pa." Harley was glad not to have to argue about it, but he could tell Seth didn't like it.

Once Seth was gone, Harley had nothing but the field and the crop and the heat surrounding him. He stopped and sat down in the middle of a row and wiped his brow. He'd packed lunch that morning; it sat where he'd left it in the shade at the edge of the field. He should go eat something; he knew. But he only wanted to sit a spell. Only wanted to be alone.

Sitting in the shade of the tobacco, soaking in the heat of the day, not moving for the first time in many hours felt right to him. There was something about the sweat rolling down every inch of his body, slipping stinging into his eyes, sopping his shirt and his pants, that was oddly comforting, in a familiar sort of way. Slipping away, he could almost hear her, calling. Almost.

He jerked up with a start, suddenly re-aware of the here and now.

"Best eat." To no one, but aloud. His voice sounded alien in the quiet drone of the field.

"Talking to yourself now?" He tested again. Then he stood up and walked to get a drink of water and his lunch. Warm as he knew it'd be, it'd still be wet, the water would. And the food would sustain him. So he went.

The shade was not quite so bad as the sun, but it was far from cool, only less bright. No breeze stirred the tree limbs above him. The shade offered solace, but little relief. He pulled off his boots and socks and let his feet dangle in the creek while he ate his sausage and sourdough sandwich, and then, forsaking the water jug, he leaned far over and drank long and deep from the cool running water of Indian Creek. The last thing he remembered before he slept was lying back in the weedy bank and closing his eyes, just for a minute. And itching. It itched so, there in the tall grass, what with the chiggers and gnats and ghosts...

He felt the rustle before he heard it, and he heard it before he woke. Off to his left. Someone coming. He opened his eyes, painfully, and found surcease in the spread of limbs and leaves above him. Ever since he could remember he'd always found ease, always been fascinated by the arboreal world that hung between dirt and sky, by the lacework of trees that provided shade. It must be such a nice world up there...

"Harley...?" Questioning, calling him up.

He thought he should answer, thought he did, but he wasn't sure. But he must not have, for it came again, the call:

"Harley?"

Sara. It had to be Sara. He came awake and sat up.

"Yeah..." Only a mumble.

"He's over here," he heard her say as he came full awake.

"Yeah?"

Deeper, more familiar: "Harl?" Burley, no doubt. What was Burley doing here?

Burley reached Harley before Sara did, before Harley had time to gain his feet.

"Don't get up on my account, boy."

"Burley?" Harley struggled with the idea of his friend here, now. Struggled to his feet. "What're you doing here?"

Burley put his ham of a hand on Harley's shoulder, pushing him back down. "Just visiting," he said.

"Oh, there you are..." Sara again.

How late was it? Harley wondered. Well past 4:00 he guessed. The sunlight was slanting now.

Burley eased Harley back to the ground, gently, firmly, just as Sara arrived.

"Sit back, bud. Relax. We were beginning to wonder where you'd got off to."

Harley looked at Burley, then at Sara, and let himself be sat back down. It was all too dim. They could tell.

"I hope you'll forgive me, Harley," she said. "Maybe I should have told you. But you'd never have let me go if I had."

He still didn't get it. She spread her dress and sat down on the opposite side of him as Burley.

"Don't be mad at her, Harley. Lord knows, if anyone does, that you're the last one to ever ask for help. You wouldn't have done any different than she did, shoe on the other foot." He tried to catch his friend's eye. "There'll be a half dozen or more here tomorrow. We ought to dang near get this field wiped out by sundown."

Now he got it. But bad as he wanted to, he couldn't get mad. He looked in Sara's direction, but she sat oblivious, watching the creek flow by. He didn't say anything.

"No need arguing," Burley went on, seeming not to notice, "we'll be here, we'll get it done. And you can come help me next week, if you care to." Then he laughed that Burley laugh that Harley knew so well. That Harley couldn't resist. Rich and deep and honest. So he did all he could do. He laughed too. And so did she.

They all stood up and walked home together.

As they passed the barn they heard voices from inside it, then hammering, then an "ouch!" Going to the big double doors Harley saw Seth and Cy huddled over a pair of sawhorses, a stack of barn wood planks beside them.

"What's going on in here, guys?' he asked.

"Tell Seth we've got to have cleats in the corners to make this box stay together, Pa. He thinks we can just nail board to board, but that'll split out and the whole thing'll be liable to fall apart," Cy said in answer.

"Aw, if you could hammer worth a crap it'd hold," Seth retorted. "Wouldn't it, Pa?'

"Anybody'd know it has to have a frame. You can't just scab boards together and expect them to hold worth a dang, can you Pa?"

"Whoa, whoa, hold on now. What exactly are you boys making?"

"Why, a box for Duke of course," said Cy.

"We can't just chunk him in the ground, Pa. That wouldn't be right," added Seth, his voice cracking a bit at the end.

As Harley looked at the feeble little start they'd made, Burley and Sara joined them in the barn, Sara lingering out of the way next to the doorway; Burley stepping up to examine what they'd done so far.

"Here, let the master carpenter take a look at that," he offered. "Y'all've got the right idea, just needs a little fine tuning is all."

"Now hold on everyone," it was Harley's turn to step up. "There's no need for any of this. We've got that old packing crate that new pump came in, right up there in the loft. That'll serve just fine, I think. We can line it with Duke's favorite rug from the front porch. It'll make a dandy... uh... box for Duke." For some reason he couldn't make himself say 'casket'.

"Duke really loved lying on that rug, and I think his shed fur is about all that's holding it together anymore." Harley felt the moisture forming in his eyes but would not allow himself to wipe it away.

"Yeah, that's right," said Cy. "I know the crate you're talking about. It's plenty big. I'll go fetch it down," he finished, heading toward the ship's ladder than gave access to the loft.

Sara stood quietly peering about the barn until she spotted the curled mass in the corner of the nearest stall, the canvas tarp from the wagon draped carefully over it, as tears began creeping onto her cheeks at the thought of Duke's wagging, his romping after the children in the yard, and his whiny little puppy yelps when he caught a scent on the air. She turned away and stared out of the barn to hide it.

Seth stood shuffling his feet in the loose dirt of the floor, and when he looked up his eyes were wet and shining as well.

"Pa," he began, pausing to draw a deep breath, "do you think we could bury him up on the knoll, on the backside, but up there with Momma?" He paused again and took another breath to steady his voice. "For the little ones, you know. They're certain he's gone to be with her, you know."

"I think that's a fine idea, son," said Harley, laying a hand on his boy's shoulder. "Your Ma would want that."

They heard footsteps, then grunting and scraping noises on the floor above them.

"I found it," Cy called. "I'm going to hand it through the hay doors up here. Can you reach it down, Pa?"

"I'll take care of that," said Burley, easing beside Sara, looking up. "And then I'll go up the hill and dig the hole while you all gather the rest of the family."

The scraping above them stopped and they heard Cy walk to the ladder well, just before his head popped down at the end of it. Hanging there, looking upside down at them, he said, "I'd like to do that myself, Burley. I'd like to dig it."

"Sure, partner, whatever you say. But could you use a little help? Me and you could get it done in no time."

"Yes," answered Cy, "I'd like some help," he said disappearing back into the loft, where the scraping resumed. "I could use some help."

The weariness of the day and the night before sunk hard and sudden into Sara. Her legs felt like jelly and her knees tried to buckle.

Harley stepped just outside the doorway, reaching up to catch the crate that was pushing over the sill above him.

"Seth," Sara said, "Why don't you go get that rug for me, and then gather up your brothers and sister. I'll stay here and prepare to get Duke properly nestled, okay?"

"Yes, ma'am," Seth said. As he walked past Sara, she reached out for his hand, and taking it, gave it a light squeeze.

"Over the rainbow bridge, right Seth?" she murmured.

"Right," Seth said, following that with a sniff. "All good dogs go to heaven." And following that he leaned into her hug, with another sniff.

Burley and Cy were finished with the hole by the time the family arrived. The two of them sat atop the little pile of dirt, talking quietly. Harley set the box on the lip of the grave, and he and Burley stepped back, allowing Seth and Cy to lay it gently into the earth and begin carefully covering it.

The sun sat low in the west, burning red near the horizon, which was fading orange and pink into deep blue above. A slight breeze rustled the chestnut leaves behind them. A few birds sang their day's ending calls from up there, and a cow lowed somewhere far off, from beyond the house. No one spoke for several seconds, and then it was Sara who broke the silence.

"A dog is the closest thing to unconditional love as there is on earth," she said, almost a whisper. Stooping, she knelt and patted the top of Duke's box, then looked up, scanning the entire group.

"Duke loved you all more than he loved himself. He couldn't have had a group of hearts that loved him back so dearly."

Bert was crying out right, as the rest cried within themselves. Even Harley; even Burley.

"Momma?" said little Amos, craning his neck to look up the rise behind them. "Heath here, Momma. Here he ith."

All around them the land glowed in soft golden aura, painting the circled faces in hues of dying light as they took up hands and started down the hill towards home.

Burley stayed the night. Harley didn't even try to talk him out of it. He was glad for the company. Suppertime was a real treat for the boys; they all loved Burley like an uncle. In fact, he was as close as they had to one. Harley and Burley unloaded the wagon-ful of sawdust while Sara cooked and tended to the kids.

"It was the Mangrums that killed your dog, no doubt," Burley spoke as they shoveled the last of the load. "Jeremiah said they came over at dusk last evening. Said they was talking about going to a funeral. Made it seem to him that one of theirs had died. But it all fit to him when I told him what'd happened." Burley spat and leaned his shovel against the wagon.

"You ain't seen the last of 'em, Harl. Something Jeremiah told me they said really bothers me..." He looked at Harley, his eyes saying 'listen now, I'm serious'. "He told me they said they was going to a burying, that they thought there was a fever running 'round, and they expected to be making more crossings soon."

"They just got rid of the watchdog last night." Harley spoke what he'd already known, but hearing it come from his own mouth tightened his throat a bit. They could hear laughter from the house and Harley looked that way. Then he spat too.

"I think they need some lessons, Harley. Once we get your tobacco in, me and some of the boys might have to pay a visit..."

"No. Leave 'em be, Burl. I know to be on watch now. You're welcome to stay tonight. And to be full honest about it, I'm grateful for the help tomorrow. But you can't stay here forever, and going after them will only make things worse. I can see to it."

"I have no doubt, Harley. No doubt about that," he grinned. "I've seen you in a scrape, and believe me, there's no one I'd rather have to my back when it comes to that than you, buddy-boy. But just like the blue mold, or tobacco worms when they come after your crop. The best way to head off trouble is to stop it before it takes hold. Catch it before it catches you."

"Yeah, maybe so. But this ain't no weeding we're talking about. This ain't about crops. Best way to cull bad seeds is to stay away from them."

"It's your business. Your call. But know that I'd sooner bite the head off a tobacco worm than see one leaf chewed holes in."

Harley had to smile at his friend, and just as he did the dinner bell rang. He clapped Burley's shoulder. "You make too much sense to pay attention to, you know that?" He stopped and put his other hand on Burley's other shoulder. It was hard for him to say. "I really do appreciate it all, Burley. More than you know. But we'll be fine. I'm on guard. Even the worms, even the mold gives signs, and anyone with half a brain knows to watch for more. I've raised many a crop. And I intend to keep on raising them come hell or high water, much less Mangrums. You ever known mold to get my crop? Or me to let worms ruin my harvest?"

Now it was Burley's turn to grin. "No, I reckon not, Harl." He clasped Harley's shoulders in return. "I reckon not. That's all I'll say about it. Just had to say I, you know..."

"Yeah. Thanks, Burley. I know it, for sure." It was getting too long for two men to stand such, yet they stood, beyond talking.

"Let's go eat," said Harley finally. "Sara's gotten pretty good at cooking. I'm actually looking forward to supper again."

They laughed, the two friends, and went to the house.

Supper was good. Despite having had little time to cook, and kids crawling over her all the while, Sara made a nice showing of salted ham steaks, fresh summer squash and decently moist cornbread. Most of the conversation centered around their guest, and at him. Burley didn't disappoint any of them, regaling with stories of young Harley and the not-quite-dead buck that placed the scar "right about there, just below your daddy's left ear." And of the time Cuthcutt about near burned away, back in the drought of '22; and of times when folks hereabouts had all they could need of anything, back before the great collapse. And then Sara produced hot blackberry cobbler just as Burley was telling them all about the time Harley and Ellie had got caught swimming naked in the quarry, just a couple or three months under a year before Cy was born. Burley had worked for Mr. Totty too, and had learned well from the old man's knack for spinning a yarn. He had them all laughing right through desert, without telling too much detail to the children. But as they finished the last of the sweet pie, the laughter died and the table grew quiet.

Sara stood and began clearing the table. Burley realized his story and stopped, and it got quiet.

Harley was tired. Tireder than he'd known. He stood, leaving the dishes, rarely, to Sara and the kids.

"Burl... Boys..." he said, trying to stifle a yawn.

"Sara." He covered his mouth as it came out anyway. "We need sleep. Burley, as much as I'd like to sit up and hear you make fun of me all night, I'm headed for the sofa. Take my room tonight."

"Harley..." Burley started, but before he could even finish, Harley cut him off.

"Goodnight." He kissed all the boys, and Cassie. Shook Burley's hand, and just before he left the kitchen, he nodded toward Sara. "See ya'll in the morning."

He slept like a log that night. A rare night, without dreams, without nightmares, without so much as a hint of waking before dawn.

He slept so deeply he never even heard Sara and Burley and Cy talking on the porch until way after the moon had set and the whippoorwills had quit for the night.

Chapter 10

Harley woke before anyone else, back in his old routine. This was beyond doubt his favorite time of day, when the house was still and dark, except for a hint of rose beginning to show at the kitchen window. The children all safely, soundly, sleeping. The world too, for that matter. By the time he had coffee boiling, the morning birds were waking one by one, beginning their song, calling the new day on. He liked these few moments, alone, rested, ready for what came today. He stood at the sink sipping his coffee, staring out at the shapes of his world growing more distinct through the window. The stock barn, the implement shed, the smokehouse nearby, and farther on, the tobacco barn, already half full, doors standing open to receive today's labor. And above it all, back-dropping the whole works, was the knoll, with the great balloon shape of the chestnut tree, full-leafed and rich.

Just as the first cock crowed he heard movement behind him.

"Morning, Pa," Cy said, just as Harley turned to see who it was.

"Good morning, sunshine." It was Ellie's phrase for all the kids.

It was plenty light for him to see Cy's creasing smile. The boy came to his father's side and stood beside him, admiring the window painting before them.

"How're you feeling today?"

"Great, Pa. I'm ready to get at it. I was bored silly yesterday. I don't see how Sara does it, put up with these kids all the time."

Harley took another sip and handed the cup to his son. Cy still hadn't grown a taste for coffee, but he was trying.

"It takes a special kind, a special heart. Just proves once more that God knows exactly what He's doing. Knew exactly what Adam needed to be complete." He put an arm around Cy and pulled him close, squeezing hard for a second, then releasing. "Want a cup of your own? I know you like sugar in yours, like your Ma."

"Yeah, I think I will have half of one anyway, sweetened, like she always said."

The roosters crowed fast now and they could hear stirrings back in the house as the rest of the family began to wake.

"What're we going to do, Pa? Mr. White told me about Duke, what really happened. I'm with him. I think we ought to go after those snakes."

"So Burley's been campaigning against me, huh?" Harley smiled, rubbing Cy's shock of thick dark hair. "I'll tell you what we're going to do, son. We'll take care of our business. As it comes up. Not sooner."

"But, Pa ..."

"Did I hear my name out here?" Burley came yawning and lumbering into the kitchen.

"Sure did, you rebel-rouser, you."

Then came the children, and Sara, and the kitchen became its usual, mad, heart of the house, place. Quiet time was done for the morning. And maybe, surely, this noise was much sweeter.

As they were finishing breakfast and things began to quiet down as the men and the older boys prepared to leave for the field, a curious sound wafted through the front door; distant, rhythmic. Harley and Burley stepped onto the porch where they could hear it clearer, growing nearer. It was singing, one voice doing the bridge and others joining in on the chorus. An old gospel song; a black voice leading. In the distance they saw the wagons turn the bend at the ford, two of them, filled with men. Romous Johnson and his clan were in the lead wagon. He was doing the singing and it was his boys backing him up. He had six of them; hardly boys at all, all well into their twenties, all still living at home with their cotton-haired old Pappy. In the second wagon, Paulie's wagon, were at least seven or eight white men, all talking and laughing up the drive.

"Well, I'll be..." Harley started.

"Look's like we'll be finishing early, huh, Harl?" grinned Burley. Seth and Cy came out on the porch and joined them.

"Gee, Pa, it's a regular army!" said Seth.

"Yeah it is, son," said Harley. "An army of angels, dressed like our friends." They all started down the drive together to meet the wagons.

Romous kept his song up right till they reached him.

"Aaaaayy..." Sang Romous.

"I say, Aaaayyyyeahhh! I said, Aaaaayeahhh... Aaaaaaaaa..."

"Mennnnnn," answered his boys as one, their voices dying quiet and reverent in the morning air.

Harley grabbed the bit of the old swayback roan that pulled them along.

"A good and glorious morning to you, Romous!" His voice was louder than he'd intended, in the sudden silence. But then a normal voice wouldn't have seemed at all appropriate in the echoing praise.

"And a good and glorious mawnin' to you too, Mistuh Hawley," smiled Romous, his great white teeth beaming in the morning sun, highlighted by the darkness of the face around them.

Harley had always liked, always respected, Romous very much. Romous was a hard worker. This was the first year in memory that he hadn't been hired to help haul in the tobacco. He was a good father (though he'd had nearly as many wives as he had kids, he'd never yet run a kid off. Unlike his women, it seemed, he took care of his kids). He lived in the midst of 'Dirt Row', where most all of the black folk of Cuthcutt lived, behind the huge, dirty warehouses that separated them from the river where they worked loading barges when they could, or lay fishing along the banks when they couldn't.

"Didn't I tell you I couldn't afford you this year, Romous?" Harley asked

"Yessuh, you most surely did tell me that. But this here ain't no matter of affording. This here's a matter of joining in," he beamed directly into Harley's eyes. Another thing Harley liked about the man. You can't hardly not like a man who looks so straight at you.

"Speaking of which, we's burning daylight. I expect brother James and his boys is already out dere in de field. They left right smart fore we did," said Romous. "Me and my chilluns'll be headed on to hep 'em now. You folk catch up when you's ready." He snapped the reins and started his wagon away before Harley had time to thank him properly. But Romous winked as he pulled away and Harley knew he'd seen it, the thanks.

"Seth, go tell Sara to make us up a proper lunch. Tell her to raid the fruit cellar, clean it out. And you stay here and help her. She'll need it with all these hands to feed."

"But, Pa, I want to work."

"I know, son, but look around you. We've got more than enough here. Best way you can help is by making up some of those famous beans of yours for 'em, to take care of our friends right and proper."

"Okay, Pa." He got a smile. "Noon?"

"Noon or a little after. I reckon we'll be about done, all but loading the barn, by then."

"We'll have it ready, Pa. A regular king's spread."

"Good. As it should be, for our royal guests." Burley and Cy were already climbing into Paulie's wagon, and Harley squeezed Seth's shoulder before going to join them.

Romous was right, his brother James and his boys were already in the field working, and had more than half a scaffold cut and loaded. There were lively greetings and handshakes and backslapping all around as the wagons emptied and the men took to the field. Everybody spread out and got right to the familiar, grinding work, side by side, black and white. There really is no color in the tobacco fields, no distinction from one man to another. No niggers, no bosses. Every hand is a nigger at this work, and every worker due his own respect. Romous fell quickly back into his song, and everyone quickly fell into the rhythm of it. The steady, hypnotic cadence had a way of easing the work, distracting the toil. The crop was going down fast, the cut line moving across the field almost visibly, like dusking shade when the sun drops close to the horizon.

Harley saw the scaffolds filling rapidly and realized that he wouldn't have enough of them to keep up with the cutters. He called Cy over.

"Yeah, Pa?" said the boy, trotting up, dragging a forearm across his dripping brow.

"I need you to pick out two or three hands and start hauling the scaffolds out and filling the barn. We can't keep up otherwise."

"Okay, Pa. I'll take Tigris and Eufrates. We can handle it."

Harley smiled. He should have known Cy would pick the Johnson twins — James' two youngest.

"Take a couple more too. I want you on the ground, directing. You're in charge of the stocking. See they get it right. I don't want you up in the tiers after the other day."

"Aw, Pa ... I can handle it."

"I'm not saying you can't. I'm asking you to handle way more than climbing tiers here, son. I'm counting on you to take over the barn for me. You, better than anyone else, know how I like things done. I need to be here and I need you there. Understand? You can handle it, can't you?"

"Yes, sir, I can. Don't worry. I'll see to it." Cy looked directly at him when he said it.

Harley took a step forward, intending to hug his child. But something in Cy's stance, something in his manner stopped him. He held out his hand instead. Cy took it and shook it, still holding Harley's eye. Man to man.

Harley stood for a time watching Cy go gather his help, lost to all but the moment. This was a crossing point, and he was lucky enough to see it.

The morning passed smooth and easy, between the singing and the quiet conversations across rows, and the fellowship of shared labor. And always, just as the last of the scaffolds was filled, back came Bess and Tigris, pulling an empty one. The sun was nigh three-quarters overhead when Romous sidled up to Harley.

"We all's been figuring a bit, Mistah Hawley," he began, working like it was an accident that they were side by side. "And we all come up with, that we can be sho 'nuff done with it all by two or three o'clock, if'n we works on through lunch..."

Harley stopped and stretched, putting his palms on his butt and bending backwards over them.

"Have ya'll figured that, sure enough, Mister Johnson?"

"Yessir. We's done come to that conclusion."

"And just what else have ya'll concluded? If I might ask?"

Romous smiled back at Harley — that sheepish sly sort of grin of his that spoke so true.

"Nuthin' much. Nuthin' at all really. Just that we could be done by two or three o'clock, if'n we skip lunch... That'd be a good thing, no?"

"Yes sir, Mister Johnson. I reckon it would be," he stopped, but Romous's wink and the grin made him go on. "A mighty good thing. What ever ya'll reckon I'll go along with. Just tell Tigris to have Cy go warn Sara to keep dinner warm till then."

"Yessuh, Mistah Hawley. Whatever's you say." Romous called out to his boy as they moved on down the line.

It wasn't much past two o'clock, by sun reckoning, when the last plant fell and every man could see every man across the now barren field. The singing was done; the last scaffold was pulling away; and there wasn't much more to be said. But there was a lively chatter nonetheless as they all climbed into the wagons, and it only grew once they started toward the house. There are few things more satisfying than friends enjoying the end of a long, hard job, well done. Together.

They stopped at the tobacco barn to help file the last of the crop on their way, but Cy and his crew were nearly done. With everyone pitching in it took less than twenty minutes to fill the barn, and when it was full there was still a scaffold and a half left standing outside. It truly had been a bumper year. Harley stood between Burley and Romous, watching as Cy closed the big double doors and dropped the latch.

"That's it, Pa. No more room. What do you wanna do with the rest? We could hang it in the stock barn, next to the tack room, and fire it there, you think?"

It wasn't even a nudge that Harley felt from Burley's side, more like shifting weight.

"No. Load it on Mr. Johnson's wagon. He can take it."

"Now, Mistah Hawley," Romous started.

"Don't 'Mistah' me, Romous. It's yours. By rights."

"He's right, Romous," said Burley. "I learned a long time ago not to argue with Harley. Waste of time." He winked at Romous, and without waiting for an answer he went and pulled a stake full off the back of the scaffold and carried it toward Romous's wagon.

"C'mon, boys! Let's finish it up," he yelled.

The tobacco barn was within sight of the house, and before they had the last of the scaffolds empty, the dinner bell began clanging, Seth pulling on it for all he was worth.

"Come on and eat, ya'll," he called across the yard.

Harley pulled up his working, looked around and said, to all and to no one in particular, "Come on, boys, you heard the man. Tobacco'll keep longer than lunch will. Let's go eat!"

Sara, and Seth, had truly outdone themselves. There was a long table, improvised from sawhorses and walk boards, draped with a fresh bedsheet for a tablecloth and loaded with food. Fried chicken, pork loins and beefsteaks for meat; fried corn, squash casserole, green beans, boiled okra, and fresh sliced tomatoes and cucumbers, and of course, Seth's baked beans, for vegetables. Apples, watermelons and pears; and at the very end, blackberry cobbler and two still steaming pies, their fillings hidden by golden-brown pastry lids. Bert and Amos were busy on the porch cranking ice cream. Makeshift tables with hay bale seats stood all about the yard, and each one had a wildflower centerpiece declaring the middle. There were even colored streamers hanging between the trees overhead.

Just as the men came gawking into the yard at the sight of it all, Sara stepped out of the kitchen onto the back porch, wiping her hands on her apron (her apron now...), blowing a wisp of hair from her forehead.

"Ya'll just help yourselves now. There'll be no waitressing here." That got laughs all around. "Except for tea. It's on the way, ice cold." She turned and disappeared back into the house.

Harley stood back and watched the line queuing up, listening to the eager, happy, talk of people filling plates, and he had to smile, once more. Burley threw an arm around Harley's shoulder, damn near pulling him off his feet, drawing him close.

"She's done herself proud, fer sure," he boomed in that too loud Burley voice of his. "She sure enough knows how to treat folks."

"I reckon so," said Harley, slapping an arm back around Burley.

"Best go fix yourself some while you've got a chance. I got a feeling won't none of it last too awfully long with this crowd."

"I'm going to," said Burley, "Right behind you, Harl. Lead the way."

As they made their way to the end of the line, Rig passed them, carrying a plate in each hand. He stopped and winked at Harley.

"See? Told you, didn't I? I knew that girl had possibilities right off. Didn't I tell you so?"

"You sure enough did, Rig," answered Harley. "You sure enough did." He shoved Burley into line in front of him.

"Fix yourself a plate now, I'll be right back." And he left, headed for the house.

Sara was busy filling a line of glasses with ice, Cassie riding her hip, wide-eyed and watchful of Sara's every move. Harley held out his arms and cooed at his baby,

"There's my little girl!"

Cassie's face lit up like kerosene on fire, squealing, kicking her legs, and leaning toward her daddy. He took her in his hands, held her high in the air above him, and began counting, "One..."

Cassie giggled, grinning down, knowing what was coming...

"Two..." He could feel his daughter tighten in his hands, waiting, anticipating... He made a "T" sound shape on his lips, prolonging it. "Oooh," she cooed.

"Threeeeee!" he burst out, drawing Cassie down fast into his arms.

"Eeeeeeee," she squealed with him, as he smothered her with kisses.

"I swear," said Sara, pausing to watch and smile at them, "if I didn't know better than to think one so young could do it, I'd say she was counting then. Sure sounded like a 'three' to me."

"She's not too young," said Harley. "Bert was counting the fall long before he ever spoke. She knew exactly what she was saying, even if you don't believe it."

"Maybe," Sara laughed. "May be..."

Harley picked up a pitcher of tea and began pouring behind her; Cassie on his hip now. Neither said a word until Sara started putting drinks on a tray and when the first one was full she picked it up and started out the door, asking behind her, "You'll bring the other?"

"Sara..."

She stopped and turned, balancing her tray.

"Yes, Harley?"

"Thank you."

He finished filling his tray and picked it up. "That's all. Just thank you."

"No," she turned and went out the door, but before she got too far he heard her. "No, once more it is I who be thanking you."

As they all ate, after everyone had got their iced tea, after Harley had fixed his plate and sat down, he couldn't help but think how the sounds of good friends enjoying a good meal and familiar company reminded him of that homecoming Sunday so long back. Sara walked up with her food and sat down beside him. The first thing she did was slip a finger under the front of Cassie's diaper — such a familiar move, why hadn't Harley thought to check — and only after she was satisfied that it was dry did she begin to eat. Seth was still up and running, refilling everyone's glass as soon as they came empty.

Again, neither spoke. Neither had to, silence sometimes has a way of going far beyond words, saying far more.

"Ice cream's ready!" yelled Bert from the front porch. "Come get it for the cobbler. It's the bestest thing that ever happened to cobbler!" Amos had his hands in the bucket, sweet white dripping down his chin and onto his shirt. He wasn't waiting for his cobbler.

"Yeath, thir!" he stopped just long enough to agree.

While the line formed at the pie end of the table, Romous stepped up to where Harley and Sara sat, bowing low to Sara.

"Missy, I got's to say that was one of the most finest meals these ole lips has ever wrapped theirselves around."

Sara giggled. "Why thank you kindly, Mr. Johnson. It's thanks like that that make cooking such a joy."

Romous bowed again, turning to Harley.

"I'se got two requests to make of you, Mistah Hawley." His teeth showed even more brightly in the late day sun than they had in the morning.

"Your request is my command, Mister Johnson," Harley grinned back. "Name your pleasure."

"Firstest," began Romous, "since we all's such pigs that we skipped proper grace for our fine dinner, I'd be honored if I could at least say thanks for our desert course..."

"By all means, Romous. Please do." Harley stood up, put his thumb and forefinger between his teeth and whistled loud, bringing all conversation to a sudden halt.

"Mister Romous here has called a serious omission to my attention," he said. "Can we all bow our heads and let him lead us in Grace."

There was a great sound of forks and glasses being put down, then of silence, overwhelming even the day cicadas. Harley nodded at Romous and sat back down, bowing his head.

"Lawd..." began Romous. "Lawd, Lawd, Lawd. You been so good to us I can't even say. You done give us fields to work in, and crops to harvest..."

Amens came from his family: brother, sons, and nephews.

"You done give us friends to sweat by. You done give us nourishment for our bellies, and for our souls too..."

"Praise God!" someone answered.

"You done give us strong backs. And you done give us strong minds and strong hearts, and the will to work those backs..." His voice took on a pulpit lilt, timed by the bugs and birds.

"And most of all, Lawd... Most of all... You done give us your onliest Son..."

His voice dropped to nearly whisper, loudest of all.

"And it's in His name that we take this meat and this drink," he paused, then added, "That we already mostly had, with Y'alls everlasting forgiveness..." Chuckles couldn't help but go up, sounding more like choir music. And then he waited, every soul waited, silent people in the afternoon noise. Until finally:

"Thank you! Thank you, thank you, Lawd! Thank you!"

There was not a mouth there, nor a heart, that didn't say a loud "Amen". Even Cassie gooed loudly with them from her blanket beside Harley and Sara.

It stayed quiet and still, heads stayed down a second more until Romous broke it by saying:

"Now we can get back to the business at hand!"

And in another second the bugs and the birds were drowned out once more by the voice of fellowship.

Romous turned back to Harley and Sara.

"Now with ya'lls leave," he said, "I'll be gettin' mysef some of dat ice cream, 'fo it's gets all gone."

"Was that the second request, Romous?" asked Harley, winking at Sara.

"Oh no, suh," said Romous, slapping his forehead, rolling his eyes, "I plumb near forgat. Would you mind very much if'n I fetched out my fiddle? I brung it in the wagon and I'd sho nuff be proud to saw on a string or two."

Sara answered before Harley even had a chance.

"Mr. Johnson, I'm sure we'd be completely disappointed if you didn't invite your fiddle!"

Romous beamed his biggest smile of all and made a great show of putting one hand to the front of his waist and one to the back , bowing his deepest bow of all. "Mighty kind of you, Missy Sara. You's a right most lady, if I may say."

Sara stood up and curtsied back, spreading her dress wide and dipping her waist low, crossing her ankles under her.

"And you, sir, are a most kind gentleman."

For a moment none of them spoke. The silence was there among them all. They knew. Then it was Harley who broke it.

"Eufates! Go fetch your uncle's fiddle. And I'll fetch you some ice cream."

It turned into a regular party before it was all done. Not only had Romous brought his fiddle, but James had brought his banjo, and Burley was even cajoled into joining in with an old harmonica that Harley fished out of a drawer, where Ellie had stashed it after a late night on the porch last summer. It didn't take long before the corn liquor came out, and even less time after that until the buck dancing and clogging commenced. There are times when a body just has to dance, and the spirit caught on as quickly as dimming took the sky. Even though Sara was the only woman there, maybe a little bit because of it, there was a camp feeling to it; men with men, doing childish things. They'd earned it. And because she sat on the side, by Harley's side, satisfied by simply seeing it happen, she became a part of it, they let her in. Allowed her to witness. Accepted her. No doubt, early on, she had plenty of invitations to join in the dancing. Her foot-tapping and head swaying couldn't be missed by any there, but her obvious contentment to stay on the sidelines, and her equally obvious condition — her six month belly — soon allowed her to sit in peace, in a place that women seldom see; a boys night out.

The music was fast and furious; happy music; get-down and lay-it-out music. Romous had a trick way of playing his fiddle sometimes that Harley had never seen anyone else do. Every now and then he would slide a little glass medicine bottle out of his pocket and slip it on his finger, laying it across the neck strings like he was playing dobro or steel guitar. When he did it, his bow and his bow hand sawed so fast they became a blur of back and forth. But the music, the changes of notes, were so soft and subtle that they blurred as well, on the slow end. About half the men were up and dancing, as fast and furious as the music, hooking each other with their elbows, damn near slinging one another off their feet, while the rest stood ringed around, clapping and stomping them on. Even Bert and Amos got up and took center stage for a few clumsy, whirling steps, until they lost track of their feet and both of them went down in a tumble of laughter and hands helping them back up.

Caught up in it all, neither Sara nor Harley noticed that Seth and Cy had cleared all the tables until Seth stepped up, offering a pair of spoons to Harley.

"Play with 'em, Pa. It's been forever since you've played spoons."

Harley laughed and shook his head. "Not tonight, son." Sara saw his face go a little bit red; saw the corner of his eyes flick in her direction then flick away as if they hadn't been there. "We've got to get Cass and your little brothers to bed."

"Aw, Pa," Cy chimed in, "me and Seth'll put the littl'uns to bed if you'll play spoons. One song. Deal? Come on, please? Seth's right, we ain't heard you play in forever..."

Harley began shaking his head again, just as the song quit, sudden and loud, with a ringing twang.

Sara stood up (no easy task for her these days — it was beginning to be a struggle for her to push herself out of chairs).

"Mr. Johnson," she called out. All heads turned her way.

"Yessum, Miss Sara?" answered Romous, pausing the tuning-plucking he did in the gap between each song.

"Mr. Felts would like to join you all for a song. Would that be all right with you?"

"Well, Miss Sara... Being as you's such a kind and pretty lady... And seeing as how Mr. Felts is so good at spoonin'... We'd even go so far as to let him name his tune, if'n you thinks you can get him to join us."

"Oh, his boys have already taken care of that, I think." She turned and nodded at Harley as she retook her seat. "Name your tune, sir."

Harley stood up and swiped the spoons out of Seth's hands, taking them into his fist and mock-shaking them around the circle, starting with Seth and ending with Sara.

"Okay, okay. Least I can do is play one with you all. After all you've done for us..."

He looked down a second, took a deep breath and coughed a small throat-clearing cough before looking back up.

"Your pleasure, Romous. You make the call. I can fall in with anything. Any idiot can beat spoons."

It seemed the later the day got the brighter Romous' teeth shown. He showed them clear across the circle, to everyone.

"That bein' the case... I reckon I'd like to hear "Sugar Babe" about now," he said. Then a second later, "One... Two... One, two, three!"

The song played on longer than most, with long improvising riffs by first Romous with his slide piece, then, getting the nod, by James, plunking the banjo for all he was worth. Then even Burley stepped up, blowing his harmonica to new heights. Harley even got in a short solo, which brought far more laughter and applause than it may have deserved, but quite a justifiable amount considering the partiality of most of the audience, and the appreciation of seeing him play again, after so long.

When the song was done Romous stood up and stretched, his arms high and spread, holding his fiddle by the neck in his left hand.

"One more and we got's to be going, I reckon. Else Jeremiah might beach the ferry and we'll all wear out our welcome on this side of the river."

"Not likely, Romous," grinned Harley.

"Not that Jeremiah wouldn't leave you stranded here..." That brought some laughs, then it got quiet around the circle "But not likely any of you could ever wear out a welcome here..." Still it was quiet, so Harley felt he had to go on.

"Guys, I've really got to thank you all for what you've done for me today," he stopped and turned, looking at his children sitting behind him, and at Sara. "For us..."

"Aw, you ain't gotta do nothing but sit down and shut up and let Romous pick us a tune 'fore we git," somebody said from the crowd, and everybody laughed.

"Amen," said another voice, a Johnson voice. "Play, Pap, before he goes speechifying!"

"As if Harley Felts would ever speechify anyone!" called another, and everybody laughed harder. Harley sat back down, shaking his head in mock shame.

"Okay, okay, I'm done. Would you please get me out of this, Mr. Johnson?"

"I'd be sho 'nuff proud to," said Romous. "But dis'n ought to be lady's call, if'n she's got a preference..." he said, nodding toward Sara.

"You've been doing just fine with your selections, Romous," she said from her seat, "I would never presume to choose better than you have. You're the boss. Your pleasure is ours, I'm sure."

"In that case, missy, with your kind permission, I'd like to play a little toe-tapping song, in your honor. It's kindly a leaving song, as befits the time fo us to be shufflin' off, but it's kinda not that either, if you catches my drift...

"Aw, heck, I'll quit babblin' now and jest play..." He looked at James. " 'Shuffle Off To Buffa...',no, make that Baltimore, double time."

James grinned and nodded and they set off into it.

It was nearly an hour later before the wagons pulled out and the last good-byes were called. Harley had let Cy and Seth stay and help the men hitch the teams and load the last few sticks of tobacco onto the Johnson wagon while Sara took the little ones to the house and got them ready for bed. As the three of them stood at the front gate, listening to the clop and rattle and song die away down their drive, Harley took a boy under each arm and held tight, enjoying the end of the day and the returned embrace of young arms around his waist. When they could hear no more of their friends, long after they could hear no more of them, Harley turned them toward the house and let go.

"Now to bed with you two, you've stayed late, earned staying late, the both of you, but we've got to start loading sawdust in the barn bright and early. Get some sleep, guys."

"Okay, Pa."

For once he was almost disappointed they didn't argue. He might've let them talk him out of it tonight. He'd had a taste or two of corn liquor himself, and even more intoxicating, a taste of company. But they were tired, no doubt. They'd earned that too. So he kissed them each on top of their heads and watched them run off to the house, walking slow behind them...

After he'd gone and shut the barn doors up; after he'd checked that all the livestock was secure; after he'd caught himself wondering for a second why Duke wasn't panting around beside him; he went to the front porch steps, of course, and sat down on the top one to take his boots off, intending to rest in the rocker a spell. Of course. But as he sat he couldn't help but overhear the quiet goodnight whisperings as Sara made her rounds, tucking the boys in for the night. And he couldn't make himself move even the few feet to the chair as he felt the lights of the house being shut off behind him. So he just sat. He couldn't make himself break the spell of peace he felt. So he didn't, he just sat.

It took longer than he expected, but when he heard the screen door spring stretch, he turned around to look and saw Sara easing the door back to with her butt, holding a steaming coffee cup in each hand, he knew why.

"I thought you might could use this before you went to bed," she said, as he stood up and met her, taking one of the mugs from her, accepting it with both hands.

"I surely could. It's just what the doctor ordered. Thank you, Sara." He blew over his cup and took a sip, slurping loud when he felt it burn his tongue. He motioned his head toward the step. "I'd been thinking about the rocker, but this seems more comfortable tonight. Care to join me for a spell?"

"I'd love to, very much. It's been a long day. Sitting sounds a bit like heaven, about now."

She took her seat, leaning back against one post, and he took his, against the opposite. They both set their coffee down, letting it cool a bit. The yard was loud with summer.

"Sara..." he started. But that quick, out-loud, laugh of hers stopped him.

"Didn't you learn your lesson at the fiddling, Harley? No need to say it. We know it. Anyone who knows you knows it. You don't have to keep saying it."

He glanced a smile at her, picked up his cup, blew on it, and shook his head.

"Shut me up. I talk too much."

"Au contraire, Mr. Felts. You hardly talk at all, but you say plenty. That's a good thing, no?"

"I reckon. If you say so..."

"I do."

Now it was her turn to pick up the coffee. She blew on it, and then set it back down without taking a drink. She turned to face him full on, staring straight at him until he had to return his eyes to hers.

"You do know how blessed you are, don't you?" Her look didn't waver; she didn't blink. So neither could his, neither could he. But he didn't answer, so she went on...

"I've never known anyone who had so much love heaped in their direction. Before I came here, I never had a clue that so much of it, so much love, was possible. Nobody has ever told me in words 'I love Harley Felts'. But it shouts itself at me at every turn. You hear it don't you?

"I saw it in your children from day one. I see in every friend of yours that I've met, one by one. I see it when you wake up in the mornings and I see it when you try to sleep at night. I know you're hurting. Everybody that comes near you knows you're hurting..."

Sara stopped herself. No longer was she holding his gaze, he held hers now, steady and unrelenting. Then she saw the screen slide down, so she stopped. He'd made her stop, they both knew.

"I'm sorry, Harley. I'm out of turn here. I don't know what made me... I'm sorry."

Harley sighed, long and deep. He picked his cup up, and while he stared down into it, he tipped it over slowly and let it pour out onto the lawn beside him.

"It's okay, Sara. You've earned it. You've got rights by now."

Suddenly Sara let out a high, quick "Ooh!" and her hands went to her belly. "It moved!" she said, "I felt it move!"

Harley watched the look on her face go from perplexion to a kind of smiling awe.

"Is that the first time?" he asked.

"Yes, it is, like this anyway. It feels... I don't know how to... Ooh! There it went again!" She slid across the step toward Harley. "Here, I've got to share this with somebody," she said, taking his hands and placing them on the underside of her belly. "It was right here. Wait a minute and see if it does it again..."

Harley smiled at the girl's excitement. This was a familiar ritual for him.

"It doesn't hurt, really," she said, "it's more like... like..."

"Like someone's moving inside you?"

"Exactly!" Then she caught the joke in his voice and giggled. "You and that dry humor of yours!"

He felt the baby move. This time she didn't squeal.

"There! Did you feel that?"

"Yes, I did. She must be trying to turn, being this active."

"She? Why do you say she?"

"Because you're carrying her so high. And because that's what it ought to be, what with your situa..." He caught himself and stopped.

"My 'situation' as you call it is very well known, Harley. You can say it. You've got rights too. It's not like I can very well keep this a secret," she said, framing her stomach with her hands. They both laughed.

"No, Ma'am, I reckon not."

He realized he was still holding her belly and took his hands away, but she caught them and drew them back. "Does it feel like a girl to you? It's funny, up until this very minute I've always thought of it as an "it". But now... She's getting real...

"Now you've got me doing it! Doctor Hall says he can't tell much by the heartbeat, 'Just a regular, strong heart' is all he says about it."

"Well, it feels like a girl to me," said Harley. "And you can tell Doc Hall I said so." He felt her belly ripple again, stronger than the first time. "Though maybe not a very gentle one. This one's strong. Like her momma."

Sara saw the familiar cloud cross Harley's eyes at the word, and he took his hands away. This time she didn't try to stop him or bring them back. He stood up and went to the bottom of the steps and stood there in the yard, looking beyond the night. She knew better than to speak, knew he wasn't there when he got like this. He was somewhere else. She'd seen him go off like this for many minutes at a time, looking blind at the world around him. But it didn't take long this time. He turned around and sat on the bottom step, looking up at Sara.

"It was cold that night, bitter cold," he began. She wasn't sure she wanted to hear this, but she knew; had known for a long time that it was something Harley needed to say, so she closed her eyes, folded her hands across her lap, leaned back and listened.

"Ellie went into labor early. The baby — Cassie — wasn't due for another two weeks. But everything else seemed normal. Right enough. So we weren't worried. I sent Cy off on Bess to fetch Doc. I was a little worried about him going off so late, it was around ten o'clock or so, I think. I had to get him out of bed to go, and on such a cold night. But I dared not leave Ellie alone; every time she delivered it got quicker and quicker. Hell, I thought I was going to have to borrow Seth's ball mitt to catch Amos. But Ben got there just in time for Amie...

"Anyway, that night, about an hour after Cy'd gone, Ellie called me in. I was out in the kitchen boiling sheets. I knew the routine pretty well by then. I thought she might be wanting a drink of water, so I fixed one before I went, and carried it in with me. Ellie was sitting up in bed, and the second I saw her face I knew something was wrong. She had this kind of scared look on her..."

He turned to sit back facing the yard again, paused and took a deep breath before going on.

"And dammit to hell, that's the face I see when I try to call up her image most times anymore. It's getting harder and harder to call her up laughing or smiling, or being just plain Ellie in the kitchen, or Ellie with the kids..." He paused again, longer this time. Sara said nothing.

"Anyway, she looked scared. And Ellie never was one to scare easy. 'What is it, Baby?' I asked her. She just looked down and then I saw it, a red spot on the sheet over her lap. No bigger than a silver dollar. Not much. But it scared her some, so it scared the hell out of me. That'd never happened before. 'Harley, we got to get this baby out, else she might not make it' Ellie told me. I tried to tell her just to calm down, wait, Ben'll be here soon, but she'd hear none of it. She started huffing and pushing, bearing down you might say, trying to force it. I kept telling her, wait Ellie, Ben'll be here soon. But she kept on pushing. The red spot was big as an apple by then. 'We've got to get her out, Harley. We've got to save her', she kept saying over and over, between grunts and puffing. I didn't know what to do, Sara. I didn't have a clue. Before, I'd always just sat by the fire or on the porch during that part, waiting for Ben or Olivia to come hand me my new young'un.

"Once I knew Ellie had her mind set and I wasn't about to change it, I asked her what I should do. 'Bring the clean sheets, and bring me some towels too. Lots of towels.' So I did what she said. And when I came back the blood was as big as a pumpkin."

A catch in his voice stopped him. He put his head down in his hands and sat that way for a full minute. Then he stood up and walked a step or two into the dark, away from the light on the porch. He looked up into the stars, then without turning or looking down, he went on.

"I told her I'd be right back, don't you move, Darling, I said. I went and woke Seth up and told him to boil some towels and wait in the kitchen until I called him. She was sweating hard and starting to scream by the time I got back. First thing I did was rip that damn sheet off her and put a fresh one back. 'Keep it off,' she told me. 'You've got to take her, Harley'. I didn't know what she meant at first. 'Get a knife,' she said. No way, I told her, no way, no way am I gettin' no knife. You hold on, Ellie, Doc'll be here directly. But she just pushed and pushed, and the mattress got redder and redder.

" 'She's coming now Harley. You've got to help her,' she said. She arched her back and spread her legs. I bent over to try to do what I could, expecting to see a baby's head come popping out. But instead there was this red, clotted looking thing hanging out of her. I pulled it out of the way and as soon as I did the baby followed. Cassie followed. 'Hold her head level, and pull' Ellie managed to say. Then she screamed and the baby came sliding out. In a river of blood."

He finally dropped his head from the heavens, onto his chest.

"Harley," Sara started, but all he had to do was shake his head to stop her. He stood there a few seconds before he looked back up, briefly, then he sat down in the grass and began talking again; very low, very soft, very slow...

"I didn't know what to do. I had the baby in my hands and my love bleeding to death right there before my eyes. Seth! I hollered. Come take this baby! Then I realized it and went to the door before he could come in and see. 'What do I do with it, Pa?' he asked me. Just take it! I told him and I shut the door. Ellie was quiet now, and still, her eyes kind of rolled back in her head. I grabbed some towels and began stuffing them between her legs, real tight, real hard, trying to make it stop. Her eyes fluttered and she looked up at me. 'That hurts, Baby. Don't', she told me. 'Please don't.' So I quit. 'What do I do?' I asked her. 'Hold me' she said. 'Just hold me, Baby.' So that's what I did."

'I'm sorry,' were the last words she ever spoke. 'I'm so sorry.'"

Sara watched his back there in the dark, beginning to heave sporadically, and when he began to lean sideways ever so slowly, she got up and went to him, sat down by his side and caught his head in her lap before it fell to the grass.

"She was so cold. She told me she loved me and to be a good daddy. She kissed me. Then she closed her eyes. She was so cold." Then he was overcome, and he cried; long, deep, hard, convulsive crying that gouged at Sara's soul. He cried until he couldn't keep his breath; then he pounded the ground with his fists and pulled clumps of grass out and rubbed them in his hair.

Sara rocked him and stroked his forehead, ssshhhed, and cried with him.

"There, there," was all she knew to say. "There, there..."

She rocked him for a long time, until gradually his sobs weakened and he came back to himself. Without word he pushed himself to standing, and leaving a soft pat on Sara's shoulder, he walked heavily up the steps. Sara followed him with her gaze as he crossed the porch and disappeared into the darkness of the house.

Chapter 11

Harley rose from his dreams to the faintly reassuring smell of lilac, and she was there with him, on his pillow, in the bedclothes. It was the familiar flowery scent that roused him, not the strong mid-morning sun that streamed through the window, even though he could remember having slept through a dawn only once before. He reached across the bed and realized even before his arm fell empty on the cold sheet where he was, and he winced. There came the sounds of frying from the kitchen, and a quiet feminine voice, enveloped by the quick chatter of children. He started to get up, but the happiness he was hearing overwhelmed the voices in his head; he lay there listening for a minute or two, then he rolled over, pulling the sheet back up to his neck.

Bacon smell came and drowned out the lilac, and he murmured, "Just this once," before letting himself fall back asleep, hoping to recapture the dream.

Sara stood at the stove, frying her heart out. The kids hadn't eaten since their late lunch/early dinner yesterday and they were fairly ravenous, scarfing up the eggs and bacon as fast as she could dish them out. But giddy as she was from lack of sleep, giddy as they were, hung over from yesterday's work and festivities, she also felt a heaviness in her heart and in her abdomen. The cooking smells, which usually reminded her of her own childhood, made her nauseous this morning. She felt as if she was going to throw up at any moment, but she tried hard not to let the kids see it; she didn't want to spoil their particular joy this morning. But she was also determined to at least keep them quiet enough so as not to wake Harley.

"Ssshhhh! Now, I told you all, keep it down, your Pa's sleeping."

"Is he sick?"

"No, he's not sick. He's just tired, and he needs rest. He's earned it don't you think?"

"Yes, Ma'am!"

"Ssshhhh, not so loud, I said."

Sara wasn't sure whether it was harder trying to hold down a kitchen full of eager children or the remnants of yesterday's meal in her stomach. But she did a fair job at both; at least Harley didn't wake, and she didn't puke.

"Cy, your father mentioned something last night about 'dusting the barn'. You know how to do that?"

" 'Course I do," laughed the boy, "and it's spreading saw dust for firing, not 'dusting'. No matter how hard you try, the Yankee in you still shows through, Sara. And the girl," he teased. Even Seth got a chuckle out of that one.

"Whatever... Can you do it? You and Seth. That's all I want to know, mister smarty-pants."

"You bet. I got it hung, didn't I? This is the easy part, firing, and getting ready for it. We're coasting now, for a while."

"Well, you two coast your tails out there and get started then. The kids and I will clean up all that 'men-mess' from the yard as soon as I finish the kitchen."

"But, Sara..." Seth started, looking a little too obviously at her swollen waist.

"Don't 'but' me, Seth Felts. The only butts I'll abide are yours and that brothers of yours, going out the door."

And they did just that without another word, unless giggles count.

Once she was out of the smoke and fumes of the kitchen the nausea passed. She had already prepped Bert and Amos for the task, making a game out of it. She told them they were going to play 'Clearing the Field', just like the big men did. She put Amos in charge of reaping the centerpieces and tablecloths and piling them beside the wash tub by the pump house. Bert would help her with the 'heavy hauling' — loading the hay bales and table boards onto his Dixie Flyer wagon and returning them to the barn: "Where they belong, so they can turn into gold, just like the tobacco." Bert wouldn't buy that line at first, arguing that "the dumb ole cows'll wind up eating it." But when Sara pointed out that he'd had two helpings of 'dumb ole cow' yesterday evening — that they (the cows) had turned hay and such into sirloin steak, he took on a puzzled look for a couple of seconds before his eyes lit like someone had switched an electric light on inside him, and he grinned up at her, saying, "Yeahhh..."

She even gave Cassie a job to do, leaning low, telling her, "And you, young lady, stay here on the porch and keep an eye on the house, like the good girl you are." And even though her voice, and certainly her words, were pointed as much at Bert and Amie as they were to the baby — making sure her brothers knew their sister was included in the game — her eyes never left Cassie's eyes. Those huge, infinite, infant eyes that are so easy to get lost in. And Cassie's eyes never left Sara's, drawing her deeper and deeper, until she broke the spell with one of those huge grins that only innocents can grin, her mouth growing so large that it covered her face to the point that no room was left for open eyes. Then she squealed, Cassie did, and tried to clap her hands, missing the clap but managing to end up with a clasp that delighted her to the point that she kicked her feet uncontrollably above her; delighting Sara to the point that she had no choice but to smother the child with kisses.

"I love you so very much!" they giggled, she and the baby, and the boys watching behind them too. "Does she have any clue how much Sara loves her Cassie? She knows, doesn't she! She does," tickled Sara. "She knows. Don't we know, little girl?"

Sara heard the words echo around her brain before she even finished uttering them; was lucky enough to catch the oh-so-rare slow motion rattle of time before it passed on by...

She was continually amazed at how fast they grew. In just two short seasons, Cassie had gone from a squalling, eating/shitting machine, into a pure bundle of joy. Amos had learned to walk more than crawl, and was actually losing some of his baby lisp and baby ways, now that he had a baby sister of his own to coddle. Bert — easily the most drastic change of all — Bert the traveler, Bert the dreamer of things beyond, had gone from toddler to boy, accepting his place as a 'big' brother to little Amos, eagerly growing into the role. Seth was still Seth, only more so. And Cy, willing himself to manhood day by day, leaving the boy behind, trying not to regret it. That spring and summer are the growing season is especially obvious in farm country, and on the Felts farm they had all grown much these past two seasons.

Sara heard the screen door slam just as they were finishing the last of the cleaning up, and she turned to see Harley standing on the porch, stretching and squinting in the bright sunlight.

"Well, you timed that pretty well, Mr. Felts. Just in time not to help. Have you been watching us?"

"No, Ma'am, Miss Sara. I've been doing nothing but being a sluggard so far today."

"Pa!" yelled Amos. "We'f been reaping the yawd!"

"So I see, Amie, and you've done a fine job of it too."

Sara took Bert's hand and started with him to the porch, intending to fix Harley's breakfast, but Amos ran ahead, throwing his arms up, beating them there to get a hug from his daddy. Harley bent and scooped the child up, raising him high into the porch roof rafters.

"I'll bet you're tuckered out after all that hard work, aren't you, little man?"

"Uh huh!" Amos beamed down.

"Well, do you think you can do one more chore for me?" Harley asked beaming back up.

"Uh huh. What do you want me to work on now?"

"Where are your big brothers?" Harley asked, as Sara and Bert reached the porch steps.

"They're at the barn spreading saw dust," Sara answered for the boy. "Cy seemed to know what needed to be done."

Harley looked at her and winked, then said to Amos, "How about going and fetching them for me, Amie. Tell them I said to get their tails back here pronto and get their swimming trunks on. It's too hot to work today. I feel a trip to the creek coming on."

Amos's eyes threw as wide and as bright as freshly minted silver dollars and his little legs were churning in that direction before Harley even set him down.

"Okay!" cried the boy over his shoulder, tearing down the steps.

"Really, Pa?" asked Bert, jumping up and down.

"Absolutely, son. We won't be firing for a couple of weeks. There's more important things to do than sweating in saw dust all day."

"Yee-haaa!" yelled Bert, banging through the door to go get changed.

Sara just smiled at this strange man who became less and less predictable the better she got to know him.

"You must be starved," she said, "the hunger's driven you mad. I'll go get you some eggs."

"Forget the eggs. I'll pack us some lunch while you go change too. You do know how to swim don't you?"

"I can keep my head above water, if that's what you mean."

Harley laughed. "You think so? You've obviously never turned your back on Cy and Seth in the creek before!" he said, opening the door for her.

The swimming hole — a slow, wide bend where Willow Creek turned back on itself, reversing its course from east to west, where the boy Harley and his friends had spent a long past afternoon piling rocks on the shoals just upstream of where the water straightened out and shallowed, wanting to pick up speed, and so had raised its depth from three or four feet to nearly six — was a little less than a half mile from the house. They walked, the seven of them together (all but Cassie of course, who rode in her daddy's arms), and owing to the heat and humidity of the day were all, (including Cassie) thoroughly drenched in sweat by the time they arrived. So it goes almost without saying that the boys were in the water nearly even before they came in sight of it; one collective splashing, jumping, diving blur, shouting, "Hurry up, Pa! Get in!" "It's cold...", "Aww, it ain't that cold, you baby", and "Come on, Sara, let's see a dive!'.

There was an old sycamore tree on the inside of the bend — the farm side — whose roots had long since been undermined by the relentless current, so that it leaned nearly horizontally over the creek. The diving tree. Harley spread a blanket near its base, where the grass stayed low and cool from the shade, and sat Cassie and himself on it, right beside the lunch basket, while Sara stood behind it all, hands clasped behind her back, admiring the scene. Seth clambered up the bank, slip-sliding in the mud, running between the blanket and the tree, dripping everywhere.

"Watch this one, Sara!" he called, starting up the trunk.

"Whoa, boy!" Harley backed-at-him, just a bit louder, "Keep that water to yourself and off your sister and the blanket. Have your fun, but if you get Cassie to crying you can come sit with her..."

"Okay, Pa," he answered, already fifteen feet from the bank, looking down into the cool, dark green pool below. "Watch this one, Sara! I'm gonna do a flip." And he did, almost; throwing his heals over his head as he spoke, splatting the water hard and loud, flat on his back. It had to hurt, they all knew, all could see it in his eyes when his head popped back up breaking water, slinging it back and forth from his eyes like a dog come in from the rain. But he wouldn't admit it and tried to show a grin through his wince.

"Hurts, don't it, show-off?" yelled Cy from the opposite bank where he lounged, arms hooked in tree roots, legs kicking lazily at the surface. There was as much smirk in his voice as on his face.

" C'mon, Daddy," urged Amos from the near bank where he and Bert were wading in, keeping clear of the big boy's splashes.

"Okay, okay, keep your shorts on," Harley said, reaching to strip off his boots and socks. He stopped and looked at Sara. "Would you mind taking first shift with the baby?"

"Not at all, sir. Go right ahead; join your boys. Matter of fact, Cassie and me were thinking we girls might just take a dip ourselves, given time enough to get ready."

She'd barely got it out of her mouth when Harley left the bank with a big 'Yee-Haaa!' and an even bigger cannonball splash.

"Look at those silly boys, Cassie-girl," Sara said, leaning over to her sole comrade, "What do you say we get out of these extra clothes and go join them?"

Cassie mouthed something like "Goo!" and waved her arms as if she were already splashing water, and Sara knew she was ready.

They stayed there for hours, the seven of them, splashing and dunking and playing war-horse and Marco Polo. Mainly playing, until the water ran brown from the soft silt bottom they stirred up under them. Without a set or formal lunch time, they nibbled on the bank, one or two at a time, until the lunch basket was emptied, and then they played some more. Sara proved to be a surprisingly strong swimmer, beating first Seth then Cy, racing from one end of the blue hole to the other. She swam with such grace and purity of stroke, with such easy power, that Harley refused to even take her on, saying, "I never claimed to be no fish, and I'll not be embarrassed by any mermaid, in front of God and the world." And then she raced Seth again, with Amos riding on her back while he taunted all the way, his head never even coming close to dipping under. Then she got her share of dunkings, and gave as well as she got.

As the sun began to lay low through the tree tops it found Harley lying on the blanket, with Cassie napping soundly in his arms as he held the stare of the dying light firmly in his eyes; while he and it reveled in the sound that surrounded them. If it had eyes, and could have read his lips, it would have seen, rather than heard, his silent 'Thank you'.

He wouldn't call them out, any of them. He would stay here until the day played itself out in its own time. And trying not to imagine being any place else but here, and now...

And when finally, inevitably, they called their own selves out, he helped them gather up and dry themselves off before heading home. But just as inevitably, he left, let them go without him.

"I'll see ya'll at the house," he told them, handing Cassie over to Sara, "I'm going to take a little walk."

Sara herded the clan together and set off with them, never having to look back to know where Harley was headed.

She knew better than to wait supper on him. Everyone was worn out from sun and water by the time they'd washed up and eaten. Seth and Cy pitched in and got the little ones ready for bed while Sara cleaned up from the meal. As she put the last of the dishes away, Cy came into the kitchen.

"I think I'll go find Pa," he said. "Wanna come with me, Sara?"

"No, I don't think so, Cy, thanks for asking though. But I think maybe he needs to be alone right now," and hearing the words, she rethought them, "but then maybe you're right. I expect he might enjoy your company this evening. Why don't you go on without me."

Cy stood motionless for a few seconds, studying this girl who seemed so much a part of the kitchen, and their lives, now. She looked up at him and his gaze held steady while things beyond words passed between them. Moments ticked by with the mantle clock in the parlor until slight smiles hinted at the corners of their mouths, and still neither felt the need to speak. Finally Sara winked at the boy, and he winked clumsily back before heading out the door.

"Good night, Sara," he said through the screen.

"Good night, Cyrus," she said to his back.

Sara was as tired as she'd ever been, but it was that good, bone-deep, satisfying kind of tired that comes only well earned. She went to her room and got undressed, pausing to study her ever-new figure in the mirror before she slipped on her nightgown, and went to check on the kids. Bert and Amos were soundly sleeping, as still and rhythmic as angel breath. Seth was asleep too, but he lay in a restless pose, one arm dangling off the bed, until he rolled over and mumbled something in his sleep. She stood there in the dark for a few minutes, looking from one face to the other before she went to them, lightly kissing each forehead and tucking their sheets gently around them. Then she went back to her room, where Cassie was.

The baby was lying on her back, breathing regularly, making a little 'hmmmm' noise with every exhale. Sara stood even longer by the girl's side than she had in the boy's room, first just staring down at her, then leaning her arms onto the crib rails and resting her chin on them. She was surprised to feel a tear slide down her cheek. She hadn't realized she was crying until it did. It ran to the corner of her mouth, where she licked it away, and its taste was sweeter than anything she could imagine. Another started down its path, then another. She didn't sob, her breathing never altered, but the tears kept falling, and the smile never left her face.

She lay in bed for a long time without sleeping, without even closing her eyes or trying to go to sleep. The darkness held her warm and tight, and talked to her. She listened to all it had to say, lost in its voice, until she heard Harley and Cy come whistling down the hill, talking and laughing through the yard, hugging and whispering good nights on the porch. Then she rolled over and finally fell asleep.

Chapter 12

Work was slow on the farm, now that the crop was in. The next few days passed slackly and easily, and Sara saw more of Harley and the boys around the house than she ever had. It seemed they were always underfoot, looking for something to do. Preparing the barn for firing took only a few hours and she'd actually gained a concept of the process of what it was they'd been talking about. A layer of sawdust, not quite a foot thick, was spread over the dirt floor. After the week or so it took for the green plants to quit oozing tar, it would be lit evenly around, smoldering the sweet oak and hickory smoke up through the hanging plants, heat curing them, drying them faster than a 'cold barn' could. The doors would be shut so the smoke would circulate thoroughly before seeping out under the eaves and between the gaps in the rough-sawn siding. More sawdust would be shoveled on as the old burned, enough to keep the fire going for two or three weeks, then they would wait while the air cooled into September and October and do it again.

Life in the Felts house took on a slow, lackadaisical pace that Sara never would have believed possible — especially after the frenzy of cutting time — until she saw it, lived it herself. There was still livestock to take care of, as always, and much of the garden was coming in, so picking vegetables and putting them up to can filled some of their days, but cooking greens is a pretty leisurely job, when you get right down to it. All in all it was just as Cy had called it: coasting time.

After three or four days Sara was growing as crazy from Harley's inactivity as she could tell he was. He fixed all the loose drawers in the kitchen, oiled every hinge in the house, shined his boots till they almost bled, and generally made a pest out of himself, like a kid rummaging through his toy box on a rainy day – 'There's nothing to do'. He was a man who didn't do empty time well.

On Friday, the fourth day after the cutting, it rained all day. Not a summer kind of storming rain, but a steady, easy, day-long kind of rain — a precursor to the fall and winter weather drawing nearer — and Harley proclaimed that the firing would commence "Tomorrow or the next day, as soon as the damp gets out of the air and the sawdust." It was dark by the time the rain began slackening. They all stayed up late, sitting on the porch as evening mist rolled in, hugging the yard and the fields low and thick; Sara darning and patching clothes; Harley alternately beating Cy then Seth at checkers while Bert and Amos rolled toy trucks and tractors across the plank flooring. Even Cassie shunned her normal bedtime, wriggling restless in her cradle, watching bright-eyed at the moths dancing in the lamplight. It was a very slow, very dull evening; one of the most pleasurably dull nights Sara had ever spent. So when Harley stood up, announcing bedtime finally, gathering his kids into the house, she asked, "Would you mind if I stayed out here a while to finish this mending and maybe just rock a spell?"

"Of course not," he answered, "but we're going to bed, with your kind permission." He mock-bowed, taking his leave; then stopped halfway through the door. "It's past due, you taking some 'Sara-time' anyway. That's a good thing; 'our' time. We all need it every so often. Goodnight. See you in the morning."

She stayed out there long after prayers had been said inside and the lights had been shut off. It was a complete night, except for the absence of Duke's snoring beside the rocker and the occasional thump of his tail when he would wake to see that all was as he remembered it being before he'd drift back off to sleep again...

She overslept that next morning, mainly because Cassie did too, and partly because she was dreaming unusually heavy (Sara rarely dreamed), ...dreams of boats drifting lazily over mirror-still water... dreams of high, thick, puffy, clouds reflected beside the boats... dreams of contented smells and sounds and sights... Dreams of hammering on the wall of her room...

Wakened by the hammering she got up, still in her nightgown, and went to the window. She raised the sash and leaned out, and there was Harley, tool belt around his waist, directing Cy and Seth to stack lumber over here and to pile the rocks over there.

"Good morning, sleepyhead," he grinned up at her.

"What in the name of..." She realized what she was wearing and pulled back into her room, crossing her arms across her breast. "What's going on out there?"

"Oh, nothing much. Been meaning to do it for a long time now, it's getting awfully crowded around here. All the boys crammed into one room and all. You know..."

"No, I very much do not know," she said shaking her hair down, thinking it must look a mess.

"The room, Sara," offered Seth. "The new room. Finally. I'm getting my own room."

"Not hardly!" countered Cy, dumping out a wheelbarrow full of creek rock. "Oldest gets dibs, right, Pa?"

"No, you don't! You had a room already before. I never had one. Don't I get a room, Pa?"

Harley interceded. "Boys! Boys! There ain't no room to dicker about yet. Let's get it built first; get something to fuss about before ya'll fuss about it..."

Sara threw her hands up, looking at Harley,

"What? In English, please. What is going on out there?"

Harley stopped his measuring and took nails out of his mouth. "We've been planning it a long time. That house is just too small. What with four boys in one room, and you in there, and babies and all... We've got time on our hands right now, and plenty of lumber. All we'll have to buy is a few sheets of roofing tin and a couple of windows." He held his hands out to his sides as if to say "Can't you see it?"

Sara blew breath out the top of her mouth, as much to get the bangs out of her eyes as in exasperation.

"Never mind," she said, shutting the window. She shook her head through the glass at them and waved a finger in front of her face that said 'I give up!' through her smile, then she raised her arm to the drape cord and pulled it, letting the curtains fall between her and the boys.

"Never mind," she said again to herself.

"What was that all about, Pa?" asked Seth.

"Women," answered Harley.

"Huh?"

"Never mind..."

When Sara got dressed and went into the kitchen, it was a complete and total mess. There were pots and pans piled on the stove and in the sink; the table was littered with plates and napkins and globs of butter and jelly; one of the chairs even lay on its side in the middle of the floor. It looked like someone had intentionally trashed the place. But she knew better. After getting over the shock of it, it seemed almost comical to her, as she tried to imagine the scene that had passed in here while she slept. As she put on her apron with an exaggerated sigh and began clearing the table, she found a full plate covered with a dishtowel sitting at her place, and a full glass of warm buttermilk beside it. And she did have to laugh at what she found under the towel. Over-cooked eggs, fried to the point of being rubbery to the touch. Under-cooked bacon sitting in a semi-congealed pool of its own grease. A doughy biscuit that she was sure would stick to the wall if she threw it hard enough, and a ball of something white – grits, she guessed. She picked the plate up and started toward the back door with it, then stopped and scraped it into the trash bin saying, "Sure do miss you, Duke." Then she freshened the fire in the stove and put a kettle of water on to boil for tea, and set about the task of putting her kitchen right again.

When she finally finished and had sat long enough to sip down a cup and a half of tea, she ventured into the back yard. She was surprised to see the perimeter bands of the floor system already in place. It looked to be a good sized room, running from the edge of her window over to the edge of the window in the boy's room, extending out from the house about 12 or 14 feet. She sat down on the rim of the back porch, sipping her tea, making herself comfortable until she was noticed. They were all as busy as a family of beavers, Harley going from one boy to the other, giving instructions and checking the work before moving on. Everyone had a job to do, and Harley was kept full time trying to stay one step ahead of them all. Amos saw Sara first, looking up from the grass where he sat working an old hammer, trying to back nails out of a piece of used barn siding.

"Morning, Thera!" he cried, jumping up to run give her a hug.

"Ssss-Ara," she said, leaning over to pull him up into her lap, "Come on, you can say it right, Amie. Remember what I taught you, start like a snake: Sssssss..."

"Sssssss..." the boy repeated, concentrating, "ara!"

"Good boy, Amos!" she said, pushing the hair away from his forehead so she could kiss him there. "My, you're working hard aren't you? You're covered with sweat!"

"Yeth, Ma'am. I mean, yessssss... Ma'am."

"Well lookie, boys!" said Harley, standing up and wiping his brow, "Her majesty finally deigns grace us with her presence!" They all laughed at that and joined in the teasing.

"She must be looking for her hand-maiden. Anybody seen a hand-maiden wandering around here?"

"Yeah, I think I saw one lying in the hog pen."

"What's a hand-maiden?" asked Bert. "What's a majesty?"

Sara waved the back of her hand at them. "You peasants may go back to your work now. I must go check on the princess; she's sleeping awfully late. I'll never get her to take her nap now."

"Aw, let her sleep," said Harley. "Missing her nap just means she'll go to bed extra early tonight. Come check it out, Sara," he said nodding back toward the new addition behind him. "Tell us what you think of it..."

She set her cup very carefully on the porch beside her, staring into it, watching the ripples settle before she stood and looked up.

"Okay."

Harley took her by the elbow and led her eagerly to the back yard, directly behind where the outline of the new floor stuck out from the house.

"I thought I'd gable the roof into the old one, leave the ceilings vaulted, and put a partition wall right down the center, under the ridge. Then I'm going to put double stacked windows on each side, facing back here, to keep it light and airy, you might say. This is a good southern exposure, so it'll get sun most of the day, and heck, we've got plenty of attic space already. The only kind of space that we do have plenty of around here anymore." His enthusiasm was contagious; she found herself getting caught up in it. "I thought I'd put one door from the boys room into this side and let two of them move back here, probably Cy and Seth since they seem so head up on it, and one from your room into the other side. You can have it and the girls can stay where you are now. Or would you rather put the nursery in the new part?"

"Harley..." said Sara, taking a deep breath.

"What?" he stopped, looking at her quizzically. "You don't like the layout?"

She looked away, out toward the fields, and up, toward the knoll.

"A nursery?"

"Oh, that. I know, I know... never mind that now. I mean just temporary, the nursery thing. But you're going to be needing one aren't you? It'll probably be Cassie's room later on. The point is we need the space, no matter. Can't very well bunk a little girl with her brothers, can I? And I've got a strong suspicion that if I keep all these boys cooped up in one room for too long, somebody'll end up killing somebody, or at least trying to." He chuckled and paused a second but pulled right out of it. "So what do you think about the plan? About the floor plan I mean? How am I messing up? I know you women well enough to know you always have a better way when it comes to house plans."

"I think you're doing just fine. I can't see a thing wrong with it." She stopped and cocked her ear a tad. "Uh-oh..."

"What?"

"Cassie's awake. Don't you hear her?"

He listened for it then, and did hear his little girl from inside the house, not even fussing yet, but gurgling and babbling; awake, no doubt.

"I'd better get her before she starts crying," said Sara, turning and walking away. "And besides, I've got canning to do."

He watched her go, watched her long, pearl colored hair swing across her back as it always did when she walked with purpose.

"Come on, Pa! What next?" broke the spell, and he went back to work.

"Bring me those joists," he said, "Let's get to it."

They were just finishing laying out the floor decking and Harley was showing the boys how to nail it off properly when Sara came back out, wringing sweat harder from the steam of the kitchen than they were from the broil of the sun.

"Harley," she said, wiping her hands on her apron and shaking her bangs out of her eyes, "do you know where that sack of sugar that was under the sink board is?"

"I sure do," he said, not missing a beat with his hammer.

She waited, thinking he'd quit his pounding and elaborate.

"Well, where is it?"

"Oh, I loaned it to Benjie Sparks the yesterday," he answered, still intent on driving his nails. "After the cutting. You know Benjie and his 'shining,'" Then he stopped, looked up at her, grinned and winked, "Come to think of it, I guess you don't." He pounded some more, driving a nail home before holstering his claw hammer with a flourish, then stopped long enough to straighten up and draw a forearm across his eyes. "Whew! Sure enough is hot, ain't it?"

"Well, I need sugar to put up the preserves, don't you think?"

"I reckon you do, at that. But Benjie needed it to liquor his corn, so I loaned it to him."

"Okay, okay, that's it," Sara said, reaching behind her, untying her apron and pulling it off. "I need to go shopping anyway. Me and Cassie are going to town; going to get away from all this infernal racket for a while."

"Too hot in the kitchen, eh? I wondered how long it'd take," he grinned.

"Whatever," she grinned back. "But we're going, and that's that."

He undid the buckle of his tool belt, letting it drop to the ground. "Break time, boys!" he called.

"Seth, how about going and fixing us all a nice glass of iced tea? Cy, go get your sister ready for a day trip. Me and Sara's going to hitch Bess up to the wagon. Time she learned how to do it, don't ya'll think?"

He took her by the elbow once more and turned her toward the barn. "Come on, missy, I figured this was coming. Besides, I've got a favor to ask you..."

She turned and yelled, "Don't you boys dare leave this yard in as big a mess as you did the kitchen this morning!" then turned back and fell into stride with Harley. He let go of her arm and they walked to the gate in the slow, easy gait of southern summer day.

When they reached the barn Harley went to the tack room and started taking gear down piece by piece, explaining what each was and what purpose it served.

"This is the bridle — we don't use a bit with Bess, she's past the need for that kind of stuff — and these are the reins. This is the harness. It goes on like this," and such.

"What favor?" she asked.

"Huh?" He was too into the mode to remember what it was she was asking.

"You said you had a favor to ask."

"Oh yeah, that..." He kept attaching the tack to the horse and the wagon, talking over his shoulder...

"You know the Whitson farm? Paulie's place?"

"I think so. Don't they live at the corner of the crossroads, where we turn to go to church?"

"Be sure when you rig the harness that's it's not too tight under her belly, but make sure it's good and snug. You've got to dress her; she can't tailor herself so you have to. Got it?"

"Yes, Harley, I'm watching. What about the Whitsons?"

"Oh yeah. Paulie's got some beagle pups that ought to be about ready for weaning now. Think you could pick up a pair on your way back? I've always wanted some good rabbit dogs." He scratched Bess between the ears, feeding leather back toward the wagon.

"Be sure you don't twist the reins; be sure you feed 'em straight through, like this..."

"Puppies, Harley?" Sara squealed, going tiptoed. "That's the favor? You want me to bring puppies home?!?"

"Yeah." He stopped, perplexed at her excitement. "Did you hear what I said about stringing the wagon?"

"I heard. You want me to bring puppies home! I'd love to!"

"But the reins, Sara. You heard about that too?"

"I heard you. Straight and flat."

"Males; two of 'em. Tell Paulie that was our deal. Take your pick; just no bitches, okay?"

"Puppies!" she squealed, reaching up, kissing him on the cheek. It was so quick and so spontaneous that it almost went unnoticed. Almost. But there was a split-second of eye contact, of recognition between them before Harley turned and went on with the lesson.

"Don't hold her tight, don't try to drive her. She knows the way better than you do."

"No need to worry about that, Mr. Felts," Sara said, climbing into the driver's seat. "We're done hitching. I've driven before, remember?" She snapped the reins and Bess lurched the wagon to motion, out of the barn. "Let's go get Cass. We girls are going to town, aren't we, Bess?"

She drove off toward the house, never looking back to see Harley pull his handkerchief from his pocket and wipe his cheek.

*

It wasn't until dusk was drawing down that Harley began to worry. By then they had the outside walls stood, and the rafters run, and were stripping them with lath, making ready for the roof tin. He'd been too busy all day to think about Sara and Cassie. But as the day dimmed around them — as he stood on the peak of the old house and wiped his face with his handkerchief — as he smelled dusk's sweet scent and saw its pink tinge, he couldn't help but look down the drive for signs of their return. Either way, it was time to call it a day, time to gather the tools and put them away.

"Okay, boys, let's get 'em up!" he called.

Just as he said it, he saw the wagon turn into the ford, smalled by the distance. He watched Bess pull them through, relieved enough at the sight to sit down on the ridge cap. But once they cleared the creek and he saw Sara snapping the reins at the horse's flank, driving her into a canter, he knew something was wrong. What was Sara doing pushing Bess so? He got up and went to the ladder so quick that he almost lost his feet on the hot tin; and he went down the ladder so quick that he nearly tipped it sideways off the eaves.

"See that your brothers get cleaned up for supper, Cy," he said without pausing when he hit the ground, as he disappeared around the corner of the house.

He was through the gate before they got there, meeting Bess by the reins, pulling her up. She snorted at him, breathing hard, foaming sweat across her back. Cassie was crying in Sara's lap and Sara looked like she had been too, and was trying to keep from doing it again.

"What?' he said, sliding his hand down Bess's side, moving to take Cassie from Sara.

"What is it, Sara?"

"Harley, those men..." She handed Cassie down and made as if she were going to get down as well, but she stopped and took a deep breath, gathering herself.

"What men? The Mangrums?"

She mouthed "Yes" but no sound came out of her, so she nodded, putting her face in her hands. Harley stepped on the axle hub and reached up to her, holding Cassie in one arm and taking Sara's hands in his, drawing her down.

"What, Sara? What happened? Tell me."

"Nothing happened. I'm just scared to hell and back. Nothing... It's just that..."

"Where are they?"

"I don't know. The last I saw them — think I saw them — was just up the road a bit..." He helped her off the wagon and the second she cleared it, she leaned against him with her arms drawn up to her chest between them. He put his free arm around her, drawing her close, trying to reassure; feeling her fists balled tight against his chest.

"Slow down. Take a breath. And tell me," he said, squeezing, then patting her back, then letting go so he could step back and see her eyes.

She dropped her hands to her side, still fisted, and took a deep breath before finally raising her eyes to his and biting her lip before telling him.

"When we got to the ferry landing to come home," she started, paused to take one more breath to calm herself, and went on.

"When we got there, Jeremiah was in a whorl. He told me that the Mangrums had crossed about an hour earlier, and that they were plenty drunk. They looked to him to be in a mean mood, he told me, and he tried to talk me into staying in town tonight. He said he didn't have the conscience to drop me on the same side of the river as they were. I made light of it and more or less forced him to take us across. He didn't like it but he did. He was scared for me, Harley. I could tell before we got halfway over. You know how he talks on his boat. He even started insisting that he shut the ferry down and ride home with me 'Just to be on the safe side', so by the time we landed I was about ready to take him up on it. I thought about it." She paused and un-balled her hands, calming down, locking her eyes onto his.

"But if he did, how would he have gotten back? I knew you wouldn't let Cy drive him back, and I knew you wouldn't leave the house to drive him yourself, what with his tales of Mangrums lurking in the woods and all. So I told him no, that I'd be fine, and I explained to him what I just told you, about how it would present an even bigger problem, getting him back.

"So he let me go. But he made me take this. He made me." She stopped and reached into her shoulder bag and pulled out a tiny 25 caliber revolver and held it dangling by the barrel between her thumb and forefinger like she might hold a dead rat by the tail, offering it to Harley; hoping he'd take it off her hands before the body of it swung too close to her.

"That's when I really became frightened. As much by the gun as I was by the Mangrums. He even walked up the road with us for a mile or so — he wouldn't even ride in the wagon, he insisted on walking beside us — until we met some folks coming the opposite way who were headed to town. Then he turned around and rode back with them, to ferry them across. It was a man and woman about your age, I think, with two little daughters. Blonde haired girls, about Bert and Amie's age... Simpson, I think their name was. Or Simpkin. Do you know them?"

"Simpkins," said Harley. Cassie had long since quit her crying, but was starting to squirm on her father's hip. Harley hitched her up a bit so she was at his eye level, and that satisfied her for the moment.

"Go on," he said, looking to Sara.

"Well, when Jeremiah left..." she began. But she was immediately interrupted.

"Pa? Sara?" It was Seth, coming through the front yard, "What're ya'll doing out here?"

"Nothing, son, just talking. Come get your sister."

"Okay, Pa. Should I start supper? I could heat us up some of those ribs we got left from the other night..."

"Fine. That'll be fine. Take Cassie and go do that. We'll be there as soon as we get Bess bedded down."

Seth took Cassie from Harley. "Hey, Sara," he said, "Didja have fun in town?"

"Hey, Seth. I did. Did you guys get a lot done?"

"You ought to see what we got done! I'll take care of supper, you and Pa stay out here and take care of ole Bess. But after we eat I want to show you what all we got done today, okay?"

"Okay, Seth, I'd love to see it."

"Shoo now!" said Harley. "We'll be in directly."

"Okay, Pa," he said, taking Cass and turning to leave. "Give me thirty minutes, ya'll. See you then. And come hungry!"

"Don't worry, Seth, we will. We will," she told him. "Now scat, like your daddy told you."

"Bye," he said, already leaving.

Harley led Sara to Bess's front where he took hold of the reins again and started walking the horse to the stock barn.

"Go on..." he said.

"Okay," Sara answered, looking over her shoulder at the retreating kids. "Okay...

"After Jeremiah left we just rode along for a bit. I always thought that was such a lovely drive — all the trees canopying the road, and the creeks. But today the woods looked dark and mean to me. I was imagining things moving deep in there, felt as if I had eyes on me the whole..." She was interrupted by a small yap, and something moving in the back of the wagon. A cardboard box under the seat began to wiggle and shake. There was another yap and scratching noises.

"Oh, the puppies! I forgot all about the puppies!" She went to the box and slid it out gingerly, handing it to Harley. It had the uneven shifting weight of life in it. He set it down, opened the flaps and leaned over to look, only to be immediately lapped on the nose as one of the dogs leapt up at him. He picked it up in his right hand and grabbed the other with his left, handing a pup to Sara.

"You done good. They're good looking dogs. Looks like they've got lots of spunk, too."

"Oh, they do have that. They got out of the box three times before they finally fell asleep."

Harley set his down and at once it went exploring the barn, running back and forth, stopping only long enough to sniff at all the strange new smells. Sara held onto hers, cradling it against her breast, scratching its ears. Unlike his brother, he seemed content enough to stay there.

"Okay, after Jeremiah left..." Harley urged.

"We drove along, no problems, except my imagination running wild in the woods. We stopped at the Whitson's and picked out these adorable little bags of kisses," she said snuggling her puppy up to her cheek.

"Why didn't Paulie ride in with you?"

"Oh, I didn't mention anything about it to them. I didn't want them thinking me some scared, flighty female. Besides they were sitting down to supper when we got there. We didn't stay long."

"Anyway, after we left, just after, less than a mile I'd say, we came upon a horse standing by the side of the road. It didn't have a bridle or anything, just a rope around its neck, tied to a tree. He was a pitiful looking creature, badly sway-backed and covered with awful looking sores. There were hordes of flies buzzing around, lighting on the open wounds, tormenting the poor thing. So I stopped, with the intention of untying it, but before I got down I heard someone walking through the woods, coming toward us. So we got out of there. But before we were out of ear shot I heard the horse kind of whinny, like it was in pain or something, so I snapped the reins and pushed Bess a little faster. I had the eeriest feeling that they were behind us, following, so when I crested the rise just before the ford I stopped the wagon and sat, watching the road behind us.

"The sun was about down and the road was dim, lying in shadows and all, but I swear I saw them way back behind. Both of them; on that poor horse. When they saw me they ducked into the woods real quick. That's when I started really driving Bess hard, bad as I hated too — I knew she must've already been beat by the long pull and the heat. But I had to get Cassie back here. Bess is okay isn't she? I didn't hurt her, did I?"

"No, Bess is fine. She's pulled a lot more load than a girl, a baby, and these two little rascals." Harley had a hard look on his face; Sara could tell he was concerned. When he noticed her watching him he bent down and whistled and clapped his hands. "Come here, you little rascal!" The puppy immediately bounded toward Harley, falling over his own feet once and banging into Harley's shin when he arrived, then he stood on his hind legs with his front paws on Harley's knees, air-licking in the direction of the man's face.

"I think he likes the name," Sara said, putting his brother down beside him.

"What name?"

"Rascal." She stooped, offering her face to the dog, which he eagerly licked. "You are a rascal aren't you?" she said scratching the tops of his long beagle ears. "Yes he is..." she baby-talked.

"Okay, okay. How about putting them in that last stall down there while I finish Bess up. We'll keep it a surprise, bring the boys out here after supper."

"Sure, Harley," she answered, scooping them into her arms. It was amazing how quickly the fear fled once she was home. The anxiety of the day, and the Mangrums, seemed light years away. But they both knew that wasn't true...

Seth had supper ready, as promised, when they got to the house. Not only was the food ready, but so were the boys, all sitting, waiting in their places. Except that they had revolved around so that Cy was seated at the end where Sara usually sat, leaving his usual place to Harley's right empty. The table was set with the good china and the silver flatware that was normally reserved for company. The ceiling light was dark, leaving only one coal-oil lamp in the center of the table to light the room.

"It's about time, ya'll," said Bert, as Harley and Sara walked in the back door. "We're starving!"

"Yeah, we're tharving" chimed in Amos.

"Hush, you guys," said Cy, standing up, taking over. "Pa... We were thinking... Uh, that is, all of us, were thinking..." He stopped and looked toward Seth, who only nodded as if to urge him on. Cy gave Seth a 'Gee thanks' look and stammered ahead.

"Why don't ya'll have a seat. You sit there, Sara," he said, tilting his head toward his old seat, the empty chair next to Harley's.

Sara glanced a quick questioning look in Harley's direction. He shrugged his eyes back at her. She went to the chair but before she could pull it out Harley stepped over and slid it back for her. She sat down, smoothing her dress under her, and as he pushed it and her back under the table, he leaned over and whispered, "You're guess is as good as mine."

"Thank you," she said, loud enough for everyone to hear.

Harley sat down in his place and looked at Cy, who sat down quickly himself, realizing he was the only one left standing.

"We was just wondering if..." He started, going red in his face and in his voice. "Well... we all thought it'd be nice if we could say grace like we used to... like when Ma was here and all... you know. We kinda miss it that way, you know?" He looked up to his Dad, asking for help.

"Sure, son." Harley reached out and took Amos' hand, "Sure we can." Amos reached out and took Seth's beside him, and Seth took Cy's and Cy took Bert's and Bert took Sara's. Then Harley took hers, and the circle was complete. "Will you lead us, son?"

"Me?" Cy gulped audibly. He swallowed hard again then closed his eyes and took a deep breath.

"Okay, Pa."

Outside the house, through the screens of the windows and the door, the crickets droned loud and steady, but the silence of nodding heads and closing eyes at the table thunderously drowned out all else.

"Lord..." Cy began, faltering, "Lord. God Almighty. Thank you." The night noise came slowly back, choiring his words. "Thank you for our many blessings. Thank you for all that you've given us, today and every day." Someone's stomach growled loudly, as if in punctuation, but none dared look up, and none, not even little Amos, giggled. Harley's hands felt damp and heavy laying lightly over the small, cool ones at his either side.

"Lord," Cy went on, "thank You for this food we are about to partake. Thank You for the harvest You have given us. Thank You for sending down your only Son to save us. And for the love and forgiveness He brought with him."

Cassie cooed a soft "Eaeeey..." from her cradle beside the table. Cy waited a second or two for her echo to fall away.

"Thank You for sharing Your spirit with this family, and thank You for taking care of Ma. And please, Lord, tell her we love her and that we miss her. And that we're alright."

"Ow! That hurts, Daddy!" Harley felt Amos' hand squirm inside his own just as he felt the pressure returned in his other; just as he realized his squeeze; just before he let go of both.

"Amen," he said.

"Amen," answered the table of boys.

"Amen." Sara said, a half syllable later.

"Pass me them ribs!" said Bert. "Let's eat!"

And so the table erupted into the quick, easy chatter of mealtime; into the passing of dishes and the filling of plates; into talk of the day's work and of what lay ahead tomorrow. Sara waited until all the boy's plates were well on their way to being emptied before she slipped away from the table and went to fix Cassie's bottle. They had thought of everything but that, and by the time she sat back down before her still nearly full plate with Cassie in her lap, holding the baby bottle in one hand while stealing bites off her fork with the other, everyone else was almost finished.

"When're we going to light the barn, Pa? Ain't it about ready to light by now?" Seth asked.

"Yeah, I reckon it is about ready, Seth. I was thinking we'd hold the ceremony tomorrow evening, after we get back from church."

"The ceremony!" chimed Bert. "Oh, boy! I get to light the first torch again, don't I, Pa?"

Then all the boys pitched in at once. "No, Bert, you got to go first last year..."

"Yeah, it's my turn this year. I never get to go first. It's my year to light first, ain't it, Pa?"

Sara listened to each in his own turn before turning to Harley, questioning him with her eyes before she asked him out loud.

"What are you all talking about? What ceremony?"

"Nothing much. No big deal really. We just all take part in lighting the barn for the first firing, same as we did in raising the crop," Harley said, looking around the table, his pride showing. "Each in his own way."

"It's really neat, Sara!" Bert jumped in. "We all get our own torch. Except Amie, he's too little."

"Yeah, and we get to make wishes for what we want to do with our share of the profits," Seth added, excitement showing unashamedly in his eyes.

"Wishes is right, if you make stupid ones like that time you wanted a phonograph player!" Cy teased at Seth. Then, looking at Sara, he went on, more seriously. "It has to be reasonable."

"Can't we do it tonight, Daddy? Bert came back. "Can't we? Pleeease?"

"Yeah, Pa, why not tonight?" Seth added. "If it'll be ready tomorrow its ready now, ain't it?"

"Whoa, whoa. Slow down, boys."

"He's got a point, Pa," Cy joined. "The sooner we get to firing, the sooner we can go help some of those that helped us."

Harley grinned and threw his hands up. "Aren't you going to help me here?" he said, looking to Sara.

"Me? If I get a vote I'd like to do it tonight too. It sounds like fun."

"Okay, okay... I know when I'm beat," Harley said dropping his hands to the table. "I was planning on staying up late tonight anyway." He felt Sara's quick glance his way. "To clean the guns. Bird season opens next week," he added.

176

"It's settled then," Sara said. "Get those plates clean, guys, and leave the dishes, I'll do them afterwards."

It didn't take any of them very long to finish eating, and before Harley was done, all the boy's plates were in the sink and they were all fidgeting around the table, trying to be patient, though doing a better job of showing their eagerness. Finally, once Harley knew he'd busted their britches for about as long as he was liable to get away with, he pushed his plate a few inches toward the center of the table, signaling that he was done too.

"Cy, why don't you and Seth go make up the torches while we help Sara clean up this mess."

"Okay, Pa!" They fairly burst out the door.

"Don't slam the screen!" he called after them, just as it banged loudly back into the jamb. "And go easy with the coal oil, we don't want to burn the whole barn down!"

"Okay, Pa!"

They were already halfway to the gate.

The sun was already set behind the west hills when Harley and Sara and the youngsters left the house, but its gloaming aftermath still hung bright enough to light their way in pale hues of lavender and rose. As they neared the barn, Harley could see no sign of Seth or Cy. His eyes quickly scanned the yard around. The stock was quiet and all seemed normal. But where were the boys? They'd had plenty of time to... His thoughts were interrupted by a yelp from the stock barn.

"Looks like the pups have found the pups," he said, relaxing and smiling at Sara. He scooped Amos up in one arm and Bert into the other, "I almost forgot, guys, we've got a surprise for you," he told them, as he took off in a gallop, giggling them along at his sides.

"Come on, Sara, keep up!" yelled Bert.

She took barely enough time to warn Cassie, "Hang on, girl!" before she broke into a canter of her own. Or at least a fair enough imitation of one, what with one baby on her hip and another swaying in her belly. But she didn't run long. Cassie she handled easily enough; Sara had grown used to having the baby girl's ever constant weight riding at her side; she felt more at home doing daily chores with one hand than with two by now. But the one in front of her — that was another story altogether. Every morning brought a new growth, a new bulge, a re-balancing. It took only a few steps for her to feel the baby inside her beginning to swing up and down, stretching the skin across her stomach to new tolerances, discomforting to both mother and child. 'To both of us,' she thought as she slowed back to a walking pace. She raised Cassie to her mouth, leaning into the baby's ear. "To all of us. Lady like," she whispered. "It's up to us to show these boys what ladies are like..."

By the time they reached the stock barn, the boys — all of them — were rolling in a jumble with the puppies, hay stems twisted up in hair and fur alike. The little black spotted pup, Rascal, was running furiously from one kid to the next, yapping all the while, dodging the outreaching hands that offered petting, preferring the sheer joy of running and teasing. Sara stood watching from the doorway for a minute before she was noticed, and then the first to see her and come wagging up was the brown and white pup. She stooped down and it immediately began licking Cassie's toes, trying to nurse on them, eliciting a high squealing giggle and an even higher grin from the baby girl.

Amos came waddling after the puppy. "Hey, Thera! Doggies!"

Sara leaned her face into the puppy licks, enjoying the sandy feel of its tongue on her cheek.

"Yes, Amie, doggies for sure." She tilted Cassie toward the brown one, the calmer one, and it shied for a second, then sniffed the baby's face before gently offering first a paw, then a tentative lick on Cassie's face, which brought even more delight to Cass. She kicked her feet and beamed brighter than noon-day sun, her mouth open in breathless glee.

"This one's the homebody," Sara said, scratching the beagle's floppy ears, swinging them back and forth. "A real homer."

"Homer! I like that," said Seth coming to join them at the door. He picked up the dog. "Hey there, Homer! You a watch dog?"

"If that one's a homer, then this one's the roamer," said Cy, lying on his back holding the other dog above his chest. "Aren't you, Roamer?"

"I like it," Harley said, sitting with his back to the door of the stall where the puppies had spent the evening. "Homer and Roamer. It fits 'em both, perfect. Looks like 'Rascal' just got his name changed."

"You're right, I won't argue that," said Sara, spreading her dress and settling in the hayed floor, trying to make room for both

Cassie and Homer where her lap should have been. Roamer made a mad dash past, nipping his brother's tail before running back into the circle of boys. Homer largely ignored the attack and climbed up and nuzzled warmly into the nest of Sara and her babies.

"Well, seems we've got one of the hardest parts of having new dogs settled, right quick-like," said Harley. "The naming. You all agree, guys?"

"Come here, Roamer!" cried Bert, and that was answer enough.

Amos sat down with Sara and his sister and picked Homer up by the neck to hug him.

"Homey..." he loved, rubbing cheeks with the dog until Sara rescued the animal and showed Amos how to hold it properly, gently.

It was a good twenty minutes before Harley dared break the spell.

"What about those torches, Cy? If we're going to have a lighting, we'll have to do it soon, or else wait till tomorrow."

Cy jumped up at once. "I can have 'em ready in a flash, Pa!"

Seth gave up his chase on Roamer and joined his brother. "Come on, Cy, I'll get the sticks, you get the burlap."

"I knew that would get 'em," Harley winked at Sara, "the only thing that might pry them away from their new dogs. For a while anyway.

"Come on, guys, help me gather these critters back up in their stall and let's get on with business."

It took a few minutes to get the pups settled, and by the time they did, Cy and Seth were back with a half dozen torches, dripping with coal oil. They all left the stock barn amidst the loud and lingering protests of Homer and Roamer, and headed as a group to the tobacco barn.

When they reached the double doors, after much chattering and jostling for position along the way, Harley dropped the latch and swung the doors open. He paused and dug in his pocket for the box of white tip matches, took one out and prepared to strike it, but stopped before he did. He looked around the circle of eager faces that surrounded him and then at the match he held against the sand-papered side of the box.

179

"It seems only fitting," he said, "That the rookie among us light the flame this year." He held the match and the box out to Sara. "Seeing as how we might not could've done it without her help..."

Sara looked at Harley, and at the boys, as she shifted Cassie from one hip to the other.

"Yeah, c'mon, Sara," said Seth, "light us up!"

Harley put the match and box in one hand and reached for Cassie with the other.

"Me?" Sara stammered. She looked around as well, then gave Cass over to her Daddy and took the match from him. Harley settled Cassie onto his left hip and took a torch from Seth with his right hand, then all five standing Felts dropped their torch tips to touch in the center of the circle.

"You can hold it and help light it, Amie," Harley told his youngest, "but let Sara help you hold it after that, okay?"

"Okay, Daddy." It took both hands and a strained face for Amos to hold the end of his torch to the others.

"Am I supposed to say anything?" Sara asked.

"Whatever you like." Harley answered.

She put the match tip to the box and hesitated a few seconds. Then she stuck the flame and held it up.

"Thank you." She said, watching the tiny flame climb toward her thumb and forefinger. "Thank you all. For everything."

One by one the fire took to the torches, and once every arm held fire she dropped the match and rubbed it out under her foot as she put her fingers in her mouth to quench the burn in them.

"Be careful now, guys," Harley warned, and they all filed into the barn.

When they had made a rough semblance of a circle around the sawdust, Harley spoke again.

"To the harvest!" He waited a moment. "Lead us off, will you, Cy?"

"Okay," Cy replied. He closed his eyes and dipped his torch. "I wish for a real rifle of my own. A deer rifle; lever action. In place of that dinky 22." He held his torch in place until a red ring of embers spread around it in the thick wood shavings, then lifted it and looked at Seth.

Seth dipped his torch and closed his eyes. "I wish for my own bed, in our new room." He picked the fire back up and waited for Bert.

"I want an Atlas book of the whole world!" Bert took his light away too quickly, so Harley had to help him hold it till the flame took properly. Then he looked to Amos and Sara.

"Y'alls turn."

Sara held Amos' hand in hers, and together they dipped the torch to their spot on the floor.

"Go ahead, make a wish, Amie," she prompted. Amos was obviously not ready for this, unlike his brothers he'd given no thought to the matter.

"For what, Ther... Ssssara? What do we wish for?"

Sara stooped to Amos' side, looking up at the tiers of crop hanging above them, then bent and whispered in Amie's ear. And slowly, as she spoke to him, a wide grin broke over the boy's face.

"Yeah..." he started. "We wish for... What was it we wish, Sssara?"

She whispered again.

"We wish for a try-thickle!" he beamed, looking up at Sara. "Is that right?"

"That's close enough, Amie," she said, raising their torch.

"Whoa, now! Hold on a minute. You're not getting off that easy, Miss Sara," Harley stopped them. "That's fine and dandy for Amie, but what about you? You have to make your own wish."

"But we've only got one torch. That's only one wish, right?"

"Not hardly," said Seth. "Come on, Sara, take your turn, else you might spoil the crop..."

"Is that so?" she said looking to Harley for escape.

"Durn-tootin' it's right," Cy spoke up. "Go, Sara. Your turn."

She sat there on her haunches, surveying the golden, fire-lit faces around her, and then she closed her eyes, squeezing them tight, thinking.

"Okay... If I must..."

Everyone waited as the bittersweet smoldering smoke began to curl around them.

"I wish for everyone to..."

"It has to be something that's yours," Harley interrupted, "and yours alone. That's the rule."

Sara opened her eyes long enough to cast an exasperated look in his direction, and as they waited one of the puppies yelped from the other barn. Sara looked at her hands, holding the torch with Amos's small hands, and closed her eyes again.

"I wish for a new oven mitt. That old one is so thin I get blisters half the time I use it."

"Fair enough, fair enough," Harley chuckled, "I think we can handle that one."

"Your turn now, Pa!" They all turned and looked at Harley.

"Not so fast. Go ahead and light your corner, Sara..." He waited as Sara and Amos dipped their torch again before he went on. "And don't forget your little sister here. She gets a turn too, you know..."

He turned to Cassie and shifted his stance so she came to near eye-level with him. "What's that, Sissy?" he said, leaning the baby girl to his ear. "You want what?" He pretended to listen for a couple of seconds then drew back and looked at Cassie with raised eyebrows. "Are you sure?" Cassie cooed and grinned at her Daddy, right on cue.

"Cassie wishes for a frilly little Sunday dress, and a new pair of shiny black church shoes. Isn't that right, Baby Girl?"

"Gaaaaa," Cassie followed right along, as if they'd rehearsed.

"I think we can handle that," Sara laughed. "And now, Mr. Felts, what about your wish? And remember, you made the rules, now play by them."

"Me? That's easy," Harley said. "Only one thing I need..."

"What, Pa? What do you wish for?"

"I wish for a trip to the fish camp. We missed our spring trip this year. I wish for us all to go for a weekend around the first of the month."

"The fish camp! You always make the best wishes, Pa!"

Harley dipped Cassie's torch and lit the last corner of the sawdust. Then, knowing what was coming, he looked at Sara before she could ask. "I'll tell you about it later," he said. "Come on, guys, let's get this barn closed up and you all off to bed. It's getting late."

"Aww, Pa, do we have to? I wanna play with Homer and Roamer a while."

"Plenty of time for that tomorrow. After church. Now git! Before I skin the lot of you!"

And so the ceremony, along with the barn, was closed for the night.

Chapter 13

There was no moon out so the night hung particularly dark, especially under the tree line along the creek bank, a hundred and fifty yards from the meager yellow lights of the house. What little relief that the past week's rain had brought was long gone, bringing back the late summer heat and the late summer mosquitoes with a vengeance, even as midnight fell past.

"Damn these bugs! Little blood suckers!" Frank spat.

Felts was still up, sitting there on the front porch, cleaning guns. At least a half-dozen of 'em by the looks of it, and by the amount of time it was taking him to do them all. Sure didn't appear as if he was going anywhere soon either. Especially seeing as how he had his liquor jug out there with him. Frank Mangrum watched him pause and take a pull on it, then set it close beside, selfish asshole that he was.

Lloyd was sound asleep in the weeds that lined the creek, snoring as he always did when he was drunk. Frank poked his brother hard in the ribs and Lloyd snorted a bit, then rolled over and quit his snoring. Frank slapped his neck at the all too familiar bite of a mosquito. He spat a stream of thick brown tobacco juice into the grass beside him, but not all of it cleared his mouth. Even though he could feel it running down his chin he didn't bother wiping it away. The last time he'd shaved and washed his face, he'd noticed the dark stain running between the left corner of his mouth and the tip of his pointy chin. It wouldn't wash off — though he hadn't scrubbed any too hard at it.

"What the hell," he said, smearing his palms over his greasy hair. The extent of his grooming was done for the day. And now here he sat, itching his ass off in chiggers and sawgrass, all because that persnickety asshole Felts had decided to clean his guns, tonight of all nights. Asshole.

Maybe that little bitch had seen them on the road today, as Lloyd'd thought. Maybe she'd tipped Felts off. More's the pity on her if she did. Mangrum spat again. It hit with a wet sound, splashing into the little pool of juice that was forming by his side. He poked his brother again.

"Lloyd," he hissed. "Wake up, you dumb-ass. You can watch a while, while I get me some shut-eye for a change."

Lloyd's eyes fluttered a second, then the big man rolled off his side onto his back again and resumed his snoring.

"Shut that racket up! You want to get us heard?" He poked Lloyd again. Lloyd didn't wake but his thick brows furrowed down toward his nose. Frank knew better than to try another poke. There were times when even he dared not cross his brother too hard.

"Alright, alright, you lazy bastard. Go on and sleep it off. I knew I shoulda taken that jug away from you sooner, what with us havin' work to do tonight and all."

Lloyd's round face slacked a bit, but his snoring went on. Frank let it be.

"Well, I expect I'll take myself a little nap too then," he muttered, taking another pull on the jug before rolling onto his back, trying to get comfortable. He stuck his thumb and forefinger into his mouth, twisting out the soggy plug of tobacco that lay molded between his cheek and what was left of his molars, then threw it into the creek where it plopped heavily into the water. He knitted his fingers together over his chest; 'deadman's pose' he called it; the only position he could fall asleep in, except for when he passed out, that is.

He was just about dozing when he heard noises from the house. Voices. He rolled back onto his stomach and saw that the girl had joined Felts on the porch — in her nightgown no less — talking to him just as bold as could be. She stood near the door for a few words before she went to the top of the steps and raised her arms up and stretched, like some kind of cat in heat or somethin'. She was bare footed, too. She leaned back against a post and commenced chattin' away with Felts, just as casual as can be; her with that big bastard belly pooching out. The little whore. All the while Felts just kept rubbing away at his rifle barrel, like it weren't no big deal; her out there parading herself in front of him like that.

"Lloyd!" he hissed again. But Lloyd was still having none of it, making noises like a growl in his sleep. Frank turned his attention back to the house. They was talkin' real intent-like now. Then Felts set his gun down, and his rag, and leaned forward in his rocking chair, resting his elbows on his knees, listening to whatever it was that the hussy was telling him. Eatin' it up, you might say. Frank went to spit, then realized his mouth was empty and he began digging in his back pocket for another chaw. By the time he found his packet and dug it out, Felts had got up from his chair and taken his jug and gone and sat down on the top step, where the girl joined him, tucking her gown under her knees. As if that mattered. Felts took another pull and offered it to the girl, and she took it and pulled long and hard on it herself, coughing a bit afterwards. Frank rolled onto his side, and in one smooth motion pulled his buck knife from his front pocket, flicked it open, cut himself a plug and slid the knife back home just as he slid the fresh chaw into his jaw.

'This could get interestin', he thought. 'Real interestin' indeed.'

They sat there for the longest time, Felts and the girl did, talking away like a couple of school kids. Then the girl put her face down into her hands and leaned over onto Felts. The big dumb-ass sat there for a second, then put his arms around the girl. She looked up at him, neither of them saying a word for a long time. Then he took her chin in his hand and pulled her closer. Then they kissed. And she put her arms around him, and they kept on kissin', just as plain as day, like there weren't no shame to it at all.

"Hot Damn, I knew it!" Frank couldn't hold it in any longer. "Lloyd! Wake your ass up! Now!"

When Lloyd still didn't answer, Frank took last resort. He pinched Lloyd's nose together with the same thumb and forefinger he'd used on his tobacco, then cupped the rest of his hand over Lloyd's mouth, cutting off his brother's air. It took a few seconds, but it worked every time. Lloyd came up snarling and coughing, fists clenched and ready, but Frank was ready for it; he knew the routine and easily dodged the rounder that Lloyd swung blindly out.

"Hush! Right now!" he whispered as loud as he dared. "Want 'em to hear us, you big dumb-ass?"

"This'd better be good, Frankie. You know how I hate to be strangulated. This'd better be good..."

"Oh, it is," Frank spat, but the plug hadn't had time to get juicy yet, so it came out as more of a feeble spray than a good hocker. He elbowed Lloyd and pointed in the direction of the house. "See for yourself. It's good alright. Didn't I tell ya Felts was pokin' her all along?"

Lloyd rubbed his fists in his eyes and followed his brother's point. Harley and Sara were still kissing. But right then they stopped and stared all goo-goo eyed at one another like a couple of love-sick pups for a little bit, then Felts leaned back and the girl nestled onto his chest; him with his arms wrapped all around her.

"Didn't I tell ya?"

Them two sat that way on the porch for the longest time. And them two on the creek sat there for a long time as well. Finally, after Felts and the girl hadn't moved in what seemed like forever, Frank turned to Lloyd.

"Come on. We might as well get to work. They ain't going to be doing no fucking, least not on the front porch anyway."

"You don't think?"

"Naw, I don't think. I said so, didn't I?"

"But I don't want to miss it if they do, Frank..."

"They ain't going to do nothing out there, you cretin. Not when they've got their nice cozy bed inside. Besides, can't you tell she's done fell asleep? Felts can't be doing her no good if'n she's gone to sleep on him. Jeez, Lloyd, do I have to draw you a picture for every damned thing?"

"Now Frankie, you know I don't like you calling me those words I don't understand. What's a cretin sposed to mean?"

"Aw, forget it, idjit. Just follow me. We could thrash around like a couple of pent bulls right now and Felts'd never notice. His dick's got his ears plum plugged by now. And we got to get this done tonight, I ain't paying another ferry charge over this shit."

"Why can't you ever be nice to me, Frankie? We's supposed to be brothers and all..."

"Just shut up and follow me," Frank spat. It was getting juicy now. "And try not to make so much noise."

The two slunk up the creek bank and started circling around the farm.

"I got the plan, brother. Just follow me."

The two on the porch didn't move as Frank led Lloyd in a wide circle around the yard.

Chapter 14

Sara knew exactly where she was even before she woke. She rose out of her sleep, lifted by his already familiar musky-glandular scent that stood out above the smoky aroma of smoldering sawdust that permeated his clothes, his skin, his hair. Though her feet and legs were a bit chilly, dampened by the wee-morning-hour dew that had settled since they'd fallen asleep, her face was warmly — almost hotly — snuggled into the hollow of his neck, and her torso drew warmth from his. His arms still covered her back as gently as his lips had hugged hers earlier, as tentatively as his tongue had searched for hers. He was leaned against a porch post, breathing softly and easily. Peacefully. She kissed his neck, trying not to linger too long so as not to wake him. It felt good here. She felt safe and loved and... well... needed. For the first time in her life she had purpose, and she liked the way that felt. It felt like home; the one she'd never known before...

But something was gnawing at the back of her consciousness; something had wakened her, something insistent, something plaintive. She cocked her head, shook her hair away from her ears, and heard it. The puppies; yapping and crying nonstop. It was their first night away from their mother, away from the warm huddling nest of their littermates. Slowly, gently, she drew her arms from around Harley's waist and slid out from under his arms, reaching behind her and taking his hands in hers — those same strong, coarse hands that had touched her so gently just a little while ago — and guided them into his lap, draping his arms in front of him. His breathing stopped and he shifted against the post. She thought she'd woken him, as hard as she was trying not to wake this man to whom rest came so sparsely; this man who deserved rest, and peace, more than anyone she'd ever known. But when he settled back and resumed his quiet rhythm she knew that she'd gotten away with it; that she hadn't disturbed it. She reached out and pushed a lock of his thick, dark hair away from his eyes, bent and kissed the top of his head, and tip-toed across the porch and into the house, quietly easing the screen door shut behind her.

Inside, the house was filled with darkness and quiet, save the light that leaked in the front window from the lantern that still burned on the porch, save the steady, almost urgent whining and crying that she could still hear coming from the direction of the barn where the puppies were. Sara resisted the urge to go check on the children and went instead to the kitchen. Even though she couldn't see a thing there at the back of the house, it was such familiar territory to her by now that she found a candle and a match after only a bare amount of fumbling. As she struck the flame and held it to the wick the puppies picked up both the volume and the intensity of their cries. She smiled at the furiousness of their yapping.

"Hold your horses, you little baby-barkers, you," she whispered as the candle began to take, spreading its feeble light dim and yellow into the corners of the kitchen, "I'm coming..."

She took a bowl down from the wall cabinet beside the window over the sink and went to get the milk jug from the icebox in the pantry across the room from the cook stove. When she lifted the lid it didn't feel as cool in there as it ought to so she made a mental note to have one of the boys go to the cave and chop a fresh block of ice for it after church tomorrow. She poured the bowl half full, intending to water it to the top, then thought, "What the heck, it's their first night and this milk is liable to be sour by the time we get home anyway," so she went ahead and filled the bowl on up. Outside, the puppies were still hard at it. She leaned to the window and sssshed as loud as she dared, knowing that they probably couldn't hear her, and that it wasn't likely they'd quiet down even if they did.

"Hush, before you wake the whole house!" she whispered hoarsely into the dark as she picked up the candle and the bowl. The clock in the parlor chimed once, marking half past the hour. She wondered which hour it was as she went out the back screen door, pushing it open with her butt, easing it back to with her foot.

She made her way across the back yard, balancing the candle in one hand and the milk bowl in the other. She guessed it was two or three-thirty, at least. Maybe even four-thirty. The smoke from the barn had spread out across the farm, lying thick and low, pushed down to waist high by the heavy night air. Even the crickets had quieted and gone to bed. "The dead of night," she thought to herself. It fit.

It had cooled down considerably since earlier. The grass was wet and heavy with dew and it tickled her feet, sending a shiver through her as she reached the gate. She turned back toward the house, wishing she'd brought a robe. Her eyes were well adjusted to the dark by now, so even with only starlight she could see the dim skeleton of the new addition; the wall studs standing vertical, slightly paler than the blackness of the trees behind them; the roof rising more distinct against the lighter night sky. And though the angle of her view blocked sight of the front porch, the warm glow of its light, and of what she knew still lay sleeping there, spilled across the front yard. As she turned back and unlatched the gate she ran her tongue over her lips, savoring the taste that lingered there...

Bess's stall was just inside the open breezeway that ran through the center of the stock barn, the first one on the right, so by the time Sara followed the small circle of light that the candle cast before her Bess had her head stretched over the stall door, looking her huge chocolate-brown eyes expectantly in the direction of the approaching glow. And even though — judging by the increasing frenzy of their yelping — the puppies had obviously noticed her coming as well, there was no way Sara could bypass Bess. As she stooped to set the candle and the bowl down, Bess snorted and hooved the ground with her right front leg, bobbing her head up and down. Sara went to the horse and hugged the long eager face to her side, wrapping her right arm under Bess's chin, stroking up and down between the horse's eyes and nose with her left hand.

"Hey, there, Bessie-girl," she soothed. "What're you doing up so late, huh? Did I wake you, or is it that you just don't you ever sleep?

"Is that it? You just stand here around the clock, waiting to do whatever is asked of you?"

Sara stepped back and took Bess's ears in her hands, pulling her head up so they were looking straight into one another's eyes. The puppies began calming at the soft lilt of Sara's voice, even though she hadn't gotten to them yet. They knew she was coming so they patiented down a bit.

"That's it, isn't it? You just live to please, don't you, girl?" Sara said, scratching behind Bess's ears. " That's it isn't it?" A smile creased her lips. "Surely it's not those confounded puppies"

Bess rattled air through her lips, blowing the soft contented sound that horses make when a cat might purr, then she nosed Sara's side gently, first sniffing at her belly then nuzzling her arm up high, begging for more petting.

Sara slid her hands down under Bess's mouth and kissed the horse square on the nose.

"Now I'll go quieten those doggies down so we can get some sleep, okay?"

As she turned and bent to pick up the milk and the candle, Bess fluttered her lips once more.

"You're welcome, girl," Sara said over her shoulder, starting toward the far stall where the puppies were. Bess watched her all the way until the light turned the corner and faded out near altogether before she turned back into her stall.

The puppies spilled out the door before Sara got it even half-open, greeting her with yips and whimpers, bouncing up her leg as far as they could reach. Sara didn't bother hesitating for them or calling them after her; she went on in, knowing they'd follow, which they did. Seeing that they had not touched the bowl of dog food the boys had left for them, she sat down between the bowl and the candle and was immediately consumed by the two licking, fawning, rolling-over-themselves balls of fur. They were obviously more interested in attention than in milk. After she'd picked them both up and lavished love over them, she put them down beside the bowl, showing them the treat she'd brought. Neither one knew what to make of the white stuff, and they bounded right back into her lap. As bright and energetic as they pups were, once she was sitting Sara felt the fatigue of the day wash over her, pulling downward on skin, muscle, and bone alike. She took Homer and Roamer in her hands and dipped their noses into the milk, trying to show them what it was, but all they wanted was to be back in her lap. After three or four tries she began to get exasperated.

"Look here, guys, I'm not about to nurse you... Though maybe I could," she said, feeling the new tug and heaviness in her breasts.

"This," she pointed uselessly toward the bowl, "is for you." Homer and Roamer's only answer was to jump even more excitedly at her face.

It took a while, but finally she got them to drinking by dipping her fingers in the milk and letting them suck it off, drawing their eager little mouths ticklish all the way up to her first knuckle. Then gradually she got them to follow her fingers under the milk and the concept of lapping dawned on them. As soon as their attention fell on the bowl, Sara took her chance and stood up and sneaked to the stall door.

"Now, will ya'll shut up and go to sleep?" she said back at them, no more able to stifle the smile that spread over her face at the sight of the two wagging tails and the two racing tongues than she was to stifle the yawn that spread her mouth wide and round.

"Good night, guys." She shut the door behind her and left while she could.

She retraced her steps down the breezeway, breathing the sickly-sweet animal dung and rotting hay smell of the barn deeply, not even pausing to bid Bess good night; not daring to raise the noise of the puppies with her voice.

The instant she stepped outside, the smell of the night changed. In the few short hours since they had set the sawdust under the tobacco crop to glowing, the smoldering scent had ranged out across the farm, taking over the land with its whispering foggy tendrils. "It sure didn't take long," Sara thought, casting a glance in the direction of the tobacco barn. Dark as it was, she saw the reason why the smell was so strong so soon; the doors had come open somehow and smoke was billowing out between them.

"Now, that can't be right," she said to no one but the night, then, "Listen at you, girl, out here muttering away at yourself in the middle of the night." Yet she went on, out loud again. "But I know we closed the doors. They should be closed." She looked toward the house where the front porch light still burned. She should go wake Harley, else he was bound to have a terrible backache tomorrow, sleeping against that post all night.

"Ouch!" she cried as a hot glob of wax dripped onto her thumb. Her candle was nearly burned up. "What the heck," she spoke, growing used to the sound of her own voice. "I'll shut it for him, seeing as I'm already out here. It's the least I can do."

She cupped her hand around the flame and blew it out, then turned and started for the tobacco barn.

There was a peace to the night quite unlike anything she'd ever known before; the peace of dark solitude; the peace of quiet comfort; the peace of mind that comes with knowing, finally. She didn't need the candle. She knew the way, and she hummed it softly as she walked.

When she reached the doors of the barn she couldn't help but peek inside. Even through the thick roiling smoke she could see the red, glowing outlines of the five circles they had lit earlier, spreading slowly, steadily, closer together. The embers burned across the surface, ringing wider toward each other, not yet overlapping; but soon they would, she knew; not burning too deeply; but soon they would do that too, she knew. Just as she reached her arms out to draw the doors together, she saw a shadow pass between her and the glow, and felt the presence behind her just as a meaty, foul smelling hand clamped itself over her mouth, forcing her scream back down into her throat.

*

The fish camp was as close to paradise as Harley had ever been, outside of his farm. There wasn't much to it, really. What they called the 'cabin' would be more rightly named a lean-to, little more than a wind break that Rig and Burley and Harley had thrown up years ago, on a trip before any of them had families or responsibilities or cares beyond those of teen dreams. But they had chosen the spot well, and that was the beauty of it. They'd stumbled onto it after three long days of lugging fifty-pound packs along the banks of the great river, in celebration of the end of their schooling and the imagined beginning of their 'independence'. It was the soft, sandy shoal that eased gently, almost beach-like, into the river that caught their attention first — as opposed to the high, weedy banks they had fought through nearly all the way from home. Cause enough to pause. It gave them a perfect spot to drop their loads, to wade in, to spend the night. It was dusking when they got there and they were more concerned with setting camp and catching super than they were with sightseeing, so it wasn't until the next morning that they all realized this was more than just another campsite. They woke, those long gone boys, to find themselves laying at the inside of a sharp bend in the river, almost a peninsula; river to the right, river to the left, river straight ahead. Directly across stream the ageless water had carved an eighty foot high curved bluff into the limestone foundation of God's land, exposing eons of sediment layers, and deepening the waters below it to depths that could support fish of unimaginable sizes. And to cap it all off, a freshwater spring crawled its murmuring way into the mighty Tennessee no more than a half dozen paces upstream.

That, and the fact that for the next two days they caught more fish than they could eat, brought them back the next fall, when they built the cabin. And they'd been going back ever since, every chance they got, together with each other, or separate with their families as they each grew their own. As they needed relief, escape, or just plain fun. And as an unspoken rule, anyone who made the trip left the place a little bit improved. A new stump-seat or table here, more rocks around the fire pit there, a patch in the cabin roof as needed...

Harley was there, and the fish were biting. It took him longer to bait his hook than it did to haul in the catch. Large mouth bass, small mouth bass, bream by the sack full. Crappie hitting the hook as fast as November sleet on a window. Channel cat as big as a man's leg. The fish were so hot he finally quit baiting at all and just threw his naked line in and hauled fish out. Damn, it was fun!

Ellie tapped him on the shoulder.

"It's time to go now, Harley. "

"Aw, El, not yet, look at how they're hittin'."

"Okay," she smiled. "You stay and enjoy it," she said, just as his float disappeared under the water, bending his pole near double with the biggest strike of all. It was a monster, this one was. He fought and fought with it, but he couldn't get it to the bank.

"El! Help me, Baby," he called over his shoulder. The rod jerked hard in his hands, pulling him to his feet, dragging him toward the water. He tried to let go of the pole but couldn't. He dug his heels in but the fish drug him on, his feet leaving furrows down the shoal behind him.

"Ellie!" he cried. He was waist deep in the river by now, being dragged deeper and deeper. When he turned and looked back, the fish camp was gone, Ellie was gone. The kids were gone. There was nothing behind him but blackness. And then he went under, and then he was flowing underwater in the current of pale green silence, sun flecked and cold.

He couldn't breathe; he woke up choking, coughing, with a pain between his shoulder blades.

Sara knew by the strength of the arms that squeezed her that it was the big one that had her. She struggled, but soon realized it was useless as he dragged her into the smoke-filled barn. The other one was inside with a bundle of empty feed sacks and tobacco sticks in his arms, and a handkerchief tied across his nose and mouth to filter out some of the smoke.

"Lookie what I found pokin' around outside, Frankie."

Frank dropped his load and stepped up in front of Sara.

"Well, well, well. What we got here?" His beady little eyes were watery, from the smoke, or from the liquor, or both. "What's a little missy like you doing out wandering around this time of night?" He reached out and drug the back of his filthy hand down her cheek. Sara wriggled and kicked out, catching Frank just above the knee, causing Lloyd to squeeze tighter until she nearly lost her breath. He wrapped a leg around the front of hers to keep her from kicking any more.

"I reckon Felts just can't satisfy her. Maybe she's got a craving for a real man, you think, little brother?" His hand continued down her neck, brushing along the side of her breast.

"What're we going to do with her, Frankie?"

Frank drew his hand back, scratching his stubbly chin.

"I don't rightly know, Lloyd. Hadn't counted on things takin' this sorta turn." His eyes traveled lewdly down Sara's front, lingering at her legs before slowly moving back up to stare into her face.

"Find some rope and tie her to that post over there while I contemplate matters. And be sure and gag her good."

He bent over and re-gathered his load while Lloyd did as he was told. He dragged her over to the post and pulled her arms behind her, tying them together behind the post. Then he took a putrid rag from his pocket and shoved it into her mouth, pulling another length of rope across it, tying her head hard against the rough cedar pole. She felt bile rising in her throat as she gagged against the foulness in her mouth. The little one carried his pile through the smoldering dust and dropped it in the center of the barn, then bent over and started arranging it, paper and burlap on the bottom, sticks on top. With a shock of horror she realized what they were up to. They were going to burn the barn! She struggled against the ropes but they cut into the corners of her mouth and she felt a trickle of blood run down her chin. Lloyd just laughed, then pulled her bonds tighter, adding one more around her waist, just under her belly. She gave up, pressing her back tight against the post, trying to ease the pressure.

Frank stepped carefully back through the embers and came to her front, spitting at her feet. She felt the spray of it splash back onto her ankle. He stood there squinting at her as his brother joined him at his side.

"What're we gonna do, Frankie? She's done seen us. We're in a heap of trouble now!"

"Shut up and let me think," Frank said, spitting again. Sara looked past the evil little man, unable to bear the sight of his leaching eyes on her. The widening red rings behind him were less than two feet from the pile of tender he'd laid. How long would it take for them to reach it? Fifteen minutes? Half an hour?

"It's a curious pickle, that's right enough, brother," Frank said, putting his hands on his hips. "Ain't but one thing we can do, way I see it...

"But we got a few minutes, might as well show her some fun before we leave her, don't you think?"

Lloyd's thick brows knit over his dull eyes, then they raised high, and his mouth fell open as he realized what his brother meant.

"But, Frankie! We ain't never kilt no woman before! And look at her — she's uhhh... got a baby in her."

Frank turned in Lloyd's direction, scowling. "You got a better idea, Mr. Genius?"

Lloyd closed his mouth and his shoulders sagged, cowing like a scolded dog.

"Well... no."

"Alright then, just shut up, less'n you want to spend the rest of your life rotting away in a prison cell up at Brushy Mountain."

Lloyd turned and looked into the smoke behind him. "You can do what you want, but I ain't havin' no part of it. Burnin' a barn's one thing. But killin' a woman and a baby is somethin' else all together."

"Look at her, you idiot! Remember what she did to you on the ferry? And I don't see no babies here. She's just swolled up with some little yankee bastard."

"Well, I just don't like it, that's all I was saying."

"Fine. You don't have to like it. Just keep your mouth shut and go find us some more sticks to put on there. Me and the little lady got us some acquaintin' to do..."

Lloyd slunk away through the gloom while Frank squatted on his haunches in front of Sara, rubbing his hand up and down his chin. "Hmmmm ..." he said.

*

Awareness crept slowly back into Harley, as it always did when he woke after dreaming. It was as if he had to climb step by step back into the waking world, hung-over by the cloudy images of his dream. He sat up and arched his back. It was stiff and he was pretty sure he felt the beginning of a crick in his neck from the night air, and from staying too long in such an awkward position. Then he remembered Sara. Where was she? And more importantly, what had they done tonight? He'd not been expecting anything like this to happen. She must've gone to bed, he thought, glad that he didn't have to deal with it until he'd had time to think about what had happened, and what was going to come of it.

He stood up and stretched again, feeling a twinge at the junction of his shoulder and neck. Yep, he'd sure enough be stiff in the morning. Realizing that couldn't be far away, he took the lantern and went inside. His mouth was dry and his lips felt chapped — what had they done out there? A wave of guilt washed over him. On one hand he felt awful about it — he'd never kissed anyone but Ellie — but on the other hand, it felt so right; felt so good to taste the sweetness of affection again. He shook his head, trying to put the confusion that crowded in there in order as he went to the kitchen for a drink of water.

When he got there, he saw the milk jug sitting on the table, and a box of matches beside it. It wasn't like Sara to leave good food out to spoil like this. She must be as rattled by the night's turn as he was. He got a glass off the drain board and picked up the milk jug, sniffing at its neck before pouring the glass full. He drank it down in one tip, gulping heavily, then went and put the milk back in the icebox where it belonged. Maybe he should go check on Sara, he thought. But no, going to her room right now would be the absolute wrong thing to do. As he turned to go to his room and get what sleep he could, the mantle clock chimed, once, twice, three times. He expected that to be the last but it chimed again a fourth time, then a fifth. Jeez, he'd been out there a long time, no wonder he was so sore.

"What the hell," he thought. "It's nearly sunrise. No point in going to bed now." He decided he'd peek in on the boys then go out and check on the fire in the barn. He tiptoed quietly down the hall and eased the door to their room open just enough to let light from the lantern leak in so he could count heads. They were all there, as he knew they would be, sleeping the deep, peaceful sleep of innocence. What would they think if they knew what'd happened on the porch earlier? As he stepped back and began to push the door to, Cy rolled over and raised his head.

"Pa? That you?" He said sleepily.

"Yeah, son, it's just me. Go on back to sleep while you can, I was just going to check the firing."

"Okay, Pa," Cy mumbled, rolling back over.

Harley pushed the door closed and went back down the hall, through the kitchen and out the back door.

Chapter 15

As Harley made his way toward the barn, across ground so familiar that he really had no need of the lantern he carried, he tried to make sense of the most unfamiliar feelings that swirled around him like the early morning mist of smoke and fog that curled and swept in his wake. Even as his mind yelled that Sara was more than a decade his junior — closer to Cy's age than his own, he realized with a bit of a shock — he couldn't deny the whispering in his heart. She had woken something in him that he had never expected to find again; something that had died last winter; something that he had buried; something he never thought would see the light of day again. He'd thought. It was almost too much for him to take. Visions of Ellie, swimming in the taste of Sara.

Life had always been so simple, so straightforward for him. You worked, you ate, you slept; then you did it again. No questions, no doubts. Ellie hadn't complicated it; she had only clarified it all. She made sense. But all at once she'd gone and left him. That wasn't part of the plan. How did that happen? And after that, nothing had made much sense at all to him. Until Sara. Until a few hours ago. Then, all at once, out of the blue, she made perfect sense to him, if only for a few minutes. She had clarified it for him again for a few precious minutes. But when he woke up she was gone, like a ghost in the night, and here he was again, left alone to find his own way through the dark. Alone with his thoughts and with his guilt. He was a simple man. Why did life have to be so complicated?

Something caught his eye then; he got the first hint that more was amiss than the thoughts that ran rampant through his mind. A flicker from the barn. The doors were open. It was brighter inside than it should be. He picked his pace up to a trot, trying to swallow the catch of instinct that rose in his throat. It was fire, sure enough. He dropped the lantern and broke into a sprint.

By the time he reached the doors, the light inside shone bright as mid-day sun. Through the smoke, past the flames that licked hungrily, sickeningly, high at the center of the barn he saw movement. It was all too much for his eyes to take in at once; too much for his mind to digest. Sara was in there, bound to a post, looking wide eyed and terrified in his direction, shaking her head violently against ropes that cut into her mouth and her waist. Her gown was ripped open down the front, exposing her breasts and her belly and the patch of hair between her legs that should have been shaded but glowed silver, lit shining by the fire that was spreading across the floor. Harley ran blindly through the smoke to her and reached around her, fumbling frantically at the knots that held her hands. All the while Sara strained against the gag that stifled the warnings she was trying to shout. Just as Harley loosed the knot he saw her eyes widen and draw focus over his shoulder, and as he turned to follow their path, the plank hit him square in the face, sending stars sparkling before his eyes. Harley crumpled to his knees, and to blackness.

Once Sara had her hands loose it didn't take her long to get free of the other ropes. Harley lay slumped at her feet, directly between her and the vile thing that had put him down. The little man was winding up to take another crack the back of Harley's head when she sprang. She got in the way of the blow just in time to take it across her ribs. She felt bones splinter just as the board did, but she refused to fall. Gathering herself up, she leapt at Frank, clawing and kicking and screaming into his face. But even as small as he was, she was no match for him. He grabbed her by the arms and slung her hard into the wall that separated the main hall of the barn from the stripping room that had been added onto the side. She hit the oak siding hard enough to jar a rack of tools loose and as she slid down the wall into a blinding yellow heap of pain, the implements rained down on her. Something sharp and heavy hit the corner of her eye, drawing blood instantly, blurring her vision. But she could still see well enough to make out the crouching form of the little one approaching her, hovering over her, leering wickedly down at her.

"Still got spunk in you, I see," it hissed at her.

"I admire that," it said reaching into its pocket, drawing something out, flicking it open. The metal blade glistened in the firelight that grew behind it.

Sara struggled to sit up, trying to push herself away from the vile thing. Her hand hit something hard and she grabbed it.

"Damn shame to have to cut spunk out of such a promising piece of meat," it reared back.

She lashed out with the tobacco knife, catching Frank just under the jaw. He stood there for a second or two with an amazed look on his face, then she drew the knife out and hit him again in the center of his throat, and blood spurted everywhere. He tried to put a hand up and stop it but he couldn't, it was done. Falling face forward on top of Sara, he gurgled and twitched a couple of times, then settled dead still in her lap.

Before she pushed him off of her and got up, she drove the knife into the back of his neck once more, for good measure.

She immediately went to Harley and bent over him, taking his face in her hands, kissing his eyes, his brow, his cheeks.

"Wake up, please, Harley!" she cried. The heat of the fire stung at her back.

When he didn't respond, she grabbed his hands and tried to drag him clear, but a blinding flash of pain stabbed through her side and her stomach. He was too heavy. She couldn't budge him. She could feel her back blistering as the flames spread over the barn, on the verge of consuming it, and them. But she wouldn't leave. She couldn't leave. Not knowing anything else to do, the mother in her came to the fore. She stomped her foot and clapped her hands hard together.

"Harley Felts! You get up right this instant!"

Then the smoke and the heat overcame her, and she laid down on top of him, to protect him a few seconds longer, laying her face over his. Just as she gave up to the blackness, his eyes fluttered on her cheeks.

"Sara?" he said weakly, "It's hot in here…"

And so it was him that pulled her out of the barn, saving the one who had saved him. He had just barely dragged her clear of the doors when there was a mild explosion inside as the year's work ignited all at once. Now it was his turn to wake her. He put his mouth gently to hers and breathed…

"Sara"

She didn't respond, so he tried it again, blowing harder this time.

"Sara!"

Then, after an eternity of two or three seconds, she opened her eyes and looked at him. And they kissed their second kiss, while the night grew blazing brighter and hotter than any noon day sun had ever shone. Lost in the warmth of the cool grass where they lay, neither noticed the shadow that fell across them.

"Where's my brother?"

Lloyd hulked over them, a pitchfork in his hand.

"What have you done with Frankie?" he said, panic hinting into his voice.

Harley rolled over quickly, but not quite quick enough. Lloyd stomped a hard foot onto Harley's chest, pinning him to the ground. Sara started to sit up, but she hurt, and when Lloyd raised the pitchfork above his head, holding it like a spear, she knew she could do no good against him.

"Where's Frankie?' he asked again, his voice rising as his weight fell harder on Harley, squeezing the breath away. He lowered the fork and pushed it against Harley's Adam's apple.

"What have ya'll done with my brother!" he demanded, crushing down. Harley felt a trickle of blood run down his neck.

The night sky lit up with a flash and a loud 'Boom!' that eclipsed even the light and crackling fury of the burning barn, and Lloyd's crush eased on Harley's chest; then the big man dropped the pitchfork and fell dead weight into the grass beside them.

Cy pumped the empty shell from the shotgun, staring down at the man he had just killed. Then he dropped the gun. Then he dropped to his knees.

For the second time that night Harley came choking and coughing up. By the time he rolled over onto his stomach and pushed himself to his hands and knees, gasping for air, Sara was already at Cy's side. The boy wore a face of pure shock. She had one arm around him and was trying to pull his face to hers with the other, but Cy wouldn't take his eyes off the bloody gaping hole he'd made in Lloyd's back. Harley struggled to his feet and went to join them, putting himself between Cy and the dead man. He took his son's cheeks in his hands and forced their eyes together, though Cy's retained their vacant stare.

"You had to do it, son. They would have killed us all." Cy's eyes slowly began to focus on his father. "His brother's in the barn. It was them or us; simple as that. You did the right thing." Cy nodded his head a little bit, obviously still in a fog. "You saved our lives, son. Just look what they did to Sara."

Sara's face and front was covered with soot and blood, some of it hers, more of it Mangrum's. Blood still leaked from the corner of her eye, which was beginning to swell already, and from the corners of her mouth. Her front and what was left of her gown was covered with red and black stains. Realizing she was exposed, she stood up and began clutching at her gown, pulling it together in front of her with both hands. Harley quickly turned his face back to Cy, and Cy's back to his own.

"You did what you had to do, Cy. I'm proud of you." Cy's eyes finally filled back up and he nodded again, surer this time.

"Yeah, Pa. I had to do it."

"You did," Harley said leaning forward, taking his son into his arms. Cy returned the hug, laying his chin on his father's shoulder, where the crick had become the least of Harley's aches. Harley turned them around so Cy wasn't facing Mangrum.

"Harley…" Sara said, and the tone of her voice sent chills through Harley's spine, even in the roaring heat the fire threw at them. He knew that tone. Pulling his face from Cy's hair, he looked up. She was standing beside them, still holding her nightgown closed, looking down at her own legs, watching the stream of burgundy red make its way from her crotch toward her feet.

"Harley…" she said again, unable to mask the fear in her voice.

"Oh my God! Lay down, Sara!" He let go of Cy and stood up, grabbing her arms and easing her back into the grass. "Cy! Go get some towe… No, go hitch Bess, fast as you can!" Cy stood up too then, still dazed and slow moving.

"No, better for you to watch Sara. I'll hitch the wagon." Harley told him. Harley could do it faster, no doubt. But also he wouldn't have to stay here and watch what was happening. He couldn't do it again. He would sooner walk himself into the inferno behind him than go through this again. Without another word he took off in a limping run toward the stock barn.

The smoke and fire smell and commotion had reached the livestock long before Harley did. All the animals were agitated, grunting and squealing, and in the puppies case, yelping frantically. Bess's eyes were wide with terror. She snorted and hooved at the floor and walls of her stall. Harley tried to soothe her but she shied away, threatening to rear up on him. Talking quietly, he opened the door to her stall, and the second he did she bolted past him, headed for open air.

"No! Whoa, Bess!" he shouted, trying to pin her flank between himself and the door. "Whoa!" But the horse pushed on. Just as she cleared the door, Harley grabbed her tail and hung on with all his might. No way was he letting her get away. No way.

"Whoa, girl," he called a little less loud, trying to take some urgency out of his voice, and out of her panic. Bess stopped and turned back, looking at him quizzically.

"That a girl," he calmed to a talk, stroking her hindquarters. "That's a good Bessie girl…"

Slowly he made his way to her front. She snorted once more, then let him slip a rope over her head and lead her outside. Thank God he hadn't sent Cy.

Bess was still skittish as hell, and Harley found his hands shaking like freezing palsy, but still and all, he had her hitched and ready to go in record time.

"Get up!" he cried, not bothering to mount the wagon, taking the lead in his hands and trotting in front of her.

When he got back to Sara, Seth was there, huddling over her with Cy. Bert and Amos were walking in their direction form the house, both crying loudly. Harley handed the lead to Seth.

"Here, hold on to her tight. The fire's got her all riled up. Cy, open the tailgate on the wagon," he said, bending and picking Sara up in his arms, "and spread that tarp out. Make a bed for her."

Cy sprang up and did as he was told, then he helped Harley settle Sara into place. He was back; too busy now to dwell on what he'd just done. That'd come later though, Harley knew.

"Hand me the reins, Seth," he ordered, climbing into the driver's seat. "And cover that thing up before your little brothers see it," he said with a nod at the dark heap of Mangrum on the ground. He jerked the reins hard, slapping them across Bess's back, and she lurched the wagon away in a gallop.

"Get the kids back to the house!" he called over his shoulder, "and see to Cassie!" Then he turned around focused on the road ahead, driving the horse like he'd never driven her before. It was over four miles to Doc Hall's house.

"God, get us there in time," he prayed aloud. "Please, Lord…

Chapter 16

By noon that day Harley's ringing headache hadn't subsided much. Ben Hall had tried to persuade Harley to take a pair of shaded glasses to wear, saying that the sunlight would only make Harley's concussion more painful. But even though Harley had deferred to the doctor about wrapping his ribs (which Ben suspected of being cracked, at the very least), he'd drawn the line at the glasses. He just couldn't imagine himself wearing such things. But now as he pulled into the ford at the end of his drive, his throbbing head made him wish he had taken the doctor's advice on that too.

As soon as he made the turn he could see his yard full of cars and wagons and people moving about here and there. It was a busy place. He hadn't seen so many folks there since... Well, not for a long time.

There were two sheriff's cars and Rig's Packard and another car he didn't recognize, along with a half a dozen wagons. The black pile where the barn had stood was still smoldering in spots as a brigade of men carried buckets of water to cool it off to the point they could start sifting through the ashes. As he drew nearer, he made out Cy, working with the men. He guessed, hoped, that Seth was in the house with the kids.

As he pulled up in front of the house he was proved right. Seth stepped out the front door with Cassie on his hip.

"Hey, Pa! How's Sara?"

"I'll be in, in a few minutes," Harley replied, reining Bess up and setting the brake. "Stay in there and watch over the kids," he said as he climbed wearily down. Seth started to speak again, then thought better of it and went back in.

"Hey, Harley!" the sheriff shouted from over by the barn rubble. He and one of his deputies started toward the house, joined by Burley.

Seeing his farm in such turmoil, seeing the ruin of the tobacco barn in broad daylight, brought the full impact of all that had happened last night crashing down on him. He'd been too occupied with Sara to think much about it till now. He was ruined. He might even lose the farm. A whole year's work, up in smoke. He watched the last wisps of smoke rising into the sky, leading his eyes to the knoll that stood almost directly behind where the barn had been. He stared hard at it for a second or two before it blurred out of his vision.

He took his hat off and used it for cover to wipe his eyes as the men approached.

Burley got there first, holding his hand out to Harley. "Damn, boy, it never ends, does it?"

Harley took the hand and shook it, trying not to hold on too long.

"No, Burl, I don't reckon it ever does," he said looking up, letting his friend catch his eye. "And I don't reckon I'd know how to act if it ever did." In spite of it all, despite himself, he smiled. Burley didn't say anything else, didn't have to. He was that kind of friend.

"Hey, Harley," Sheriff Jeffers interrupted, a bit sheepishly, almost apologetically. "Been a while. Damn shame we only see one another at bad times."

"No doubt, Jimbo. How're Evelyn and the kids doing?"

Harley was one of the few people who still called Jim Jeffers by his first nickname — Jimbo, the name Harley had grown up knowing him as. Jimbo Jeffers, the big, soft, fat kid, who'd become 'Mutt' the first time he'd run for sheriff, calling himself 'Lawdog' Jeffers on his campaign posters. Lawdog hadn't stuck, but Mutt had.

"Great. They're all doing just great." He paused, seeming guilty about that. Then he went on.

"Your boy," he said, throwing a nod over his shoulder toward the barn where Cy toiled amongst the men, "told me most of what went on…" He paused a second. Jimbo never had been one to get right to the point.

"We've got the big one bagged and tagged. There ain't no problem, mind you… It's just… We got to find the other. For the coroner, you know. And we'll have to get a statement before long. Not today, mind you, wouldn't dream of it today. Ya'll can come in when you get a chance, no rush, you know…"

Harley had known Jimbo, 'the fat boy from town', since first grade. Now he was their sheriff, their 'protector'. Still the fat boy, still from town.

"Sure, Jimbo," he said. "Day after tomorrow soon enough?"

"You bet. That'll be plenty soon enough," said Jimbo, "or the next day… Whenever ya'll can make it…" He had a bad habit of leaving his words hanging in the air, a terrible habit for a sheriff, Harley'd always thought.

"You and your boy... Whenever ya'll can make it." He looked over his shoulder toward the crew at the barn, as if he was in charge, as if they missed him. Jimbo Jeffers always seemed to be looking for someplace else to be. "We'll ask the girl about it when she's able..."

Harley couldn't help but follow his gaze, where he saw Cy looking their way; saw Rig take Cy by the shoulder and begin leading him their way.

"She will be able to give us a statement, won't she? There won't be no charges or anything. It all seems pretty clear cut, them on your property and all. Hell, ya'll did the town a favor if you ask me. But we got to have statements anyway. For the record and all, you know..."

"She'll be able, Jimbo. Me and Cy'll be in Tuesday." Harley said. He shook the sheriff's hand and walked past him to go meet Cy.

Burley stayed behind with Jimbo, and Harley walked away he tried not to hear what Jeffers said before Burley cut him off in mid-sentence. Good ole Burley.

Halfway between the house and the barn remnants, Cy shook loose of Rig's arm and ran to his Daddy's.

"How is she, Pa?" he asked as they hugged.

"She's gonna be okay, son." He hugged his boy tight, so tight it hurt his ribs, and then he hugged tighter.

Cy looked up, his face darkened with soot, yet bright and shining at Harley.

"Really?"

"Really." Harley held his boy at arm's length, where they could look one another at full face. "Would I lie to you?"

Cy's only answer, his best answer, was to fall into Harley's hug once more.

They would have stayed that way a longer time if Rig hadn't stepped up, 'A-hemming' beside them.

"Don't let me get in the way, you guys," he said, by way of intruding, "but here I am, in the way."

Harley looked up and released his hold on Cy.

"Hi, Rig." His son smelled like fire.

"Hey, Harley," Rig held his hand out. Harley took it and shook it.

"What does Doc say about the girl?" Rig asked.

Cy stepped back and coughed slightly in the background, clearing his throat.

"Sara'll be fine," Harley said. "Ben says she'll be fine, in a few days. She lost her baby, but she'll be fine, Ben says."

"Well, you needn't worry about her no more. Cloie should be there by now, at the Hall's. She'll see to her proper, Clorise will, believe me on that. She's probably got half of Maryland woke up by now. You know Ben and Liv got a telephone, don't you?"

"Yeah, I know, Rig. Clorise was there before I left," Harley said. "She hadn't got a hold of Sara's folks yet, but she was going to keep trying."

"Well, knowing my Cloie, she'll get through to her sister one way or another. When she gets her mind set, she could probably scream loud enough to be heard plumb to Baltimore. I pity any operator who gets in her way." He tried a chuckle, but it fell away alone. A little bit self-consciously he turned around and looked at the ruins behind him. "Damn, what a bitch, Harley. What're you going to do now?"

"I don't know, Rig. Pick up the pieces and start over, I reckon. I haven't really had time to think ahead any."

Four men were lifting a long burlap-wrapped bundle that was tied off in rope, trying to load it into one of the wagons, being none too gentle about it.

"Did a real number on that one, you did, boy," Rig said, reaching out to tousle Cy's hair. Harley snapped his arm out and knocked Rig's hand away before it touched Cy. The smile dropped from Rig's face and he stepped back a pace at Harley's glare.

"Cy, why don't you go see to Bess and the rest of the stock. She's plenty wore out and the rest of 'em are bound to need some calming down."

"Okay, Pa," he started away, then stopped and nodded toward Rig, "Mr. Gambil," he said. Then he took his leave.

"Jeez, Harley. I didn't mean nothing by…" Rig started.

"I know you didn't, Rig. Sorry to be so quick. He just doesn't need it right now." Harley watched Cy walking away, saw his son's eyes fixed on the county wagon as he passed it.

"I know, Harley. Sorry. It's just… He's sort of a hero, way I hear it."

"Not in his eyes, Rig. Not in his eyes, he ain't."

"Sheriff!" One of the men working at the barn called. "We might have us something here!"

"About the girl," Rig said, changing the subject, "you needn't worry about her no more. We'll take her to our house once Doc lets her go. At least until her folks come for her."

"That's what Clorise said," Harley started, not quite sure where to go from there. He looked at the bustle around them, then took a deep breath and looked square at Rig. "I didn't argue much with her, but..." He saw the quizzical look creeping into Rig's eyes, the same one he'd seen in Clorise's when he'd brought it up with her back at the Hall's.

"But what, Harley?"

"But... Well, I'd like to bring her back here when she gets well enough."

He'd started now, he had to finish. "We can look after her for a while, till she gets back on her feet. I figure it's the least we can do. After all she's done for us."

Rig chuckled again. "Don't be silly, boy! You've got more than enough on your plate as it is, what with your young'uns, and all this to deal with," he said, tilting his head at the mess behind them. "The last thing you need right now is another one to look after, another mouth to feed. Especially one that ain't even kin. We won't hear of it. You've done Cloie and me enough of a favor already, taking her off our hands. Now it's our turn to take her back off of yours."

"But you don't understand, Rig. It ain't like that at all..." He stopped, caught by the question in Rig's eyes; stopped by the same puzzled look he'd seen earlier in Clorise when he'd tried to talk to her about it.

"Understand what, Harley? What're you driving at?"

"It's just..." he stumbled ahead, hoping to get it out in time, before the look of perplexion was replaced by the dawning he'd seen — or at least imagined he'd seen — in Clorise's eyes. Just before he'd left to come back home. "It's just I feel like I... like we owe it to her. After all she's done for us. You don't know what a Godsend she's been around here. It'd only be right if we could pay her back just a little."

"I can understand that, Harley, right enough. But now that her, uhhh... 'problem' has been solved, there's no need for her to stay around here anymore. She'll be headed home soon enough, back to where she belongs. And she is Cloie's niece, after all. It's our place now. We can manage for a week or two. And besides, Cloie always loved playing nurse. This'll give her a good spell at it. Something to hang over that uppity sister of hers, for a change."

There was another yell from behind them.

"We got him, Sheriff! Sure enough!" Jimbo and Burley started walking in the direction of the barn.

Harley put his hands on Rig's shoulders, hoping he'd said enough. Hoping he hadn't said too much.

"It's the least we can do, Rig." He lowered his voice before they went to join the others, "Talk to Clorise about it for me, will you?"

"Sure, Harley, if you want. Not that I think it'll do any good, but I'll tell her what you said."

Harley let his hands fall from Rig's shoulders just as Burley and Jimbo reached them.

"Come on, Harley, I don't want to miss this," Rig said, falling into stride with the sheriff. "I ain't never seen no burnt up man before. Have you, Mutt?" he asked, turning his attention to the matters at hand.

Burley stopped at Harley's side and put his hands in the pockets of his overalls. They both stood quietly watching the scurry toward the middle of the ash pile.

"Lookie here, boys!" one of the searchers shouted. "Mangrum, well done!"

"That's the first time I ever heard a Mangrum called well done," someone else said, provoking laughs and catcalls.

"I'm not sure I've got stomach for that," Burley said, as much to himself as to Harley. He turned his back on the scene and waited until Harley did the same before he spoke again. They were facing the house, fenced and yarded so familiar, so unchanged, except for the clutter of wagons and automobiles in front and the skeleton of the new addition in the back; standing so solid and sure against the surrounding turmoil.

"I don't know about you, Harl, but I sure could use a walk about now." Burley turned his head just enough in Harley's direction to draw his friend's attention. Harley turned toward Burley just enough to catch the hint of wink aimed at him. "Unless, of course, you're too tired. Or too busy."

Harley smiled. Burley could always do it, because Burley never tried to be anything but there. And Burley was always there.

"Who, me?" Harley spread his hands from his sides, arms down, palms facing out, pretending to beg answer. "Busy? Do I look busy? Do I look tired?"

Cy was heading back toward them, coming to fetch Bess and the wagon. The front screen door at the house burst open and Seth stepped out, dragging Bert behind him. The men where the barn had been were homing their black footed circle tighter and tighter.

"Those dang puppies have got loose and run the hogs out of their pen!"

"Pa, tell Bert to mind me and quit picking on Amos!"

"Get over here quick! You've got to see this!"

Harley drew a deep breath, rolled his eyes and looked at Burley.

"Come to think of it, I do need to move the cattle over to the creek bottom. Care to give me a hand?"

"Absolutely!" Burley said, clamping a hand over Harley's shoulder. "Cy! Let them pups run. We'll fetch the hogs up later. Bert! Mind your big brother and help him look after your little brother and sister." He turned toward the men at the barn and yelled, " Guys! There's still farm to tend to. We'll be back directly. There's plenty of ya'll to handle that mess without us."

And with that they walked away.

Harley's herd consisted of about sixty Herefords, about half steers and half raising stock, and of course, Big Red, one of the finest bulls in the county. It'd been a good year, calving a dozen and one (though Harley wasn't a particularly superstitious man, he never counted thirteen — it was always a dozen and one to him). He and Burley walked in silence until they reached the gate separating the upper pasture from the lower one. The cattle were all at the far end of the field, grazing on the side of the hill that led up to the ridge that marked the rear boundary of his farm.

"Whoooooop!" he called. "Heyyyyyyyydeee!" At the sound of his yells the animals started slowly moving in his direction.

"The herd's looking good as ever," Burley commented. "I'd give anything to have a bull like that one of yours."

"Yep, he's a dandy alright. He not only breeds like a maniac, he makes good steak stock, nice and lean. Not much fat in his young'uns." Harley clapped his hands and whooped again and a few of the cows picked up their pace, thinking they'd be getting hay.

"I reckon I'll be thinning the herd considerably now. Beef prices are shit right now, but if I sell all but Red and a half dozen breeding heifers then I can sell most of my hay too." As the first of the cattle reached the gate, he and Burley started circling to the back of the herd to shoo the stragglers through. "It won't be near enough to pay the bank note for the seed and supplies, but maybe enough for me to buy an extension, keep them from foreclosing on me."

"Harl," Burley began, "it's been a good year for tobacco. I pretty near doubled my yield from last year…"

"No, Burl." Harley shook his head, trying to cut his friend off.

"Now hear me out, Harley. I can be just as stubborn as you can and I'm going to say this. I bought my seeds with cash this year. I don't owe anything on my crop and I expect I'll make enough at auction to bankroll some into savings."

"Burley, I appreciate what you're getting at, I really do. But …"

"Shut up and let me finish, will ya? Jeez, you're thick headed! I'm just saying, let me deposit it with you instead of the bank. Hell, I trust you more than I do them, especially after what happened in '29. You can give me some out of next year's crop, some the year after that. Whatever. I know you're good for it."

"I do appreciate it, Burley, you know I do. But I can't take your money. There's no guarantee there'll be a crop next year. Could be drought, could be mold. You know how risky farming is. If something happens you'll be needing that money. And besides, with this new government insurance on the banks there's no way you can lose it there."

"Just think it over. That's all I ask."

The last of the cows went through the gate and Harley swung it closed and dropped the latch.

"Thanks, Burl," he said, clamping an arm over his friend's shoulder. "Now come on, we'd best get back to the house. The commotion ought to be about over by now, and I need to talk to the boys. I know they're worried about Sara."

"How is she doing anyway?" Burley asked, falling in stroll with Harley. "It sounded like she's in pretty rough shape, the way Cy told it."

"She's banged up right smart, no doubt. She'll be laid up for a while, but Ben says she'll be fine. He had her knocked out on pills when I left. She was pretty tore up about losing her baby..."

"I saw you talking to Rig. She going to stay with them now?" Some of the cows were lowing behind them, disappointed at not being hayed.

"Seems that way. But I'd like to bring her back home with us. She's as close to a momma as Cassie has ever known. And the boys..." he paused, "...and we've all gotten attached to her."

"I'm sure you have. All of you. But, still, don't you think it'd be best for her to be with her family now? Rig and Clorise, I mean. How would you take care of her and the kids too?"

They walked, the both of them, looking straight ahead. Harley waited a long time before he answered.

"It just seems the fitting thing to do. We'd find a way. The boys have grown a lot since last spring. They're big enough to help. It'll be hard for them to understand if she doesn't come ho... If she doesn't come back."

Now it was Burley's turn to wait before answering. As they walked, Harley could feel Burley chewing the silence like the cows chewed on their cud behind them. When he finally spoke, his words came slow and measured, as if he was being careful not to spill any.

"We're best friends, aren't we? You and me?" He didn't even have to wait for an answer; he wasn't looking for one. They both knew. "And best friends owe it to one another to speak their minds to one another, right?" Again, it was rhetorical, but Harley nodded anyway.

"Yep," he said, walking on.

"There's been a lot of talk around, ever since Sara got here. I know you've got wind of some of it." Burley bent and picked a stalk of broom sage and put it between his teeth without losing pace. "Not that I believe any of it. But you know how some folks are; they'll talk about anything, if for no reason other than to hear their own smug little voices. Not that it makes them right, or even worth listening to.

But some folks just have a habit of it." He waited a few seconds to let it soak in before going on.

"There was always a reason for her being here, before. She was here to help out. But now, well... Now, she'd just be another burden to you. And Lord knows, you, of all people don't need any more burden." They were coming in sight of the house now, a couple of the wagons and one of the cars were already gone; things were beginning to look a little more normal again. Burley stopped walking and waited the four of five paces Harley took before he stopped and looked back. The two friends fixed eyes on one another before Harley said:

"It ain't like that, Burl. We... I owe it to her." Then he turned away first. "You don't understand..."

"Maybe I don't, Harley. I know you want to pay her back. But am I making sense here?" Burley asked. "She needs to be with her own now, doesn't she?"

Harley started walking again, and Burley started after him, staying just close enough to hear the whisper.

"I reckon so."

Burley had never seen such slouch in his friend's shoulders before.

Chapter 17

"Come on, Pa! We're ready to go!"

Harley hurriedly bagged the last of the sandwiches he'd made for lunch.

"Okay, okay, I'm coming already. Hold your horses." He picked up the bag and the jug of tea he'd made earlier and surveyed the kitchen, making sure he hadn't forgotten anything. He went through the front of the house and saw the kids squirming in the wagon out front, and Bess squirming in her harness in front of them, looking nervously around at the prospect of being driven by such an anxious bunch. He amended, "Hold your horse, I mean."

"Finally!" Bert said when he saw his daddy coming out the front door. "It's about time. We've been waiting forever," he whined, his eagerness to get underway overwhelming any fear of being called down for sassing. And he was right. It never occurred to Harley to take exception to such talk today; it only made him step quicker. The boys had made it unanimously clear last night that they would see Sara today, as soon as possible. Not that Harley needed any convincing; he hadn't even pretended to argue otherwise. He knew that he was going anyway and the force of their adamancy, their demand to go along, only reinforced the decision he'd made, only made him prouder of them. Like any father, he'd always thought they were all special, each in his own way. But in this morning's light, he felt it even more so. The halo of unconditional love that he'd always seen around them was enhanced by a new glow — the glow that usually comes so hard, so painstakingly, and so much later in the lives of parents and their children — the glow of respect. Respect for who they are and what they are; individuals, each worthy of the love heaped on them regardless. This was the glow of earned love, outshining love simply given because they were his offspring.

Harley leaned over the side of the wagon and put the sack of food and the jug of tea under the seat where Seth sat holding Cassie. Cy laid the reins down and started to climb to the back with Bert and Amos.

"Hold on, son," Harley stopped him. "Why don't you drive us today?"

"Sure, Pa!" Cy beamed, throwing a smirk at Seth as he sat back down, taking the reins back up.

"Oh, Pa, let me drive. Please?" Seth pleaded, looking down at his father.

"He wants me to drive, didn't you hear him?" Cy defended.

"You can drive us back home, Seth," Harley said, stepping up on the hub of the wheel and reaching for Cassie. He was able to suppress the groan that sprang from the pang in his side, but he couldn't hide the wince.

"Now give me my girl. You ride up here with your brother. We're going to ride in the back with Bert and Amie, where it's fun," he said, leaning down close to Cassie's face, returning her grin. "Ain't that right, little girl? We'll go back here where we can play, won't we?"

Cassie ga-ga-ed something that sounded like definite agreement.

"Oh, boy! Daddy's going to ride with us, Amos," Bert clapped. "Can we play slap-the-snake, Daddy?"

"Sure we can, Bertie," Harley said, settling in.

Cy looked back, making sure they were all set.

"Ready?" he asked.

"Let's go!" Amos answered.

Cy snapped the reins. "Hup, Bessie!" he called, and wagon lurched into motion.

Harley scooted himself over so he could lean against the back of the seat, crossing his legs Indian style, making a nest for Cassie.

"Come on, Daddy, I'll be snake first," said Bert sliding over to face Harley.

"I wanna play!" Amos whined.

"Hold on, boys. There'll be plenty of time to play. We've got to get your Sissie situated first. And don't worry, Amos, you'll get your turn." He was facing back toward the house as they made their way down the drive. It sure looked different with only a black smudge to the left of the yard where the barn should have been. There was a gap in the familiar picture, like one of the kid's mouths when they lost a tooth.

"Ready, Daddy?"

"Yeah, I'm ready now. But let's take it slow to start. We need to teach Cassie how to play, you think?"

Cassie squealed, once more in obvious agreement.

*

It was a bright, clear, day, and hot, but mid-eighties hot, not the nineties hot it had been for so long; and there was a bit of breeze blowing, pushing the humidity away. Fall was coming. Not here yet but definitely on its way.

They rode along chattering and laughing, unusually gay; partly at the prospect of seeing Sara, but also, Harley guessed, because they were all equally eager to let the bright sunshine chase away the weekend's nightmare.

They were perhaps three-quarters of the way to the Hall's before the novelty and excitement of the outing wore down and they settled into a calmer, quieter mode, still enjoying the ride and the day and each other, just a bit less exuberantly and a bit more peacefully, lulled by the steady clop of Bess's progress and the sun/shade dappling of the road. Then Seth brought it up, turning in his seat.

"Do you think Doctor Hall will let her come home today?"

"I wouldn't count on it, Seth." Harley hadn't gone into any details of his conversations with Clorise and Rig to the boys. And though Cy and Seth had a pretty good grasp of what had happened, they had instinctively spared asking too much around their little brothers. Bert and Amos still weren't clear on any of it. All they really knew was that they had been woken in the middle of the night by the flames, and that Sara was gone.

"Was it the fire that hurt Sssara, Daddy?" Amos asked.

"Yes, the fire hurt her a little bit, Amie. And some other things too. She just had an accident and she's got some boo-boos, but she'll be fine in a few days. Now why don't you and Bert play slap a while?"

"Okay," Amos said turning to Bert, satisfied enough at the answer.

"Me first, Bert!" It took so little to satisfy Amie.

He was the easiest one so far. Harley could see so much of Ellie in him. Day by day as he grew, he showed more and more of the heart and spirit of Ellie in him, even as his memory of his Momma and his questions about where she'd gone faded to dim flickers. Bert, he was different from the rest. Bert the wisher; Bert the dreamer. Bert

217

stood apart from the others somehow. Harley often thought that Bert would be the one, out of all the boys, who was most likely to make his mark on the world. Harley had his own secret wishes and dreams for little Bertie; that he might be the first Felts ever to make it to college. Harley had determined long ago to make every effort see they all had a chance to do just that.

Seth… He was so, so, Seth. So much like his mother that Harley sometimes thought he should have been their first daughter. Seth wore his heart on his sleeve, just like Ellie did, unashamed and proud to let the world see exactly what he was feeling, just like Ellie.

And then there was Cy… Harley knew that Cy would be the one to take over the farm, when the time came. Cy was as plain and sturdy as they come; salt of the earth, stubborn as a mule and as steadfast in his beliefs as Harley was. Cy knew 'right' and would not tolerate anything but.

All together they made as solid a team as ever there was. And now there was Cassie. Even as young as she was, Harley felt he knew her future. She was the binder. Her brothers already doted on her so much that it seemed as if she were already exercising her sway over them. Cassie would be the center; the compass; the heart of the family. Just like Ellie… had been.

Still was, even so.

"When do you think she might come home?" Cy asked, keeping his eyes fixed on the road ahead, trying to seem intent on his job of driving.

Satisfied that the younger boys were caught up in their game, Harley squirmed himself around to face the front.

"I'm not sure, son. It could be a while…"

"What do you mean, Pa?" Cy quit pretending and turned to face Harley with the same questioning look that Seth held.

"Well, it's likely she'll go to the Gambil's for a while. Until she has time to recuperate."

"The Gambil's?" Seth shot out. "She don't belong there. She needs to be home."

"Whoa, whoa. Wait a minute there, son. Sara's home is in Maryland. You forgetting that?"

He saw the same pained flash cross their faces that he felt crossing his own ears at hearing the words spoken out loud. It took two or three seconds for Seth to come back.

"That's not what I mean, Pa. You know what I mean…"

"Sure I do, Seth. I absolutely do know what you mean." Cassie reached her arms out high and wide then, yawning so mightily it made her shiver in Harley's arms when she cut it off.

"Reach under there and hand me a bottle out of the lunch sack, will you?" Harley asked Seth, grateful for something to distract his eyes from the two pairs of the boys' eyes that looked so hard at him.

"Oh great. We're nearly there and now she wants to go to sleep," Cy said, turning back to face forward again.

"But, Pa." Seth started, then paused, his eyes trailing off with the same tone of distant study that his voice carried. "She'll be back, right?"

Harley fussed way more than he needed to, settling Cassie and her bottle in his lap, focusing so much attention on her that he didn't even have to look up when he answered.

"I don't know, son. I reckon you'll have to ask Sara about that. I can't answer for her on that."

If Harley had been looking, he'd have seen a bit of relief in Seth's face before he turned around and leaned back in his seat.

"We're here," Cy announced. "There's the Hall's mailbox, right up ahead."

"Oh, boy!" Amos cried, jumping up. "Thera!"

"Sit back down, son," Harley said quietly. "You'll get yourself hurt, getting all excited like that."

"Oh, boy!" Amos exclaimed again, as he obeyed and sat. "Sssss-Ara!"

Cy had called it right. They were no more in sight of the Hall's house when Cassie let the nipple of the bottle slip out of her mouth, and fell asleep. And she made it squallingly plain that she didn't like the jostling she got when Cy reined up. Harley struggled to his feet as gingerly as he could, trying as hard not to disturb his baby's sleep as he was trying not to arouse another stab in his rib cage — though failing equally at both.

Before Harley even got his feet on the ground the boys were all tumbled out of the wagon and rumbling up the front steps. He and Cassie would have been left behind in the yard if Olivia Hall hadn't stepped through her front door just then, wiping her hands on her yellow-flowered apron, admonishing the boys.

"Ya'll quieten down now. Sara's sleeping," she hushed. She paused long enough to give Cy and Seth a quick hug before she started down the steps, rubbing the tops of Bert and Amos' hair as she went to the yard. Seeing Harley struggling down from the wagon with Cassie screaming in his arms she added, "and get over there and help your daddy with that baby." She knew them well enough, and they her, to know her fussing for what it really was. They all respected her lead and followed, quieting behind her.

"Lord, I've seen every one of you boys come into this world, and I've seen how you've been raised, and it was a durn sight better than you're all showing right now." Though Harley was the only one who could see the smile on her face, he had no doubt the boys could hear it beyond her mock-stern words.

"Hello, Harley," she said, taking Cassie from him with one arm, hugging his waist with the other. "How are you?"

"Hello, Liv," he said hugging back, gently. "I'm fine."

She turned her face up to his without letting go.

"Really. I am." He repeated.

She held him a second longer before releasing him.

"Well, we'll see what Ben has to say about that," she smiled, more satisfied by the answer in his eyes than his words. "Now, where's this baby's bottle?" She asked, turning her attention to Cassie, who was quickly soothing at the feminine voice that held her now.

"It's up here," Bert volunteered, climbing back into the wagon. "I'll get it for you, Mrs. Hall!"

"Why thank you, Bertram. You are the gentleman I thought you to be after all, aren't you?"

"Yes, Ma'am," he answered, handing her Cassie's bottle as he beamed proudly back at his brothers, who were gathering unsure around.

"When can we see Sara?" Seth asked first.

"I can't tell you that, Seth. That's up to Doctor Hall," Olivia said, managing to cuddle and feed Cassie in one arm while crooking Harley's elbow in her other — displaying the singular talent that mothers have of seeming to do three things at once with only two hands.

"He's tending to her now," she said quietly to Harley as she led him up the steps with Cassie sinking hungrily sleepy into her breast. Then she raised her voice again to speak to all.

"But I'm certain he'll want to see your daddy next. And I need to get your sister fed and napped. Why don't you all find a game to play out here until we call you? Or I could find some chores that need doing…"

"That's okay, Mrs. Hall. We'll be okay."

Olivia winked at Harley and closed the door on the answer.

"Works every time," she said, nuzzling Cassie close to her face and leading Harley in the door.

The Hall's front parlor was dim after the bright sunshine. It was a very formal room with high wingback chairs in the corners and an ornate cherry hutch that served as a bookshelf along the back wall opposite the front door, with a matching curio cabinet filled with antique medical instruments on the end wall. The polished pine floor was covered in the center of the room by a dark wool rug with a floral pattern similar to the fabric of the chairs and of the long settee that bisected the rug, facing the door and fronted by an equally long cherry coffee table. Despite Olivia's attempts to cozy the room up with intricate lace doilies on the arms and backs of the chairs and sofa, the abundance of seating still spoke 'waiting room'.

"Have a seat, Harley, Ben'll be out in a minute. And now if you'll excuse me, I'm going to get this girl laid down where she can sleep in peace. It smells like she could use a fresh diaper too," she said, sniffing faintly, turning her attention back to Cassie.

"Did you make a stink, little girl? Have you pooped your pants?" she baby-talked out of the room. "Make yourself comfortable, Harley," she called over her shoulder as she disappeared down the hallway.

He took his hat off and hung it on the coat rack by the door, looking at the fancy furnishings around him. Instead of sitting, he went to the window and gazed out into the yard where the boys were already hard at play, scrambling up the low hanging, nearly horizontal limbs of the huge bodock tree that dominated the front lawn. Cy was just settling into a perch near the crown while Seth and Bert climbed up behind him. Poor little Amie was still struggling to pull himself onto the lowest branch that split off the trunk barely within his leaping reach. But it was too thick for his hands to find much purchase. Harley watched Amos kick his legs furiously under him until the commotion they made broke his grip and he fell; watched him spring back up to try again only to fall again, and jump back up to try again. That was the thing that stood out about Amos — his determination. Though he wasn't the fastest learner of the kids (that'd be Seth, no doubt), he was certainly the surest. Once he set his focus to something he wouldn't let go until he got it, with help or without. Ellie had seen it in him first (of course), and ever since the night she had pointed it out to Harley — the night Amos had come padding down the hall just in time to interrupt them preluding to lovemaking on the sofa in the front room and she'd gone and scooped him up, saying, "Baby, you're too young to be walking, let alone freeing yourself from the crib. You won't be denied, will you?"— Harley had seen it too.

But still and all, he leaned to the window screen and called, "Seth! Bert! Help your brother up. And see he doesn't fall."

"Okay, Pa," It was Seth, of course, who answered and started down to help Amie.

"You never stop looking out for them, do you?" Harley spun around, startled by the voice behind him. He hadn't heard Ben Hall come into the room.

"Always the daddy, huh, Harley?" Ben went on. "Now if only I could get you to take half as good care of yourself as you do of those children…" He'd obviously seen Harley's wince at the stab of pain in his breastbone at the sudden move.

"Hello, Ben. How's Sara doing?"

"She's fine. But right now I'm more interested in how you're doing," the doctor said, laying a hand on Harley's shoulder. Harley glanced out the window just in time to see Amos being pulled up by his brother. "They'll be fine. Come on back and let's have a look at you," Ben said, leading Harley down the hall.

Doc Hall had two 'examining rooms' — bedrooms actually, but with high hospital-type beds and a washstand and credenza for his instruments in each. The door to the first was shut. Harley tried to pause but Ben took him firmly on past into the next room.

"She in there?" Harley asked.

"Yeah, she's sleeping right now. Have a seat on the bed and take your shirt off."

Harley did as he was told and Ben began un-wrapping the bandage around Harley's chest.

"Will I get to see her?"

"Sure. You can peek in when we're done here," he said. "Hmmm, not as much bruising as I expected." He held the stethoscope receiver to his mouth and exhaled slowly onto it before placing it on Harley's chest, but it was still cold enough to make Harley flinch. "Take a deep breath for me." Harley did while Ben listened. "Does it hurt when you do that?"

"Naw, not much."

Doc Hall chuckled as he removed the earpieces and let the stethoscope drop to his chest. "Naw, not much. As if you'd let on even if it was killing you. Fat lot of good you are. I'm just glad all my patients don't make me doctor in the dark like you do."

"It ain't too bad, really, Ben."

"I know, I know, Harley. I'd just hate to see what you call 'too bad'," he said, picking up a fresh roll of bandage. "I suspect that anything that qualified as that for you would have most folks needing Reverend Adams more than they'd need me. Now hold your arms up for me, will you? High as you can, without hurting too bad."

"How bad is she, Ben?"

"He cracked your sternum, that much I'm sure of, but I don't think he punctured a lung or anything like that. You're lucky there. You haven't coughed any blood have you?" He looked up at Harley long enough to see him shake his head and open his mouth to speak before he cut him off, going back to his wrapping. "I want to keep it wrapped for a week at least, as tight as you can stand it. That's about all I can do. That and tell you to *Take it easy*. Give it time to heal. I mean it, Harley. No work till I see you again, okay?"

"Ben…" Harley's tone was too serious to be denied any longer.

"She's pretty banged up. You know that as well as I do," Doctor Hall answered, going on with his work. "She's got a mean gash over her eye, and a real shiner to go with it. Mild to moderate concussion. Separated shoulder; sprained wrist. Maybe a fractured thumb. Two or three broken ribs — further back around her side than yours — not near as serious," he paused long enough to cast a pointed look at Harley before finishing his wrap and continuing. "Lots of bruises and abrasions. And several deep burns. Hand me that tape, will you, Harl?"

"Deep burns?" Harley asked, reaching for the roll of white tape on the table beside the bed. Doc Hall took the tape from Harley and began tearing it off in long strips, making a bigger show of hanging them on the rail of the bed than he needed.

"What do you mean, 'deep burns'?"

"I mean very deep, very localized burns," Ben answered, not waiting for the implications of what he'd said set in before he began winding tape over Harley's bandages. "Is this too tight?"

"No." It sounded more like a denial than an answer.

Once the bandages were secure, Ben sat down on the bed beside Harley, going from doctor to friend.

"And she lost the baby, of course. That's where the complications came from."

"Complications? What kind of complications, Ben?"

"Nothing too serious. Just a little bleeding we couldn't get stopped. That's why she's knocked out today, I had to do a little minor surgery on her this morning but I think we got it taken care of. She'll be fine, with a little rest. She's a strong girl. But I put her under pretty deep; she won't wake up and come to herself before morning at least." He paused, but Harley could tell he had more to say, so he said nothing back, waiting Ben out.

"She's been asking about you quite a lot. Both when she was awake and when she was pretty much out of it, if you know what I mean. Calling your name in her sleep and such." Ben waited for Harley to comment until it became clear that Harley wasn't going to. "Oh well, it's none of my business anyway," he said standing up, getting back to doctoring. "Let's have a look at that neck, then I'll be done with you." He pulled the gauze off the puncture wound the pitchfork had made just below Harley's Adam's apple. "One more thing though... She wouldn't let me anesthetize her until I promised her I'd talk to you about it if you came by today. She can be one stubborn girl when she gets her mind set to something," he leaned close, looking hard at Harley's neck, touching his fingers gingerly on either side of the hole, "Sure enough is infected. I expected that, considering where that fork's been. I'm going to give you some cream to take with you. I want you to put it on this twice a day, and keep a clean bandage on it."

"What, Ben?"

"How long has it been since you had a tetanus shot, Harley? Do you remember?" he asked as he daubed antiseptic cream gently on Harley's neck.

"Talk to me about what?"

Doc Hall concentrated on smoothing the cream over the wound and cutting a fresh piece of gauze to cover it.

"Her baby," he said almost absently, tearing a piece of tape off with his teeth. "She talked to Liv about it some before she even brought it up to me. Just between me and you, I think she was kind of afraid to ask you herself anyway. She wasn't sure if she should or not." He was taking great pains to place the bandage just so, pressing the tape firmly around it. Stalling.

"Will you quit fussing over that scratch and just spit it out, Ben?"

Ben stopped and looked straight at Harley.

"She wants to know if she can bury the baby on your place. Next to Ellie." Harley had known Ben Hall all of their lives and he'd never seen so much as a trace of awkwardness in the man before. As Harley let the thought roll around his mind, Ben turned and began straightening the room. "She said it's as close to a home as her baby girl ever came to knowing." As he put the last of the supplies into the credenza and closed the drawer, he turned back. "She said to tell you she'd understand if you'd rather not."

"Where is it now?" The words sounded cold and flat, said aloud. "She, I mean."

"In the fruit cellar. Olivia insisted on dressing her and laying her in one of her cedar chests. It's not a proper coffin by any means, but it works. Listen, Harley, we can take care of…"

"Nonsense, Ben. We'll take her with us when we leave today… Did Sara name her?"

"Yes, she did. Hope. She told Olivia that she'd picked that name out months ago."

"Hope," Harley repeated, "That's a nice name…" His words hung in the room, blending with the cries of the children playing outside until Ben broke the spell.

"Now you just sit tight for a minute," he said going to the door and opening it. "I'm going to have Liv give you a tetanus booster while I go check on Sara. She'll show you in as soon as she gets done with you."

"Okay," Harley answered as the door closed softly behind the doctor.

It wasn't long before the door opened again and Olivia came bustling into the room, flooding it matter-of-factly with her energy.

"That girl, that girl," she said, holding a hypodermic up against the light of the window. "You'll have your hands full with that one, mark my word," she continued, thumping at the syringe with her index finger. "I finally got her to sleep, but boy did she fight it. She doesn't want to miss a thing. She'll do just fine in a house full of males. She'll hold her own." She glanced a smile in Harley's direction, then squinted back at the needle. "I dare say you all had best watch out for her; she'll have the lot of you wrapped around her fingers before you know it, Cassie will..." she said. She squeezed the plunger until a drop formed at the needle tip and she was satisfied. "Roll up your sleeve."

Harley did, while she tipped a bottle of alcohol over a cotton ball.

"Ben tells me you're going to take her baby and bury it at your place."

"Yep. Seems like the thing to do."

"It is, Harley. It absolutely is the right thing to do." She didn't look up as she swabbed the sterile, cold, alcohol onto his biceps, going on: "You learn a lot about people when they're hurting. They say a lot of things in that ozone between asleep and awake. I've spent a lot of time with Sara in the last day or two... This might sting a bit, try not to tense on me," she said as she drove the needle home and began slowly plunging the medicine into him. "Ben's heard a bit of it too; the babbling part. But she talked to me a couple of times when she was full awake."

She glanced up at him, knowing him well enough not to expect to catch his eyes in such a delicate subject, yet trying anyway, before going on. He remained focused on the progress of the emptying syringe.

"No details, mind you... All I know is that Sara loves you and the children very much. Very much.

"And that she is one scared, confused little girl herself." She put the swab over his arm where the needle pierced before pulling it out.

"I don't know the answer Harley, any more than you do. I don't pretend to…" she said, turning away from him as she pulled the needle free of the syringe and dropped it into a stainless-steel sterilizer. "But I do know one thing… You deserve it. All of you. Every last one of you. Don't listen to Ben, or anyone else," she paused washing the instruments enough to barely turn.

"Heckfire, listen to me, telling you to not even listen to me." She went back to her sterilizing. "You know what I'm saying."

He nodded, not sure at first if it was her or him that said it. Or either.

"Listen to your heart."

They looked at one another, long and steady, he and Olivia, as she wiped her hands against each other, then on her apron, until she said, "Come on, I'll take you to see her."

Sara looked bad, worse than he'd expected. Her upper left cheek had swollen her eye to a slit. She was pale and her breathing was ragged. Harley would have thought her dead if not for the heave and sink of her chest and the rattle of her lungs. Her hair clung damp and matted to her head, though it was obvious that either she or Olivia had made some attempt to brush some of the tangles out of it. Ben was holding her wrist in one hand and a pocket watch in the other, counting her pulse. He ignored Harley for a few seconds before laying her arm gently to her side and turning. "She's doing fine," he said.

Harley stood just inside the door, halted there by her appearance and by the queasiness that welled up in his stomach; whether from the shot he just gotten or the shock he just had.

Dr. Hall walked over to Harley, put a hand on his shoulder, led him to the bedside. "Talk to her, let her hear your voice. I firmly believe that even under the anesthesia she can hear you. It always helps patients to know that folks that care about them are close by."

"How long will you keep her here?" Harley asked, keeping his gaze on Sara.

"Depends. I'll examine her tomorrow. If she wakes up alert and there's no sign of bleeding then I've done about all I can do at this point. Sara and time will have to do the rest of the healing. She'll

definitely have to stay off her feet as much as possible for a while."
He paused just long enough to punctuate what he'd said. "I'll leave
you with her for a bit." He walked to the door and paused again, his
hand on the knob, "Should I have Cy or Seth help me go ahead and
load the… uhhh… chest?"

Harley looked up, pulled from Sara's frailty by the question.

"No, Ben, I don't think so," he began, studying how he was
going to handle the logistics of the situation. He didn't want his
children handling such cargo until he'd had time to explain things to
them in his own way, in his own time.

"They all came here hell bent and determined to see Sara
today. But seeing her like this… I don't think I want the little ones to
see her today. Like this. But Cy and Seth… That's another matter
altogether…" Sara coughed weakly from her sleep. It sounded wet
and gargled to Harley but Ben seemed unconcerned by it so he went
on. "They can handle it. They've earned it. I know I wouldn't want to
be the one to deny them, and even though I know you could without
starting another Great War like I would if I tried, I won't ask you to
do that."

"Thank God and you for small favors," Ben chuckled, wiping
his brow in exaggerated relief. Seeing the grin he'd drawn from
Harley he knew he had just practiced his best medicine of the day.
He'd learned early on that there is nothing quite so infectious or
nearly so curative as a smile.

"But…?"

"What makes you think there's a 'but'?"

"There's always a 'but' behind a reprieve, isn't there?"

"Yeah, yeah, yeah… You're the doctor." Harley felt suddenly
hot and flushed and he wondered if he really was having a reaction to
the shot.

"Yes, I am. But…?"

"Okay, you win. But, if you could figure a way to distract Bert
and Amie long enough to let Cy and Seth come take a peek… Let her
hear their voices, like you said…"

But the door was already shut, and Ben Hall was already gone,
leaving Harley suddenly alone to wonder whether the echo of the
word 'Done' had been left in the room or had simply sprung into his
mind. Leaving him to wonder whose shadow it was that lay on the

bed beside him — to wonder what he'd heard or seen and what he'd imagined in his swimming thoughts.

He sat on the edge of the bed, and when he covered her forehead with his palm, he saw her eyelids tighten, then relax. He pushed a strand of hair away from the corner of her eye, and she let out something like a sigh. She was responding. She was alive. He leaned over, ever so slowly, ever so gently; closing his eyes just as his lips brushed hers. And though they made no sound, he knew the movement well enough; heard his name on her lips, as he'd heard it silently so many times before.

So he answered automatically, as he had so many times before.

"Ellie."

Her forehead tightened. Her eyelids clinched and she turned her head and began coughing, spitting up. Behind them, a door opened.

"Pa?"

Harley was sick before he could get out of the room.

Chapter 18

The earth was packed and hard, baked almost to powder by the long, fierce summer sun and the dry beginning of fall. For most of the first foot down it raised little brown clouds of dust every time Cy cleared the shovel, but gradually as he worked, it began to lose its pale beige color, darkening to hues of chocolate milk, then of coffee, and the digging grew easier. And it was a small hole, after all.

He wondered how deep he ought to make it, thinking at first that since it was only about half the size the one next to it had been that it only need be half as deep. But remembering the height of the chest he and Pa had carried to the cave and set among the last remnants of ice there, he finally reckoned he should go at least shoulder deep, to get enough cover. It seemed proper cover was the main thing, more so than depth.

It was hot, unseasonably hot for this time of year, but when he paused and sat, wiping the sweat from his brow and dangling his legs into the grave, it was from the weary more so than from the work or the heat. Laying the shovel aside, he put his hands into the grass behind him as he arched his back and closed his eyes into the strong morning sun. Feeling it; hearing it; letting it in.

He saw the stone before his eyes a half second before opening them, before speaking a quarter-second later.

"Momma…"

He waited long enough to hear the answer that he knew wasn't coming before he drew his feet up and went to her.

"Momma…"

The stone felt warm on his back, from the heat of sunshine it held or from the expectations he held. Either way, it was warm. No matter. He closed his eyes — squeezed them almost tight enough — waiting, giving her a chance before he went on, hoping he wouldn't have to go on even as he knew he would, even as he knew she wouldn't answer for him or to him, until finally he went on.

"I miss…"

His voice echoed back and forth through his head, reverberating so very many sleepless nights of thoughts, here on the hill where the sunlight and the faintest hint of breeze stole the words gale-force from his mouth.

"We miss you, Momma," he amended, growing used to, and more comfortable with the sound of his voice.

"But we're doing okay. Really. All of us.

"I finished that arithmetic book you gave me last Christmas. Every problem. Maybe not right, every single one, but most of 'em. I know I got most of 'em right. I passed sixth grade and'll be going to seventh next week at the town school across the river, just like you wanted." He waited a second or two, before going on. "Seth's done pretty good himself, too. Miss Joyce skipped him right over fifth and has got him starting sixth this year."

And before the words, finally spoken, had time to trail away he heard the call, rising up the hill behind him.

"Cy?"

He gave no answer, except to scramble up and renew his work, wanting to be caught busy at his task; wanting not to be caught wisting. He was back hard to it by the time he felt the presence shadow over him.

"Can I spell you a bit?"

"No, Pa," he said without turning, bending so deeply intent at shaving the sides of the hole to the most purely vertical planes imaginable that it would have been impossible to hear the faint exhalation of breath above him, or to imagine such a slight sound to be a sigh, without an ear cocked for such.

"I'm almost done," he said.

Harley stood and watched his son work for a long time, without word from either of them. It seemed all too familiar.

They buried Hope the next day, without much pomp or ceremony. Cy led what little service there was. He seemed bound to do so, and Harley had neither the heart nor the voice to have it any different. They walked the box up the hill; Cy and Seth did, with Bert and Amos in close tow, while Harley lagged behind, carrying Cassie. The kids had Olivia's chest lowered into the grave by the time he got there. They stood, his four sons, one to a corner, looking silently down at the rounded-up cedar lid below. Harley stopped six or seven paces short of them and pulled Cassie upright to his neck. Without any signal except his presence, Cy and Seth took up shovels and began moving the mound of dirt from beside the hole back into its rightful place. The first dozen or so blade-fulls made a terribly horrible hollow sound as they landed, reverberating across the hilltop. But after that, the sound of the falling dirt timbered into soft thuds, almost comforting, in a gentler sort of way.

No one spoke, or even caught another's eye until the pile was complete, moved back over the spot of earth from which it had been removed. Then the sudden silence of cessation assailed them all. When it became apparent that Harley was not about to step up, Cy did. He dropped his head in prayer and everyone else followed suit.

"Here's a baby girl for you, Ma. Like you always wanted."

The only sound that came back was Cassie's sigh as she settled under her daddy's chin, peacefully.

"Take good care of her," Cy said. "Her name is Hope."

And that was the end of it.

*

Harley saw it almost as soon as they started for the house, Burley's roan mare grazing at the long grass that plumed under the short picket fence that defined their yard, but no one else noticed until they were going through the second stock gate. They were well off the hill and into the flat when Bert saw it too and cried out.

"Pooh Bear's hitched at the house! Mr. White's here!" Just as he said it, Burley stepped around the far corner of the house, pulling up the zipper of his overalls. Bert took off in a run, waving his arms.

"Woo-hooo! Mr. White!"

Burley had always been like a favorite uncle, or more rightly a second father, to all the boys. He usually brought them some little treat like hard candy or such when he visited. But Burley and Bert had always had a special relationship. Burley always went out of his way to pay extra attention to Bertie, slipping him an extra piece of candy when the others weren't looking, or trying to make sure Bert's fishing line was cast in just the right spot to help his chances of catching the big one.

"Bert's a middle child," he'd told Harley once, "Cy and Seth are close enough in age to be friends for each other and Amos is the baby, the one who gets all the fuss. It's easy for a middle one like Bertie to get lost in the mix — to feel overlooked, if you know what I mean."

Hearing the cry, Burley looked up, waved, and began ambling his big frame toward the yard gate. He reached it just as Bert burst through. He scooped the child up in his arms and continued on to meet the rest of them while he whispered conspiratorially in Bert's ear. Bert turned and looked back in their direction and giggled.

"Guys, how about getting your feeding done while me and Cassie go pry Bert off of Burley."

"Okay, Pa."

"And take Amos with you. It's time he starts learning the routine, ya think?"

"Yeah, Pa," said Seth, taking Amos' hand in his. "Hey, Mr. White!" he waved with the other as he veered off behind Cy toward the stock barn, with Amie in tow.

"Howdy, fellers," Burley called back. He set Bert down as he closed the last few yards between them. Harley saw him slip something into the boy's hand as he did. "Hold up a sec, guys," He called to the other boys. "I got ya'll a little something to help with the chores."

He squatted on his haunches and held his fists out at arm's length as the boys reversed courses and ringed around him. He asked them each in turn, "Right or left?" before dropping something from the thick meaty hand of their choice into the cupped palms that waited below.

"Thanks, Mr. White!"

"Thanks, Mr. White!"

"Yeah! Fanks, Mista Wite!"

Bert giggled again and Burley winked at him as he stood up, wiping his hands on his overalls.

"You got your treats. Now get on," Harley smiled. "We'll see you at the house in a few minutes."

They turned almost as one and started away, his sons did.

"Not you, Bertie. Amos can take your turn today. Cassie's getting awfully heavy on your old Pa. Reckon you can carry her to the house for me?"

"Sure, Daddy!"

Harley bent down and handed the baby gingerly over to her brother.

"Keep her head up and watch your step. That's precious cargo you're handling there."

"I know, Pa. I will."

Cassie gooed softly as she settled into her new charge, then grinned when Bert rubbed his nose to hers and said, "I got you, Sissy. Bert'll take good care of his Sissy."

Harley watched the others going away for a second or two before he turned to Burley and put his hand out for a shake. He knew his friend well enough to know what a stickler he was for a handshake – or a 'manshake' —as Burley had named it to every one of Harley's boys.

"A lot of folks don't get how important a 'manshake' is," he'd taught.

"You can tell a world of things about someone by how they shake hands, stranger and friend alike. There's two parts to it. The hand is one; you gotta be firm and strong with your hand when you take another's. Grip him like you mean it, firm and tight, without trying to show off, without turning it into some kind of squeezing contest to see who's strongest. But far and away, the most important part is right here…" at which point Burley would lean close into his pupil's face and hold the first two fingers of his left hand – his free hand – in a V and move them back and forth between his eyes and theirs. "The eyes. You can see it all in the eyes. Never let go of a man's hand before he lets go of your eyes. Never trust a man who doesn't look you in the eye when he shakes your hand. Always look a man in the eye. You can tell it all by looking a man in the eye. Friend and foe alike."

It was a good lesson for boys to learn, and God bless Burley for drilling it into the kids so early and so adamantly. And not exactly goddamn him for practicing so well what he preached, Harley thought as his friend took his hand as he always did; not quite too firmly; shaking it just almost too vigorously; staring nearly too deeply. But yes, goddammit Burley, for once, just this once, can't you stay out of here?

"How goes it, Burl?"

"Finer than frog hair, Harl. You?"

"Gooder'n snuff." He dropped the grip, looked away and started after Bert and Cassie toward the house.

"Bullshit."

"Come on, I'll fix us some coffee."

He heard Burley hock and spit behind him, and murmur again.

"Like bullshit."

Within two paces Burley was at his side.

"I know what you need, and it ain't coffee. You can't bullshit no bullshitter," he said, taking hold of Harley's elbow. "I brung us a jug. I know what you need."

Harley didn't say anything, he just went along. When they reached the house and Burley steered him onto the front porch and handed him the jug that he'd brought Harley went along with that too. He took it and drank, surprised at what a hard pull he took from it. He handed it to Burley who took an equally long pull and handed it back. They repeated the procedure without a word or even a glance at one another. They knew each other that well, were that comfortable together. Silence was enough. Silence was plenty. It takes a long time to get to know somebody that well.

Before Burley could offer the jug back Harley sat down on the top step and began loosening his bootlaces. Staring across the same field, Burley joined him, setting the jug between them.

"Pa! She's pooped herself!" Bert called from inside.

"Well change her then," Harley answered. "And fix her a bottle too. She changes a whole lot easier with a bottle."

"Paaaw..." Bert whined in protest.

"Would you rather me do it, and you go do chores with your brothers?" Harley winked at Burley, knowing what the answer would be.

"No, that's okay, I'll do it."

"Damn, you do handle 'em well, boy," Burley winked back, taking the jug up. "You do know your stuff there, I've got to admit." He took a quick swig and handed it over to Harley, who took it and put it into his lap, knowing Burley wouldn't drink more until he had. And it was too early for Harley to take another drink just yet.

"Ewwwww..." They heard from Bert, and they both smiled at that.

Harley knew something was coming from Burley, but he wasn't sure what it was, so he went on and took his swig and handed the jug back, and when Burley set it back on the porch between them without drinking, he knew it was coming.

"I know what you need, Harl..."

"Oh, do you now?" Harley said, tempted to pick the jug back up.

"Yep. I sure do. I know exactly."

"And what, in your great wisdom, might that be?"

Burley picked the jug up and swallowed, wiped his mouth with his sleeve and let out a slow "Ahhhh," before he went on.

"You need the fish camp, is what you need."

There it was. He was relieved. It was less than he'd expected.

"You think so, do you?"

"I know so."

"Well, that ought to solve everything."

"Damn straight it will. The biggest part of it anyway."

"You think so?"

"I know so. Told you I knew what you need, didn't I?"

"Yeah, it sounded like you said something like that."

"You heard right."

"Sure would be nice if you knew what you were talking about, at least every once in a while."

Burley turned toward Harley and dropped his tone a notch.

"Seriously, Harley. Let's do it. I got it all worked out. Tom said he'd go, and Paulie's up for it too, if he can put it to Maude right. I talked to Anna Mae and she said she'd come stay with the kids."

"Oh? Been talking to Anna Mae have you? Again? Seems to be gettin' a regular thing, eh, Burl?"

"Don't go trying to off-track me here, Harley. We can leave in the morning and be back Sunday evening. Doesn't school start back next week? This'll be our last chance for a while. Come on, it'll do us all good."

"I don't know, Burley. I've got to go to town this afternoon and talk to Jimbo."

"I know, Harley, that's why I'm here, remember? To keep an eye on the kids while you go."

"And they're having a fit about me not taking them. They don't know what's going on with…"

"I know, Harley! Hello? You hearing me?"

"I don't know either. I've got to figure out what's…"

Burley leaned close and snapped his fingers under Harley's nose.

"Wake up, pard. Quit talking to yourself in front of me, will ya? Go talk to Jimbo. Go see Sara. And by the time you get home I'll have your shit packed and ready to go. I'll drop Anna Mae off by dawn tomorrow and we'll head to camp."

"But she might..." Harley trailed off, realizing what he was on the verge of saying.

Burley waited quietly a half-minute before he spat, picked up the jug and handed it to Harley.

"Here. Have a drink." But he didn't let go of it when Harley reached and took hold of it, he held onto it until Harley looked up at him. Then he held Harley's eyes as firmly as he held the jug.

"Might what, Harl?"

Burley outwaited him, not dropping his grip from the jug until a split second after Harley dropped his eyes.

"Never mind," said Harley. Then he took his hardest, longest pull yet.

*

He went to town first, resisting the urge to turn toward the Hall's as he drew up on the crossroads – a decision made harder still by Bess when she tried to turn that way. She was a much better draft horse than she was saddle horse. It seemed the lighter her load the more headstrong she was. She didn't turn the first time he pulled her reins left, and if she hadn't turned on the second pull, he would probably have let her have her way. But she did, with a loud snort, and Harley caught himself wondering whether he was really glad she'd given in so easily. He leaned forward far enough to scratch behind her half-cocked ear and whisper into it, "Business first. Right Girl?" He ran his hand scratching and patting its way up the underside of her neck — knowing that was her weak spot — as he drew himself back up into the saddle, thanking her for not making the decision any harder. Then he kicked her into a trot toward the river.

The ferry was on the far bank, docked and empty, when he reached the landing. Harley dismounted Bess and draped the reins over her neck, looping them around the pommel so she could go drink and graze while they waited.

Though Jeremiah was dependable, running the ferry seven days a week, sunup to sundown, he was not at all regular. He kept no schedule except his own, or whatever the fares demanded. And though it was well past lunch time, by most reckonings, Harley knew that Jeremiah was sometimes prone to taking 'extended breaks', spent mostly at the Hog's Head. So he didn't bother ringing the big cast iron signal bell that was mounted atop a cedar post at the end of the loading pier. He had time to kill; something he was not used to having; something he normally did not welcome, nor do well. But this was no normal time. He welcomed the chance and valued it far beyond those who take such for granted. Just as he valued the river and loved the simple act of sitting near it, dangling his feet in it, watching it flow past, feeling its tug on his toes. Just as those who lived beside it rarely even gave a second thought to the current at their feet.

He unsaddled and unbridled Bess and she followed him to the low mud-flat bank upstream of the landing. She waited while he took off his boots and socks before she plunged her nose into the water beside his feet, as grateful for the easing wet as he was.

He laid there for a long time, an hour or more. It was at least that long, he knew, because for most of that time he was awake; feeling the sun-cracked mud soften and mold into his back; feeling the tickle of shad minnows nibbling along his feet; feeling Bess's exuberance and exhilaration with the water — splashing and bubbling, first on one side of him, then on the other. But maybe it was longer than that. He wasn't sure because somewhere in there he napped, lulled away from the day by the heat of the sun on his face and the cool of the river over his legs. Wasn't sure because he so rarely napped during daylight. He wasn't even sure he had napped at all. But he was pretty sure he had, because he'd never seen such flocks of birds before. Long-legged, long-necked, wide-winged birds swarmed all around him. He could have believed that they were real and not dreamed, but for their vivid colors — pink and lime-green and chartreuse. If they hadn't all flown and waded in such alien, kaleidoscopic pastels, he might have convinced himself that they were real, rather than idle vision. And if they hadn't seemed real enough to confuse him, he might have laid back and tried to summon them again instead of jerking awake and standing up so abruptly that he startled poor Bess out of the water. And he might not have gone and rung the signal bell so violently.

It didn't do any good of course, as far as fetching Jeremiah any quicker. Harley knew the little boatman was comfortably beyond earshot of the bell, yet he pulled away. Even though every clang split between Harley's ears like a new ax through seasoned wood, he pulled away. Maybe it did help. If nothing else, it scared the birds away, so he kept ringing, right up until he saw the dark little figure come scurrying down Commerce Street, up the ramp and onto the ferry. He rang and rang until the little figure across the river untied the ferry and started in his direction; he rang until he realized Bess was snorting and pawing angrily on the road behind him. And then, finally, he quit, sat down, and waited as the sudden silence rang awesome in his ears.

It was plain enough to Jeremiah that Harley was in a mood. He'd ferried folks back and forth from one bank to the other long enough to know when someone was in a mood or not. All the rest of ferrying — the piloting, the docking, the judging of the ever-changing currents, came easy to him because he understood the river. The river was the river. It was the moods that had taken him so long to learn, partly because he so loved to talk, to hear the sound of his own voice, and partly because folks were so different. Not only different from one another, but also different from one trip to the next, back and forth. Same folks every time, but they carried different water every time, just like the river. He knew the river from the start; he could feel its ebb and flow, its rise and fall. That part came to him naturally. But it taken him a long time to recognize his fares for what they were. It had taken him years to see them in terms he understood, each a river of their own, ebbing and flowing and rising and falling according to the weather of their own lives. Once he got that, he went from liking the ferry business to loving it. He'd always loved the river because he'd always known it, was born into it. He lived on the surface, but he could feel every bump and dip of its bed under his feet, every stream and trough of its water. And somewhere, atop the water, gradually and without a namable flash point, he realized that the people he carried were no different than the river they crossed. Their names stayed the same and they all flowed within their own well-defined banks, so you knew them, but the water between their banks was pushed downstream, renewed and replaced every second. Different water, same path.

Yep, Harley was in a mood all right. He was deep water today, slow current, and cold.

"Howdy, Harl" was the least he could say and the most he dared as he eased up to the landing.

Harley touched his thumb and forefinger to the brim of his hat and tilted his head forward a notch in a tipping motion.

"Afternoon, Jeremiah."

A bit too polite that, proving he'd sounded Harley right.

Jeremiah cut the engine and slid the ferry into the bank with a nod and a soft *cusshh,* then he went forward and began cranking the ramp down while Harley whistled his horse up.

Jeremiah stayed quiet as long as he could, waiting for Harley to start up the talk. But by the time they were half across and Harley still hadn't said a word, still leaned over the rail watching the wake roll by, Jeremiah figured he'd waited long enough, so he started it himself.

"You're going after her, ain't you?"

"Huh?" Harley looked up from the river, not quite sure if he'd heard what he thought he had.

"Good for you. Soon as she went across I figured I'd be seeing you today. Ole Jeremiah knows more than what most folks give him credit for…"

"Huh? What are you talking about?"

"I just knew it, that's all. And here you are, and I was right."

"Knew what, Jeremiah? What the hell are you talking about?"

"When the girl went across," said the little boatman, peering past the current ahead of them.

"Are you talking about Sara?"

"She looks pretty durn bad. She never got out of the car, but I seen enough. Ask me, them Mangrums got off easy, compared to what they done to her. If it'd been me, I'd a hung out 'em out to dry for a while. They got off easy enough, from what I've heard. But good riddance to bad rubbish is good enough, I reckon."

"You took Sara across? You've seen Sara?"

"Yeah. Early this morning. First run. Rig and his old lady went across first thing. That damn Packard of theirs really makes us ride low. Puts a hell of strain on my motor. I'm thinkin' I need to charge a premium for cars from now on."

Harley straightened up off the railing and turned full toward Jeremiah and almost let it out. If he'd found the words quicker he would have let it out, to the worst person he could possibly have let it out to. The old joke went through his head – "Telephone, telegraph, tell Jeremiah". He caught his breath and himself before he spoke. He turned back to the railing.

"How long ago?"

Jeremiah turned to look at Harley, scrunching his brow in thought.

"Oh… Mid-morning sometime. Two or three hours ago, at least." He turned back to the river, studying the current and the dock ahead, judging his angle of approach. "If you ask me, I'm glad you're going after her, no matter what folks say. I knew you would. But you'll have to hurry, you ain't got much time"

Harley didn't say anything, he stopped and gathered himself before 'I didn't ask anything,' came out, then he sat down on the starboard bench. It took a couple of minutes before the silence dawned on Jeremiah and he turned back to Harley. The little river rat had learned his trade well.

"You didn't know, did you?" he squinted.

"I'm on my way to see Jimbo."

"Damn, boy! You didn't know. I thought you knew. I knew you'd be coming but I figured it'd be 'cause you knew." He waited, looking at Harley with an expression of disbelief on his face, as if he'd seen a ghost, and as he out-waited Harley as it gradually clarified into an expression of disbelief in the fact that he'd been wrong.

"What do you mean 'I don't have long'?"

"Rig's taking her to Memphis to pick her folks up. They're coming to fetch her. Damn boy, I coulda sworn you knew. You really didn't know?"

"I'm on my way to see Jimbo," Harley said again. They both heard the lie, lying flat as the water, so they didn't say any more until they landed. Harley tied the ferry off and was mounted on Bess by the time Jeremiah got the ramp cranked down.

"Thanks," he said.

"Hurry," grinned the little boatman.

Rig and Clorise lived in a big Victorian house on Main Street, about a quarter mile beyond the business district. Rig was a trader at heart — a classic middleman — and the business of buying local commodities and shipping them out on the empty barges that brought outside goods he ordered on speculation had treated him well over the years. But the depression had hit him harder than most, and his house was beginning to show it. Past due for paint, past due for fence pickets, past due for shingles. Harley and everyone else knew that the past-dues on his house were the least of Rig's worries. As risky as farming was, at least it let a man rely on his own sweat, rather than someone else's.

He trotted Bess past the howdy's and waves of the folks downtown, trying to ignore the pace of his heart, which was considerably more than a trot. But as he topped the rise that hid Rig's house from view until you were suddenly there, and saw that the Packard wasn't sitting out front, he couldn't ignore the sinking in his chest. And though he wanted then to turn away and go back, he couldn't, having come this far.

He whoa'd Bess, got down from her and tied her beside the gate in the three-foot high fence that ringed the tiny front yard. Before he made it halfway up the walk, Clorise stepped out the front door to greet him.

"Well hello, Harley! What a nice surprise!"

"Hello, Clorise. How are you?"

"I'm fine. Just fine." She was wearing a full front apron over her plain cotton dress, with a red checked bandanna tied over her hair and a dust rag in her hand. Work clothes.

Harley took his hat off and stopped just inside the gate, six feet short of her, suddenly feeling very awkward. Clorise reached up and pulled the bandanna from her head and shook her hair loose as she put the hand with the dust rag behind her back.

"I was just getting ready for company, but I wasn't expecting any this soon," she said, trying at a smile.

Harley didn't know what to say. Didn't know why he hadn't turned around in the road. Didn't know why he'd stopped, while knowing exactly why.

"You just missed Rig and Sara," Clorise said. "They left not more than ten minutes ago…"

"I was just… In town. To see Jimbo," Harley stammered. He stepped back a half step back and put his hand atop the gate. "Just thought I'd stop by… To say hello."

Clorise brought the hand with the dust rag back out in front of her and began wringing it in her other.

Harley put his hat back on and swung the gate open behind him.

"Tell Rig I came by," he said, backing out.

"I will, Harley." She just stood there while he climbed onto Bess's back. "I'll tell them."

"Bye, Clorise," he said.

"Bye, Harley."

He kicked Bess away, hoping Clorise hadn't noticed the heat in his face or the burn in his eyes.

"Git up, girl," he said to his horse, knowing full well that she had.

Chapter 19

Burley was mostly right, as usual. Of the few things that Harley had ever been able to trust outside of his own voice inside his own head, Burley's voice was one. Burley was far more than neighbor, more than best friend; he was the closest thing to a brother Harley had. Burley White was Harley's sounding board, his anchor, and his compass. And though Harley rarely agreed with Burley's reasons, he never doubted the man's direction. Burley had never married, had never had children of his own, and so, could never really *get* it (the closest they ever came to spatting was when Harley tried using that phrase as argument), but Harley knew one thing about his friend. Burley was rarely wrong. He was usually right, for all the wrong reasons maybe, but right nonetheless. So the fish camp it was.

Camp was always tonic for Harley's soul. It was healing, soothing, clarifying medicine, and no one can ever overdose on that. Burley was right in thinking that was what Harley needed just now. He only missed by thinking it a solve rather than a salve.

It was still full dark when they left. Things went amazingly quick once Harley admitted he was going. Even though Burley and Anna Mae showed up a half-hour early, Harley was up and packed, ready to go when they got there. He liked roaming the house when it was dark and quiet, when he could hear every sigh and cough of his children safely dreaming. He liked tiptoeing his way around with only a candle for light; liked trying not to rattle the pot or cups when he fixed coffee; liked the creak of the floor under his feet — house-talk that could never be heard during the day, reserved for hours like this. This was the kind of quiet he liked. Most nights he hated the quiet, because most nights he was in bed alone with it, fighting to go to sleep before all the voices and doubts and images in his head filled up the quiet and chased it away. But when he was up and busy, moving around in it, his head stayed quiet for a change. He heard the rhythmic clop of the horses from a hundred yards down the driveway, telling him that Burley and Anna were early. Hearing it, he drew the sooty glass chimney from the lamp on the kitchen table and touched the flame of the candle to its wick, waiting long enough to make sure the fire took and had been safely passed along before blowing the candle out and going out to the porch to greet his friends. He liked it all.

They sounded almost to the gate by the time he stepped out. He had to trust his ears because what little moon there had been had long since set, and the light he held pretty much blinded him beyond the feeble yellow circle that it spread around him. He set the lamp on the porch and stepped into the yard just far enough to escape its glow, giving his eyes a chance to adjust to the dark. He heard that they were still far enough away to not be able to hear him unless he raised his voice loud to maybe wake the children, yet close enough that he had no doubt they could see him. He waved at them, and once the light was behind him he could see them wave back, riding side by side, not talking. Anna Mae on Pooh Bear, Burley's usual mount, and Burley on Juniper, the small, skittish paint that Harley would ride to camp. They would leave Bess here so the boys would have a ride in case of emergency.

He was waiting for them when they stopped at the gate, touching his cap and tipping it to Anna as he offered a hand to help her down.

"Good morning, Miss Anna."

"Good morning, Harley," she answered, taking his hand as she dismounted.

"I sure do appreciate your doing this for us."

"Oh, it's no problem at all, Harley. You know I love spending time with those darling children of yours. I'm happy to do it, truly I am."

"I know, Anna Mae, but I still thank…"

"Enough with the formalities," Burley cut in. "You ready to go, pard? Where's your gear?" He climbed down from Juniper and began untying Anna Mae's luggage from behind the saddle.

"It's on the porch, packed and ready."

"Well get it strapped on and let's get going. I told Tom and Paulie we'd meet 'em at the crossroads by first light." He started toward the house, lugging Anna Mae's bag at his side. "Jeez, Anna! What've you got in here? Bricks?"

"Now, Burley, you know ladies don't travel lightly," she teased back. Harley thought he saw her wink at Burley but it was hard to tell in the dim light.

"Where's she going to stay, Harl? Your room?"

"Pa?" They turned as the screen door spring stretched whiningly and Cy stepped onto the porch in his nightshirt, rubbing his eyes with his fists. He peered into the dark yard for a second then murmured "Good morning, Mr. White, Miss Anna," as the scene before him came into focus.

They both good-morning-ed back, then Harley said, "Morning, son. How about taking Miss Anna's bags to my room, will ya?"

"Don't worry about it, Cy, I got it," Burley said, starting up the steps to the house.

Cy stepped gingerly down the steps, walking tender-footed into the dew-covered grass. He let out a yawn that turned into a shiver as he reached the gate, then crossed his arms across his chest to hold out the cold and hold in the warmth, obviously not yet fully awake.

"When will ya'll be back, Pa?" he asked, yawning again.

"Sunday evening, like I told you."

"I wish I could go," said the boy, walking absently over to Juniper to rub and pat her flank. He always been taken by that horse — the Indian pony, he called her.

"I know. Maybe next time, son. We'll all go later this fall, I promise. But I need you here this time to stay and watch the house for me, right?"

Anna Mae stepped up and put an arm around Cy's shoulders. Harley saw his son draw his arms back across his chest in a motion that spoke 'I'm too old to be babied' to Harley, but was lost completely on Anna Mae.

"Oh, let those men go off and act silly on their own, Cy," Anna Mae said, dropping her hug. Maybe she had noticed it after all. "We'll have a big time here ourselves. I brought chocolate chips with me, and cracked walnuts. I can almost smell those tollhouse cookies baking already."

"Yes, Ma'am," said Cy, almost too politely, then he looked up at Harley, his eyes, his expression saying it all, asking one more time.

"Come on and help me with my stuff," Harley said in answer to the silent question. He turned to Anna Mae, offering his arm to her. "Come on in, Anna, make yourself at home. There's coffee brewing in the kitchen." She hooked her arm in his and they all walked to the porch.

Cy held the door for her and after she went in, he helped Harley pick up his packs, and they went to tie them onto Juniper. They worked quietly for a minute or two, intent on the task at hand, until Harley spoke.

"After your brothers get up and get their feeding done, I want ya'll to start stripping the boards off the back of the house."

Cy stopped in the middle of cinching Harley's bedroll on the side of the saddle. "But, Pa! What about the new rooms?"

Harley went on about his business, checking that everything was tight.

"I reckon we'll just have to wait on that a bit. We need a tobacco barn way worse than we need more rooms in the house, don't you think?" He knew Cy wouldn't answer, but he waited anyway, giving him a chance to before he went on.

"We'll need every scrap of lumber we can get, and then some. Take them down carefully. Don't split any more than you can help. Have Bert clean the nails out and show Amos how to straighten 'em. Stack everything nice and neat beside the stock barn."

Juniper snorted and stamped in the gravel of the drive, unaccustomed to the dead weight on her back. Harley rubbed her neck and whispered soothingly into her ears, knowing that if any more protest was coming, it'd come now. But before there was time for such, Burley, with his usual impeccable timing, burst through the screen door, letting it slam loudly behind him.

"You ready yet?" he called, lumbering down the steps. 'We're wasting time. Can't keep those big bucket-mouths waiting!"

Deep in the house behind him Cassie started crying.

"Oops!" Burley said, suddenly aware of his racket, going into an exaggerated tiptoe walk.

"Forgot about the babies. Anna Mae'll take care of 'em. That's what she's here for, right, Cy?" he said tousling the boy's hair.

"Yeah, I reckon," Cy answered, smoothing his sleep tangled, Burley-ruffled hair back down to his head with the palms of his hands. He looked square at Harley and said "Okay, Pa," then he turned and started up the walk toward the house.

Burley climbed aboard Pooh Bear and looked down at Harley. "C'mon, boy! Time to get a move on! What're you waiting for?"

Harley watched long enough to see Cy reach the door, open it and start through before he turned and mounted up, so he missed seeing his son stop in the doorway and wave back, but he heard it clearly enough; Cy's voice, backgrounded by Cassie's squalling.

"Ya'll have fun."

The doorway was empty by the time Harley turned back to say, "Next time, I promise," too late. He tugged Juniper's reins, turned her away and spurred her off.

It wasn't until they'd gotten beyond the lights of the house that Harley noticed how crisp and clear the dying night was. There were no clouds to hold the earth's heat in; no summer haze to dim the stars; no sounds except the eager step of the horses to Burley's excited chatter about what a great trip this going to be, and about how many fish they would catch, and how good they would taste, spit-grilled over a campfire. He kept it up, Burley did, all the way to the crossroads, while Harley just listened. But with every step of the horses' way, guilt nagged at the back of his mind. Some sort of unclear, undefined guilt. It felt wrong, him going off like this... And every time guilt reared its doubt in his head, he pushed it away, tuned back into Burley's talk for a moment, and told himself he didn't know why he should feel so.

It was full light by the time they reached the crossroads, without Harley ever being conscious of the process. Suddenly they were there, and suddenly it was light. That was all he could tell of the trip. When they arrived, they were greeted not only by Tom and Paulie — who gave them proper hell for being late — but also by Tom's cousin Earl, from over in Giles county. It seemed Cousin Earl needed, or rather that Cousin Earl's wife Edna had demanded, 'a respite from matrimonial bliss', due to her discovery of Earl's attentions having been lately directed a bit too much toward a certain schoolteacher at Shiloh Elementary. And so, after introductions and the brief history of Cousin Earl's straits had been given all around, they set off toward the river amid the banter of boys out on a lark, with Earl (who immediately proved himself to be quite a talker) leading the way to a place he'd never been, with everyone else in the middle, and with Harley following behind.

They rode that way for a long time, long enough to feel as if they all knew far more about Cousin Earl, the stranger, than they did about each other — guys they'd grown up with. No matter what subject came up, no matter who else tried to talk, it was Earl's voice that rose up, drowned out, and one-upped any story that anyone else began. Earl had caught and seen bigger fish, had fucked and turned down being fucked by prettier girls, and fought and beaten bigger men than anyone alive. Cousin Earl was a non-stop monologue on the virtues and adventures of Cousin Earl, and no one had a shimmer of a chance of forgetting that as long as Earl was around. At first, right after they'd started out, Harley felt bad about lagging behind the group; had wished he were up there laughing and joking along with them; wanted to be happy like they seemed to be. But he couldn't. He just couldn't. Once again, his mind was not his own anymore, and no matter how hard he tried, no matter how much he wished he could, he couldn't turn off the thoughts. They rose in him just as surely and evenly as the sun rose into the sky, surrounding and engulfing him in their heat and brightness without mercy. There was no thing in the world that didn't contain some memory, some reminder of her. She dwelled in every leaf above, every gravel below and every molecule between. There was nothing he could do about it. No amount of friends or morning or talk could steer his thoughts away from her, and he hated it. Hated himself for being so weak about it. He had been here before and had sworn he'd never come back to this place, yet here he was again, damn it to hell, going down a damnable road he'd traveled before. Even though she was gone, she drew on him as surely and as regularly as he drew breath. He could no more choose to keep her from his mind than he could choose to keep oxygen from his lungs. He'd heard tell of a pipe fitter at the steam plant in Cumberland Furnace during its first run; a poor sucker caught in the vent stack who was boiled from the inside out, breathing steam because he couldn't keep from breathing, no matter how bad it hurt. Harley knew exactly why that tale crossed his mind this morning, and even though he knew that Earl wasn't the steam that seared his gut with every breath and every thought, he knew right off that the man was hot air, more than Harley could stomach just now. And it didn't take much longer for the others to realize it too.

Burley was the first to drop back and join Harley, quietly and sneakily, with a silent meaningful look and roll of his eyes that said all that needed be said between them. Paulie was next, a bit more animated, a bit more obvious than Burley had been, as was Paulie's way. He just stopped his horse dead in the road and with an undisguised look of apology at Tom (which Earl, of course, completely failed to notice amidst his account of the time he had supper with and rebuked the affections of none other than Jefferson Davis' 'prettiest' grand-daughter'), he waited to fall into pace with Harley and Burley's silence, leaving poor Tom with nothing to do but look back at his friends, shrug his apology their way, and ride beside his cousin, pretending to listen.

It was nearly noon by the time they reached the camp. Earl had finally relinquished the lead, and his imagined control, when they reached the new Memphis/Bristol Highway — old state route 70, which they had to follow for about two miles or so east before veering back south toward the river. The horses were not accustomed to the heavy traffic, nor the frequency and size of the big trucks of the highway, but they made it back into the quiet of the woods with only a couple of minor rearings.

No one was in a hurry to set camp, but everyone was pretty hungry after the long morning's ride, so as soon as they unpacked the horses and turned them out to graze, they all sat down and lunched on the sandwiches they'd brought. It was nice to be here with no agenda except to fish and relax. They ate mostly in silence, listening to the sounds of the river current flowing beside them, and their own chewing and swallowing, and the crunch and tear of the horses pulling clumps of grass from the sandy shoal. One by one as they finished eating, each man went to his gear to dig out their poles and tackle to begin rigging for the business of catching supper. Everyone but Harley had opted for spinning reels and artificial lures — jigs and spinners and such — and he took a bit of good-natured ribbing about his old cane pole and the can of nightcrawlers and red wigglers that the boys had gathered for him the night before.

"Still fishing in the nineteenth century are you, Harley?" Paulie teased as Harley tied his minnow trap to the wood stake that would hold it in place just off the bank. "Damn, boy, this here's the 1930's. You got to be so all fired old fashioned about everything?"

Harley got up and walked to where the spring fed into the river as if he hadn't even heard. He set the peg with his hand and drove it tight with his heel. He tossed the trap and watched it sink into the deep green water before he answered.

"I don't know nothing about no new-fashioned fish," he said, turning back. "I never heard tell of a fish keeping a calendar. All I know is, fish have been eating shad and worms since there's been fish, and I reckon they'll eat it still, no matter the year."

Just then Earl called out from downstream.

"You fellars stay out of my way and watch, cause even if ya'll don't know it yet and they don't know it yet, every bucketmouth in this here river has my name on it."

Harley looked at Paulie and saw by his friend's expression that they were thinking the same thing. Harley just said it first.

"I believe I'll take the john boat across river and fish under the bluffs a spell. Where it's nice and quiet."

"Not by yourself you ain't," Paulie said, breaking into a grin, "I'll row both ways if I have to, but you ain't stranding me over here. Let's go get the boat before someone else takes it."

Despite it all, Harley couldn't help but grin back.

*

Sara rode weakly, dazedly, dreamily; lulled by the drowsy, flat sameness of the land blowing past the car window; hypnotized by the steady, even drone of the motor, and non-stop chatter of her mother trying to sound lively and eager. The miles and the words floated by distantly, unconnectedly. She was not here; not a part of any of this. She was somewhere else, sometime else, hungover by the weight of the drugs that lingered in her mind and by the pain that gnawed steadily deep inside her. The easiest thing was just to sleep. To dream her way through here and now, back into other, more enticing places and times. So nearly all of the drive from Memphis was a dim less-than-memory, just like the last few days. She was not a part of it; it was not happening to her; was not her life. She had become a mere spectator to what she was living, waking occasionally just long enough to remember she wasn't interested in the play; just long enough to yawn and wish herself back to sleep. But it didn't always work.

There was soft, gentle warmth on her forehead, but it was only the afternoon sun streaming through the window. There was a steady, droning voice from the dark, but it was only her mother, nagging her awake.

"I'll swan, for the life of me I cannot see how these people live such a life in such a horrid climate. Here it is onto September and I am positively melting, even with the car windows half down at 50 miles an hour."

Sara heard what her mother said as she felt her push the wet bangs from her brow, but she remained still and kept her eyes shut.

"Open your window some more, Clive. Your daughter is perspiring profusely back here."

Daddy sat up front with Uncle Rig. Even though they were brothers-in-law, the two men were not very familiar with one another, had never spent much time together; so after the first few miles, their small talk of motor cars and topography and local game conditions petered out, and they rode pretty much quietly, gratefully allowing the running commentary from the back seat beside Sara to keep the silence between them at bay. When Sara felt the breeze freshening, she peeked up long enough to see the back of her Daddy's head bob back and forth in time with his shoulder as he worked the window crank. He had such a quiet head, especially from behind as she saw it now, such a gently quiet head. Sara thought he must be the only man on earth with patience enough to live with her mother. When he twisted around in his seat and saw Sara looking at him, he reached back and brushed her bangs away from her eyes.

"Is that too much wind, Baby?"

She couldn't leave him alone any longer.

"No, Daddy," she said, pulling herself up in the seat. "It feels good." He smiled at her — that knowing smile of his that warmed her like no other could — and for a second they were alone together, just as they had always been. For a second, until mother broke the spell, again.

"Well it's about time, young lady! I'm beginning to think that quack country doctor needs his credentials checked. What kind of medicine has he got you on? You've acted like a zombie ever since we got here."

"Dr. Hall is a good doctor, Mother. I'm just very tired. And the car makes me sleepy. It always has, you know that."

She caught the 'getting out of the way' little half-wink of her Daddy before he turned back around to stare into the road ahead. She leaned toward the window and put her arms on the slot where the glass disappeared into the door.

"I'll find out how good a doctor he is, you may rest assured. I wonder if he even has a diploma. Do you know what school he went to?"

Sara knew her mother didn't really want an answer, and that she wouldn't accept one if she got it. So she just rested her chin on her forearms and let the wind blow her hair into a train behind her, while the sound of it roared in her ears and filled them up, almost loud enough to drown out the voice of her mother, nagging. "How much further is it, Rig? Is there no end to this horrid road? It seems as if we're on some sort of dreary treadmill."

It occurred to Sara that the air that tore at her was actually still and quiet, to any standing in it, and it was she who was tearing through it.

"No more than twenty miles or so," Uncle Rig said without turning, "We'll be there in half an hour or so, tops."

Sara closed her eyes, feeling the stillness rushing past, and didn't open them again until it stopped.

*

The river was more than a quarter-mile wide where it bent around the camp. The deepest water was at the foot of the limestone bluffs straight across, but just upstream on that side they tapered sharply off into pasture land where hardwoods stood close to the bank, shading and cooling the water. And along that stretch, on the outside of the Tennessee's curve, the current crashed hard into the land, eroding the dirt from under the trees, exposing their roots until they dipped limbs into the water, creating valuable cover for spawn and little fish. But cover is a mixed blessing, because big fish know that's where little fish swim, so that's where they go to eat. Harley and Paulie knew it too, so that's where they went, to catch the big fish that feed on little fish. They didn't speak much along the way; didn't have to, or care to. After the long morning's ride, quiet was a welcome thing.

It didn't take long for Harley to rig his pole, simple as it was, so he took the oars by the time they were halfway across. That gave time for Paulie to get his casting rod ready, but more importantly it gave Harley something to do besides sit with his thoughts. More than ever, busy was a good thing. It felt good to let his muscles take over, pulling steadily and surely upriver; felt so good that he didn't realize he'd taken them far beyond the point he could've stopped and let them float back along the stretch they aimed to fish, until he heard Paulie.

"You can let her drift now, Harl. We're plenty far up, don't you think?"

Harley put the oars down, picked up his pole, and sat still for a minute. By the time he nodded yes, Paulie had thrown his first cast and was too busy fishing to see it. Though he wasn't sure why, Harley felt embarrassed. He picked up his worm can and stuck his thumb and forefinger deep into the warm, damp mulch and pulled out the fattest worm he could feel. The wiggler was as lively as it was plump and long, so it took some doing to impale it up the hook from tail to head, and by the time he set his float and dropped his line into the water Paulie had caught the first fish — a nice palm-sized bluegill.

"That's one to nothing," Paulie said, unhooking the fish and throwing it into the live bucket at Harley's feet. He'd no sooner gotten the words out of his mouth than Harley saw his own float bob, bob again, then go under. Harley set the hook with a quick upward jerk, then raised his pole and lifted another keeper-sized bluegill out of the water. As he raised the bamboo cane toward vertical to swing the fish inboard, his eyes traveled up the line to the tip of the pole just as it passed between he and the strong late-afternoon sun. He was blinded for a second, by the light, and by the whispered boyhood memory.

"Dang, this is gonna be fun," Paulie exclaimed.

Even though he heard the words clear enough, it wasn't until he heard the whir of Paulie's reel, casting line, that he came back to whose voice it was. He circled his thumb and forefinger around the line just above the head of his catch and ran his hand down the fish, smoothing its fins down so as not to be spined by them.

"Gonna have to fish deeper to catch us a big cat," Harley said as he unhooked the fish, tossing it in the bucket and reaching for another worm.

"Hot damn! I've got another one," Paulie answered, snatching his rod upwards. "Forget the big ones," he reeled. "We've done found us a honey hole. We've got to milk these babies while they're hittin'. Then we'll go after the catfish if you still want to. Right now I'm after supper. And by the looks of things, supper's chomping at the bit to all but jump in the boat with us." He unhooked the fish and tossed it toward the catch bucket, missing all but the right rim, which 'supper' bounced off of, landing in the bottom of the boat, flopping itself end over end, trying as best it could to swim out of water.

They fished that way for over an hour, during which they caught over a dozen keepers. By the middle of the third pass, the bucket was nearly full.

"Let's let her drift further down this time, Paulie," Harley said, "I want me a channel cat."

"Okay, Harl. But I want to take it a little closer into shore this time, ride the shade and cool off a bit before we hit open water." He grabbed the oars and steered them toward the overhanging branches and the shade they offered.

Harley was intent on baiting his pole, not looking up. The alternating splotches of sun and shade on the bottom of the boat reminded him of riding the road between the farm and the river, and even that called up memories and hurt now. He didn't notice how close they were to the bank until Paulie said, "Dang it, watch out," just before a low limb swept across Harley's head, knocking his hat into the river.

"Dadgummit, Paulie," he said, leaning over to fish it out. As he did, he heard a loud thump in the bottom of the boat, at the same time he heard Paulie's shriek.

"Moccasin!" Paulie screamed, and before Harley could even turn to look, he heard the splash as Paulie bailed out of the boat and into the water.

When Harley did turn, he saw why Paulie had been so quick to abandon ship. A huge water moccasin — as thick in the middle as Harley's biceps — lay coiling itself less than a yard from Harley's feet.

"Jump, Harley! Get outta there!" Paulie yelled, dog paddling about ten feet from the boat.

Harley eyed the snake as it settled itself into a spiral and raised its head, looking square back at him. It flicked its long black tongue once, then again, smelling the fish in the bucket at Harley's feet and feeling the heat of the man before it. Its dark, slitted eyes came to focus directly on Harley as it adjusted to the strange turn of events, and to the alien place it suddenly found itself. Those eyes, Harley thought, were as purely evil, as purely malevolent, as anything Harley had ever seen. They seemed to narrow as Harley stared back. They darted to the bucket at his feet, sizing up the situation, trying to decide if its unexpected drop, almost literally into the lap of such abundant food, was serendipitous, or if the proximity of the huge warm-blooded thing before it was more threat than the food was worth. As slowly, as gently, as easily, as he could, Harley lowered his pole into the water beside the boat and dropped it, but the movement was enough to alert the snake and take its mind off the fish, directing it solely to the danger of the man before it.

"Get the hell out of there, Harley! What're you doing?"

Paulie's ruckus was loud enough to catch the attention of the others on the far bank, and through the corner of his eye Harley could see them running to the water's edge, peering across at the boat, trying to figure out what was going on. Harley considered rolling off the side of the boat into the river, but a threatening hiss from the snake jerked his attention full on the beast. It eyed Harley unwaveringly as it pulled its huge arrowhead back into striking position. Its long, thick body shined gray-brown in the sunlight they had drifted back into. It flicked its tongue again as if taking aim on its menacing prey. Harley stared transfixed at the thing before him. He thought the snake was as prime an example of seething evil as he had ever seen. The serpent. The devil himself. As if the snake could read Harley's mind, it reared its head a bit further back and opened it mouth wide, showing its inch and a half long fangs and the snow-white maw that gave this breed of slithering poison the nickname 'cottonmouth'. Poised there like that, the snake seemed to Harley to be the epitome of all that was vile and wicked and selfish in the world, the embodiment of all that had beset and ruined his life. But as he stared into the thing's eyes, he saw something different there, something almost familiar; something the snake, for all its vicious show just could not hide. Yes, it was mean. Yes, it was deadly. But somewhere deep in the vertical slice of its pupils, Harley thought he saw a flash of fear as well. He realized that it was as afraid of him as he was of it. The two of them sat unmoving, neither wanting to be where he was, but neither knowing a way out, save confrontation. Then Harley made his decision. Without moving, without taking his eyes from the eyes of his 'enemy', he took a shallow breath and began to hum, softly at first, then louder and louder. He was two or three bars into the tune before he realized what it was that he was humming. It was one of Ellie's songs, one of her nursery songs. The one that Cy had hummed at the funeral. The snake cocked its head almost imperceptibly, like a dog does when it hears or smells something it's not quite sure of. Harley went on humming, a little louder with every note. Slowly, ever so slowly, the cottonmouth drew smaller and smaller as the white maw drew a bit less wide, the fangs a bit less bared. But its eyes never wavered from Harley's. As its jaws slowly relaxed, Harley began just as slowly to lean forward.

"Dammit, Harley! What the hell you think you're doing?! Get the hell out of there!"

Harley ignored Paulie — very nearly did not hear him at all — so intent on the snake he was. He continued humming, and he continued leaning closer and closer to the thing before him. Though the beast never entirely closed its mouth, it came near enough to doing so that the bottom tip of its fangs became hidden under its lower jaw. Its eyes showed obvious confusion. It was as unsure of what exactly was happening here as Harley was. And still Harley leaned closer. And closer. The foot high pedestal of body that held its head cocked and reared seemed to waver. It swayed back and forth just a bit and Harley knew he must be imagining that its sway was in time to the nursery song.

Still neither flinched, neither blinked, and neither lost eye contact. Harley was so close he could actually see into the black depths of the pupils, past his own reflection on their surface. Was so close he could smell the foul stench of poison and dead fish in the creature's mouth. So he stopped.

The others across the river finally understood what was going on, and they all waved and shouted desperately across the water. But their distant imprecations had no more meaning to Harley than did the drone of late day cicadas. Paulie had finally quieted down and was treading water behind the boat, watching intently.

"Jeez, Harley," only a whisper now.

All the world was reduced to only two things now. Harley and the snake. This close, the eyes before him didn't seem quite so evil after all. They were just eyes. As unsecure and fearful of what the future held as his own. If he had seen fear in them before, as he'd imagined, he saw something else there now. Not confusion really, but…perplexion? Doubt?

Harley knew the time was now. Knew he'd have only one chance. Knew what a dose of such venom would mean, this deep in the woods.

"You don't want to be here anymore than I do, do you, partner?" Harley whispered.

The snake flicked its shiny black tongue again, this time closing its mouth behind it.

"Okay then," Harley said. He held the water moccasin's gaze one second more. Then he lashed his right hand across the distance between them quicker than lightening fades from the night sky, and he had the snake around the neck. It thrashed violently, slapping the bottom of the boat with the full strength of is four-foot-plus length of muscle. It thrashed so violently that Harley thought for an instant he wouldn't be able to hold his grip. But just as instantly as the writhing had started, it stopped, and the snake fell limp in his hands, knowing it was caught. Harley stood in up in the boat and hung the fire hose body he held to its full length. It was every bit of five feet long, Harley saw now — he had to hold his arm out above shoulder height to clear its tail from the hull — and must have weighed close to 10 pounds. He picked up its midsection with his left hand and it immediately coiled its body around his forearm. His heart was slowing to a racing pound, and, still humming the nursery tune, he brought the snake's head to within an inch of his nose, staring once more into its eyes.

"You ain't never done me no wrong, Mr. Cottonmouth. And I reckon you'll be as glad to get shed of me as I will you." The snake held still for a second, wrapping tighter around Harley's arm, as if the sheer power of its squeeze would set it free. Harley sat back down without taking his eyes off the snake. Gently he untwined the coil from his arm and leaned over toward the water.

"Go on home," he said. But before he moved the snake away from his face, he lowered it slightly and kissed the top of its head. It felt cold and surprisingly hard on his lips. Then he leaned and dipped the hand that held the snake into the water. He held it there for a second, watching it try to swim, still in his grip, going nowhere. Then he released.

"Have a nice day," he said.

The snake s-curved its way toward the bank as fast as it could, never looking back.

*

    Though nothing is ever the same from one day to the next, or even one moment to the next, some things never change. The camp was the same as it had ever been, though the fire burned new logs, different logs than had ever been burned before, and the light they cast, though oh so same to all the firelight that had shone here in the centuries before, was new light. The evening was cool enough to keep them all around the campfire while they ate.

    "Damn fine supper, boys." Earl was a new log, same light. "A bit under cooked and over salted for my taste, but a damn fine supper."

    There was always an Earl at camp. Someone always played Earl. It was tradition in camp that everyone shared the chores, except the *Three* (providing there were more than three in attendance that is, which wasn't always the case). Whoever caught the biggest fish of the day, whoever caught the most fish, and whoever caught the most poundage, were exempt from duties for the evening. Until supper was done and all remnants cleared, the Three had to do nothing, save enjoy leisure and being served. No cleaning fish, no gathering of wood or feeding the fire, no cooking and no cleaning pots and plates afterwards. Only once in all the years had Harley ever not been one of the three, and that was in the worst of cases — a four-man trip. And as if wasn't bad enough that he alone had to cook and serve and clean up after everyone else, it was right after he'd married Ellie. The first time since he'd slept with her that he would not be sleeping with her. His heart wasn't in camp then, it was on its way home the whole time. Home. Where they lived, he and she, together. Home. Where it was so easy to discount her and take her for granted because they two were always there together, just a couple more fixtures in the house. Home. Where his mind could travel to other places and think about other things while he pretended to deny what he valued most, while refusing to admit to the only thing on earth that mattered to him. Home. The only place that she did not invade and saturate and permeate every instant of his world for as long as he was there, with her, and she wasn't gone.

    Home. The only place he had ever had so much company, feeling so alone.

Hell, he hadn't even been able to keep his mind on fishing that day, so how could he be expected to concentrate on catering to Burley's and Tom's and Rig's demands, much less abide their ribbing? Rig was the Earl that trip, nagging and riding and reminding Harley why home was so enticing. Earl was the Rig this time. Not so much because he'd bent the rules by counting a throwback — a thigh-sized carp, huge but inedible, even by Earl's own not so lofty standards — as biggest fish, nor because he had refused to hear any argument that only eating fish count. But more because he was the one, this trip, who made home seem so far away.

"Fetch us a jug back when you get done with those dishes, will ya, cuz?" Earl said, spitting into the fire, oblivious of the limits pushed.

It was quiet for a spell, except for the hiss and pop of unseasoned wood burning. Everyone was full and tired, and it was well past dark, and the fire was enough. Harley shut his eyes and leaned back against the log seat behind him, soaking in the tonic of camp. Burley had been right again; this was the one place he could empty his mind of the ghosts that haunted his thoughts. This was the nearest he'd been to peace in too long a while. It felt good to be so... vacant. This was as close to a vacation as Harley had ever known. A place where he could feel rightfully tired enough, with a full belly enough, surrounded by friends enough, and just far from home enough to luxuriate in nothing else but here and now. Unburdened enough to forget past and future long enough to saturate in nothing but the present. A rare place where more than one person can sit in silence and feel not the least bit awkward about the lack of words, and to respect the quiet enough to feel no need for them. For interminable seconds the reverie of the elements of the night — Fire, Earth, Air, Water — stood pure and clear and visible enough that none among them, not even Earl, failed to recognize the sanctity, nor dared violate it.

Then someone farted, loud and long and greasy sounding, and the spell was broken.

"Damn beans'll do it ever time," admitted Paulie.

"Jeez, boy, get away from the fire next time, before you blow us all up with a gasser like that," said Tom.

"Sheee-it! You'd better change them pants," Earl chimed. "They bound to be drippin' after that."

"Better yet," Burley said, standing and stretching his back over his arms, hands bent backwards on his hips." Why not use some of that wind blowing on that harmonica of yours? You did bring it along didn't you, Paulie?"

Chapter 20

Even knowing what scarce commodity rain had been these past few weeks, Sara was still surprised at the amount of dust that clouded behind the car, following them like a reluctant ghost down the driveway. She had grown up traveling at the speed of automobiles, but the few short months she'd spent here made her feel out of place with the rushing pace of engines and tires. Cars belong in the streets of Baltimore, not here. This was Bess's territory, slow and steady and gradual. Behind Bess there is time to think about where you are going, and why. Time to soak in the nuances of the countryside rather than to simply pass them by. Time to actually smell the flowers along the way rather than simply coat them with a layer of dust.

"Oh my," her mother said as they crossed the ford and accelerated toward the house.

Sara watched the heart of the farm growing larger and larger in the windshield before them, and for a moment she was thankful for the speed. And she was glad that they reached the end of the drive before her mother had time to comment further. It occurred to her that maybe, just maybe, given time enough and leisure enough, even her mother might learn to appreciate the view of approach through Bess's ears. But as they pulled up to the front gate and the noise of the motor dwindled, taken over by the sound of tires crunching slowly over gravel, she said it again, looking at Sara as if asking forgiveness for banishing her daughter to such rude wilderness.

"Oh my."

Her tone bore more indictment, more judgment, than any diatribe could ever have carried.

No, not mother, Sara realized. Mother would never, could never, *get* it.

Before the car was even at full stop Sara threw the door open. She had to get out.

"Where is everybody?" she thought aloud. Not to anyone in the car; not even aware she'd spoken until she heard her own voice. The house was quiet. The yard was empty.

"Sara. Darling. I had no idea..."

"Shut up!" Sara spun on her mother with a ferocity that she'd never known herself capable of. She watched her mother's face go from shock, to indignance, to something that looked like... perplexity. For the first time ever, Sara locked eyes with her mother and didn't look away first. Looking straight and deep past Sally's fierce facade, Sara finally saw her mother for what she really was — a person. Just another scared, defensive, walled-up person. She's just like me, Sara realized. She felt her own face soften from a glare to a stare, then to a simple searching look. She was curious more than anything else. She saw the exact instant that Sally saw it too, and saw that it was more than Sally could take. Her mother looked away, down and to the left.

"Be quiet, Momma," Sara whispered, knowing that her whisper was loud enough to be heard, now. "Please be quiet."

Her mother didn't look up, but her head moved almost imperceptibly, in something like a nod. Daddy and Uncle Rig sat motionless in the car, not a part of this, pretending not to be even witness to it.

Something on the edge of Sara's vision caught her eye. Movement. And just like that, Sally and Daddy and Uncle Rig were periphery.

"Sara?" called Cy tentatively, coming from around the corner of the house.

"Cy!" She threw open her arms and ran at him so boldly as to make him take an involuntary step backwards.

Before she reached Cy, before she could, even as fast as she flew, the rest of the boys appeared behind him. She took Cy in her arms first, because he was nearest, and before she could let go of him all the others joined in and they became one single mass of hug. Everyone talked at once until Sara drew herself up.

"Hush, ya'll!" she stomped, putting her hands on her hips in mock sternness, and they hushed. "One at a time, okay?" Her attempt at a harsh demeanor fell away, giving in to her huge smile.

She started with Amos.

"How's my biggest little man been doing, Amie?" she asked, squatting down to look him eye-level.

"Thhher... I mean Sssssara! We missed you!" Amie threw his arms around her and buried his face in her neck. She picked the baby boy up in her arms and spun him around.

"Oh, and Sara has missed you so very, very much too, Amie!" She buried her face into his neck, and the sweet little boyness of him nearly overcame her, so she tickled his ribs to hear his giggle and distract herself from the tears that welled in her eyes.

"Me next! My turn. Hug me now, Sara!" cried Bert, jumping up and down, tugging at her arm.

She set Amos down and spread her arms wide to Bert.

"Come here, my Bertie."

He needed no more prompting than that. He threw himself into Sara's arms and welcomed her squeeze. She pulled him into her lap, nuzzling kisses through his thick dark hair, all the way up his scalp.

Bert suddenly released his hold and stepped back, taking her cheeks into his little hands.

"Are your ow's better now? They look like they still hurt. Are you all better, Sara?"

"Yes, Bert, Sara is all better. Now." She grabbed him back into her arms and kissed the top of his head again. Never, ever, had she smelled any purer scent than his dirty little hair. She could have stayed that way forever. Until she saw Seth.

Seth, in his bib overalls, standing so Seth, quietly in the background, patiently waiting his turn.

She kissed the top of Bert's head once more then turned his face up in her hands and kissed both of his cheeks in turn. As she did she winked at Seth.

"Come look at all the work we've done, Sara," Bert said. "I worked *hard*!"

"I'm certain you have, Master Bertram," she said, standing him up beside Amos. "And I want to see what you've done," she said, standing herself up and smoothing her dress on her thighs with her palms. "Just as soon as I get my hello's out of the way..."

She turned and smiled directly at Seth, as brightly and strong as early sun shines on fresh morning dew. Seth reflected it back to her equally as bright. She spread her arms and before she'd taken the two steps to him his hands were out of his pockets and spread just as wide to meet her. He hugged her as tight, if not tighter, than she hugged him. It hurt her ribs, but not so much that she was willing to quit it. She couldn't help but feel the earnestness and the honesty in his arms. But he didn't hug her as long as the little ones had. Though she was mostly certain she hadn't turned her head as her eyes scanned the yard beyond, she felt the awkwardness creep between them, and she knew for certain that he had felt her searching over his shoulder.

Seth let go and stepped back, looking down at his feet. He cleared his throat and took her biceps in his hands and looked up at her.

"He's coming back. He'll be back soon."

She saw his eyes mist over, saw him trying so hard to be a man. She saw something else too. There was a softness in his look that betrayed his matter-of-fact words, and she knew it was a bit of Ellie she was seeing in those eyes.

"He'll be back," Seth said again, looking away.

Sara wanted so badly to hug him again, but somehow she knew not to, so she didn't. Instead she put a hand on his forearm and stroked it ever so lightly. She needed the touch and the time even more than Seth did; so many thoughts whirled through her head. As badly as she wanted to ask the question that hung between them, she was afraid her voice would give it all away, so she waited.

She wanted to say something, anything, but she didn't know what. She was about to ask anyway when Seth looked back up into her eyes, and she saw the Harley in his eyes now.

"Trust me," Seth said, unblinking. "He will. Sunday, in time for Sunday dinner."

She wanted so badly to ask, but Seth held his gaze so dead on her that she didn't say anything. Then suddenly he turned his eyes and had gotten away.

Sara wasn't sure what to do, except finish the rounds she'd started.

"Where's Cassie?" She asked, looking around, suddenly unsure of what was going on. "And where did Cy get off to?"

Before anyone had a chance to answer they heard the pounding of a hammer from behind the house, and everyone but Sara and her folks knew that Cy was back at work, tearing down the new rooms.

She knew soon enough, all too soon. The instant she stepped around the corner and saw the half-dismantled skeleton of the addition hovering before her, she froze. Though Cy worked on as if he didn't see her, he worked far too intently to leave any doubt that he knew she was watching.

She was still trying to understand what it all meant — Harley gone and the room coming down, when she heard the voice behind her.

"Sara?" It was Mother, in a tone that Sara had never heard before. Mother's voice was always so certain and in charge, but not this time.

"Hey, guys, come here," Sara said, fending off the imagined implications of what she saw going on here at ... She stopped her thoughts before they got to the word.

When she turned to face her mother, Daddy and Uncle Rig were walking up behind Sally. She took her mother's hand in hers and led her closer to the children.

"Boys, this is my mother." She dropped Sally's hand and went and put her arm around her father. "And this is my Daddy." She introduced everybody, one by one. Her mother smiled politely and said 'How do you do' to each in turn, and her father bent to each one and shook their hands, smiling broadly and repeating their names, making sure he had them right. While that was going on, Sara had enough time to remember who was missing, and just as she was about to ask, Anna Mae stepped through the back porch door, wearing Ellie's apron over her dress, with Cassie on her hip.

"Well, hello, Sara!" Anna Mae smiled. She shifted Cassie a bit higher and started down the steps.

Sara wanted nothing more than to run and take Cassie into her arms, but she hesitated. She had looked so forward to getting back here, but suddenly she felt like a visitor, as outsider as her mother acted. So she ran through the introductions again, while Cassie stared curiously in her direction.

"I was just starting on supper," Anna Mae said, hitching Cassie again. "Y'all will stay, won't you?"

"Oh, no," Sally answered. "We wouldn't dream of it. Uhh, imposing that is."

"Oh, there's enough for everybody. That is if you'll take potluck. I wasn't expecting company."

"No, no," Sally shook her head. "Clorise is cooking dinner for us. We really must get back there soon."

"Well at least let me make us some tea," Anna Mae said.

Sara could stand it no longer and she stepped up to Cassie, holding her arms out.

"May I?" she asked, smiling at Anna Mae.

"Of course, Sara! Where are my manners?"

But Cassie was on the bad side of Sara's face, the strange looking, swollen and bruised side. The baby wore a look of puzzlement, trying to register this new face with Sara's voice. As Sara reached out to take her from Anna Mae, Cassie turned and kicked and broke into squalling, afraid of what she saw. Sara dropped her arms and left Cass with Anna Mae.

"I'd love some tea, Ann Marie, after those terrible dusty roads," Sally said, freezing her face into a kind of tolerant smile.

"Good, come inside then and I'll send one of the boys to fetch some ice from the cave."

Cy was still at his pounding, backing another lath from a rafter, Cassie was crying, and Bert and Amos were tugging on both of Sara's hands, talking into both of her ears.

Sara felt dizzy, overwhelmed by everything she'd found so different than she'd left it.

"You all go ahead. I need to take a walk. I've been sitting far too long. My legs need to move."

"Sara, you absolutely do *not* need to walk, in your condition," Sally started, but Sara cut her off.

"I *am* going for a walk, Mother," Sara said, just too loud enough to aggravate Cassie's crying. "Go enjoy your tea. I'll be back soon."

She was turned and was on her way out of the yard before anyone had a chance to argue with her.

She took her time, walking slowly, taking in the familiar sights and smells of the farm around her. But one smell overrode it all. The smoldery scent of ashes. She skirted far around the black circle where the tobacco barn had stood, even though she really did feel too weak to take any more steps than necessary to get to where she was going, but she was definitely not strong enough to pass too close to that place yet. The afternoon sun reassured her pained face as she made her way uphill. A cow lowed mournfully away toward the creek, and she remembered that #14 was due to be calving. Any other time she would have given most anything to go and watch and help with the delivery. But not now, no way, no how. It hit too close to home. When the cow lowed again a wave of dizziness washed over her, so she sat and rested halfway up the knoll.

Down from the house the steady rhythm of Cy tearing down the new rooms assailed her. She could see the yard, empty except for Cy's movement — everyone else was already inside sipping afternoon tea and making the smallest of talk, she had no doubt. Sara knew her mother well. And she also knew herself well enough to know that she mustn't sit too long here, else she might never make it up the hill. So she took a deep breath and gathered her courage up as she gathered her legs under her, to make the final climb.

When she crested the rise and saw the small pile of raw dirt beside Ellie, it was all she could do to keep herself from fainting. It was not mere dizziness that hit her this time. Her vision blackened into the smallest of focus, pulsing lighter and darker in time with the thudding in her ears, and her legs buckled her into a near crouching position. But she didn't stop moving because she couldn't. If she didn't walk it now, she never would. She could blame it on the medicine and the physical pain now. She wouldn't be able to next time. So when she found herself sitting between new dirt and the tombstone, it surprised her, as if she'd just woken from a dream, unclear where she was or how she got here. Unclear on anything for that matter, except that this was no dream. Of that, there was no mistaking.

She heard panting, and when she realized it was her own, she forced herself to concentrate on breathing. That was as much as she could do now. Slow her respiration and deepen it; regulate it before she hyperventilated. Number 14 still moaned in the distance and Cy still hammered. That was all she knew and all she cared to think about, for the moment.

But she wasn't having much luck doing even that, so she lay down across the fresh dirt and hugged it to her breast. It was warm, and dark, and soft under her. But far too dry for proper hugging.

*

After a time Sara realized that the soil was not so dry after all. At least not the part that lay under her cheeks. And she also became aware of the sobs of little girl crying. She never for an instant thought it her little girl she heard. Hope had never had a chance to find voice. For an instant though, she did think it might be Cassie's voice. It reminded her of Cassie's voice until she paid attention to it, and then she knew at once that it was her own. And as soon as she realized that she sat up, dried her eyes, and crossed her legs Indian-style, as painful as that was. Then she smoothed her dress over her lap and began speaking.

"That's no way for a Mommy to act now, is it?" But her voice didn't sound a bit Mommy-ish, even to her own ears. It was far too small and far too weak. She sniffed hard but there was way too much snot for a mere sniff to send away, so she raised the hem of her dress and blew hard into it, clearing her nostrils. And she smiled, thinking of the picture that must make, were anybody to see it. She patted the top of the little mound softly and smiled again, soft and wistful. She held her hand on the dirt as long as she dared, then turned herself around without uncrossing her legs. And she smiled again.

"Ellie..." she started.

"It's okay if I call you Ellie, isn't it?" The sun was low and dimming, and she knew she wouldn't have long before somebody came looking for her.

"You may not know me, but I feel like I know you. I've seen your hand a thousand times in your family. I never even got to meet you and it's painful for me to see how much they miss you. I can only imagine how much they hurt for you...

"I only hope that when God takes me, I'll leave as much love behind as you have."

She paused for a moment, listening to the sounds of dying day around her.

"I have been honored to take care of your babies for a time. Now I'm asking you to honor me by taking care of mine for me. Her name is Hope." Sara's voice broke at the last. She took another breath and went on…

"Maybe I have no right to say this... But I love you, Ellie. I love what I've seen of you in those that love you. I love what you gave up, what I've been privileged enough to get a glimpse of. I love..."

"Sara?" Came the call from downhill. It was Daddy.

"Oh, drat it!" Sara said. "I knew we wouldn't have enough time." She leaned forward and lowered her voice to a conspiratorial whisper. "But I'm glad it's him. I'd like you to meet him. You'll like Daddy, I think."

She turned her head and shouted, "Up here, Daddy," over her shoulder, then she leaned back toward Ellie and lowered her voice again. "Sounds like he's only halfway up, and believe me, Daddy doesn't move too fast. We can get it done before he gets here..."

"Sara? Sweetheart? Your mother says she's ready to go. She sent me to tell you."

"Okay, Daddy. Come on up," she answered. Then back to Ellie. "I really wanted a bit more time with you, but at least it's him. I figured it would be. We can still do this."

She leaned down and tugged a clump of grass from Ellie's grave, right over the spot where she guessed Ellie's heart would be.

"Thank you," she whispered. Then she turned around to where Hope lay. With her left hand she dug a small hole over where she guessed Hope's heart would be. She gently placed the grass into the hole and smoothed the soil around it.

"Grow deep, roots," she said. And as if on cue a single tear slid from her cheek and fell into the grass.

"Sara. Honey," came Daddy's voice, softly, from just behind her. She wasn't startled by it; she didn't turn around right away. She'd been expecting him. Daddy, wise as he was, didn't say anything else; he just stood, puffing from the climb up the hill, waiting for Sara.

When she finally did turn around he was still breathing heavily, standing there quietly in his big frame, with dark sweat stains at each armpit and his suit coat draped over his right forearm like an over-sized napkin on a wine-steward. She didn't bother wiping her eyes, or saying anything. She just stood up and walked slowly to him and laid herself against his chest. He dropped his coat and wrapped his arms around her and held her tight while she heaved and sobbed against him.

When finally she stilled and had sniffed a couple of times, trying to dry up, he put his face to the side of her head, nuzzling her golden, silk-spun hair.

"It's beautiful here. This is a beautiful place," he said.

Sara leaned back from his chest just enough to look him in the eye. As soon she saw the old familiar loving look in them and that oh-so reassuring smile of his, she had to smile, and let out a little half-laugh.

"I know I must look a fright," she said, wiping her hands across her eyes to clear away the tears. Then she reached up and wiped his tears off of his cheeks.

"Nonsense," he said. "You look lovelier than you ever have, Sweetheart. Except for that shiner; it's not quite your style," and they both smiled again. "There is nothing frightful about you, Baby. And I should know. After all, I wake up next to your mother every morning, don't I?"

Sara stretched up on her tiptoes to kiss his cheek.

"I love you, Daddy."

"I love you too, Darling. More than you'll ever imagine."

They hugged again, briefly but fiercely.

She stepped back from him and slipped her hand into his.

"Come here," she said, tugging him gently toward the graves. "There are a couple of young ladies I want to introduce you to."

*

Juniper stepped quirky and skittish on the road. It must have seemed odd to her to have Harley on her back, the same evening of the day they'd arrived at camp. It seemed odd to him too, to be on Juniper's back, the same evening of the day they'd arrived at camp. But he'd run in the wrong direction for long enough. He wasn't running away anymore. He was running home.

Chapter 21

Once he made up his mind, the rest was easy. He'd thought that leaving camp would be awkward, imagining that no matter how he tried to explain his sudden departure to the others, everyone would see right through it for what it really was. And while he was trying to decide, that thought kept popping into his mind, confusing the issue. But he hadn't really been comfortable since he'd left the house that morning and it seemed like some kind of ... *violation*... to the spirit of camp, to be there and not be relaxed and soothed by it. He had brought doubts and confusion and unease into a place where they had no right to be. And it seemed to him that if he stayed there, if he allowed them to stay there with him, he would somehow rob the camp of its power, tainting the very purpose of the place.

Still and all, he might have stayed anyway had it not been for Earl. It was one thing to have the constant nagging voices in his head, but to have one in his ears also, well that was just too much. And he knew the instant he decided that he'd made the right choice, because suddenly all the nagging thoughts disappeared, and even Earl's non-stop monologues lost their ability to irritate him. He didn't give a damn what anybody thought, once he convinced himself.

"I'm going home to my family," was all he told them. "That's where I ought to be."

It didn't matter what anyone else thought about it or how much they tried to argue him out of it, which they all did. Except Burley. He was glad Burley hadn't joined the chorus of the others. Maybe Burley didn't understand the reasons any better than they did, but he understood Harley better enough to not try and change his friend's mind. Burley was the one who helped Harley load up, without saying a word. Burley was the one who walked out of camp with him, beyond the range of the sights and smells and sounds of it, without a word. And it was Burley who shook Harley's hand and looked him in the eye and said, "Do what you gotta do, boy."

Burley was the one who'd helped Harley into the peace of mind that he enjoyed now, quiet and solitary and sure, on the way home.

Juniper had long settled down, perhaps lulled as much by the hypnotic rhythm of the clop and crunch of her hooves on the road gravel as Harley was. She carried him calmly and easily through the night. It was still early enough for the crickets and tree frogs and fireflies to fill the dark with their singing and dancing, but late enough in the season for their volume and number to be noticeably diminished from the peak of summer. Just as the swirling and buzzing of Harley's own thoughts had subsided to the point that they began to blend invisible into the background, the bugs, though not gone completely away, had quieted enough so as not to demand constant awareness of their presence.

He didn't know what the future held any more than he ever had. It was, if anything, less clear than ever. The only difference was that he was ready to accept whatever came without questioning, and so he could finally rest, free of worrying. And that felt good.

Though he never slept along the way, from time to time he found himself snapping out of that surreal neverland that lies between drowse and wake, where images unbidden and barely dreamed float up briefly and mingle with the conscious world. He was in just one of those states when a new noise — at first seeming dreamed, then growing real — pulled him from his fugue. It was a deep steady hum from far away, but growing closer quickly. As he peered into the darkness of the road ahead he realized he was approaching the crossroads and that the depth of night was weakening up there, lightening gradually by an approaching glow. A car was coming, headed toward the river. Harley checked his watch, thinking it awfully late for traffic, and was surprised to find that it was not even nine o'clock yet. He would have guessed it much later than that. When he was within fifteen or twenty yards of the intersection the car roared by, leaving a cloud of dust and fumes in its wake. The noise and aftermath of its passing seemed foreign and out of place in the peace of the night. But once passed, its intrusion faded as quickly as it had come. Harley didn't care if he ever owned an automobile. He didn't understand the need for such rush and hurry. Life is short enough without speeding past the pleasure of journeying. He hocked and spat the dust of the road he'd been forced to breathe by the passing of the car, then he tugged Juniper's reins, turning her onto the final leg of the road home.

*

"Where are we?"

Sara raised her head with a start. She hadn't been asleep, exactly, but neither had she been awake.

"Uncle Rig?"

Rig turned from the wheel, silhouetted by the dashboard lights.

"We're halfway to the river. We just passed the crossroads."

Sara twisted around to look through the back glass behind her. All she could see was the cloud of dust they left in their wake, red-tinged by the taillights. She must have been asleep after all. She must have been dreaming. But still she peered backwards, unable to accept it. She had a sudden urge to scream at them to stop, to go back. But they'd humored her all evening, Mother and Daddy and Uncle Rig had, and she knew if she pushed it again they'd begin to more than just wonder why she was acting as she was...

And besides, he wasn't coming anyway.

Sara had convinced them to stay for supper, had insisted on it actually, so she could have a little more time with the children, she'd used as excuse to them. And that was true, too. But she'd spent all evening looking past whoever was talking at the time to steal glances down the driveway, toward the ford.

She ate with Cassie propped on her lap, spooning tiny bites of vegetables into the baby as often as she could. The rest of the kids chattered gaily through the meal, delighted at having Sara with them again, unaware of what was coming. Except Cy, who sensed the real reason she was here today, with her parents. He sat quietly sullen, barely picking at his food. And maybe Seth sensed it too, but he hid it better, denied it better, though he brought up his Pa at every chance, talking about how soon Harley would be back and how delicious all those fresh fish would be. But when he invited Sara and her folks back for a fish fry on Sunday evening and Sara's father answered, saying, "That sounds great, Seth, but I'm afraid we have a train to catch in the morning. We have to get our little girl back home and get her well again," then Seth had to face it too. That was when Cy got up from the table, mumbling something about having to go feed the animals, and left the house. Sara didn't say anything; she just put her fork down and bowed her head and kissed the top of Cassie's head. She left her lips planted in the baby's wispy-fine angel hair for a long time, and she didn't eat any more after that. When she finally lifted her head back up, her eyes strayed deliberately through the window and down the drive again, while Bert and Amos kept up their happy talk, oblivious to the situation.

Sara had already decided to keep it that way. She wasn't going to tell them goodbye— she didn't think she could even if she wanted to — she would simply kiss them goodnight, as she had so many times before.

If only Harley were here. Maybe then...

But no, she couldn't allow herself to even think such thoughts.

He wasn't here. That was fact. Everything else was just wishes and guesses.

He wasn't here. She hadn't even seen him since... that night.

Even so, she tried to delay the inevitable for as long as she could. She kept looking out the window even after it got too dark to see much beyond the yard. Even when her Daddy pulled out his pocket watch, saying as he opened it, "Well, it's getting late and we'd best be getting...", and she cut him off in mid-sentence by jumping up and beginning to clear the table, insisting that she and Seth do the cleaning up — "Since Anna Mae has been hospitable enough to invite us to such a fine dinner" — she couldn't keep from looking out the window. And when her mother started to argue that they really should be leaving, Sara thought that as much as she'd always loved her Daddy, she had never loved him more than when he cut her mother off with a simple, "Sally, let's go out on the porch. I could use a cigar before we go."

They started the dishes, Sara washing, Seth drying, without speaking for the first few minutes. Sara simply didn't know what to say, or at least not how to begin, so she waited for Seth to break the silence between them. They were halfway through before he did. Then, without looking up, focusing intently on the already dry plate that he kept wiping with his towel, he finally asked in as monotone a voice as he could manage.

"Do you wanna go?"

She handed him a clean plate and he put the one he had been drying for so long into the cupboard, carefully avoiding looking in her direction. Sara kept to the business at hand, taking a pot off the sideboard and dipping it into the soapy water. When she answered, her tone was as flat as Seth's had been.

"What choice do I have?"

Seth turned suddenly and faced her.

"You can make them wait until Pa gets back!" He said, his voice anything but flat now. "You can't leave without talking to Pa. He'll explain it to them. They'll understand if he tells them."

"Tells them what, Seth? What do you think your Daddy would tell them? What could he tell them?"

"He'd tell them that we ought to get our turn to take care of you. He'd tell 'em at least that. He'd tell 'em it's only right, and he'd make 'em understand. He just didn't know they'd try to take you away this quick, that's all."

All pretense of dish washing was gone now. They stood face to face, eye to eye, Seth still holding his plate and Sara still holding her pot. They heard Bertie's squealing laughter from the front porch, and Sara knew her Daddy was tickling the boy; that he'd already won Bert over — and vice versa.

Again Sara didn't know what to say, so she said nothing. Except with her eyes. And as she and Seth stood there staring into one another, she knew he'd heard her.

But she had no clue of the bomb he was about to drop on her.

As he turned away from her and went back to his drying, he said it, very quietly.

"I saw ya'll on the porch."

The pot slipped out of Sara's hands and clanged loudly on the kitchen floor, followed immediately by the voice of Sara's mother calling in through the front window.

"Is everything okay in there? Sara?"

"Yes, Mother. We're almost done," Sara answered. Then there was a moment of silence before she lowered her voice again and drew a deep breath.

"Seth... I... I don't know what to say."

Seth put the dish he'd been drying into the cupboard and stooped to pick up the pot she'd dropped.

"Seth. Darling. I know how you must feel. I know how much you all miss your mother, and how much you all wish she were still here with you. I would never..."

Seth looked up and handed the pot to her as he rose.

"You don't know how it made me feel," he said.

Sara dropped her eyes from his and took the pot he held out to her. Then she dropped her head to her chest and drew another deep breath until she trusted her voice enough to say the only thing she knew to say.

"I'm sorry."

Seth held his eyes steady on hers and his voice never wavered when he answered, and though the words were barely audible, hardly above thought, she heard them clear enough to have no mistake as to what he said. She heard them as clearly as if they'd been shouted at the top of his lungs instead of barely whispered.

"It made me happy."

*

As Harley turned Juniper into the ford and kicked her across it, he saw his home ahead, all the windows dark except for the one in the parlor, which was dimly lit from a light in the kitchen beyond it. He didn't know what that meant, but the hope that it didn't mean Anna Mae might still be up flashed across his mind. He didn't want to have to explain any more to anyone else today. He didn't know what he'd hoped to find, until the image of the car that had rushed past him back at the crossroads flitted darkly and disappointingly across his mind.

He was just tired, he told himself, that was all. That was why he felt the sudden queasiness in his stomach. He was just tired.

He decided he wouldn't even bother turning Juniper out into the pasture tonight. He'd just get his gear unloaded from her and let her graze the yard. And then he'd crawl into his bed and get some sleep. But as he led her to through the front gate and tied her reins off on the porch post, his thinking changed. He didn't really want to go inside after all. Not yet.

Maybe he'd just sit in his grand-daddy's chair and rock a spell, and not even go inside the house tonight; stay out here in the dark for a while, where it was less crowded. Besides, Anna Mae was probably sleeping in his room, and he sure didn't want to go in there and deal with that. So as soon as he got Juniper free of his luggage, he slapped her bottom and sent her off into the darkness and sat down on the porch and shucked his boots. Then he eased himself into the old rocker, and before he knew it was happening, he was asleep.

Chapter 22

Jeremiah had three lines in the water and none of them were biting. But he didn't have any place else to go and he still had bait, so he reckoned he'd stay and fish some more. That is if laying back with one eye halfcocked, half-heartedly watching the lines laying slack and un-tugged by anything but the current can be called fishing. Besides, the little missy and her folks hadn't crossed back over yet, and he was curious to find out what was going on with all that, so he'd give them a little longer, waiting on this side.

He pulled his lines in to check the hooks. Two of 'em were empty — the little suckers had robbed him again — and as he fingered for fresh worms in his bait can he squinted up at the sliver of moon above. It looked to be drawing nigh onto nine o'clock. He decided he'd feed the river-buggers one more meal, and then head back across to the town side. The way he figured it, if Miss Sara and them weren't here by then, they wouldn't be coming back tonight. He smiled at the thought of what that could mean as he plucked a fat juicy nightcrawler from the can and strung it up his hook. After he loaded the other hook likewise, he spat in the river and settled back to wait a spell longer.

After maybe a half-hour or so with no action, he stood up and stretched, then began reeling his lines in. The first two came clear and easy — empty — so he was surprised when he felt drag on third. But the sluggishness of the rod tip told him right away that it was a carp. He picked up a paddle, intending to knock the 'trash-fish' off his hook, but then thought better of it and gabbed his net and scooped it out of the water, thinking he'd drop it off at the Johnson's on his way home. They ate carp as eager as other folks eat catfish, and Jeremiah knew as well as the Good Lord did that the Johnson's could use a free meal whenever they could get one, so he unhooked the carp and tossed it onto the deck behind him. As he went to start the ferry motor to let it warm up for the trip back, he heard the fish flop a half dozen times before it gave up and stilled, resigning itself to its fate. He untied the mooring ropes, watching the poor thing working its mouth slowly open and shut, in round silent protests of being snatched so unexpectedly from its home, gasping for breath as it drowned in the cool night air. So as he cast off and throttled the ferry away from the landing, he stomped his boot hard on the doomed fish's head, putting it out of its misery.

*

Sara had allowed herself — no, had forced herself — to drowse, until Rig braked the car up to the ferry landing. Then she could pretend no more so she sat up, awake and grateful to have something to do; something to occupy her mind, rather than just to sit and let it wander.

"Shit!" Uncle Rig said from the front seat. "The little fucker has already gone back. And he said he'd wait for us."

"Riggins!" Sara's mother said in that oh-so-icy tone of voice that she used so well and so often, "There's a child in the car!"

Rig twisted around in the seat, turning toward Sara.

"Sorry."

Even though it was too dark to see his face reddening, his voice showed that he'd been properly chastised enough to appease Sara's mother.

That was Sally's primary weapon, that dripping tone of reproach, and she wielded it masterfully. That, and 'the stare', as Sara called it. Though this was only the second time Sally and Rig had ever met, it was clear enough that she had him in her power already. As Rig looked askance in his sister-in-law's direction, though she was in his car, on his turf, it was Daddy, as usual, who came to the rescue, getting Rig off the hook.

"I think I see him. Look there, across the river. Isn't someone moving over there, on the ferry?"

They all turned to look, and sure enough a silhouette crossed between them and the single lamp that burned on the ferry.

Relieved, reprieved, Rig began honking the horn and flashing his car lights. The figure of the little boatman straightened and peered back in their direction, then waved and began undoing the work he'd been at, preparing to head back their way.

"Thank God," Sara heard Rig say, half under his breath. Then she saw his eyes flash immediately up into the rearview mirror, scanning past Sara, straight toward Sally.

280

"I mean... We got here just in time. Thank goodness we caught him."

The motor of the ferry coughed and started, and they watched in silence as the flat boat pulled away from the far dock, heading their way.

*

As soon as they were under way, headed back across, Sara opened her door and stepped gingerly out of the car, being careful not to let her mother see her wince. Perhaps she had overdone it today after all; she was hurting more than ever. But she needed fresh air; she needed respite from the confines of the back seat, if only for a little while. Daddy and Uncle Rig got out too and headed for the front of the boat, while Mother sat where she was, preferring to remain cramped in the car rather than risk contacting any more of the dirt of the ferry than absolutely necessary. Sara went back to the stern where Jeremiah sat steering their way across.

"Howdy, Miss Sara," he greeted her, moving his hand toward the brim of his dirty little cap in a mock tipping motion. He eyed her from top to bottom, not caring if he was being obvious or not. Then he looked up into the sky.

"Nice night," he said. He waited what he deemed a proper spell before looking back at her and continuing. "Isn't it?" There was barely more question in his voice than in his look, but he was too honest to turn away. He wanted to know.

"Not really," Sara said. "I mean, is it? I hadn't noticed."

Jeremiah settled down beside her, keeping his gaze fixed directly on her, while she stared steadfastly at the wake their passing left in the water behind them.

"Now look here, Missy Sara. We'll be acrost in a coupla minutes, so I got to say this quick-like. But I'm bound to say it, so you just hush up and listen whilst ole Jeremiah clears his chest, okay?"

Sara neither answered nor moved, and he took that as a go-ahead.

"I've heered all the talk that folks has been makin'. Believe me, I've heered it all. Something about the river makes folks open up and talk. Like it's private or XXXoundaryXXX', not bein' on either side of the XXXoundary. So believe me when I tell you I've heered it all," he paused for effect, then spat and went on.

"And you know what I say? Wanna know what I think? I hope you do, because I'm fixin' to tell ya anyway..."

The boat, her Mom, the night, had all dissolved away in a vapor of curiosity.

"I says 'Go for it', that's what I says. I may not be no Tom Edison nor such, but I knows what I thinks. And I thinks... I says... just go for it.

"I've seen the way you two look at one another. And I know what good folks you is, the both of you. And I says go for it, no matter what folks think or say.

"Ol' Harley, he deserves it. He's been pining long enough if you ask me. And you too, Missy. I don't know all the details of what all you've been through that brung you here, but the fact of the matter is, here you are. And you're good folk too, just like Mr. Harley is. So don't ya'll pay no never mind to what all them busybody, goody-goody church ladies and townfolk says. And don't you let Harley allow them to run his life either. I don't care how embarrassed he acts about you being here when he's around them kind. Don't pay no attention to his acting like you and him ain't nothing. There ain't no shame in wanting somebody, no shame at all. Sure, he might act like he's ashamed of you and him hankering for one another. Sure, he might pretend like he don't care, but that's just his way is all. Don't you put no stock in such, you hear? I know for a fact there ain't no finer fellar than Harley Felts, least not in these parts, no how. Let a year or two get by and nobody will even remember Miss Ellie." He paused, hearing how awful what he'd just said sounded, spoken aloud. Then he went on, stammering a bit at first. "I didn't mean that, least not how it came out. She was a fine lady, God rest her soul. But she's dead and moldering, and y'all — you and Harley I mean — y'all are still alive and kickin'. Let the dead keep the dead is what I say. And let the livin' keep the livin'. I don't care how ashamed of you Harley acts right now. Shame is a durn sight better than lonely, the way I see it. And I oughta know. What I'd give to have someone as fine as you to be ashamed of..."

"Shit," he hollered, jumping up and turning the rudder hard left.

"We about missed the landing all together, what with my babbling and all."

He set to the business at hand, leaving Sara suddenly alone with the words he'd spoken, hanging limp in the air above her, settling cold and sodden in the pit of her belly. Her freshly empty, newly hollow belly. She thought she was going to be sick — wished in a way that she would be, to clean the awful feeling out of her stomach. But it wouldn't leave her that easily, so while Jeremiah was busy docking them she went quietly to the car and got in, slouching low in the back seat, feeling more selfish and ashamed of herself than she had ever imagined possible.

After he'd lowered the ramp, just before they drove off the boat onto shore, Jeremiah came to her window and leaned close in to her, putting his stale tobacco breath so near to her face that she gagged a little. But she held it in and swallowed it back down, hoping he hadn't noticed. Jeremiah was nice, had always gone out of his way to make her feel welcome, and he did mean well, after all, through all his blunt, child-like candor.

"Remember what I told you, Miss Sara, you hear me?"

She gagged again, held it again. Lucky for Jeremiah, else she would have thrown it all up in his face. Fearful that the next time the wave washed over her she would do just that, she began rolling up her window as she looked at him and said, "Thank you, Jeremiah. I'll miss you." She could see by the look on his face that he realized how badly he had missed his mark. Then she stopped when the glass was only halfway up, and she sat up. She suddenly knew what she had to do, and once she realized it, the urge to be sick left her, solidifying the turmoil in her stomach into something as heavy as lead. But no matter the weight it added, it was solid and no longer roiling.

"One more thing, Jeremiah," she said, looking dead at him, as thick as the lead she felt inside her now, "and make no mistake about it. Mr. Felts has absolutely nothing to be ashamed of. You be sure and tell that to all your gossipers, will you? There is not, has never been anything at all 'between us', as you say, except that I was his boarder and he was my employer for a time. And now that the need for that... uh, situation... has been resolved, I am returning to my home. Going back where I belong. It's as simple as that."

The little boatman opened his mouth and before he even spoke she could see the protest forming on his lips.

"Do you understand, Jeremiah?" He closed his mouth and she knew that he did, even when she heard the faint "No, Ma'am," escape him as she closed the window to the top.

Then she slid back down in the seat and continued to stare at his face as the car lurched onto the ramp. And before they were even clear of the ferry, she let the tears she'd held back for days roll unchecked down her face. She allowed them to flow freely, knowing it was too dark for anyone to see them. But she would no more allow the choking sobs to escape her mouth than she would the vomit that was rising there again, lest her mother and father get a taste of her real pain.

Chapter 23

Harley woke up gradually and easily, rising out of the dark as gently as the dawn crept rosy into the sky. Despite having slept in the hard-backed rocking chair, he felt no stiffness or discomfort, only peace and gladness at awakening home. He sat for a minute, reveling in the serenity of the scene around him. Even the gap where the tobacco barn once stood had lost the power to upset him. When at last he stood up and the chair rocked backwards and banged into the house siding, even that racket seemed friendly and familiar to him.

He raised his arms high above his head and arched his back hard behind him, tilting his head up toward the faint hint of daylight in the east. As he stretched, the euphoria of dizziness swelled over him as the blood fell from his head, made giddy by gravity's pull. He bent forward and put his hands on his knees, dropping his head low to allow the blood to rush back there easier, and also to give him proper stance for his morning prayer of thanks.

He was standing that way, talking silently to the Lord, longer than usual, when he heard the unmistakable click of the hammer of a gun cocking behind him.

"Hold it right there, Mister," came an ominous sounding voice.

Though he was startled by it, he wasn't the slightest bit alarmed. Without turning to face his assailant, he answered.

"Oh come on now, you wouldn't shoot you own Pa in the back, would you, son?" As soon as he said it he immediately regretted it, realizing his error. It was too soon, too true. But Cy seemed not to notice at all.

"Pa! What're you doing home so soon?"

"I just decided I was missing ya'll more than those fish would miss me if I came back where I belong in the first place." He took a step toward Cy. "You can point that thing elsewhere now, unless you think me a burglar disguised as me."

Cy was still holding the shotgun level at his Pa. He dropped it to his side and went to meet Harley's hug.

"We'd have been okay. You could have stayed, you know."

"I could have," Harley said, tousling the boy's hair. "I just didn't want to. Rather be here, that's all. And I can see that ya'll were well protected." They both laughed at that.

Harley went to the top step — his booting up spot — and began loosening the laces on his heavy boots to make them easier to put on. "How is... everybody?" he asked, sounding a bit too nonchalant to his own ears. But Cy was busy swinging the gun up to his shoulder, arcing it across the front yard while he made shooting noises with his lips.

"Everybody's fine," he said absently, dropping another quail from the imaginary covey. "Did you bring any fish home?" He shot again. "Puh-kush!"

"Naw, I left 'em all in camp. I almost brought you a pet home though, but thought better of it and let him go."

Cy dropped the gun to his side again and looked at his dad quizzically.

"A pet? What'd you catch, Pa?"

"Never mind. I'm sure you'll hear all about it as soon as Burley gets back."

Cy shrugged and raised the barrel for another bird. When he swung left toward the corner of the house, he saw Juniper grazing at the far corner of the yard.

"Juniper's here! Can I ride her before you take her home, Pa? Can I?"

"Sure. You can take her back to Burley's yourself if you want to."

"Oh boy!" Cy laid the shotgun gingerly on the front porch, a forgotten toy now, and started off in Juniper's direction.

"Whoa there, boy," called Harley. "How about you and me going and starting breakfast. We'll have a hungry brood up soon. And I forgot, Anna Mae can take Juniper home when she goes, she'll be needing a ride, don't you think?"

"Aw, Pa. Can't you take her in the wagon? She'd be more comfortable, and she's got luggage and all."

"You'll have time to ride Juniper some before she leaves, I promise you. Now come on, let's go rustle up some grub. I could eat a horse." Juniper snorted and hoofed the ground as Cy stopped short. She liked having the young spirit on her back as much as he liked being there. "Sorry, girl," Harley grinned. "I didn't mean that."

As he started walking toward the back door Cy trotted over and fell into step with him.

"What kind of pet, Pa? What'd you catch? Was it another baby coon? I sure do miss little..."

The slam of the front screen door and Seth's cry of "Pa!" cut Cy off in mid-sentence. Seth was still in his nightshirt, but that didn't stop him from running to his father.

"What are you doing here? I thought you were gone for the weekend."

"I just decided to come home early. It didn't feel right, me going off and leaving all ya'll here..."

"I knew you'd come back! I told her you'd be back. Didn't I tell her, Cy?" Cy turned and began walking toward the back again without answering.

Harley started to ask, "Told who, what? What're you..." but Seth bubbled on, near breathless.

"I knew you'd come back. Now you can stop her, Pa. But you have to hurry, you don't have much time."

"What are you talking about, Seth? Stop who? You told who what? Are you talking about Sara?"

Seth stopped dead in his tracks. "Didn't he tell you?" His brows furrowed as a look of realization, a troubled look, sank into his face. He turned and called at Cy's back.

"You didn't tell him?" He asked, his voice rising. He turned back to Harley. "He didn't tell you?" Then he spun back to Cy, fairly screaming now.

"You didn't tell him, Cy?"

Cy continued walking away, pausing only long enough to turn his head sideways and mumble something over his shoulder.

"What?" Seth yelled.

He left Harley's side and ran to catch up with Cy, grabbing his brother by the shoulders, spinning him around.

"What did you say, Cy? I can't believe you didn't tell Pa!" His troubled look had melted into a pained expression.

"I said, 'She don't belong here anyway'. I knew all along she'd leave us too, sooner or later."

Cy spat the words out as if they were some vile thing that had crawled into his mouth.

Seth yelled something else then, not a word, just a sound. A raging sound. He lashed out with a roundhouse left hook that caught Cy square on the jaw, sending the older boy sprawling. Seth was on top of him before he even hit the grass, kicking and swinging wildly, screaming his rage all the while.

Harley couldn't believe his eyes. Though the boys often quarreled, as all brothers do, they had never actually gotten into a real fight like this. He'd never seen, never imagined that Seth harbored such a vicious streak. He ran and pulled Seth off of Cy, who wasn't even trying to fight back. He had just curled himself into a defensive ball, arms covering his face. Harley couldn't believe that either, but he was seeing it with his own eyes.

"Boys!" He shouted, holding Seth up in the air by his armpits. Seth kicked and struggled to get back at Cy for a couple of seconds, then went limp in Harley's grip. "What the hell is going on here?" Harley demanded.

Cy pushed himself up to a sitting position.

"Ask him," he said, rubbing his jaw. "Ask the maniac."

Harley lowered Seth to the ground, but held on to his shoulders, turning the boy to face him.

"What's this all about, Seth?" Tears were streaming down Seth's cheeks now, and his face glowed as bright red as the sunrise behind him.

"She's leaving, Pa! They're taking her away. Back to Baltimore." He sniffed and drew a sleeve of his nightshirt across his nose, then, turning to Cy he said, "I can't believe you didn't tell him! We don't have much time!"

"You're talking to me, Seth," Harley said, taking Seth's jaw in his right hand, turning the boy's face back to his own. "Now take a deep breath and tell me...."

Seth did as he was told , looking up at his Pa.

"Sara came home yesterday. Her parents brought her. Her father said they had a train to catch this morning. They're taking her away, Pa! We gotta stop 'em!"

Harley stood there amidst the sounds of morning, the sounds of the farm wakening around him, having been rudely roused by the ruckus. He heard the back screen door spring stretch and then Anna Mae's voice, questioning.

"Harley? Is that you? What's going on out there?"

He answered without letting his eyes leave Seth's.

"We'll be in, in a minute, Anna. Thank you." It was more dismissal than thanks and she heard it. The spring sighed softly back out of tension without another word.

Seth took up the cause anew.

"Isn't that why you're here, Pa? Isn't that why you came back? For Sara?"

Again, for moments there was only the sound of the rising day; hens beginning to cluck; hogs snorting; a rooster crowing sudden and loud, startlingly close.

He didn't know what to say. He had never in his life been at a loss for words around his children, until now. He turned slowly to Cy.

"Why didn't you want to tell me, son?"

Cy looked away, up toward the knoll, but his face wasn't angled far enough to hide the tear that slid down his cheek now.

"Cy?"

Cy sniffed hard, then coughed to try and hide it. He took a deep breath, still looking away up the hill. He sniffed once more, then turned and looked at Harley, defiantly.

"I knew she'd leave us," he said, turning toward Seth, even more defiantly. "I knew it!"

Seth stepped over to his brother and put out a hand to help him up. Cy looked at Seth's hand a few seconds, then took it and stood up. Seth was between Harley and Cy now. The father said nothing, nor interfered, he just watched.

"Don't you get it, Cy?" Seth said quietly, back in his normal, gentle Seth voice.

"Momma sent her to us."

Tears streamed down Cy's face now, faster than Seth's had flowed moments earlier, but he didn't turn away, didn't try to hide them; showed no shame in them.

"She sent her, Cy. She did."

The two boys stood eye to eye, and neither spoke for a long time.

Harley took it for as long as he could, as long as he thought they could, and then stepped between them, draping an arm around each's shoulder.

"Come on, boys. Let's go visit your Mother."

*

They walked mostly in silence, each lost in his own separate thoughts, each alternating in private reverie or personal nightmare, yet each linked together by the unfailing arms of the parent among them, connecting the three of them in trilateral chain. In fact, they were three-quarters up the knoll before anyone — before Harley — said a word. He would leave them to their own hearts if that was where they chose to stay, but the father in him had to warn them, had to protect them, had let them know it was allowed, before they came in sight of her place.

"We don't have to say a word. All we have to do is listen."

That was enough. Neither of the boys felt need to respond, nor did the father feel need to say anything more. Though it is true that silence can sometimes be the biggest lie of all, so can it sometimes be the ultimate communication, untainted and uncolored by oral language.

No one said a word when they first saw the carved stone; there was no need. No one spoke when they first saw the cut flowers on the small mound next to the stone; there was no need. And no one commented at the sprig of grass transplanted from one place to the other. There was no need. They all knew equally that mere words could only violate what lay before them. As if under a spell they sat, they listened, and they were eased as the sun rose in the sky over them, unfolding the day around them.

And when their prayers were done, it was Harley who broke the spell simply by standing up a half second sooner than did his eldest or his second born. They turned as one to each other and hugged, and this time it was Seth who broke the spell, simply by saying 'Amen' a half-second before his father and his big brother repeated it. And it was Cy who broke the hug a half-second before his father and his little brother did.

As soon as Cy stepped away he simply said, "Race you to go hitch the wagon, Seth," as he turned and took advantage of his head start down the hill.

Harley walked slowly behind his children, watching them fly down the knoll with the grace that comes only through total abandon. But as he reached the edge of the crest he knew he couldn't start down; not just yet. And besides, he had time before the boys had the wagon ready for him. He should let them do it themselves this time.

He went back to the foot of the grave and stood there, letting the tears flow freely down his cheeks. It was his turn, finally. He tilted his face heavenward, letting the sunshine and the morning breeze dry his eyes, allowing them time to.

"Into Thy Hands," he whispered.

Then he knelt down and kissed the spot where the remains of Ellie's earthly heart lay.

"I love you."

As he began to leave once more, he tasted raw dirt on his lips, and he stopped. Turning back around, he saw the tiny green sprig over the heart that lay next to Ellie's.

Bowing his head this time, he prayed once more.

"According to thy will."

And he kneeled again, kissing the sprig of green, taken from one heart spot, given to another.

Chapter 24

Harley was still at least a mile from the river when he heard the train whistle, faint and distant. It was coming from the west, riding under the thunderheads that gathered in that direction, most likely giving its warning blasts as it approached the grade crossing below Joe Trotter's place. Since it was eastbound Harley knew it was an L&N line, headed to Nashville and points beyond. And since Cuthcutt was a river town, it was usually a water stop for the trains coming out of Memphis. Sometimes they made it a coal stop too, but more often they took on coal when they came from the other direction. But in either case Harley knew he'd have time enough to get to the station before it left. Unless Jeremiah was laid up late in bed sleeping off a Friday night drunk, which was all too likely. But no, he reassured himself, it was Saturday, Jeremiah's money day, and it was after ten o'clock already. Somebody would have dragged Jeremiah out of bed by now. Harley knew he'd have time, barely, but time enough to get there. Nonetheless, he flicked the reins and hupped Bess into a trot.

As he neared the last bend before he would come in sight of the crossing, he strained to hear the chugging of the ferry engine, but heard nothing except the rumbling of not-so-distant thunder. That didn't necessarily mean the ferry wasn't running yet, he told himself, just that it was probably idling at one landing or the other. When he cleared the last stand of hardwoods that guarded the last curve, he saw that was the case. Jeremiah was on the far side, lowering the ramp to unload the two cars and the someone on horseback who waited onboard. Looking westward, Harley saw a bank of low, dark clouds rising on the horizon.

Harley climbed off the wagon to stretch his legs and lead Bess down the ramp so she could drink from the river. Since he was there, he decided to ring the big cast iron calling bell at the end of the dock, to make sure Jeremiah knew he was over here and wouldn't decide to wait for an outbound fare before crossing back, or maybe slip off for a nip or two at the Boar's Head.

He saw the little ferry captain straighten up and squint in his direction at the sound of the tolling, then begin waving his arms at the off-loading fares, hurrying them along. He waved broadly back in Harley's direction while he waited at the ramp, ready to crank it back up as soon as they were off the ferry. Harley could see that no one was waiting on that side to cross back — it was still too early for folks to be leaving town yet — and since Jeremiah had just cleared this side it looked like it'd be just Harley and Jeremiah making the return crossing. At the thought of that Harley found himself hoping that someone would show up from the road behind him before the ferry got back over here. He liked Jeremiah, despite, or maybe because of all his bluntness and lack of tact. But the man loved prying into everybody's business — not to mention spreading it around to any who would listen — and Harley didn't relish the idea of having to fend off Jeremiah's questions and opinions on this particular morning. That and besides, in all the ride here Harley hadn't really figured out what he would say to Sara when he saw her, and he could use some more time to think it out. Were it just Sara, that'd be one thing, but her folks would be there too, and probably Rig and Clorise as well. How could he say what he wanted to say with a crowd standing around?

An image of Ellie's daddy standing on the church steps so many Sundays ago flashed across his mind.

He watched the last car drive ashore and saw Jeremiah immediately begin cranking the ramp, working furiously, compared to his regular pace. The train whistled again, much nearer this time. One long blast followed by three short ones, then two more long ones. It was approaching the station. Jeremiah heard it too. He jerked a bit at its sound as he left the ramp cranked less than three-quarters of the way up, threw off his lines, and started across the river, pushing the ferry motor wide open.

Harley went and scratched Bess behind her ears, oddly calm, considering what was going on.

"Strangeness, huh, Girl," he whispered to the horse, keeping his eyes fixed on the approaching ferry.

"Strange things going on about..."

Bess snorted and clomped a hoof on the shoal, agreeing. Or maybe just caught up in the eagerness, and the coming storm that filled the air around her.

The wind kicked up and the first of the clouds slid under the sun, turning the river from glinting glass to leaden swells. As Harley led Bess back up the ramp to the loading line, she nosed the air for the scent of rain and began high stepping, snorting again.

Once Jeremiah had the ferry turned around for landing he waved again and called out, "Ho there, Harl!" and some other words that got lost in the wind. Harley just waved back and watched the ferry slide into the ramp with long-practiced ease as Jeremiah cut the engines abruptly and immediately bent to pick up the docking rope, throwing it to Harley.

"Don't bother tying her off, you ain't got time," Jeremiah said, already cranking the ramp down, "Just hold 'er snug and I'll lead Bess on."

"Howdy, Jeremiah. What's all the rush about?"

"Don't go playing no coy shit with me, Harley Felts. I know good and well why you're here and you know I know," he said, as the steel ramp settled onto the shoal with a soft crunch.

"Now hold tight agin' it," he ordered, going for the wagon reins.

Harley didn't say anything; he just pulled hard and held on.

As soon as he followed the tail of the wagon onto the boat Jeremiah went to start the engine. "Get that ramp cranked up, will ya?" He pushed the start-button and the big Ford engine began to turn over. But it didn't fire. Jeremiah let off, waited a second, and tried it again, cranking and cranking this time. But the plugs never hit.

"Shit! Shit! Shit!" He said, spitting into the river. "Shit fire and be damned. I know'd better'n to cut it off on full throttle! It floods her every time." he spat again, bending over to lift the engine housing. "Shit fire," he cursed

"Does this mean I can take my time cranking this ramp up?" Harley said. His grin was wasted on Jeremiah's back, and he realized that was probably a good thing because it felt a bit too tight on his face.

Just as Jeremiah raised the cowling a fresh gale came up, ripping it from his hands, banging it loudly against the railing. "Shit fire," he spat again as he began twisting the wing nut that held the carburetor breather in place.

"Don't worry, I'll get you there on time. Fact is, this wind helps matters, it'll dry the thang out quicker."

"You need a hand there?"

"Naw, I done this a million times, no problem. I can do it faster without no other hands in my way," then he thought better of it and said, "Yeah, come over and take hold of the housin' while I try and start'er again."

The wind kicked up another notch, white-capping the river and pushing the un-moored boat sideways from the landing. There was a flash of lightening and a half-second later a loud boom of thunder, close down river. The starter cranked again, fast at first, then quickly slowing. The battery was going down. Jeremiah let off the button and swore under his breath, not as angrily as before, but the knit in his brow seemed not quite so optimistic as before.

"Hand me that gas can under the bench behind ya," he yelled at Harley. Harley had to pull the cowling down to reach the can, and when he did, another gust caught it like a parachute, throwing it against the railing again. He let it stay there and grabbed the can and handed it to Jeremiah, who took it and unscrewed the cap.

"Pour me a lid full," Jerimiah said, holding it out.

Harley was standing upwind of the motor, so when he tried to pour the gas into the cap the wind ripped most of it away, spotting both the engine and Jeremiah's overalls. But the cap was over half full so Jeremiah went ahead and dumped it into the carburetor, then pushed the starter again. The motor turned sluggishly, once, twice; then it picked up speed and turned fast. There was a loud bang as the motor backfired, sending an arm of flame as high as their heads. But the motor caught, immediately revving to high end. He had forgotten to shut the throttle down.

"Shit!" Jeremiah yelled, just as the props found purchase in the water, launching the boat, which had swung tail end upstream leaving them facing directly into the dock now. They rammed it hard enough to knock Harley off his feet, hard enough to knock Jeremiah's hand off the throttle, leaving the ferry pushing into the dock at full tilt. Bess tried to rear against the wagon pulls and Harley grabbed for her reins just as Jeremiah reached the throttle and shut it down. The engine died at once and they began drifting upstream again, at the mercy of the on-setting storm. Just as Harley got a hold of the reins, huge splotches of water began plopping sporadically across the deck, and another crack of thunder rent the air, this one deafeningly loud, accompanied simultaneously by another streak of lightning that hit the river less than a thousand yards below them. When it struck the water it scattered in a spider web pattern, licking fingers of sun-heat in all directions for a hundred yards around. Harley felt the hairs on his arms and the back of his neck tingling, reaching for the energy, and he tasted a metallic, coppery flavor in his mouth. The boat lurched again in the opposite direction from the first hit. The wind pushed them into the bank below the landing. Jeremiah yelled out something Harley couldn't understand, but by the tone and bite of it there was no doubt it was cussing of some sort. The rain lost its randomness and picked up its pace, and in another instant they were as drenched as if someone had dumped a bucket of water on their heads. Lightning thundered again, this time bolting down on the far side of town, toward the ball fields.

"Damn good thing I wasn't trying to start'er. Woulda busted the prop for sure." Jeremiah had to shout to be heard above the tempest that surrounded them now.

"Might have anyway," he added, not as loud, but loud enough for Harley to hear it, even though he knew Jeremiah was talking to himself on that one. Bess stomped and pulled against her harness, jerking the wagon back and forth. Even she had enough sense to know the water was no place to be in a storm like this. Harley leaned into her and dropped an arm across her neck, trying to soothe her. No sooner than he did another Crack-Flash-Bang split the heavens over them. It was raining too hard for Harley to look up, but he knew that if he did he would see a boiling, foaming, flying ocean hovering over them, looking more like Hell than Heaven. He had not seen a storm this fierce since... well, since the day Sara had arrived.

Jeremiah was back at the helm, and this time when he pushed the starter the engine fired at once.

"Close that housing before this shit drowns the carburetor out." He yelled

With a last pat and reassuring word in Bess's ear Harley made his way back astern, walking like a drunk on the rolling deck. The rain was coming almost horizontal now and it actually stung where it hit bare skin. He grabbed the handle of the cowling and began trying to force it down against the rush of air that pushed into its cup. He almost had it closed when a sudden fist of wind slammed into them so violently that it tilted the boat , which had ungrounded itself and was once more headed upstream, sideways, as it tore the handle out of his grip. This time when the metal cover hit the railing the hinges gave way and the cowling flew off downwind as light and easy as a kite in

March winds. Jeremiah shouted again, not words, just a noise full of curse.

"Get that breather cover on, quick! If the motor dies we're sunk for sure!" he yelled as he opened the throttle full, trying to regain control of his wayward ship.

Harley found the cover but he couldn't find the wing nut so he fitted it in place and held it there with one hand and held his brimmed felt hat on his head with the other. He wondered how far upriver they had been pushed, but when he tried to look back at the landing he could barely keep his eyes open against the sheet of water that assailed them. Even when he tried squinting, he could see no sign of the dock. He felt the boat shudder and begin to turn into the wind, and slowly, ever so slowly, it begin inching back in the direction of the crossing. The howl of the wind in Harley's ears gained volume, and for a second of two he expected to see a funnel cloud swinging below the writhing black ceiling above. But when the wind fell back to its previous roar, he knew it wasn't a tornado he'd heard.

Maybe that wasn't the wind at all. Maybe it was a train whistle.

He realized Jeremiah was shouting at him over the din of the engine and the rage of the sky.

"Huh?" He said, hardly louder than a whisper, as if startled out of a trance. He turned his head and yelled back.

"What?"

"I said we're going to have to make for some lee up at the bend beyond town. No way can we dock in this blow."

Harley had already guessed, knew, that trying to land in this storm would be impossible. Every variation of gust and gale that blew past his ears sounded like a train now. There broke another flash of heat and boom of thunder, but they were separate now, a little apart in time, and upstream, east. The center was past. He looked to his right and saw that they were just about abreast of the town side landing. The wall of water they were plowing through abated for a second, then hit hard again, a last slap goodbye, and then the front was gone, taking the biggest part of the wind with it. Another Flash-Boom, but more widely separated this time, father away. And as suddenly as it had started, the rain dropped intensity by half, almost as if God had turned a faucet valve partly back from the wide open He had twisted it to so suddenly a few minutes ago. There was still a fair amount of wind trailing the brunt, and it was still a hard rain that fell, but not nearly so violently as before.

"Maybe we can land in this," Jeremiah called, louder than needed now. Lowering his voice back to a notch or two below shouting, he added, "I'm gonna give it try."

Harley straightened up from his post over the engine, feeling safe that the breather cover would stay in place by its own weight now. Jeremiah hunched over the rudder wheel, his hair plastered down into his face, his clothes hanging so heavy on his skinny frame that they looked as if they would fall off him at any moment. Harley knew that he himself must look no better, and a laugh sprang out of him before he saw it coming, as he got an image of what a sight they must be.

"Talk about a drowned rat! You ought to see yourself, Jeremiah."

"You ain't so dad-gummed pretty yourself, pardner," the little captain grinned back. A shivering spasm ran over him and he shook like a dog fresh out of water. The passing front had taken the warmth of the day with it, dropping the temperature drastically.

"At least not to me anyway. But I know one certain young lady that I'd wager would disagree."

Harley went to the wagon and patted Bess on the neck, saying "Good girl" as he passed. He reached under the seat of the wagon and got his old black duster coat out from under it and carried it back to Jeremiah.

"Here, put this on before you catch your death," he said holding it out.

"Naw, you take it yourself. But I will let you fetch me my jacket under the seat over there, next to where the gas can was."

Harley bent and dug the jacket out and took it to Jeremiah, who throttled the engine back slightly before he took it. The landing was only a hundred or so yards away. Harley held the wheel steady while Jeremiah pulled his jacket on.

"We damn near lost 'er, boy, you know that?"

"I figured that out, even before the second wreck."

"It ain't never even crossed my mind before that she could get away from me. I ain't never been afra... I mean I ain't never come that close to losing her."

Jeremiah's face showed that his mind was wandering, thinking thoughts that had never occurred to him before. Harley poked him in the arm and brought him back.

"Hell, I knew that for sure when you couldn't even miss something as big as the south side of Tennessee."

They both chuckled at that. One, two, three booms of thunder rolled away, already distant afterthoughts, and as they died, the whistle of the train, unmistakable now, took their place. It stopped at exactly the instant the sky flashed again from their left.

"How many whistles was that? Did you hear?" Harley asked. There was no point dodging or denying it any longer.

The wind was still stiff enough to fish-tail the boat a bit, and Jeremiah stared ahead, intent on his fast approaching target, working his tongue back and forth over his lips in concentration.

"No. I thought I heard it a time or two during the blow though," he managed to pull his tongue in long enough to say before it went right back to its stroking. He still hadn't cut the throttle back anymore. He was usually barely above idle this close in.

"Grab that fending pole under the bench where my jacket was and man the front, will ya? It's way back in the back there."

"Take it easy, Jeremiah, two wrecks in one day is plenty for me."

The train whistled again, "Woo-Woo, Wauoooooooo."

The second boarding call.

Harley bent low and grabbed the pole and took his station on the forward right corner.

"And get the mooring rope ready," Jeremiah added, throttling back hard and reversing the engine. As soon as the propellers took purchase the bow began swinging upstream. Jeremiah spun the wheel to correct it and they nosed back toward the dock. But the current was back in play, freshening from the water being dumped upstream from them, so the bow turned way too much, throwing the boat nearly parallel to the bank. Jeremiah threw the throttle wide open again and spun the wheel back hard the other way. The ferry slowed and began to yawl back to perpendicular, but it was maddeningly slow to respond. Trying to maneuver the wide flat hull was like trying to push a snowball up a hill — it was hell to get it going in one direction and hell to stop it in the other. Jeremiah threw the throttle from reverse to forward a half-second too late to swing the right front clear of the dock. Harley braced the push pole against the dock, but with not only the momentum and the weight of the ferry and its load against him, the current was pushing them that way as well. He might as well have been trying to stop the world from turning. Though they hit with a glancing blow, but it was vicious enough to break the railing off at its base and swing the rear of the ferry into the far end of the dock almost as soon as the front bounced off. Bess neighed loudly and reared her front legs as high as the wagon harnessing allowed.

"Whoa, Bess!" Harley yelled. His tone was strictly stern command — it was too late for soothing now.

"Hang on!" Jeremiah yelled an instant later; "I'm going for it!" He gunned the motor just as the train whistle began blowing the final boarding call.

*

They stayed inside the little depot while the sky played out its tantrum. Mother stayed by the door the whole time, peering into the steel-colored curtain of rain that slashed and flashed between her and the train, as if she were afraid she might miss the boarding call. She was so eager to get on her way home that Sara believed she would have actually ventured out into the storm, if that meant she could just be on her way. Daddy stood next to the ticket window talking to Aunt Clorise and Uncle Rig between the crashings of thunder. Sara sat on a bench with her back to the wall, trying not to think of any of it.

She looked at the clock on the wall; she looked at her hands; she looked at the wear pattern in the ancient wood flooring. She looked anywhere and everywhere except out the window. That's why she sat where she did, back to the wall, so she wouldn't have to look into the storm. But she could still feel it rattling into her through the wall behind. She closed her eyes and gave the fury free rein, feeling the vibrations die deeper and deeper inside her.

But the storm had no sooner calmed in her than a simultaneous blast of the train whistled behind her, as another round of thunder roared above her, wrenching her back tight against the wall again.

"They're ready, Clive," Sara heard her mother say. But she wasn't ready to open her eyes yet.

"Come along now. You too, Sara. Wake up over there, we're ready to leave now."

Sara felt a wave of cold wash over her as Sally pushed the door open. She opened her eyes. She couldn't hide in here any longer.

"Oh, Porter! Porter!" her mother called out the door. "Our bags are in that black car there." Sara couldn't see who she was talking to, but she heard the reply.

"I'm not a porter, Ma'am. I'm a passenger, just like you."

"Well, could you find me a porter then, if you please?"

Sara shut her eyes back and turned her ears off before she heard the response from outside. But she couldn't shut them tight enough to prevent hearing the next

"Sara, I said come along now."

Sara heard the door swing shut and felt the cold retreat as soon as it did. Then she heard Sally's footsteps approaching. She could pick out the brisk, no-nonsense rhythm of that stride even in the densest of crowds, she'd lived her life in tune to it, much less here in the empty, echoing train station.

"Darling, are you okay?" she felt a hand push her bangs off her forehead. "You're not having another one of those concussion things that country quack mentioned, are you?"

Sara had to open her eyes again. It was still raining hard, but not quite as hard as before.

"No, Ma'am. I'm just tired, that's all. May I sit here just a minute longer?"

"Pshaw to that, young lady! What you need is fresh air. Come along, we'll wait outside in the breezeway while you father finds a porter," Sally said, taking Sara by the forearm, leaving no room for argument. "Clive. Clorise. And you too, Rig. We're leaving now."

Sara let herself be pulled up and led to the door. Daddy held it open while Sally passed, but he stopped Sara before she went out.

"Are you okay, Sweetheart? You don't look like you're feeling well."

Sara looked up at her Daddy, and for a moment she was on the fence; she almost slipped off. Then she regained her balance and reached up on her tiptoes to kiss him.

"I'll be okay, Daddy. I just need a little healing time, that's all."

"Okay, Punkin. If you say so. Whatever you say."

He pulled the door wide, and Sara stepped out into the sudden chill.

Chapter 25

The ferry was far from square to the bank, but Jeremiah didn't hesitate or back off a bit. They slammed ashore at something like a 45-degree angle, so the only part of the boat that actually hit the ramp was the front right corner. There was a sickening sound of tearing metal and Harley knew the hull had most likely been gouged open by the huge rip-rap stones that lined the landing. As the deck of the ferry rose and canted to the left and to the rear, Bess whinnied loudly, wanting desperately to run, even knowing she had nowhere to go. The ramp wench let go when they hit and the chain clacked itself out of the sprocket, spinning the handle wildly as the big plate of reinforced steel banged loudly into the graveled shore. Only the lower corner of the ramp hit, just at the water's edge, and from there it tilted steeply uphill, leaving the upper corner three or four feet above ground. Jeremiah lay on the deck where the impact had thrown him, his head bare inches from the handle of the crank that had just spun out with the weight of the falling ramp at skull-smashing speed.

"You git, Harley," he called, struggling to his feet. "I'll sort this here mess and get Bess taken care of while you go tend to business."

Harley went to give him a hand up.

"Are you okay?"

"Git, I said. I'm fine. Can't say the same for my boat though. But never mind that now. Git on, boy!"

"Jeremi..."

"Shut your fool mouth and go. Don't make me have wrecked her for nothing."

Harley pulled his coat on and went to the front of the boat, holding onto the broken rail for balance on the cockeyed ramp. He squatted and jumped down to shore. The train station was only a block away. He could still make it. He started up the hill, walking fast.

"And don't you pay no never mind to that babble she tried to feed me," he heard Jeremiah call after him. He stopped and turned around.

"What babble? What did she say?"

"All that crap about 'There was never nothing between Mr. Felts and me'." Jeremiah raised his voice an octave or two in poor imitation of feminine pitch, and he bit the 'Mr. Felts' part off in a sharp, contemptuous tone. "And that bullshit about 'He was nothing more than my employer', or the part about 'I can't wait to get back home'. Bullshit, every durn word of it. Ole Jeremiah may not look so smart, but he knows bullshit when he hears it."

Harley said nothing; he just turned back toward town and looked up the hill. Even from this distance, even in the rain, he knew Jeremiah would see it if he kept facing his way.

"Now you git on, you hear me, boy. Go show her she ain't fooled nobody."

Harley took a step, then another, and then he was on his way up the hill again. But this time all trace of urgency was gone from his pace.

*

It was not only cold in the breezeway that separated the passenger side of the depot from the baggage-handling side; it was loud. There was no ceiling above them, just the open webbing of the trusses and the underside of the roof decking. That and the shingles were all that stood between them and the driving rain that drummed and echoed around them, amplified by the empty tent of air above, so they had to shout to hear one another.

"Thank you for everything, Sister," Sally said, leaning to air-kiss just beside each of Aunt Clorise's cheeks.

"Oh, posh, Sally. We loved having her. I only wish we could have spent more time with her. But it worked out for the best."

"Yes, it did." Sally reached over to Sara's face to push a strand of hair off her cheek, while Clorise smiled gently in her direction.

"It certainly did," Sally said again, speaking more at Sara than to Clorise.

Two soaking wet porters excused themselves past, carrying their luggage to the train. Sara left the conversation behind and looked back in the direction the porters had come from, until Sally's sharp voice jerked her back.

"Sara! Your aunt is speaking to you. I swan I'll be happy to get you away from this horrid country and back to where you belong, so you'll start acting yourself again."

"I'm sorry," Sara said turning to face Clorise. "I didn't hear. All this noise...."

The bell on the locomotive began clanging loudly, insistently.

"I said, I bet you can't wait to be back home again." Clorise said, almost in a shout, raising her voice a bit louder than necessary, the way people do when they talk to the deaf or the senile.

"Yes, Ma'am," Sara answered, but she could tell by the quizzical look on Aunt Clorise's face that she hadn't spoken loud enough to be heard. So she spoke up, matching the volume Clorise had just used.

"Yes, Ma'am. I can't wait to get back home." Just as she said it the bell ceased its clanging, but she didn't drop her voice soon enough to keep her words from echoing up and down the platform, loud enough for everyone around to hear.

The porters came back, holding open umbrellas to escort them to the train. Sally hugged Clorise and Rig, then turned and walked out onto the platform, leaving the porter hurrying to keep up behind her. Daddy shook hands with Rig, pumping his right hand while he reached out and took hold of Rig's upper arm with his left.

"Thanks for everything. We're still waiting for that visit you promised us. You'll like Baltimore, and I dare say you'll benefit from some of those business contacts we talked about."

"We'll do it, Clive. Before spring."

Daddy let go of Rig and turned to Clorise, hugging her tightly. When he stood back he took both her arms in his hands. "Hold him to that for me, will you, Clo?"

"I will. I can't wait to see all those shops Sally told me about."

Daddy looked hard into her eyes, still holding her arms.

"Thank you." He said. He dropped his grip and turned to Sara. "Come on, Cupcake. It's time."

He put an arm around Sara's waist and started her toward the train. The porter followed, holding his umbrella over them while Daddy helped Sara up the steps and followed her on board. As soon as they were clear of the doorway, the porter picked the wooden step up from the platform and handed it to the conductor that appeared in their place. The conductor leaned far out of the train, holding a handle beside the door, and waved his free arm in big sweeping arcs toward the locomotive. The engineer gave a long blast of the whistle and the conductor disappeared back inside. As soon as he was gone Sara took his place, holding onto the same handle, still warm from his grip. She looked from one end of the depot platform to the other, swinging her eyes slowly from back to front.

As the train began to inch forward in its agonizing battle to overcome inertia and get the immeasurable weight of itself and its cargo moving, she left the doorway and went to her seat. But as soon as she sat down her eyes went back through the rain-glazed glass of the window. She watched the depot slide away behind her, not turning around until her car cleared the platform and her window replaced Cuthcut Station with a tall fence of autumning trees.

Had she waited a half second more, had she turned a bit to look behind her, she might have glimpsed the figure of a man wearing a felt hat, pulled low over his face above a long black duster, step out from under the shadows at the end soffit of the depot. But she would have had to open the window and lean out to see him walk to the end of the platform and stand in the rain until he could no longer see nor hear any trace of the train as it wailed its way away.

Epilogue

The white was all around, unstained and cold, falling furiously upon the city in flakes as big as quarters, so wet and heavy that each and every one could be heard silently landing on the streets; on the lamp posts; on the finely manicured lawns; on the carefully trimmed hedges. But there was neither hint nor breath of wind, so it was a purely vertical snowing, lacing the black night sky neatly in half with white falling stripes. And since it was so freshly begun, and since it had been a rather warm day in late December terms, the quiet of nighttime snow spread its blanket of silence over the land before the white had a chance to.

Directly ahead an oasis of light shown through the eighth inch thickness of glass that separated the chill from the warmth, light from dark, company from solitude. Music seeped through the glass too, radiating farther than the heat that followed it. In there was laughter, food and spirits, fellowship. Things familiar. Things he understood. Things he almost felt a part of, even from the distance of the street; even though he stood in a world not his own and not of his own choosing. He didn't belong in there, with them, but neither did he belong out here, in the cold and the dark. He belonged elsewhere. Yet here he was. He turned and looked down the street behind him and almost took a step away, but realizing where that first simple step would lead, he turned back and drew in a deep breath of the night air, then exhaled it and put his hand on the gate latch. Another breath – cold in, warm out – and he stepped through. Another breath – cold in, warm out – and he took a step. And so on and so on, walking aware of the tracks he left on the sidewalk behind him, yet refusing to look back at them.

And then he was on the steps, and then he had climbed them, and then he was on the stoop, staring into the brass face of a brass lion with a brass ring through its nose, mounted on the center of the door, staring back at him at eye-level. He took another breath, the man in the worn felt hat and the worn black duster did, but this time it failed him, it didn't help. They wore tuxedos and top hats in there. They belonged here. So what was he doing here, staring at a brass lion?

He turned around and looked behind him. Inside, the music stopped, replaced by polite clapping. There were footprints in the thin snow, leading up to where he stood. A peel of laughter rang out from the other side of the door. White covered everything except where he had stepped. Someone clanged silver on crystal. He thought about all the miles, all the steps that had brought him here. A single voice began speaking, breaking the silence of the night, and he realized a toast was being given in there. He took his hat off and shook the snow from it. A multitude of voices chimed in a single syllable before quiet returned as they drank up. He put his hat on and turned back to the door, and just as he reached for the brass ring in the lion's mouth the music started anew, fast and loud. And the world stood still.

The snow fell with all its might, intent on nothing more than laying itself into every corner it could possibly reach. Even knowing that its victory and its presence would be fleeting and temporary at best; even knowing that even on the coldest of days in the darkest of winter, the sun would eventually shine again, melting all its efforts to defeat and defy warmth.

Too bad for the snow, that it worked so hard at being the best snow it could be, that it failed to notice one warm door open for one lone soul. All it saw was its chill defeated by the golden arms that bounced out and embraced the unexpected visitor.

Made in the USA
Coppell, TX
09 May 2023

16636468R00174